CRIMSON DEEPS

Mary B. Lyons

WORDPOWER™

CRIMSON DEEPS

Copyright © Mary B. Lyons BSc(Hons) 2013

First Edition 2013
Firstclassy Fiction series

Published in England, Great Britain, by Wordpower™
P.O. Box 1190, SANDHURST, GU47 7BW

www.wordpower.u-net.com

A CIP catalogue record for this book
Is available from the British Library

ISBN 978-0950821276

Cover Design by Mary B. Lyons BSc(Hons)

Typeset by Wordpower™

Printed and bound in Great Britain by
Witley Press Ltd

CRIMSON DEEPS

About the Author

Mary B. Lyons, an established writer in several genres, was born in Surrey, England and has been writing since the age of eight years. Those who know her will agree that she pours boundless energy, innovative creativity, positive thinking and attention to detail into any project that she undertakes. Following the success of her first novel, AIRSHOW ILEX in 2010, this new crime thriller, CRIMSON DEEPS, is the second of many blockbuster novels to pour from the fingers of this talented writer who deserves every success.

Writing my first novel, AIRSHOW ILEX, was a huge undertaking. The journey was utterly amazing as my characters progressively interacted. I set out to write an entertaining and interesting book, not realising that the process would be so excruciatingly, creatively productive. Some of the characters from AIRSHOW ILEX go forward to do other things with their lives in CRIMSON DEEPS. However, new and fascinating people join them in a cliff-hanging, entertaining read with its share of romance and humour. This book is a real page turner.

I could not have achieved it without the unstinting support and encouragement of my husband Pitt who always finds time to take an interest in my work. Many thanks to all my friends, colleagues and adult children for their uplifting, continuous enquiries about my progress.

Mary B. Lyons
Hampshire, England, 2013

Also by Mary B. Lyons

The Lonely Shade © 2009
Original, comforting, bereavement poetry
With monochrome illustrations
ISBN 9780950821214

The Lonely Shade CD © *2009*
Spoken by the author
ISBN 9780950821221

Airshow Ilex © 2010
A riveting novel full of glamour, technology,
double-dealing, romance and fun. Trust nobody!
ISBN 9780950821238

Caravan Hitches © 2011
Entertaining short stories and cartoons
for owners of caravans and motor homes,
campers and anybody else who loves a good read
and a laugh. Received a great review in
The Caravan Club Magazine.
ISBN 9780950821245

Sporting Hitches © 2012
Entertaining short stories and cartoons
for sportspeople and couch potatoes.
Set in the world of bogies, fouls, rowlocks,
racquets, disasters, romance and revenge.
ISBN 9780950821252

Baby Boom © 2012
Quirky humour in verse and cartoons
about Mums, bumps, babies and tots.
Also suitable for grandparents and
maiden aunts with a strong constitution.
ISBN 9780950821269

**Available from: www.wordpower.u-net.com
or from libraries and bookshops.**

Published England by
Wordpower™, PO Box 1190, SANDHURST, GU47 7BW

In memory of my mother,
Patricia Campbell-Lyons

Chapter 1

Casslands Estate, East Anglia, England
New Year's Day

'Just try and relax. Hold still. Open it wide. I promise you I'll be gentle.'

Eleanor Framp stood in the knee-high, glistening, white snow, clutching nervously at the arm of Grant Landscar. Their breath combined in the frosty January air as, using a tissue, he dabbed cautiously at the corner of her eye.

'Got it,' he declared. Eleanor blinked rapidly as tears welled up and spilled down over her cold cheeks.

'Oh, that's better. What was it?'

'It looks like a piece of fluff from your scarf. Here, honey, keep the tissue.' The tall Texan put his arm comfortingly around her. 'We ought-a be getting back. Look, the sun's going down and so is the temperature. It sure looks mighty pretty over there though.' He indicated towards the horizon where a red-orange glow glimmered through the mist, outlining the bare branches of the water willows that fringed the frozen river, tinting the undulating snow drifts in shades of pale pink with a hint of purple in the hollows.

'There's something magical about snow,' Eleanor said, putting on her mittens again and placing the end of the offending scarlet, cashmere scarf firmly over her shoulder, 'and snow on New Year's Day is especially enchanting, don't you think?'

'Pretty special, like you.' He pulled her towards him and planted an affectionate kiss on the top of her woolly hat. They turned and began to trudge across the estate, back towards the house, the trail of their footprints embossed in the pristine snow behind them as if the only two people on Earth had passed that way on this icy, winter's day.

Casslands stood in the distance, coated in a white blanket of snow, windows shining with golden light. Curls of smoke rose lazily from its three chimneys into the fading winter afternoon sky. A tall Christmas tree, bedecked with multi-coloured lights, stood in the middle of the virginal, white lawn.

The path back to the house took them through an evergreen copse where conifers and glades of ivy-covered tree stumps were sprinkled as if with icing sugar. There, an open-sided log gazebo was hung with long icicles, glinting like glass in the twilight. A robin took flight, twittering sharply, from his perch on the circular wooden bench in the centre.

Eleanor stopped. 'Oh I just love it here,' she declared, breaking away from Grant, raising her arms and turning around in slow motion, her brown leather boots stamping the snow down in a delayed action flamenco.   'There's something enchanting about East Anglia, the huge skies, all the watery inlets of the Broads and spaciousness.'

'We get a lot of snow though,' Grant said.

'Yes, but it's so beautiful. I could stand out here forever.'

'You'd soon be frozen stiff, my lady,' he joked, pulling his black stetson down. 'My ears are real cold.'

'It's time you took up the great British tradition of the silly, woolly hat,' she teased.

'My darlin' woman. There's nothin' whatsoever macho about a woolly hat.'

'Oh, there would be on you.' She came back to him and looked up adoringly into his face, raising her mittened hands to cover his ears. 'Is that better?'

'I can't hear what you're saying.'

'I said, is that better?'

He reached up and took her hands in his. Then, without any warning, he dropped down in front of her.

'Grant! Grant! Are you alright?'

'Shucks! These pershin' tree roots!'

Then she realised that he was kneeling on one knee. All her life she had dreamed of this moment and now it was here. She felt a cold shiver run down her spine. He gripped her hands more firmly. The world seemed to stand still. The snow white land became as if in a dream. Crystal flakes began to fall gently, sprinkling his black stetson and shoulders, catching on his grey eyelashes as he looked up. Her heart skipped a beat.

'Marry me Eleanor. Be my wife.'

She couldn't breathe properly for a moment and shook her head slowly in disbelief, swallowing, struggling to keep her composure.

'Eleanor I love you. We are soul mates. We belong together.'

'But Grant, we've only known each other since the airshow six months ago and you've told me that you've been married three times before,' she whispered.

'It's different this time, my honey-bunch. I want to share the rest of my life with you. Marry me and come and live at *Casslands* with me. Make my world complete.'

Eleanor thought of her little flat in *Isabel Avenue*, her Reverend Mother aunt who had brought her up, her past career as a journalist and her new venture as a magazine editor that was to start this very week... had this been where her life was intended to go?

'Oh Grant,' she said.

'This is not the dress rehearsal. This is the show, Eleanor. Take this chance to be happy and enjoy life together. Please say 'Yes' so that I can get up off this freezing snow. My knee is giving me gyp.'

She took a deep, cold breath that made her lungs ache. What else was there? A lifetime of lonely nights. Meals for one. He was offering her everything. She helped him up.

His lips were cold against hers as they clung together in the ivy-strewn copse, caught in that eternal moment of time when man and woman know, really know, that there is no other choice.

'Yes,' she said. 'I love you, Grant. It would be an honour to be your wife.'

*

Eleanor found Grant a little later in his study on the ground floor of *Casslands*. It was a massive house and estate, backing onto the Broads. She wondered whether she would ever feel at home here. He was just finishing a telephone call and swung the executive chair around towards her.

'Come in, my dear. Good timing. Are you feeling a little warmer now? Coffee?' He indicated the machine.

'No thank you, Grant. I'm just thinking about having a little light tea.' She saw him glance at his watch.

'Yes, I guess that would be a good idea.'

'Then, if you have time, we really ought to go to the convent to see Aunty Rev to tell her the news.'

'Yes, I suppose we'd better get it over with. Jeepers, I've faced a lot of things in my time, but your nun aunt sure scares me.' He pretended to tremble all over. 'Come here, you lovely woman.' She took his extended hand and he guided her around the edge of the desk and onto his lap. She draped her arm around his neck and rested her cheek against his silver hair. It smelled so good. It felt so good.

'Anyone important on the phone?'

'Nobody for you to worry about. I'll have to meet up with the client at some point, but not immediately.'

'Where are they based?'

'In the Mediterranean.'

'Big company?'

'Nope, but I think you might know the boss.'

'Now,' said Eleanor, 'let me think...'

'Save your energy.'

She looked puzzled. 'The lady pilot from last year's airshow?'

'Bingo! That's the very one. Only she's not flying anymore. She's opening a hotel in Milloncha. We're in partnership.'

Eleanor felt her heart sink. She remembered last summer when he had taken the woman out on his boat, the *Lucky Lady*, during the airshow. Grant felt her stiffen in his arms.

'Now, now. Don't you go being all silly on me. You know she was only ever after a business partner.'

'She's young and very pretty.'

'Not so young and definitely not my type.'

'Am I your type?'

'Let's just say I've grown up in my later years and have learned to appreciate more than the superficial. You are one gorgeously loving woman. What more could a man ask for? Give me a kiss.'

He embraced her tenderly and then slid his hand suggestively along her quivering thigh.

'Oh! Sorry, Sir. I thought this room was unoccupied.'

The pair sprang apart like naughty teenagers.

'I just wanted to close the curtains.'

'It's fine, Synth. You do that and then you can take away this coffee cup, please.'

'Yes, Sir. Sorry Miss Eleanor. Didn't mean to disturb you.'

Eleanor froze and breathed slowly as Synth went to the window to draw the heavy, sage green curtains and then took away the tray as she left.

She was never going to get used to having staff intruding all the time, especially not somebody she'd vaguely known before. The moment was lost, though, and she got up and rearranged her clothing, giving Grant an 'Oh well' sort of regretful smile.

'We'll have to order some *Do not disturb signs*,' he joked. 'Just let me make a note here and then we'll go and have a look in the kitchen.' He scribbled something firmly on a small pad, placed it in the desk drawer, locked it and put the key firmly in his waistcoat pocket.

'Are we allowed in the kitchen?' Eleanor queried as they made their way across the ground floor, through the wide marble hall with its massive staircase sporting convoluted, carved handrails.

'Sure we are. I own the joint, don't I?' He placed his arm around her shoulders in a conspiratorial hug.

'Do you know,' she said, 'although I've been coming here since the summer, it didn't quite dawn on me how much help you would need to run a house and an estate like this. I should have guessed really. This is a huge place and must need a lot of looking after.'

'Well, as you know, there's only Synth living in. She does all the housekeeping and cooking. You've never seen her staff quarters, have you?'

Eleanor shook her head. He continued, 'Oh it's real nice up there and very comfortable for her. When those singing star people owned *Casslands* before I acquired the estate, it was their nanny's quarters and they spared no expense. She's even got her own piano.'

'That's nice for her and I'm glad she's turning out well for you. Aunty Rev wanted to get her settled somewhere useful and away from...' Eleanor hesitated. 'Well, you know.'

'Temptation?'

'I didn't mean...'

'Sure you didn't.' He opened the door that led to the kitchen corridor. 'Your aunt said that Synth needed a respectable occupation and I have provided it. When a nun recommends somebody, it's not gentlemanly to question it.' He grinned. 'Of course the pool man comes in early a few times a week in the season and the gardener keeps himself busy all year round and there's a maintenance man but they're all mostly fairly unobtrusive. If I stage a conference or party then we call in agency staff.'

*

Grant pushed open the kitchen's interior door.

'Mr. Landscar! Miss Eleanor!' Synth wiped her hands on a teacloth and hastily pulled out a couple of kitchen chairs for the visitors. 'You should have rung for me.'

'Don't let us disturb you, dear. We're not stopping. Just looking for a little snack before we go out. What have you got for us?'

Synth turned her huge watery, green eyes ceilingwards and thought for a moment. 'How about some carver ham on granary bread and a little side-salad? I could do that for you very quickly.'

The pair nodded to each other in agreement and sat down.

Feeling slightly awkward, Eleanor looked around the massive kitchen, taking in the stainless steel walls, triple cooker, shelves of pans, several fridges, numerous electrical gadgets and the end wall adorned with food related paintings.

'Bitterly cold today, don't you think, Synth?'

'Oh yes, Mr. Landscar. Deep snow everywhere. It's a good job we are well stocked up.' She busied herself.

'Will you be wanting something to drink with this, Sir?'

'We'll have some of that delightful peach-flavoured, spring water you hide in that fridge over there.'

'I keep it specially for you, Sir.'

'You haven't tried it, have you, Eleanor?'

'I think I'm about to.' She paused. 'This is a very big kitchen.'

'Yes, Miss Eleanor,' Synth replied, 'but I think we need the space for all the entertaining. I've heard it said that Mr. Landscar puts on some lovely dinners, don't you, Sir?'

'The success of my events is entirely down to the culinary skills of others, young woman.'

'I'll just get the salad made,' Synth said. 'Will you be eating here or would you like it served in another room, perhaps the dining room, Mr. Landscar?'

'I think in the library, thank you.'

'I'll see to that right away. It'll be with you in a moment. Won't keep you long.'

She arranged some napkins on the edge of the tray and collected the peach water from the refrigerator. The master of the house got up to leave with his lady.

'Come along, Eleanor. Let's go and wait for our snack.' Then, with a wink to Synth, 'Thank you.'

'Pleasure, Sir.'

The couple left, retracing their steps across the marble hall. Eleanor asked Grant, 'Why didn't you carry the tray through yourself? We were coming back this way and it would have been a nice gesture.'.

'It's her job to do that.'

'I'm sure she'd have appreciated it.'

'She's just the housekeeper.'

'She's a person.'

He gave her a quick glance.

'It's a fluid situation. I don't know how long she'll be here.'

'What about the tray?' Eleanor persevered.

'Why keep a dog and bark yourself?'

'You're much stronger than she is... little slip of a thing.'

'She has a trolley. Let it rest, my dear.'

Eleanor noted the set of his jaw and dropped the subject as he guided her along a picture-lined, deeply carpeted corridor and stopped before a heavy mahogany door marked LIBRARY. As the pair walked into the room, hidden lights came on automatically to show walls lined with fitted book cases from floor to ceiling. A ladder on wheels stood in the corner.

'What do you think of my collection?'

'It's wonderful.' She walked across the room and stretched out her hand towards a gold-embossed, leather-bound tome.

'I'd appreciate it if you didn't touch, my dear.'

She hastily pulled her hand away.

'Sorry. Sorry.'

'They are very valuable.' He paused meaningfully and then said, 'So is this.' He turned to her and, from his trouser pocket, produced a small, square, black leather box with ornate gold embossing. He flipped it open. She gasped.

There, nestling in black velvet, lay the most exquisite emerald ring she had ever set eyes on. The gloriously faceted oval stone was surrounded by a border of sparkling white diamonds and the whole glinted wickedly and enticingly as the box lay in Grant's open palm. He looked at her with his head quizzically on one side.

'Do you want me to get down on my knees again?'

Eleanor shook her head, lost for words.

'Cat got your tongue?'

She nodded. Then, recovering her composure, she looked up into his kindly eyes and asked, childlike, 'Is that for me?'

He didn't reply but placed the box on the shiny surface of a side table, took the ring and kissed it. She stood there, arms dangling by her sides, unable to move. He reached down and took her left hand in his. She trembled. This was a huge step.

'Wait. Please wait.'

'Don't you like it?'

'It's too good. Too valuable for me,' she whispered.

'Nonsense. It suits your long, elegant fingers. Come on, my lady, be brave.' He slid the gorgeous ring onto her third finger.

'There,' he said. 'That wasn't so bad, was it?'

She smiled up at him. 'Oh, Grant.'

'Oh Eleanor,' he teased. 'Come on. Get used to it. I'm gonna spoil you rotten.'

He tipped one finger under her chin and lifted her face to his before placing a single, tender kiss on her quivering lips.

There was a knock and Synth wheeled in the meal.

'Oh! Sorry,' she said, pausing just inside the doorway as she surveyed the couple clinging together. Grant turned towards his housekeeper.

'You can be the first to congratulate us. Miss Eleanor is going to be my wife.'

*

'St. Bede's Convent. Reverend Mother speaking.'

'Er, hello, Reverend Mother. It's... it's Synth here.'

'Hello, my dear. How are you?'

'Very well, thank you. Are the sisters all alright?'

'Yes, my dear, although a few colds have been going around. It's to be expected at this time of year. Is everything working out satisfactorily for you at *Casslands*?'

'Oh, yes. Yes, thank you. It's lovely here. That catering course you sent me on has been so useful and the flat Mr. Landscar has given me is really nice.'

'Excellent. Excellent.'

'I can't thank you enough... '

'No need. We are all here to help each other.'

'I just wanted to wish you a 'Happy New Year' and to tell you that I went to see my mother yesterday in the care home.'

'She seems to be quite content, don't you think?'

'Yes, she does. She still talks about the cottage, and the fire. You were so kind to put us up in the convent last summer.'

'It was our pleasure. As for your mother, well, she's getting on rather, like all of us and, with her problems, she needed some support, but I see the care home has a resident cat so she's very happy about that, as you can imagine.'

'Yes, she is. Oh, did the cat rescue lady come and get the rest?'

'Yes, all fourteen of them, and I must say it was a relief to see them go at last. The stables here were fine as a temporary measure but... '

'Reverend Mother,' Synth interrupted. 'I... I... there's something I think you should know but perhaps not from me...'

'What might that be, Synth?'

The kitchen door swung open and Grant popped his head around.

Synth said, 'I have to go. 'Bye,' and hung up. Then, turning calmly to Grant she said brightly, 'I was just wishing somebody 'Happy New Year.'

'Well, we're just off to do that too. We're popping over to the convent and then I'll take Miss Eleanor to her home and be back here for dinner at eight. That smells good.'

'Just a casserole in the slow cooker, Sir. I'm going upstairs for my usual music practice but I'll come down again to serve your dinner.'

'Thank you, Synth. By the way, I meant to ask, how was your mother yesterday?'

'She's well, thank you, Mr. Landscar. The dementia comes and goes.'

'Fine. Fine. See you later.' Then both he and Eleanor were gone, leaving his housekeeper alone in the great house.

Synth heard the whine of one of the automatic garage doors opening and closing, followed by the crunch of tyres on snow as Grant's Hercedix made its way down the long, poplar-edged drive in the luminous glow of the snow under the floodlights that turned on and off as the vehicle passed.

She took off her frilly, white apron, hung it on the back of a chair, turned out the lights, closed the kitchen door and, ignoring the glass-sided lift, climbed up two flights of stairs to her self-contained apartment. Switching on one side-lamp, she walked over to the window. The spread of *Casslands* estate lay before her, glimmering in the twilight, as gentle snowflakes drifted down to settle on the white of nature's counterpane. She looked at her reflection in the window pane, her slim figure semi-silhouetted, her long, red hair piled on top of her head and the warmth of her cosy sitting room a back-drop behind her.

'What a different life,' she murmured to herself as she drew the pale blue, damask curtains across, shutting out the panorama of glowing white, turning her thoughts inwards to the loneliness of her position. She kicked off her shoes, padded across to the electronic piano and sat down, flexing her fingers. Her time was her own for a couple of hours until the boss came back. 'Some blues,' she thought. 'Yes, I'm in the mood for some blues.'

*

'Why, Eleanor, my dear! Grant! What a delightful and unexpected surprise!' Reverend Mother's face beamed as she peered through the square grill at the visitors lit by the glare of the porch security lamps outside the big front door at St. Bede's Convent . She closed the grill and laboriously drew back the heavy bolts.

'Come in! Come in! Fancy driving through all this snow!'

The pair brushed their shoulders clean, wiped their feet and stepped into the not very warm, oak-panelled entrance hall, Eleanor carrying a large, flat box in a plastic carrier bag,.

'Aw, it wasn't so bad, Reverend Mother,' Grant said. 'I've got these real good tyres on my auto.' His glance swept around the large hallway, taking in garlands of holly and other greenery, the remains of Christmas. A small manger scene still stood on a card table in the corner.

Reverend Mother Veronica pecked her niece fondly on her cold cheeks and then turned to shake hands with Grant Landscar, who promptly removed his stetson.

'Well, Reverend Mother, it sure is a pleasure to meet you again,' he drawled. 'It seems no time at all since Eleanor enjoyed your splendid Christmas eve midnight mass here in the chapel last week.'

'Yes, the days have gone by so fast. This time of year is very busy for us, what with the sisters out distributing food to the homeless. The festive season is a bad time for some. It's a good job we've got the people-mover, although I do worry about the sisters going out in this weather. However, the needs of others are paramount just now.'

'You should have said. I'd have been happy to make a donation.'

'That's very kind of you, Grant. It's willing hands we need more than anything, though.' She led the way, smiling. 'Come and take your coats off in the warm. We're in the front parlour with a nice log fire going.'

The pair followed and found themselves confronted by a circle of nuns, all seated and working at some handicraft or other. There was a miniature Christmas tree on the sideboard. The statue in the alcove bore a garland of ivy. More greenery hung from the picture rails. The sisters started to get to their feet at the sight of Eleanor, their faces wreathed in smiles.

'Miss Eleanor!' they exclaimed in a cacophany.

'Happy New Year everybody! Please don't get up,' she replied as she slid the large box of chocolates from the carrier bag and onto the oval dining table. This elicited a murmur of approval. Then Reverend Mother lead Grant by the elbow to the button-backed leather sofa where he and Eleanor both removed their gloves and coats and hung them over the arm before sitting down. Eleanor tucked her left hand down beside her. Reverend Mother joined with the others in reciprocating the greeting, then returned to her winged chair by the fire.

'May we offer you some refreshment?' She indicated a tray bearing a glass decanter of home-made elderberry juice and a plate of biscuits on a white, crochet lace doiley.

'No thank you kindly, Ma'am. We have just eaten.' Grant took Eleanor's right hand in his and turned his gaze towards her.

'We just came over to tell you the good news,' he said. Eleanor smiled apprehensively at him.

A flicker of concern flashed across Reverend Mother's plump face. The sisters, who had resumed their needlework and knitting, paused in mid-stitch, holding a communal breath.

Grant cleared his throat. They all waited. Eleanor looked down at her lap, a feint flush painting her thin cheeks as she bit her lower lip.

'I have asked Eleanor to be my wife,' he said.

There was an audible intake of breath as all the sisters turned to look expectantly at Reverend Mother who, with only the slightest of perceptible hesitations, grabbed the claw-shaped arms of her chair and raised herself up to her feet again. Did she sway ever so slightly?

Then she was across the room and holding her arms open, bending over the couple, embraced them.

'Eleanor and Grant. What wonderful news. May I be the first to wish you every happiness?'

The sisters set aside their work and clustered around the happy pair. 'Congratulations! Oh, a wedding! How lovely!' They twittered on like happy starlings, turning to pat each other on the arm or shrug in group conspiratorial delight. As brides of Christ, a wedding meant something entirely different to them.

'Thank you. Thank you,' Eleanor said, quite overwhelmed by the reaction. She had been dreading telling her aunt.

'So, when is it to be then?' Reverend Mother clasped her hands across her ample waistline and beamed encouragingly. Grant reached across and took Eleanor's left hand in his, displaying the gorgeous emerald and diamond ring.

'We thought Easter.'

The sisters gasped as they peered at the ring.

'Perfect,' said Reverend Mother. 'In the chapel here, of course, or will you be choosing somewhere bigger?'

'In the chapel. In the chapel,' repeated the sisters hopefully, eyes wide and eyebrows raised.

'Well, actually...' Grant and Eleanor looked nervously at each other. 'It will be in a Phillipstone Register Office,' he said.

Chapter 2

Eleanor Framp stood and surveyed her Sunday morning domain. The fully serviced suite of offices on the first floor of *Curtis House* in *The Circle* in Phillipstone, was a dream come true and Grant had made it all happen. She cast her mind back to the romantic dinner they had shared at last summer's airshow in *Clouds Restaurant*, how he had placed the keys to her enterprise on the snowy white table cloth together with a confirmation letter from the solicitors. She had one year in which to prove that she could be an editor as well as a reporter.

The suite of offices overlooked *The Circle*, true to its name because it was a circular park with iron railings around it and a pedestrian walkway encompassing the whole. Modern offices had been constructed overlooking it on all sides. Any traffic passed to the rear of the buildings, allowing this oasis on the outskirts of town to be enjoyed by the office-workers at lunchtime.

Eleanor hugged herself with muted joy as she gazed out of the window of the main office. She could see bench-style seats and young saplings devoid of life on this snowy winter's morning. In the spring, the park would burgeon with flowerbeds and blossoming bushes.

It was comfortably warm in the office. She removed her coat and hung it in the closet. It felt like the first day of the school term. Her own magazine! Imagine! What challenges lay ahead? She looked around at the two L-shaped desks with their PCs and telephones, the swivel chairs, wood-finished filing cabinets and tall stationery cupboard. Pin-boards adorned the walls, empty apart from a planning chart and a calendar showing views of the Broads. The pale green carpet and white blinds gave the room a fresh feeling. So did the big *Swiss Cheese* plant in its blue ceramic pot over by the door.

She walked across and into the side-office with its shiny, woodblock floor, noting the photocopier, mailing ephemera and a working side with a sink and kettle socket. Next to this room, a modestly sized conference salon offered a shining table with six chairs and a display screen for video-conferencing. There were also a couple of black leather sofas with colourful cushions. She was pleased to see that there were two cloakrooms, one for her exclusive use and one for staff and visitors.

Eleanor was going to be happy here. After years at the beck and call of recalcitrant editors, this moment of literary freedom was to be savoured. She opened the office door and peeped out gingerly into the long corridor edged with windows that looked down across the rear service road and onto the backs of some shops. All was quiet. The plaque on the door stated:

Embroideryworld
Editor, Eleanor Framp

With a deep, contented sigh, she went back in to the urgent ringing of the telephone. Who could be calling her?

'_Embroideryworld_,' she said crisply in a business-like tone into the mouthpiece. 'Eleanor Framp speaking.'

'Good morning, Miss Framp. This is reception,' a man's voice said. 'Just checking everything's in order for you in your new offices.'

'Yes. Fine, thank you. It all looks lovely.'

'That's good then. Anything you need, just dial double zero for reception. The desk down here is manned from 7a.m. until 10 p.m. Happy New Year, Miss Framp, and good luck with your magazine.'

'Thank you. Happy New Year to you too.'

She hung up and sat down at her workstation next to one of the panoramic windows, put her elbows on the desk and clasped her hands together under her chin. This was going to be such an exciting year. She reached down beside her for the bulky, brown briefcase, a legacy from her days as a freelance journalist. Once open, its contents spilled out in a mêlée of notes, plans, photographs and artwork. A flick of the wall switch and soon the pc was on and ready to accept the memory stick crammed with her dreams of a magazine devoted entirely to decorative needlework. Her little flat in _Isabel Avenue_ contained just the tip of the embroidery iceberg that was her passion.

Through *Embroideryworld* she was going to revitalise the world of needlework and lead her readers along the pathways of history to discover the roots of decorative embroidery in Asia, the Americas, Europe and Australia. They would follow her into the intricacies of tribal and Inca designs, the glories of Victorian gold and the subtleties of fine, drawn thread-work. She would transport them on a magic carpet of discovery that would thrill and inspire.

First though, she had to look at the magazine mock-up she had cut and pasted together... sixty-two pages to be filled with illustrated articles, advertisements, letters, a help section, features, travel and special offers, as well as great personalities. Colour. That was the most important thing. The publication had to be attractive to all ages and both sexes. She smiled at the knowledge that embroidery was originally the province of men.

Soon, her assistant would arrive to take up her position at the other workstation. Grant had recommended his only daughter, Pandora. 'She's got a career history to die for,' he'd said. 'You'll need somebody who knows all about editing, photography, design, advertising and copy-writing. She's going to be such an asset to you, Eleanor.' A little shocked at having her staff selected for her, the embryo magazine editor had been too stunned to respond. She'd met Pandora at *Casslands* and had been impressed by her easy, friendly manner. So maybe it would work out.

Grant had told Eleanor, 'You must understand that I move in very useful and influential circles which Pandora shares. Her professional pedigree is outstanding and she is just what you need to get your publication off the ground.'

Somewhere at the back of her mind Eleanor felt a passing whim that maybe she would have liked to have chosen her assistant herself, but then Grant was so much more worldly than she was. He probably knew best. After all, he had given her the use of this lovely suite of offices. Her eyes swept around her little empire and she took in a deep breath of pride. She was going to make this work. She really had to.

Only three months to Easter and then she would be his wife. Eleanor took out her spiral-bound note-pad... no hand-held, note-making, electronic devices for her. At the front was the growing list of things she needed to remember to do with the magazine. At the back were the wedding plans.

She perused the details of her dress, bridesmaids, flowers, cars, register office... oh dear! That hadn't gone down too well with Aunty Rev, but then she knew it wouldn't. She grimaced slightly at the memory of that rather awkward moment that had followed their announcement in the convent parlour. Of course, her aunt had made the best of it but Eleanor could see how hurt she was at the thought of her only, beloved niece, entering a heathen marriage.

*

'Gonzales, is that you?' Grant Landscar shouted irritably into the telephone handset.

'Yes, Señor.'

'You took your time getting to the phone.'

'I was attending to the pool, Señor Landscar.'

'You should have emptied it.'

'It is empty, sir. I was sweeping it out.'

'Getting kind of short of odd jobs, are you?'

'No, sir. There is always much maintenance to do during the winter here in Milloncha.'

'I believe you, you rascal.'

'Please?'

'Never mind. Now, listen to me carefully, Gonzo.'

'I am listening, Sir.'

'I will be arriving at the *Villa Estancia* after Easter and I will be bringing my new wife with me for our honeymoon.'

'That is very good news indeed, Señor Landscar. Many congratulations. I heartily wish you both every happiness for the foreseeable future.'

'Thank you. Now, down to business. It is very important that everything is in first class order when we arrive. So I'll be sending you a list of my requirements by email today.'

'I will await your communication with alacrity, Sir.'

Grant winced at the wordy overload.

'We will also be bringing our maid with us, so there's no need to hire in help from the village this time.'

'That is a pity, sir. The ladies like to work here at your *Villa Estancia.*'

'Not this time, Gonzo. We are self-sufficient... which brings me precisely to my next thought. Have you started sowing the vegetable seeds in the greenhouse?'

'Yes, Señor Landscar, and I have planted new roses last autumn. We will have a very nice display in the summer for you, Sir.'

'Swell. Swell. Look out for my email later and be sure that you follow my instructions exactly.'

Yes, Señor Landscar. Adios.'

'Adios to you too.'

Grant put the handset back in its cradle, extended his long legs under the huge desk and stretched his arms above his head. Gee, this was going to be an exciting year!

The phone rang.

'Hi, Pops.'

'Pandora! It sure is good to hear from you. I was wondering where the heck you'd gotten to.'

'Just a little shopping trip to New York, but I'm back in the UK now and raring to go at that little venture of Eleanor's.'

'Cutting it a bit fine, aren't you? She's gone into the new office today. I take it you'll join her tomorrow?'

'Well, I'll sort it out with her. I'll probably go in later in the week. Get over my jet lag.'

'Now look, Pandora, you're my only daughter but sometimes I think I have been a little bit too lax with you.'

'Loosen up, Pops. I know why you want me there. I won't let you down.'

'You'd better not. Let Eleanor know when to expect you. It's the courteous thing to do. She'll soon be family.'

'Haven't I always adapted to your latest conquest?'

'This time, it's different, Pandy. This one is for keeps. She's special.' He paused. 'Aw, by the way, how's that fine grandson of mine?'

'Charlie's gone on to stay with his school friends in London for a little while. He's at that age when he just wants to hang out with the guys. Don't forget his birthday coming up next week. I can't believe he'll be thirteen. How time flies! It seems like only yesterday when he was toddling around.'

'Give me some credit. I don't need reminding. I've already fixed up a mighty good present for him.'

'You're in danger of spoiling him, Pops.'

'Well, the kid's got no Dad, so he deserves a little bit extra.'

There was a silence from the other end. Then Pandora said, 'He had a father. He's not illegitimate.'

'I know that, honey.'

'Well, must get unpacked and try on some of my fabby January sale bargains. You should have seen it in *Stacey's*. A real bun fight but fabulous designer clothes at real knock-down prices.'

'If there's one trait you didn't get from me, it's the ability to spend wildly.'

'All bargains, Pops. All bargains.'

'Hey, by the way, I've got somebody interested in one of those two adjacent shops on that little parade of mine.'

'About time. They've been empty for ages. Who's taken it?'

'Aw, some woman's after the one with the dry rot under the stairs. The agent said she's got great references so it'll be OK. She's wants to open a moms and babies retail outlet there.'

'And the other one?'

'Nothin' yet.'

'I hope it's taken soon.'

'I hope so too, although that little parade has been a good investment so far... and there's something else interesting that I'm thinking about in that neck of the woods. Tell you when I see you.'

'Sounds mysterious. Talk again soon. Mind how you drive in this snow. We skidded a bit when we landed.'

'I will honeybun. You be careful too. Love yah.'

'Love you Pops. Bye-eeee.'

Then she was gone.

*

Celeste Blagden wrestled with the bunch of keys outside the retail outlet on the main road. It was a bitterly cold morning and she could see her breath in the air. The shop windows were whited out and she couldn't wait to get inside and see what it all looked like. The slush on the forecourt had partly refrozen and the shopping parade was deserted. The agent had said she could go in anytime over the new year to see what she thought of it.

The lock turned but she had to put her shoulder to the door to get it to open. The action pulled the muscles on her abdomen, still tender from the Caesarian last October. A musty and unused smell hit her like a wall as she peered into the gloom. A counter stretched across at the back. There were adjustable shelves on brackets. She fumbled for the light switch and the fluorescents flickered on uncertainly, as if surprised that they were needed after all this time.   The chipboard flooring was dusty and gritty and cobwebs hung from the high ceiling that was dotted with a plethora of hooks. It was a depressing sight.

Starting up and running a mother and baby shop was going to be such a huge change from an executive position at the airshow company. As a single mother of triplets, she'd had to draw on all her resources to get through these past months and had come up with the idea of this retail outlet because it ticked all the boxes. She was going to be self-employed and live above the shop.

'You can't go into trade,' her mother had said disparagingly.

'Bit of a step down, Celeste,' her father had added.

'Come and live with us, dear,' Mrs. Blagden had wheedled.

Discovering that her only daughter was to be an unmarried mother hadn't gone down too well in their large, detached on the outskirts of Phillipstone. That the pregnancy was to produce triplets had ameliorated the situation somewhat because of the novelty value. So the new young mother had moved into her parents' five-bedroomed pile with her brood and two hired nursery nurses.

Celeste looked around the shop.The stockroom at the back was dismal but there was a sink and a socket. The dimness in there was caused by a big, overhanging, wooden balcony attached to the rear of the flat above. Iron bars at the large side window further enhanced the cell-like look of the place. She stifled a sob. Rupert. Rupert, the father of her three babies, was now incarcerated in a Hamburg jail serving an immoral earnings sentence. 'I hope he rots!' she muttered, blinking back the tears. He had sent her a pathetic Christmas card with *'Fröhliche Weihnachten'* on the front.

She went on, unlocking, to find a rudimentary store attached to the back of the stockroom. A foul little toilet, home to a spider colony, came off that. Outside in the long yard, two large concrete sheds stood, their rusty green-painted roofs iced with frost. At the end was an open-sided barn with padlocked gates leading out onto the rear access which was in a dreadful state. Celeste stood looking up at the back of the three storey building. The massive, wooden balcony projected outwards like a ship's jetty. Then she turned to peer across beyond the service road at the huge, new circular building. One day she would have somewhere like that.

The *Put and Keep* lease would eat up much of her savings just getting started. Two bedrooms were ideal because it meant that the two nannies wouldn't be able to come to stay with the triplets. So they'd all have to live with her parents. She looked at her watch and wandered back in through the outhouses and stockroom, into the shop. A connecting door opened onto a minute square of hallway and a steep staircase leading up from the private front door at the front of the building. It was dim and narrow with a turn at the top. The lightbulb had gone. She groped her way upwards, finding the door-handle in the semi-darkness. A long landing gave onto an extensive lounge-diner. Further exploration yielded a kitchen, bathroom and study on this first floor. A twisting staircase rose to the bedrooms. There was no bathroom up there.

She looked down from the front bedroom window onto the dual carriageway that tomorrow would be congested with streams of noisy traffic. The patient and ever-changing traffic signals cycled their fruit-drop colours on this quiet, January morning. The service road in front of the shop's wide forecourt was almost empty. Celeste took a deep breath. This was a challenge she had to meet and that meant leaving her children safely down in the Phillipstone countryside so that she could get on with her life.

*

Schriftenvolle Prison near Hamburg was a stark and miserable place, one of Germany's older penitentiaries. Rupert Skinner sat with his head bowed on the lower bunk in the yellow glossed cell that he shared with another inmate who refused to speak to him. How had it come to this? How could he have been so stupid? Seven years! A trumped up charge of 'living off immoral earnings', set up by that ignominious rat he had fallen in with in this city last summer.

He ran his fingers through his dark and greasy hair. Celeste. Celeste. The triplets. He had thrown it all away, after all those years together. Yes, she could be forthright and over-organised but she had been dynamite in bed... too much of a good thing sometimes. Rupert took her photograph out of the top pocket of his regulation grey and white striped shirt. She looked back at him, her shoulder-length dark hair gleaming and those arched eyebrows eternally questioning him.

'Do you want to see a photograph of my girlfriend?' he called to his silent companion on the bunk above. No reply. Just the rustle of a German tabloid newspaper. Rupert ducked his head and got to his feet, holding the photograph up for the other prisoner to see.

'She's good looking.' No response. The man, who had been lying on his back, turned away from Rupert.

'Hey! Don't do that! Talk to me! Ich spreche ein bisschen deutsch. I speak a little German. Comprende?' It was useless. The other prisoner had been moved in with him two days ago. It was like living with a robot. Rupert felt as if he himself was invisible. He put the photograph away again and walked over to the end wall beneath the high barred window. All he could see was a heavy grey sky and the occasional screeching seagull that had followed the Elbe all the way up from the North Sea and into the port. It was a sure sign of bitter weather.

Last night he had heard the church bells ringing in the New Year, the ships' sirens hooting in the harbour, the fireworks and rockets and the sound of cheering.

A guard hammered on the cell door and the key turned in the lock.

'Frühstück! Raus! Raus!'

'Breakfast.' Rupert said. 'Come on! Essen!'

His fellow prisoner slowly folded his paper and climbed down from the top bunk, pulling his grey striped trousers up over his enormous stomach and shambling out into the corridor behind Rupert. Columns of striped figures walked dejectedly towards the spiral, metal staircases that led down to the communal area and through to the dining hall that always stank of Bratwurst and fried potatoes.

It all started so suddenly! A chair over-turned, a plastic plate flying through the air and ricocheting off the wall, the insistent drumming of fists on tables. Whistles blew! Alarm bells rang! Kitchen staff and their trustee helpers made a hasty exit via the store-rooms. Then the sprinklers came on, drenching the rioting inmates with cold water. Guards dived out into the passageway, slamming and locking behind them. A few didn't make it and rapidly found themselves held hostage.

Then the chanting started. 'Fröhliches Neues Jahr! Fröhliches Neues Jahr!' Rupert looked around in panic. Somebody shoved him sideways, bruising his ribs. How could he get out of this chaos? He dropped to his knees and scuttled along, half-crawling, to the end of the room where the waste-bins stood in a row, and squeezed past the last one to crouch in the corner. The noise was deafening. The food throwing started.

Serving trays were up-ended, cereal packets flew through the air and prisoners were skidding and sliding on porridge that had been tipped all over the tiled floor. Sporadic fights broke out everywhere. Bloody noses and black eyes abounded. Then the loudspeakers crackled into life.

'Alle auf den Boden sitzen mit den Händen über die Köpfe.' The loudspeaker request for everybody to sit down on the floor with their hands on their heads was lost in the chaos and hiss of sprinklers. Somebody vaulted over the serving counter and started throwing trolleys and cooking pans about.

Rupert tucked his head between his knees and hugged himself to be as small as possible. A fried egg hit the wall beside him and slid down to land on his laceless trainer.

A television monitor suspended from the ceiling came on. The governor appeared, appealing to the rioters to calm down and discuss their grievances in the prescribed manner. It became the target for a pie-throwing contest.

It had all started with food and it would be food that ended it. Three days later, the waste bins were full of bodily wastes. Every scrap of food in the dining hall had been scraped up and consumed. The large freezers and fridges had been pillaged and management had turned off the gas and water from outside. Thirst was becoming a problem.

Two nights of sleeping in filthy clothes on a fast-becoming rancid floor was starting to pall. Those needing medication were not faring well. Rupert felt weak and disoriented, stretched out behind the stinking bins.

'Achtung!' shouted a burley prisoner, stripped to the waist. He righted a chair and stood up on it.

'Das ist genug. Ich bin gelangweilt. Stille!'

Whoever he was, Rupert guessed that he had some power over the others. Having told them that was enough and he was bored, he'd ordered them all to be quiet. Like lambs, the entire company sat on the floor and put their hands on the tops of their heads.

The burley prisoner looked up at one of the recessed camera lenses in the ceiling and called out in German that the protest was over and that everybody was ready to return to their cells. The hostage guards were bundled towards the door and their hands untied.

With a feeling of relief, Rupert crawled out from behind the bins, stood up, took a step forward, then slipped over and cracked his head on the corner of a table.

*

Celeste Blagden pulled the pastel blue *Fabula* over to the side of the slushy road as her mobile phone beeped its banal jingle for the third time in quick succession. She had returned the shop keys to the estate agent, dropping them into the office letterbox, and was keen to get back to her parents' house out in the sticks beyond the fringes of Phillipstone. What now? She turned off the ignition and slammed on the handbrake. A quick rummage in the depths of her voluminous *Du Prève* handbag on the front passenger seat beside her, produced the offending item. There were three SMS messages from an unknown number requesting her to return the call. Who could it be? Was it a scam? Oh, she'd try it later.

She did, much later, in the sumptuous bedroom that her doting parents had decorated and furnished lavishly for her comfort and relaxation. Her three-month old triplets, April, May and June, were ensconced in the top floor bedrooms with their two nannies, well out of earshot of their not very interested mother.

It was nearly midnight. Celeste turned off the bedside light and snuggled down under the softest of duvets in her lonely bed. As her eyes closed and she sought sleep, there was this nagging feeling that something had been forgotten. Was it failing to go and see her baby daughters when she'd arrived home? No. That didn't trouble her at all. She sat bolt upright, groping for the lamp switch.

The SMS messages! Hauling the big handbag up from the thick carpet beside the bed, she undid the clasp and took out the mobile phone. Oh heck! It was too late to ring now. Or was it? She looked at the message envelope and punched in the number. It was answered by a guttural German voice advising her that the prison office was closed until nine o'clock the following morning and that she should call back then. If the truth be told, she didn't understand the message fully until it was repeated in English. Then the penny dropped. Celeste switched off the mobile and put it back in her bag. She sat with her head resting against the oyster pink satin bed-head. This was about Rupert, the imprisoned father of her babies, the beast who had abandoned her last summer upon receiving the news of her pregnancy. Now what? She had cut him out of her life entirely, resolute in her belief that his immoral earnings sentence was well deserved in view of his attitude to her and their unborn children. Let him go to hell! The lamp went off. The duvet embraced her. She lay awake for a very long time.

Chapter 3

St. Bede's Convent nestled in extensive grounds adjacent to the airport. Today, with a blanket of snow adorning its fields and woods and coating the edifice's ancient eves like cotton wool, it was straight out of a picture book or Christmas card. The old sandstone building glowed in an early January afternoon sun that shone weakly across the terrain, glinting on molehills and sparkling on icicles clinging to the wainscots and soffits. The hazy, orange globe would soon sink below the horizon and condemn the nuns to another night shivering in their unheated cells as a hard frost gripped the East Anglian Broads, those meandering waterways abutting to the market town of Phillipstone.

'Good day again, Sister Catherine.'

'Hello, Reverend Mother,' replied the other nun with a smile as they fell into step on their way to the chapel where they had already heard mass in the darkness of the early morning.

'You have your usual chores, Sister?'

'Oh yes indeed, Reverend Mother. It's my day for changing the altar cloth, replenishing candles and topping up holy water.'

'Yes, we must have everything in good order for today.'

'Father Guyler's arrival. Of course! I had quite forgotten.'

'He should have been here on the midday train but I very much doubt whether it was in on time. They said there was ice on the rails. I heard it on the five o'clock news this morning.'

Sister Catherine paused for a moment. 'Is there some special reason for his visit?'

Reverend Mother took her gently by the elbow and steered her forward. 'I shouldn't really say much about it but there is talk of new plans for some of the larger convent estates such as ours.'

A look of alarm spread across the other nun's face as she stopped in her tracks again but Reverend Mother was quick.

'Oh, no, my dear. Don't worry. They just want us to make the best of our assets after that most distressing land-grabbing attempt last year.'

'By Miss Eleanor's fiancé...'

'Yes, yes, but it's all been sorted out. The council is paying us a substantial rental for our land that they sub-lease to the airport. It was all a misunderstanding. I'm sure Mr. Landscar didn't mean to harm us personally. He just wanted what he thought was his by rights. Grant Landscar is, I believe, a basically good man.' She gave a look askance at her elderly companion. 'He'd better be or he'll have me to answer to.'

They paced onwards along the parquet floored passage-way that was imbued with the scent of wax polish from decades of kneeling nuns buffing the wood until it gleamed with a patina laced in history but this convent had been a stately mansion long before the nuns had come into residence.

'Here we are, then. I'll leave you to your work, Sister. The novices are getting the guest suite ready for Father Guyler. It will be most interesting to see him again after all these years. Do you know, I don't believe I have set eyes on him since before we went on that mission to Kridblikistan. That was so long ago. Now, let me think. Eleanor was at college then, doing her journalist's course. Father Guyler went off to India and then Eleanor, on the spur of the moment, took that post in Italy for a year. Do you remember? When we got back from Kridblikistan she had quite grown up. Now look at her, middle-aged and about to get married for the first time.'

'The register office wedding must be very disappointing for you, Reverend Mother. After all, she's your only niece.'

'Yes it is, my dear, but I would rather Grant Landscar was honest about his lack of belief. It would be far worse if she were to marry a hypocrite.'

'Still...'

'We can always pray. I'll see you at teatime, Sister.'

Reverend Mother touched her friend on the sleeve as she left on her way down to the basement kitchens. The two elderly nuns were harnessed together in belief and humility that would bind them until their dying days.

*

'Pandora! How good to hear from you!' Eleanor Framp perched on the edge of her desk at *Embroideryworld.*

'Hiya, boss lady. I'm just back from the States and raring to go!'

'How did you know I was here in the office?'

'Dad told me. I've just got off the phone to him. So, is it OK with you if I come in on Thursday? That'll give me a bit of time to sort myself out.'

'Yes. That's fine,' Eleanor replied, silently grateful that she would have her magazine office to herself for a few more days. Then, observing the niceties, she added, 'Did you have a good flight back?'

'First class, in every sense of the word. Well, I won't keep you. I expect you've got masses to do and I must unpack all my lovely sale bargains and try them on again. See you later in the week. 'Bye.'

'Goodbye, Pand...' Eleanor peered at the receiver as if expecting her to pop out of it. She put it down. Her future stepdaughter was quite a lively type. 'I hope it works out,' she half-whispered to herself. How would it be, harnessed to the dynamic daughter of her future husband? What if they didn't get along? Too late now. The die was cast.

She glanced out of the window down at the empty *Circle*, still caked with slush and frozen snow, its park benches vacant, trees and shrubs bare. New Year's Day was well behind her now. People would soon come out of their offices for an early lunch.

She looked at the wall-clock. There was just enough time to ring Aunty Rev before the morning silence. Eleanor sat down at her workstation and speed-dialled the telephone number of *St. Bede's Convent*. Reverend Mother answered promptly.

'Ah! Eleanor! How lovely to hear your voice! You've been very much in my thoughts since your visit here with Grant on New Year's Day. The sisters were all very excited about your news.' There was an awkward silence. 'It's all alright, Eleanor. You're a grown woman now and must make your own decisions.'

'I'm terribly sorry if you're disappointed about the venue for the wedding ceremony, Aunty.'

'It's up to you both to do as you see fit. It's your special day. I'm only a little bit sad that the sisters and I won't be there to see you getting married.'

'You wouldn't consider...?'

'That would be impossible. Surely you can see that, my dear? As nuns, our first duty is to a higher authority.'

'I suppose so.' Eleanor played with the telephone base, tracing her finger around the edge. 'I don't want to lose him. He may be my last chance at real happiness.'

'Then you have to do what you have to do, even if it's not in the way I had hoped for you.'

'Thank you for being so understanding, Aunty.'

There was a hesitation before Reverend Mother said, 'I have to go now. It's time for the morning silence. Don't worry. All will be well. Remember me in your prayers.'

'Goodbye Aunty Rev.' The line went dead. Eleanor felt tears well up. She hated hurting the woman who had brought her up and provided a home-life of sorts but she couldn't bear to risk losing Grant, the man of her dreams... tall, elegant, polite, self-assured Grant with his silver hair and ever-present stetson.

Eleanor took the first issue file of *Embroideryworld* and flipped it open on her desk. The cover of the February edition bore a photograph of a beautiful, gold-embroidered, Victorian valentine card set against a deep plush, red velvet background. The magazine's title was emblazoned across the top in faux embroidery in rainbow-shaded colours in a stylised script that could have been Asian but, there again, oriental or even Turkish. Instructions to the designer had been specific. It was to appeal to as many ethnic groups as possible.

She turned the plastic-covered pages, her eyes hungry for colour and interest, trying to view the mock-up as if she were one of the readers. No irritating dotted lines around the columns. A good, clear font without serifs. The list of museums and suppliers of embroidery paraphernalia was not exhaustive and would grow with time, perhaps having to be moved later on to the web-site.

The workstation was powered up and she found and logged onto the launch page. It came up to the sound of tinkling bells and the sweep of harp strings. Then a husky voice intoned, '*Embroideryworld*, your very own passport to embroidery paradise.' Eleanor wrinkled her nose. That was rather over the top. She imagined hordes of angels cavorting about in smocked tops but the home page was attractive with 'buttons' contrived from coiled silk threads which, when clicked, took the surfer to yet more delights, such as the embroidery picture gallery, the special offers page and the regular feature on celebrity embroiderers.

The face of a well-known comedian came up. He was sitting in his dressing room backstage in the *Phillipstone Theatre*, working away at a large tablecloth bearing the names of all the famous performers he had encountered on his tours. He looked up and smiled disarmingly at the camera, like a little boy caught doing something naughty. Then, with a look sincere enough to make a skylark sing, he extolled the virtues of his hidden hobby, telling how it sustained him backstage, how his mother had taught him to sew and how important it was to allow your creativity to flow. The camera panned away and a disembodied voice said, 'Overture and beginners, please.' The solitary sewer reluctantly put down his work, dabbed some powder on his nose and left his dressing room wearing baggy, plaid trousers and signature, silver, fuzzy wig as the magazine title came up. It was great advertising.

Eleanor closed the web-site. The web-master had done a good job there. The television campaign would start in a couple of weeks' time and she herself was scheduled to appear on an afternoon programme aimed at women. There was no doubt about it. Grant had the connections. Having lived a life where she had figuratively always had to pull herself up by her bootstraps, it was strange to have magic doors opened in front of her, but rather nice. She felt she didn't deserve it. The convent humility never left her no matter how she tried to overcome it.

There was a knock at the office door. Eleanor looked up sharply. Who could it be? She wasn't expecting any visitors to the office today.

'Come!' she said, getting to her feet. It was the janitor bearing a large bouquet of pink roses and gypsophela tied up with a huge, multi-pastel shaded ribbon.

'Sorry to disturb you, Miss Framp, but these just came for you. There's a card with them. '

She looked puzzled.

'Thank you. Thank you.' The janitor gave her the flowers, tipped his forehead in mock salute and left her to enjoy the thrill that unexpected flowers always brings.

Bewildered, she nursed the huge bunch and extracted the small envelope, ripping it open. *'To my Darling Eleanor. Good luck with your magazine! Your Grant, xxx.'*

'Oh! Oh! How thoughtful!' She buried her nose in the blooms and sniffed in the heady perfume. Then, realising that she had no vase to put them in, she hurried into the kitchenette and half-filled the circular-bowl sink with water, plunging the flowers into it. She'd have to bring in a vase tomorrow.

'Hello,' said a young voice behind her.

Eleanor whipped around to see a boy in a grey anorak standing in the doorway. She became immediately stern.

'Who are you and what do you want? You shouldn't be in here.'

'I'm Charlie Brand and my Mum's going to work here with you.' He pulled a string of pink bubble-gum out of his mouth, folded it in half and popped it back in again, wiping his fingers on the sides of his long, maroon trousers. He went back and kicked the office door to and then sauntered across to Eleanor, gazing cheekily at her, eyebrows raised in expectation, cheeks ruddy with January cold.

Eleanor blinked hard as she emerged from the utility room. 'You must be Pandora's son. Does your mother know you're here?'

'Course not! She wouldn't let me come to the office.'

'Then why do it?'

'I just wanted to have a look at you. You're going to marry my grand-dad, aren't you?'

'Yes, I am.'

'Are you after his money?' Eleanor was outraged and placed her hands on her hips.

'How dare you say that! I love your grandfather. Money has nothing to do with it. I'm going to telephone your mother right this minute.'

'Please don't do that, Eleanor, I just thought I'd better check. He's quite good to me and I wouldn't want some fortune-hunter after him.' She suppressed a smile and walked towards him with her hand out.

'Delighted to meet you, Charlie Brand. Your grandfather would be pleased that you look after his interests so well, and you may not call me by my first name.'

'You can't be too careful, you know.' He winked. 'What am I supposed to call you, anyway?'
Eleanor glanced at her watch.' I'll think about it. Where does your mother think you are now?'

'Staying with friends.'

'How on earth did you get here?'

'Train and taxi.'

'How can a boy of your age afford such a thing?'

'I'm nearly thirteen, you know. I'm not some kid. Oh, I've got loads of money. Grand-dad gives me plenty of spends.'

'Well, the first thing we have to do is to tell your mother where you are. She'd be worried to death if she thought you were roaming the countryside.'

'I can take care of myself.'

'Maybe but I'm phoning your mother straight away and you are going to speak to her.'

'OK. Keep your hair on. I'll do it myself on my mobile.' He pressed the call button. 'Hi Mum. I'm at the office with Eleanor.'

There was the sound of a machine-gun rattle of angry words. The boy looked at the ceiling.

'Stay cool, Mum. Is it alright if I treat her to lunch?'
Another round of expletives.

'I'll take it that's a 'yes', then. Be home later. 'Bye.' He clicked off and turned to his new-found friend. 'I think that's sorted then. Come on, Eleanor! Let's go to the *Chicken Grillo*. I'm starving.'

If the mature lady was nonplussed to be so familiarly addressed by a juvenile, she covered it well.

'I was just about to get something to eat, as it happens. Very well. We can go and lunch together but I think that you shouldn't address me by my first name. I am very much older than you are.

'I don't mind if you don't.' He held the office door open for her. 'Come on! We want to beat the lunchtime rush.'

*

'Celeste! Celeste Blagden! Yoo-hoo!'

The young woman pushing her airport trolley, slowly ambling along the concourse outside *Departures*, was impervious to the shouts of the baseball-capped, middle-aged man running after her as planes screamed overhead. The stench of taxi diesel hung like a low-level cloud around the area. Armed police were everywhere.

'Celeste! Are you deaf or something?'

She turned distractedly to face Roland Dilger who panted and skidded to a stop beside her, dropping one of his heavy cases onto the ground with a clatter and thud.

'Oh,' she said. 'It's you. Haven't clapped eyes on you since last year's airshow.'

'Are you alright?' he queried, puzzled at her distant demeanour. This wasn't the woman he had last seen bossing and snapping as she managed the Press Centre. 'Are you still working for the airshow people?'

She gazed off meekly towards the terminal building. It was then that he noticed that she wore no make-up and that her eyes were very puffy. 'No. I had to leave last year. I'm flying to Hamburg today. Rupert's dead.' He noted her black coat.

'Dead? Rupert?'

'Yes. My ex-partner. He died in prison. A riot or something. He slipped and cracked his head open.'

Roland adjusted his camera strap and placed his hand on her shoulder. She shrugged it off. 'I can't stop. I'll miss my flight.'

'Celeste. I'm really so very sorry.' His breath was steamy in the frosty afternoon air. 'I heard you were expecting a baby last year...'

'Triplets, actually,' she said, ignoring Roland's dropped jaw and adding hastily, 'stupid idiot was involved with some immoral earnings scam and got caught. Serves him right.' Tears brimmed over and streamed down her blotchy cheeks. 'I've got to go.' She pushed the trolley handle down and trundled off towards the pedestrian crossing, ignoring his pleas to meet up sometime.

Roland stood and watched her go, mystified. She was usually somebody to be reckoned with but her fighting spirit seemed to have been broken now though. He picked up his case and caught the eye of a cab driver who had just pulled over. The man got out and opened the boot, grabbing the items from Roland. The engine was still ticking over and the stench of exhaust overpowering.

'Be careful with that lot. It's fragile,' Roland said, fussy as always, about his equipment.

Celeste didn't look back as she struggled to push her trolley through the large, revolving glass door. There was a long queue at check-in. Security was tight. There had been another alert. She studied the tiled floor, not wanting to meet anyone's gaze, remembering how she had flown back from Hamburg on the Sunday night before the airshow had opened last June, how, before leaving, she had told Rupert that she was pregnant. He had calmly and unceremoniously dumped her only minutes before he had been arrested by the German police. That had somehow made it easier, although telling her parents had been something of a trial.

That was all over now. The triplets were safely delivered, her job with the airshow organisation abandoned and she was on the brink of becoming a small business owner. She ground her teeth together and shuffled forward. Another check-in opened and the clerk beckoned her over. Celeste placed her passport and ticket on the high desk-top and humped her weekend case laboriously onto the conveyor.

'Did you pack this case yourself, madam?' the girl enquired genially.

'Yes.'

'Are you carrying any electrical or battery-operated items?'

'No.'

'Would you prefer a window seat?'

'Yes please.' The check-in clerk briskly attached a label to the case and it disappeared into suitcase hell. Then she swiftly printed out a boarding pass and handed it to Celeste with her passport and ticket remains.

'Seat A, row thirty. The departure lounge is open. Have a pleasant flight.'

'Thank-you.' Celeste placed her one item of hand luggage on the top of the trolley and meandered through to the departure lounge, laconically showing her passport and boarding pass, almost robotic in her actions. The flight was uneventful.

Hamburg Airport looked the same as usual. The huge Christmas tree was still up. Muffled, piped music echoed around the rafters. The long traipse from *Arrivals* was a time for thought. She walked straight through to the baggage hall, seeing with diluted envy other pairs of travellers by the snaking luggage transporter as they waited for their cases.

'*Willkommen in Hamburg!*' a large sign declared. She collected her case and walked through the EU exit.

'*Hotel Kleine Eichhörnchen*, bitte' she said in school-girl German as she got into the taxi. 'Sind Sie Deutscher?'

'Jawohl,' returned the driver. 'Ja, but I can speak English.'

She breathed a sigh of relief. Last time, an illegal immigrant posing as a taxi driver had stolen her case and she had arrived at her hotel in a terrible state. After what had happened with Rupert's arrest in the hotel's back garden, there was no way that she was going to stay at the same place again. She had chosen a new one.

After ten minutes, the cab pulled off the *Strasse* and into a gravelled drive that led to a large Bavarian-style hotel with the picture of a squirrel on the signboard. Warm, amber lights shone through the old-fashioned sweet-shop style windows with pale blue shutters thrown open. Winter pansies bloomed in the flower-painted window-boxes. The funeral was tomorrow.

*

'Fraulein Blagden, how goot to see you.'

The prison Governor greeted Celeste outside the mortuary chapel in the large Hamburg cemetery. She stepped out of the hired car, glad to be wearing her long, fur-lined boots as the Governor escorted her and they crunched across the frozen snow. Their breath hung in the air like a veil. Crisp leaves clung to the margins of the kerbs like the ghosts of last autumn, littering the mounds of white. Over beyond a copse of naked birches, a reluctant bonfire smouldered.

'He iss coming already here,' the Governor said in a low and comforting voice, indicating with a glance in the direction of the glacéed drive. Celeste blinked slowly and gravely, nodding almost imperceptibly once in acquiescence as she hugged herself against the harsh winter morning. In the distance, a solitary black funeral car made its way slowly towards them along the empty roadway, parting the mist as it changed from a dot to a presence, grinding the ice beneath its winter tyres with a sound like tearing bubble-wrap.

'We should go in now.' The governor took Celeste by the elbow and guided her into a small, dim waiting room from where, after five minutes, they were led through to a right-hand pew at the front of the chapel. The dark, oak coffin standing in the aisle before the altar was so near that she felt she could almost have reached out to touch it. She stifled a sob and bowed her head. The strong smell of chrysanthemums nearly took her breath away. A brief glance showed that the top of the coffin was decked with yellow blooms and long, trailing white ribbons.

Muted organ music emanated from somewhere. Across the aisle there were two plump ladies clad in black, both wearing felt hats, also clutching white tissues..

'Who are those women sitting there?' Celeste asked quietly.

'Church visitors. They used to come to see Rupert in prison.'

For what seemed an eternity, Celeste studied her hands in her lap. She hated wearing black. It was so depressing. It was chilly in the chapel. How could Rupert be dead? The man who had shared her life for seven years now lay cold and still in a wooden box in a foreign mortuary chapel. The father of her triplet daughters would never see them. The lover she had adored would love no more. If only she had made her peace with him. Now it was too late. It was all too late.

A door in the panelling to the left of the altar opened quietly and a sad-looking priest came in carrying a large prayer book. Everybody stood up. The music stopped. He turned to face them and started to chant something in German. It was like a surreal dream. Celeste felt spaced out.

The priest said, 'Bitte setzen.' They all sat down. Celeste tried to control her panic by breathing slowly. Then the Governor got up and walked to the lectern to haltingly read an English poem, *'Don't weep for me for I am going to another place...'* Then he rejoined the sobbing young woman.

CRASH! The main doors of the chapel flew open and a shaft of brilliant sunlight flooded in. Celeste turned in panic to see four tall men in black cloaks, wide white collars and black tri-corn hats striding down the aisle, trundling a hand-cart that rumbled like thunder and reverberated around the room. Celeste was startled.

'Don't be afraid. They have come to take him to the grave.'

'The grave? It will be a burial?'

'Yes, Miss Blagden,' he whispered. 'As you haf not ask for a cremation, we arrange a burial. So he will always be here in Hamburg when you come to visit.'

Celeste swallowed hard. Oh no! She would have to stand and watch Rupert being put into the ground. It was unbearable.

Deftly, the four sepulchral bearers transferred the coffin onto the purple-draped handcart, rotated on their heels with military precision and solemnly trundled their cargo to the doors.

'We must follow. Come along my dear.'

Celeste got to her feet in a rather wobbly manner and clutched at the Governor's arm as, led by the priest, they followed her former lover out into the icy wall of a Hamburg January morning.

Along gravel paths under winter trees they paced, past monuments and obelisks and a gardener who doffed his woolly hat to stand respectfully as the small group crunched its way to a mound of earth and a grave space already dug.

The two women in black gave wan half-smiles of sympathy to Celeste as the coffin was suspended above the earthy pit that would inevitably and finally swallow it. More German prayers from the priest. The straps were grasped, the coffin lowered. Celeste watched in horror as Rupert went into the earth. The governor stepped forward and, bending down, grasped a small ladle to scoop up sand and sprinkle it into the grave. Celeste followed suit, and then stood and gazed down onto the sand-spattered coffin lid that bore a brass plate with the dates of the deceased's birth and death and also bearing the English inscription:

> *Rupert Skinner,*
> *Partner of Celeste Blagden*
> *and father of*
> *April, May and June.*
> *RIP*

Chapter 4

'Synth, I'm just going out. If Miss Eleanor calls or comes in, please tell her I'll be back in time for lunch.'

'Yes, Mr. Landscar. Shall I set the table for two?'

'Better to be on the safe side.' He placed his stetson on his silver-haired head and then was gone, out of the huge marble reception hall of *Casslands*, through the double doors, down the steps and into his Hercedix 3i.5 with the lustre finish and gold stripe along the side.

He took the ring road past the airport and out towards the shopping parade that he had recently bought further away from the town centre.

The area was ripe for development and Grant had earmarked the small group of shops as a promising investment because it was on the most heavily used route into town. Additionally, it backed onto the set of buildings containing Eleanor's new office. However, his next target of interest was a dilapidated bungalow that stood immediately opposite to his newly acquired parade. He pulled up outside the bungalow and switched off. The continuous stream of traffic roared past on the main road.

Access was good. The site looked about a hundred metres wide. He couldn't see how far back it went so he got out of the car, locked it and strode around to the front gate. It was hanging off its hinges. He lifted it and walked along the weed-encrusted garden path. There were some vandalised broken windows and litter on the front lawn. He pushed an overgrown, evergreen japonica out of the way and unlatched the side gate. It scraped open. A passage led to a rear patio and beyond that a lily pond with a statue in the centre. The rest of the back garden was a jungle of large oak trees, a decrepit greenhouse, a rotting summer house, abandoned chicken coops surrounded by wire and, at the very end, a crazed, hard tennis court and green, soupy swimming pool. It must all have gone back two hundred metres. Perfect. He took out his digital camera and snapped away. High hedges all around. Just what he needed.

Back at the car, he sat and perused his shopping parade on the other side of the busy A-road. The previous landlord had sold it to him with two tenants installed and two vacant shops with flats over. The group of four retail outlets with flats would yield a steady income. His agent had leased one of the empty ones to some woman opening a mother and baby shop. He'd been told that she was a pushy type but she might do well in her own business. That's what was needed, although the agent had also hinted that she was an unmarried mother without male support. The two sitting tenants were easy meat... a small general store and a chemist. He needed one more watertight tenant to complete the set of four and then he could sit back and enjoy the quarterly rentals rolling in.

Across the road, in her soon to be Mother and Baby shop, Celeste peered out through a hole she had made with a wet finger in the whitening painted all over the inside of the shop windows. What was stetson man doing snooping around that bungalow over there? She remembered him from the airshow. He hadn't been particularly friendly to her. Now he had walked back to his car and was sitting in it in the service road on the other side of the dual carriageway, looking across at her. Surely he couldn't see her?

It was cold in the empty shop. No heating at all. She'd have to get some installed. After returning from Rupert's funeral, she'd gone straight to the agent and said, 'Yes, subject to contract and survey.' She needed to get on with her life. Her father had lent her something towards the deposit. Together with her savings, she would have enough to get started. Despite everything, her heart still ached for Rupert when she allowed it to. That was all over though. She flicked on the reluctant fluorescent lamps. They flickered and came to life with a ping.

From the exclusive and privileged comfort of his very expensive Hercedix, Grant Landscar saw the shop lights come on. The new tenant must be in. He couldn't see much, just a shape moving about behind the whitened out plate glass windows. He'd go over and introduce himself. Well, why not?

He got out of his limousine again and crossed the wide dual carriageway via the zebra crossing a little further on. Walking along the pavement with the shop forecourts abutted to it, he could hardly think because of all the traffic noise. Good. The more the better! He stopped outside the lit-up shop. Yes, this would be a little gold mine to fund a rent review in due course.

Celeste paused as she was about to go through to the stock room. 'Rap, rap, rap!' Who could it be? Nobody knew that she was here. She hurried over to the shop door, pulled aside the orange curtain on the central, half-glazed door and stared into the eyes of stetson man himself. Their surprise was mutual.

'What do you want?' Celeste mouthed.

Grant, unaware that although he couldn't hear himself speak, his words would be very loud inside the shop, yelled, 'I'm your landlord, Grant Landscar. Open up!'

Celeste, angry at his confrontational approach, switched immediately into managerial mode and mouthed, 'One moment please.' She allowed the curtain to drop back into place and took a couple of steps away from the door. How to deal with this? He was an odious, bullish type, in her opinion. If she'd known he was the owner, she would never have signed the lease with TexRmist Holdings. It was too late now. Taking the keys out of the pocket of her cargo pants trousers, she jangled them loudly, rattling the lock. The bolts were already off. The door swung open and her landlord stepped inside.

'Why, Miss Blagden,' he drawled patronisingly. 'Quite a change of life-style for you, I see.' He removed his hat, clutched it to his chest and perused the empty and scruffy shop as he paced about, his chukka boots thudding and reverberating on the chipboard flooring. He looked upwards. 'High ceiling,' he commented.

'How can I help you, Mr. Landscar?'

'Jest poppin' by to see that my new tenant is safely in. When do you propose to start tradin'?'

Celeste stifled an urge to say, 'When I'm good and ready you pin-head' but instead she smiled demurely and replied, 'Well, Mr. Landscar, as you can see, there's a fair amount of cleaning and decorating to be done and I need to instal some heating, create a changing room and to upgrade the shop toilet.'

'So we're lookin' at about a month, I suppose.'

'I'd like to try and open on the 1st March.'

He looked down aloofly at her.

'That's a good six weeks away. You'll be payin' rental without any income. Sure you can manage that? I kinda heard that you had some problems, personal like.'

Celeste tilted her chin upwards and replied, 'My personal life has never intruded on my work.'

Grant had the knife in and wasn't going to let it go. 'I believe that congratulations are in order. A baby, I believe.'

'Triplets, actually,' she said with an air of supreme pride and finality.

'Well, I'll be jiggered! A little thing like you.'

'Will there be anything else, Mr. Landscar?'

'I bet their Daddy is well pleased...'

'Their father is dead, Mr. Landscar. I attended his funeral last week.' Celeste blinked rapidly as her heart pounded.

'I'm mighty sorry to hear that, Miss Blagden.' His emphasis on the word 'Miss' was not lost on her. 'However,' he continued, 'please also accept my sincere condolences.' His words sounded anything but sincere. 'So, I'd better leave you to get on with your little venture.' He extended his paw-like hand and she was forced to reciprocate. 'Remember that if you want to make any structural changes to the premises, you'll need my permission.'

'I'd like to reinstate some internal doors, both in the shop and the flat. I'm not a fan of open-plan living.'

'That's not structural. Go ahead but you will have to bear the costs.'

'Yes.' Celeste walked over and opened the shop door as a clear hint that he should leave. With a final, cursory glance around and a hint of chagrin he said, 'Good luck with your venture.' She didn't see his smile of smug doubt as he strode away.

*

'Well, where's she working now?' Roland Dilger shouted into the receiver. 'Celeste Blagden. Surely you remember her? She used to be the Press Centre Manager there at the airshow. You, know, attractive girl with dark, shoulder-length hair.'

The receptionist at Phillipstone International Airshows said she had no idea but wasn't she the one that had...?

'She can't have just vanished,' he cut in. 'Didn't she perhaps leave a forwarding address or phone number?'

'Who did you say you were?'

'I'm Roland Dilger. I worked with her last year and I was the Airshow's official photographer. Don't you remember me?'

'Mmmmm,' the girl replied with hesitation. 'Weren't you the one whose picture was in the local paper without any...?'

'Yes, yes but that's old history now.'

'I remember you.'

'Good. How about Celeste Blagden's mobile number?'

'It's confidential. I haven't been on reception for long. They promoted me from the office. This is a big step-up for me.'

'I'll make it worth your while.'

''How?'

'Some glamour photographs? I'll take them in my studio.'

'Where's your studio?'

'Oh, local,' Roland lied. 'How about it?'

She gave him Celeste's mobile number and then her own.

'Be sure to call me,' she said.

'I'll be in touch.' Then he rang Celeste.

'*Mums, Tums and Tots,*' a female voice said.

'Celeste? Is that you?'

'Who's calling please?'

'Roland Dilger, photographer extraordinaire. I bumped into you at the airport last week. How did the funeral go?'

'Oh, it's you.' She had a long memory. His escapade of being photographed nude on the airport roof had nearly cost them both their jobs last year during the airshow. She had hung on there until the seventh month of her pregnancy when a premature labour had ended her career in PR.

'Just like any other funeral, incredibly depressing.'

'Can't we do lunch today, just for old time's sake? Come on, old thing.'

'Roland, your behaviour was ghastly last year at the show. Why would I want to have lunch with you?'

'Because I'm a cheery chappie and you sound like one girl who needs a bit of a lift.'

She glanced at her watch. 'I'm at the shop. I'm busy.'

'Are you out shopping?'

'No. I'm in my shop. I'm going into business for myself.'

'Get away!'

'No, really. I'm opening a Mother and Baby retail outlet.'

'I'm gob-smacked. Why that?'

'Well, with the triplets, it seemed the best sort.'

'Triplets? Oh yes, the triplets.'

'I've got three baby girls.'

'I knew you had a bun in the oven but the grapevine failed. Congratulations. Rupert's, I'm presuming?'

'Yes, of course. Don't be so crass.'

'That's why you answered with that *Mums* thing. What do you know about shop-keeping?'

'Not a lot but I'll learn. It's got a flat over, so I can live here. I had to give up Rupert's and my old place.'

'Well, I have to say one thing for you, Celeste, you're certainly full of surprises.'

'I have to get on with my life.'

'Come to lunch and tell me all about it.'

She relented. 'OK. Pick me up. The shop's on *Pitt Parade* along the dual carriageway.'

'I know. Be with you in twenty minutes.'

She was standing on her forecourt when he arrived. He pulled into the service road immediately outside, leaned across and opened the passenger door of his two-seater sports car.

'Hop in, lovely lady,' he said, turning on the old charm. 'So that's the start of your empire,' he added, nodding towards the scruffy and dilapidated shop.

'It'll be fine when it's done up,' she replied defensively. 'I have great plans for it.'

'The one next to it's empty too.'

'Yes, it is. I don't know what will go in there. I hope it's not something ghastly like a fishmonger or a firework shop.'

'It might suit me.'

She stopped in the middle of strapping up her seat belt and turned to stare at him with mock horror. 'You? What on Earth do you want that for?'

'I've quit working for the air industry. I want to be a serious portrait photographer. All that trailing about and flying here there and everywhere. I've had enough. I need a more settled lifestyle.'

'I'm astounded. Why would you give up your well-paid job for the risks of the self-employed? I don't have a lot of choice, given my situation, but you... you can go anywhere, do anything. You don't really want to be stuck on a suburban parade, do you?'

'Besides,' he said, 'Debbie and I are through. She's gone off to open a hotel in Milloncha... you know... that island in the Mediterranean.'

'She probably got fed up with your philandering.'

'I wanted to marry her.'

'A wise lady to wriggle out of that one.' He gave one tut of exasperation and looked out briefly through the car window.'

'How much rent do you pay?'

'Mind your own business.'

He leaned ingratiatingly towards her, appealing like a child.

'You'd love to have me next door. We could help each other. Hey! You could send me customers for baby pictures.'

She looked at him askance. 'You'll help me with some DIY and things?'

'Of course I will. Tell me where the agent is. I really want to look inside that unit.'

'After lunch,' she replied.

*

'Father Guyler! How wonderful to see you again!' Reverend Mother Veronica shook the priest's hand warmly. 'Did you have a terrible journey? They said there was ice on the rails.'

'After visiting my sister in Scotland I got held up at Crewe, Reverend Mother, but doesn't everybody?' he joked. 'I'm so sorry I'm late.' He smiled benevolently at the short, chubby nun as she closed the front door of *St. Bede's Convent* behind him.

'Not to worry, Father, we kept something back for you. Perhaps you'd like to have it on a tray by the fire in the sitting room here?' She opened the oak-panelled door. 'Please come into the warm. Let me take your coat.' The priest put down his case and divested himself of his heavy, black woollen, double-breasted coat with the astrakhan collar.

'Thank you kindly, Reverend Mother. My! Isn't this grand!' He briskly rubbed the palms of his hands together and strode over to the fireplace, showing his fingers to the blaze. 'It's wonderful to see a real log fire.'

'Please make yourself comfortable while I put your things away and get your hot lunch organised. Would you care for a little glass of our home made elderberry and ginger juice while you're waiting? Do help yourself. It's on the small table next to you there.' She made a little bow and shuffled out of the room. It was a shame he'd arrived just as she had been going to her study for a short nap... or some 'contemplation' as she called it. With the passing of the years, examining the insides of her eyelids after lunch each day became an increasing necessity that she gave in to graciously. There had to be some concessions to the relentless and inexorable march of time.

The clanging of the front door bell disturbed the silence. The priest cocked his ear to try and hear what was going on in the hall. He heard women's voices and then the sitting room door opened and Eleanor Framp appeared. He rose, took a second to realise who it was and then came forward to greet her.

'Eleanor, my dear. How delightful to see you again.'

'Father Guyler, what a surprise!'

Reverend Mother beamed from the doorway. 'How many years must it be since your two last came face to face?' she asked.

'Reverend Mother, please don't embarrass your niece. She doesn't look a day older than when we last met.'

'You're too kind, Father,' Eleanor smiled as she gritted her teeth and fought a desire to scream and run out of the room.

'Your meal will be here shortly, Father, and I'm so glad you've popped in, Eleanor. I'll get some tea and biscuits for us and we can have a nice chat.' Then she shuffled out again.

The newcomer took off her beige, camel coat and put it over the back of one of the dining chairs. She peeled off the brown woollen hat and placed it on the table with her gloves. Then she walked over and settled down in the easy chair opposite the priest.

'Well! Let me look at you!' he said. Eleanor opened her hands in mock display and replied, 'Not much to see.'

'Don't put yourself down, my dear. You were a charming young girl and you've grown into a splendid woman.'

Eleanor smiled dismissively. 'I think I have changed quite a lot in the intervening years.'

'You will always be little Eleanor to me,' he replied with a patronising nod. She stared hard at him.

'So, Father, what have you been doing since you disappeared from my life when I was seventeen?'

'We were both very young and foolish.'

'You betrayed your position of trust.'

'Shhhhh!' He hissed. 'That kind of talk isn't helpful.'

'Neither is denial.'

'I have long regretted what happened. Please accept my apology, Eleanor. I know that nothing can undo the past but we all have to move on.'

'I was in love with you.'

'And I with you.'

'My aunt would have had you thrown out of the church if she had found out. You went away so soon afterwards. I was heart-broken.'

'I took that position in India for both of our sakes.'

'You could have written. One day we were in love and the next you had disappeared. It was so cruel.'

'I didn't want to arouse suspicion. I was filled with remorse. I made ten novenas to try and receive forgiveness. I made a full confession to the bishop.'

She took in the 'I, I, I' with disdain. He was so self-centred.

'You ruined my young life. After you, I cared for nobody else. I didn't even have a single photograph.' Her eyes brimmed with tears. He reached forward to pat her hand but she snatched it away. 'Don't!'

The door opened and a Filipino novice came in bearing the dinner tray. The priest sat back hurriedly in his chair, changed his mind and then stood up. Eleaner quickly turned her head away.

'Good afternoon, Miss Eleanor and Father. You like it here, Father, or you like it there?' The young nun indicated the highly polished, oval, dining table that was rarely used. The priest took a few paces forward and relieved her of the tray.

'It will be fine just here on my lap. Thank-you.' He looked down at the small lamb chop, mashed potatoes and mushy, over-cooked cabbage. There was a small dish of rice pudding with a blob of jam in the middle. Convent food didn't change much.

Another novice came in with the tea tray and placed it on the sideboard. Reverend Mother had also returned.

'Thank you sisters. Thank you.'

The young nuns beat a dignified retreat. The priest sat down. Eleanor relinquished her chair to her aunt. It was, after all, her usual place by the fire.

'Shall I pour the tea, Aunty Rev?'

'Oh, yes please, Eleanor.'

She raised her eyebrows enquiringly towards the priest who gave a slight nod as he tucked the paper napkin under his chin.

'I'll pour one for you too, Father.'

The priest took up his knife and fork and attacked the chop. Dried yak dung sprang to mind.

'Yes please. This looks delicious,' he said diplomatically.

'Only simple fare,' Reverend Mother said.

'I'm ravenous. Forgive me for eating in front of you.'

'Oh please go on. I like to see a man with a healthy appetite,' she replied, completely missing the darting, reproachful stab of a look that Eleanor directed at the priest.

'Well, Father,' the elderly nun continued, 'you have to tell us about your time in India. Where was the orphanage?'

'Glyderabad,' he mumbled through the gristle.

'If I'm right, that's in the middle of India somewhere.'

He swallowed with difficulty. 'Yes, it's the capital of the state of Undshra Pragesh and is very highly populated. It's also called *The City of Pearls* but I'm not sure why.'

Eleanor handed her aunt and the priest their cups of tea. She herself perched on a dining chair and sipped delicately, feeling anger born of grief and desertion. She looked down at the pompous, balding priest, a few years older than herself. How could she ever have loved him? How could he have so taken advantage of a young and innocent girl? She blinked rapidly. Sorrow had sown the seeds of revenge. No, revenge was wrong. It was against everything she had always been taught but should the perpetrators of evil get away scot-free? She wanted to smack him and shout at him and kick him. This was not how she had been taught to behave so she sat there primly on the edge of her dining chair as they talked about India, orphanages and the weather.

'Just think,' said Reverend Mother, 'you haven't been back here for over thirty years.'

'Well,' he said, 'that's not strictly true. I used to have to return periodically to report to the bishop... only flying visits of course,' he added hastily, when he saw Eleanor's expression change.

Eleanor froze and her jaw dropped. Reverend Mother, however was keen to move on to her niece's forthcoming marriage.

Father Guyler gravely put down his cutlery and stared in mock amazement. 'You are getting married?' He had already noted the emerald and diamond engagement ring. Shocked, she responded.

'Yes, I am, Father, to a wonderfully kind and considerate American man.' Was the priest aware of the wobble in her voice?

'Congratulations, my dear.'

'Thank you, Father.'

She wished he wouldn't call her 'my dear'.

'When will the wedding take place?'

'At Easter, Father.'

'Will it be in a church or here in the Convent chapel?'

'Neither, Father.'

Reverend mother stopped in mid-sip.

'Eleanor's fiancé is not of the faith.' She took a couple more sips of her tea. 'The ceremony will be in Phillipstone Register Office.'

There was a stunned silence. The priest blinked in surprise.

'But surely he would like you to have your union blessed?'

'Grant is an Atheist,' Eleanor said blankly and shrugged.

'You have to introduce me to your fiancé. Perhaps he doesn't understand the implications for your immortal soul. Doesn't he realise...?' He was cut short.

'He doesn't believe in souls,' Eleanor replied, stony-faced.

'But you do, surely?'

Eleanor cast her eyes around the room, nervously glancing at the statue of the Virgin Mary in its alcove on the far wall.

'Perhaps we could have this conversation another time. It's rather a sensitive matter.'

'Surely, dear Eleanor, surely,' he replied, returning to his cabbage. Reverend Mother put her cup and saucer down on the side table and yawned discreetly.

'Did you notice our solar panels on the roof, Father?' she enquired by way of changing the subject and fully aware that her niece was on the edge of tears.

'No, Reverend Mother. I can't say that I really did. The roof was covered in snow. Please do tell me about them.'

She was keen to bolster Grant's reputation to the priest.

'Eleanor's fiancé is an environmentalist. He kindly provided the convent with solar panels so that we have free hot water from April to September each year.'

'That sounds grand but what do you do in the less sunny months?'

'You explain it, Eleanor. You understand it better.'

Eleanor said, 'The convent also has a gas boiler as well.'

'It sounds as if your future husband must be quite well off to pay for all those panels.'

Reverend Mother interjected, 'Grant is a business man and a very good one too.'

Eleanor nodded. The priest tipped his head on one side and raised his eyebrows. 'I see.' Then he put his knife and fork together with an air of finality. The cabbage had beaten him.

'That was delicious, Reverend Mother. I'll just tuck into this rice pudding.' He took up the spoon but the elderly nun didn't hear him for she had drifted off to sleep by the heat of the fire. The priest gave Eleanor a wink.

Chapter 5

'Pandora, how good to see you!' Eleanor got up from the desk in her office at *Curtis House* and walked across the carpet to greet her future stepdaughter who exploded into the room in a welter of over-dressing and packages.

'Hi boss lady!'

'What have you got there?' Eleanor asked with trepidation as Pandora struggled to dump things on her desk. She ripped off her mock-fur coat, wrap and hat, nimbly crossed the room to hang them on the rack and then turned to embrace her future stepmother who was rather taken aback by the gusto of the greeting.

'Just a little gift from New York for you,' she said, proffering a beautifully packaged box with red ribbons.

'You shouldn't have...'

'Nonsense! I had to. Go on! Open it!'

Eleanor meekly obeyed. Out came a gorgeous negligee with matching night-dress in shell pink with silver embroidery.

'This is lovely.' She held it against herself. 'I don't deserve such pretty things.'

'It's for the honeymoon... or earlier if you feel the need,' she said with an air of nudge-nudge wink-wink. Eleanor held it up to the light. She could see right through it. Gosh, that was a bit racy!

'How can I thank you? This is just too kind.'

'I got it in a sale at *Stacey's*. Hopefully, it's the right size.'

'Yes it is. How clever of you to guess.' Eleanor held it against her front and did a little twirl, quite out of keeping with the tweed two-piece suit she was wearing. Pandora continued, 'You and I should go on some shopping trips. You know, to start to get your trousseau together. Hey! Why don't we spoil ourselves and go for a session at the beauty salon?'

'I don't think...' Eleanor began.

'You'll love being pampered. I'll book us in.'

Eleanor could see that there was no point in arguing.

'Would you like a coffee?'

'You bet. Gasping for one. By the way, I'm sorry about my naughty son ambushing you the other day.'

'Charlie? Oh, he was a delight. A very forthright child,' Eleanor replied from the kitchenette. She put the kettle on. It was one of the new fast boilers and sang loudly.

'You can say that again.'

'We had a lively chat. He seems rather grown-up for his age.' She came back into the office.

'True. He's a very independent child. It comes of my being a single parent. One of the advantages, I suppose. Now, what do you want me to do first?'

Eleanor hesitated. She wasn't used to giving directions but it was something she was going to have to master.

'Why don't we sit down and have a look through the mock-up? I've got it on my desk here. Pull a chair over and we can view it together. I'll show you the web-site too.'

'I can't wait to get started. When does the first issue have to be put to bed?'

'It'll be out on 1st February, a Valentine's day theme, so the printers will want it by the end of next week.' Pandora joined her and they pored over the mock-up together. 'What sort of work have you been doing lately?' Eleanor asked.

'Stuff for Dad and little bit of freelance design. I can turn my hand to most things. Say, who did your photographs?'

'I had to buy them from a photographic library. For the March issue I want us to do our own.'

'Very nice,' Pandora said as she slowly turned the pages and the kettle clicked off. The flamboyant assistant went to make the coffee.

'We'll take turns, shall we, boss lady?' The boss lady wasn't too keen on the whimsical title. It sounded as if Pandora was making fun of her but she didn't want to say anything.

'Black, no sugar. I'm looking forward to working with you, Pandora. Your father says you have a wealth of experience. I'm going to need a lot of help. This first issue has been rather a struggle but I have had six months in which to get it together. I've already got story-boards for the March and April issues.'

Eleanor held up some artwork.

'Here, have a look at the front cover of this first one.'

'OK,' Pandora said, returning with the coffee mugs as Eleanor rummaged and shuffled papers. 'We're going to have such a good time working together. Keep it in the family, yes?'

'Absolutely.'

'I say, this is a really neat cover design on the February issue but have you thought about putting the price in a box to make it stand out more? Oh, and that heart shape could be a little further up the page. Wait a minute, how about lace around the edge?'

'Don't you like it how it is?' Eleanor queried.

'Yes, of course. You've done a lovely job with it. I just thought a little more pizzazz might boost sales.'

Eleanor's heart sank. This was going to be a lot tougher than she'd thought.

*

'Good morning, Councillor Springstock. Please come in,' Synth said as she politely ushered the future Mayor of Phillipstone into the grandiose hall of *Casslands.*

'You're new,' he remarked as he dabbed at his moist nose.

'Oh, I've been here for a while now,' she remarked, taking his coat and hanging it on the Victorian rack. 'Please come through.'

He followed her along to the side of the large, central staircase and down a wide, well-lit passageway the walls of which were adorned with gilt-edged oil paintings of flower studies. He was torn between looking at the pictures and at Synth's hypnotically and rhythmically swinging hips ahead of him. He decided to enjoy the hips. She stopped outside a door with a *Do not Disturb* sign on it and knocked tentatively.

Grant's voice could be heard on the telephone. He paused and called out, 'Come!' As soon as he saw Councillor Springstock he glanced at his watch, hurriedly ended the call and rose in greeting.

'Councillor. Councillor. So glad you could make it.'

Springstock thought it was rather ingratiating but smiled bravely with his yellow dentures and put forward a hand to shake.

'Pleasure, Mr. Landscar. Where would you like me to sit?'

'Please. Take a seat there.' He indicated a low chair on the far side of his massive desk so that he was now in a position to look down on his guest. As he settled in his seat, Springstock cast his eyes around the generously proportioned study, taking in the ormolu clock, velvet drapes and crystal chandelier. The walls were rich with framed pictures of Grant's past projects.

'A very nice room,' the councillor commented.

'Glad you like it. I find it conducive to my work. Now, what are we here for?' He was playing silly games and the councillor knew it full well.

'The plot of land right next to the dual carriageway. You are interested in buying it for development.'

'Yes indeedy. I had a quick look at it yesterday and the size is about right. However, there are some issues associated with it that may need your assistance.' The councillor's heart sank. He had been here before, last summer, when this beastly entrepreneur had tried to pressure him into supporting his ill-fated wind generator project for the airfield. It had been very stressful. He broke out into a sweat at the memory of it all and wiped his forehead with the edge of his hand.

'I understand that you own the plot,' Grant continued. 'It's clearly in a state of decay so why haven't you sold it off before?' Councillor Springstock fidgeted with his handkerchief, cleared his throat and hesitated.

'Well... well... it used to be my mother's...'

'Not a politically good time for you?'

'One can't be see to be too avaricious when the position of Mayor is on the horizon. Things move slowly in local politics, you know.'

'True,' Grant agreed.

'So, may I rely on your confidentiality?'

'Of course, of course.'

He struggled to look sincere and wondered what the Texan had up his sleeve this time.

'I think we can arrange for the transfer of ownership to be done discreetly. Yes. I can arrange that. It's now a matter of agreeing upon a price subject to the usual.' Grant took a note-pad.

He scribbled a sum onto it, tore the sheet off and slid it across the leather-topped desk. Springstock unclipped his half-glasses from his shirt pocket and put them on his thread-veined nose. He perused the amount, pursed his lips and sniffed deeply.

'I had hoped for somewhat more. The bungalow would do up very nicely with a little investment.'

'You misunderstand me, Councillor. I intend to demolish the bungalow.' Alarm registered on the older man's face.

'What will you put in its place? Another house? It has to be in keeping with other properties along there.'

'Actually, no.' Grant unfolded a plan and spread it out before the Councillor. 'As you know, I am somewhat environmentally inclined, and it is my intention to build an electric vehicle refuelling point and heavy lorry cleaning complex on the site.' He indicated with the tip of his very pointed pencil.

'Out of the question, Landscar. That side of the road is purely residential. It would never get through Planning.'

'That's where I need your help, Councillor. My refuelling depot will be entirely at one with nature. It will be for electrically driven vehicles only. The cleaning facility will recycle its water so that ninety-nine percent of it will be re-used. With the new spur coming off the motorway next year, heavy goods vehicles will be using the dual carriageway more than ever. I also need you to help a little with changing the Council's own vehicles over to electric power. That would be a grand point to make at your Mayoral inauguration speech in the spring. It would gain tremendous public support.'

'I told you before. I can't influence democratic decisions.'

'As chairman of the Planning Committee, I think you can. May I remind you that I still have that cutting?'

The Councillor's face flushed with embarrassment and anger. 'I was a young man protesting against my local council over a matter of principle. Spending a few weeks in jail was unfortunate but I had to stand by my life ethics.'

'It mightn't look good if that came out right now, would it?'
The older man trembled with rage.

'Here, Councillor. Have a little water.' Grant poured some from a carafe into a crystal tumbler. It was gratefully accepted.

His host continued, 'It doesn't have to be unpleasant. We are both well versed in the ways of business. Haven't you ever thought of a nice, holiday place abroad, perhaps somewhere warm?'

The Councillor's beady eyes lit up. Grant went on, 'I have a little flat out in Milloncha that might suit you. I could put it in my wife's name and you could have the free use of it for your lifetime. How does that appeal to you?'

'Interesting. I might need something for expenses too. In cash.'

'I'm sure that could be arranged. Did you have a sum in mind?' Grant was playing him like a fish.

'Perhaps ten percent of my bungalow's valuation price?' The weaselling little man looked slyly at Grant.

'Five percent.'

'Agreed.' He put forward his hand. They shook on it.

Grant Landscar leaned back in his brown, leather chair, satisfied. He loved to do deals. 'I'll get my people onto it right away.'

Springstock stuffed his handkerchief into his trouser pocket and smiled. A flat in Milloncha. Respite from English weather. A suntan.

'Does it have a balcony?' he enquired.

'Oh sure, it does, with plants and an awning and pool use.'

'It sounds delightful. When can I go there?'

'As soon as this deal is done and dusted. I should think in about three months.' The Councillor looked disappointed.

The telephone rang and Grant picked up.

'Yes? Yes. A photographic studio? Fine. I'll leave it with you.' He hung up. 'Sorry about that interruption, Councillor. Oh, there is one other little matter.' Springstock's stomach pitched. 'The oak trees in the bungalow's back garden. They all have preservation orders. Those need to be revoked.'

*

Eleanor Framp snuggled warmly and drowsily against Grant Landscar's shoulder on the plush, uncut moquette sofa in the main lounge of *Casslands*. They were watching a wildlife television programme. The sound was on low.

'Darling,' he muttered.

'Mmmm?' she replied.

'How would you feel about staying tonight?'

Her eyes shot wide open. She pulled away from him.

'Oh Grant. I couldn't possibly. It's against everything...'

'We're going to be husband and wife in only a few weeks,' he added.

She bit her lip and folded her hands in her lap. Men always spoiled the romance. She shook her head slowly.

'I do love you so much, Grant.' She looked shyly sideways at him, but I want to save all that for our honeymoon. Would it be so difficult for you? I mean, we've waited this long.'

He sighed. She sighed. Maybe he was getting old, but it wasn't as difficult as this in the past. Three wives and umpteen mistresses hadn't given him all the trouble that this lady had. The others had just rolled over and complied. This one wanted the whole fairytale. He hadn't even got past first base.

Eleanor stroked the creases on the sides of his tanned face. Even in January, he still looked touched by the sun. She planted a kiss on the stubble. He nuzzled her. This was all very relaxing. Late afternoon light glimmered around the edges of the heavy drapes. Soon, Synth would bring in tea.

'My sweet,' he murmured.

'Yes, my love?'

'How would you like a special, little, early wedding present from me?'

'That sounds exciting? What did you have in mind? Something to keep for the coming years?'

'More of an investment, actually, my treasure.'

She looked up at him in surprise.

'That's your department then, Grant dear. I'll just see to *Embroideryworld* and make you proud of me.

'This is something that I would like to just put in your name,' he said with closed eyelids flicking.

'Very well. Please tell me about it.'

'I want to buy you a small flat in the Milloncha. The leisure business is good there. You don't have to deal with it in any way. It's just something for you for the future.'

'Oh Grant! That is so generous of you but you already have the *Villa Estancia* out there. I can't wait to see it for our honeymoon after Easter. It looks lovely from the photographs.'

'That's always going to be my province.' He struggled to sit up, unwrapping her arms as he did so. 'The holiday flat would be yours.'

'If you think it would be a good idea... yes of course... thank you.' She sat up more. 'You'll tell me exactly where it is and what it's like?'

'Yes, of course. You can see the brochure. It's well appointed and overlooks the bay. I'll get it organised then.' He noticed her new red shoes. 'They sure look pretty. Where did they come from?'

'Oh, I bought them in the January sales in town. Do you like them?'

'Absolutely lovely. Not in your usual taste though.' He pretended to pinch her cheek and she simpered. 'You'll have to let Pandora have a go at your wardrobe,' he added.

Eleanor felt slighted affronted.

'Don't you like what I wear, Grant?'

'Sure I do, Honey, but you're not a hack now. You're goin' to be the wife of a billionaire entrepreneur. We have to keep up our image.'

'Yes, of course,' she said humbly. He was right. She knew it but there was something comforting in her old clothes.

'All in good time. You can't rush a girl into these things,' she said.

If he thought to himself. 'You're not kidding,' he kept quiet, slapping his hand affectionately on her thigh. She squirmed with delight.

'So! Tell me truthfully. How're things going with you and my precious daughter?'

Eleanor didn't miss a beat as she replied.

'We're getting along really famously. She wants to take me to a beauty salon.'

'You sure don't need that or any other type of treatment but I hear the ladies find it kind of fun.'

'Should I go?'

'Why not?'

'I've never been before. It seems such a waste of money.'

'Pleasure is never a waste of money,' he remarked sagely.

'I'll pay for it myself, of course.'

'Nonsense. I own the health farm. Go and have a good day, or two or three.'

'You didn't tell me about that.'

'You don't need to know everything at once. You'll learn.'

Suddenly she was eager like a young girl. 'Tell me! What sort of things do they have there?'

'It'll spoil it if I give away all the secrets.'

'Well, what does Pandora have done?'

'Heck, Eleanor! She's ma daughter. I don't pry into her beauty treatments.'

'Will they do things like mud wraps and massages?'

'I daresay. They run the place very well. Go and see what you think of it.'

'Perhaps we'd better wait until after the magazine launch.'

'Forgive me for saying so, my darlin' woman, but if you're going on television, don't you think that a visit to the beauty salon at the health farm would be better done before the event?'

'You're right, of course. Yes, I must look my best for television.' She hesitated. 'Pandora's going to take me shopping for clothes for my trousseau.'

'There's a thing.' He scratched his head and yawned. 'You girls get it together. I'm sure I don't need to be involved. By the way... when are we supposed to go that perishin' Register Office to do all the necessary?'

'It's booked for the ceremony on Easter Saturday but we need to go in with all your legal papers. Divorce.' She muttered a trifle embarrassed. 'They're expecting us next Monday.'

'I'll get the papers ready. This one's for keeps.'

'We have to pay...'

'Aw, shucks! I'll see to all that kinda nonsense. You just start preparing for a really great day.'

'It's a very busy time, these next two or three months, what with the magazine and the wedding.'

'Life's like that sometimes. All or nothing.'

There was a knock at the door and Synth came in with the trolley bearing a selection of naughty-looking cakes and tea..

'Good afternoon, Synth,' Grant said bluntly.

'Mr. Landscar. Miss Eleanor,' she said.

'I'm never going to get used to this,' Eleanor remarked, after the woman had gone.

'You'll be surprised how quickly you'll adapt.'

Grant took a fine, bone china tea plate and helped himself to an exotic, cream swirled cake. His fiancée picked delicately at a salmon and cucumber sandwich. She was watching her figure, not that she had any need, but Grant observed that brides always did this nonsense with paltry rations.

'Let's go take the world by the throat,' he said, grinning at her with cream all around his mouth.

*

'Shove it over there, Celeste,' Roland commanded as his shopkeeper neighbour helped him unload and stash equipment in the new studio. 'Absolute brainwave! Brilliant! Two ships in a storm. Two little lambs who have lost our way!'

'Cut the metaphors. Where do you want this stand?'

'Bung it in the corner.'

'I hope you've done something about insurance. It looks as if there's a lot of valuable stuff here,' his helper remarked. 'What are you going to call the studio, anyway?'

'That's the fun part, thinking up a name. How about something a bit up-market like *Personality Portraiture Studio?*'

'*Snaps for Snobs.*'

'*Negative Equity* if it doesn't take off,' he remarked grimly. 'I wonder what was in this shop before? It smells farmyard-y.'

'The agent said it had been a dog-grooming parlour.'

'That explains it. Actually, look through here. There's a separate little room with basins and showers and things.' Celeste followed him and remarked how handy that would be for his photographic lab. 'You're not doing all that film stuff though, are you? Surely you'll be digital?'

'Yep. I'll be putting a pc in here and plenty of filing cabinets. What I really need to do before I start, is have a proper think about how the studio itself will look. Who will be my clientele? I see streams of dignitaries, anniversary portraits, children... the little darlings will come via you. I'm sure a convenient kickback could be arranged. Then there will be family groups, pets, brides, glamour models...'

'Glamour models? When did that side of the business come into your plans?

'Right now. Get 'em off.'

She glared at him. 'Roland! Don't start all that again. Your reputation goes so far ahead of you it's in another universe. Not sure having you as a neighbour's a good idea.'

'You could do a bit of posing for me, just so I can get my eye in, so to speak.'

'Dream on, lover boy. I'm a respectable mother of three.'

'But they're not here and you look gorgeous.'

'Give it a rest. I've got work to do. All that's off-limits.'

'Spoil sport!'

'Over-grown teenager!'

'OK. OK. I'll be good.' He waved his hands downwards in a calming gesture. 'We need to discuss how we are going to do all this to our shops. If we pooled the costs of buying decorating materials and carpets and things, we could save a bit. Who's going to paint your sign?'

'Oh the agent recommended some guy who'll do it for cash only but he's quick. He knows somebody who will clean the awnings too. I'll give you their details.'

'Ta. I'll tell you something, Celeste,' he said, looking around his dreary shell of a shop, 'I was over at a shop fitters' recycling place near the river a few weeks back. I went to pick up some sheets of aluminium to make into reflectors. Anyway, while I was there, I noticed they had some other stuff, like dress rails, carpet tiles and ex-shop mirrors. That would be interesting for you, wouldn't it? I could certainly use some of their adjustable wall shelves. I bet you could too.'

'Absolutely. Why pay for new? When can we go?'

'If I borrow a van, we could take a look tomorrow. I'll see if I can lay my hands on one. Are you staying here?'

'Not yet. I'm still sleeping down at my parents. I need some furniture for my flat here. All my other stuff got sold to the people who bought Rupert's and my place...' She suppressed a half-sob and nodded meaningfully upwards and next door. 'I need loads of things to make it habitable.'

'Righty-ho. If you can be here at ten, I'll pick you up.'

The next day was another crisp one but dry. The last of the snow was melting on the verges and Celeste was standing shivering on her forecourt when Roland drew up into the service road in a battered, white van. She looked at it askance, vaguely shocked by its dreadful appearance.

'Hop in,' he said. It chugged like a clapped out steam engine. Celeste climbed into the passenger seat and strapped in. The windows were steamed up. He peered uncertainly into the wing mirror and pulled away very fast, eliciting a loud hooting from somebody behind whom he had failed to see. He wound the window down and waved an apology, receiving two more hoots in response.

'I hope things improve,' she remarked.

The traffic was at its mid-morning usual level. School runs were over, buses were crawling, delivery vans were jostling and car-driving shoppers bumbling about looking for parking spaces. Roland manoeuvred the van through town and out towards the river, to an area steeped in small manufacturing and wholesalers. The retail recycling centre was at the end of a business park cul-de-sac, in a place where normal shoppers never went. He parked up and they got out.

'Remember to bargain,' she hinted as they opened the heavy metal door and found themselves in Aladdin's cave. Inside the huge, corrugated steel roofed warehouse was a graveyard to commerce. Everything that had ever appeared in shop fittings was stacked in sections throughout the area. Cardboard signs hung on wires declaring *'Carpet Tiles'* or *'Mannequins'*. There were alcoves full of plain and globular shop mirrors next to piles of peg-board and spikes to stick in it. Adjustable shelving sat cheek by jowl with dress rails in chrome and mud brown. There were stacks of serving counters, kitchen equipment, signs, chairs and stools. In tubs along the sides were hundreds of bits and pieces of bankrupt stock.

A miserable little man, face blue with cold, blew into his hands as he sauntered over towards them.

'Alright mates?' he enquired.

'Just looking,' Roland replied, making off along one of the aisles with Celeste in hot pursuit.

'What's the rush?'

'He'll start trying to sell us things we don't want.'

She pulled on his coat sleeve. 'Look, I've got a list. Shouldn't we take one of those heavy-duty trolleys from over there?'

In the end they needed two trolleys. It took them half an hour to fit all their purchases in the van. Roland paid cash and obtained some discount. Celeste was full of admiration. She sat up beside him in the van, feeling like a child out with Daddy as he wiped the steamy windows with a dish-mop on a stick and revved up the dubious engine.

Back at their shops, they unloaded onto their forecourts. Not only had Roland bought shelving but also a job lot of frames. Both had picked up dozens of washable carpet tiles and a fight was on the cards as to who had which colour. Celeste was over the moon at her cornucopia of cut-price shop equipment. She'd got everything she'd wanted, including some very classy mirrors from a London store and a huge quantity of white shelving with brackets and stays. Roland had the same.

Like somebody wrestling with a long-legged bird, she handled the dress-rails into her shop and through to the stock-room, wheels skidding all over the place. The dismembered rails clanged onto the chipboard flooring, sending up clouds of dust.

About one o'clock, the van had to go back and Celeste was left in charge of all the remaining gear standing on the forecourts. It started to rain, icy rain. Everything was getting wet. She cast around in desperation, trying to find something to put over it all.

'Here, lady,' an Asian man called out from the doorway of the chemist's shop the other side of Roland's studio. 'Take this!' He waved some, large, crumpled sheets of polythene at her.

'Thank you. You're so kind,' she gushed.

'Pleasure, lady. You can keep them'

When Roland came back in his sports car about an hour later, he found Celeste sitting on a box outside the shops under an umbrella in the midst of a sea of goods. Everything was swathed in plastic. She looked cold, wet and very fed up.

'Where have you been?' she grumbled, getting up.

'The van conked out. I had to get help pushing it. You're lucky I'm back at all. You should have pulled the awning out.'

'I'm not tall enough to reach right up there.'

'Don't be daft. There's a pole with a hook on. It's parked up the side of your staircase. I've got one too. Come on, let's get some shelter from this downpour.'

The pair of them worked until late afternoon. With a borrowed vacuum cleaner they gave both shop floors a good going over. Two mugs of tea had come along from the chemist's and were gratefully received. By nine o'clock that night, some sort of order had been established. All the wall shelving was up and the carpet tiles were stacked neatly in the back rooms. Celeste had wanted pink and blue alternates. Roland had enough to do his studio floor in blue. They sat slumped on swivel chairs in his shop, exhausted, surveying the fruits of their labours.

'Thanks for putting up my mirrors,' she said.

'How about a bit of rumpy-pumpy?' Roland replied.

Chapter 6

'Bless me, Father, for I have sinned. It is one week since my last confession and these are my sins. I was uncharitable to one of my sisters, Father.'

'Were you indeed, my daughter, and which particular form did this uncharitable act take?'

Sister Catherine adjusted the pain in her knees as she tilted her veiled head towards the black, iron grill that separated her from Father Guyler. 'I was impatient, Father. I wanted her to pass the salt more quickly to me.'

The priest smiled discreetly behind his hand. He knew it was Sister Catherine, one of the purest and most conscientious of all the nuns, second in holiness only to Reverend Mother Veronica.

'Little faults of impatience can be forgiven by a private act of contrition, Sister,' he said. She knew that too. 'So, what is it you'd really like to talk to me about?'

'Am I that transparent, Father?' She queried.

'I'm afraid so, my dear. I sometimes think that you ladies have no need of confession at all. Please go on.'

'Well,' said the elderly nun rather conspiratorially, 'I am deeply concerned about Miss Eleanor's wedding ceremony. I mean, a Register Office and she a nun's niece!'

'Life isn't always perfect, Sister.'

'I was wondering, Father, whether we could put a little, shall we say, 'pressure' on her to perhaps have a sort of pseudo-wedding or a blessing here in the chapel.'

'It's really up to the couple,' he replied.

'Reverend Mother is so upset. I know she is. Can't we help?'

'Let me think about it a little, Sister Catherine... er... I mean Sister, and perhaps a small prayer on your part might help too. For your penance please say three *Hail Marys* and now make a good act of contrition.'

*

Eleanor was passing along the lower corridor of the convent on her way to the kitchens. Grant had sent her over with a big box of dried figs from his villa in Milloncha. The chapel door was a-jar and so she put the box on a velvet-covered stool outside and went in. The scent of incense still hung about from yesterday's benediction and there were some candles lit on the side altar and on the stand where the nuns prayed for indulgences. She slipped quietly into a pew at the back and crossed herself. Old habits die hard. She could hear somebody mumbling away in the confessional. Then the door of the little cupboard opened and Sister Catherine came out and went to the front pew to say her penance.

Father Guyler sat there, able to see out through the grill and the door that had been left open. He spied Eleanor deep in prayer. He coughed. She looked up. A moment of hesitation and then she came into the confessional.

'Good afternoon, Father,' she said. 'You know it's me.'

'Hello, my dear. What have you to say to me?'

'Well, I don't intend to come to confession any more, for one thing.'

'I'm very sorry to hear that.'

'There will be no point as I intend to live the rest of my life in mortal sin.'

'Things can look very black and white sometimes.'

'Tell me, Father. What did you do about your big sin? I went to another parish and confessed mine when I was a girl of seventeen, but what did you do apart from tell yours to the bishop and then spend your life working in an orphanage?'

'Please keep your voice down, Eleanor. This attitude isn't helping anyone.'

'How did your working in an orphanage in the middle of India help me? How was I supposed to cope on my own when the love of my life had evaporated? Did you never think of me, alone and lonely here in the convent?'

'Yes, of course I did but I had to put all thoughts of you out of my mind, to try and rise above such worldly feelings.'

'I didn't even know where you were.'

She shook with rage and emotion, tears flowing, throat tight.

'It was felt it was best for me to go on a special mission for the bishop, privately. I'm truly sorry that you were hurt. Can't we at least be friends now? It was all a very long time ago.'

'It's like yesterday to me. The cherry blossom was out.'

'Yes, I believe it was.' He hesitated. 'This isn't getting us anywhere. What do you want me to do? I can't change the past.'

'Are you made of stone?' she hissed. 'Do you think you can hide behind that garment? That it sets you apart from the feelings of normal human beings? You say you returned to this country over the years. Did you never think to come to see me?'

'We priests are set apart. We are not the same as other men.'

'Illusion!' she snapped, quite uncharacteristically. 'You live in your selfish world of illusion handing out platitudes while the rest of us get on with real life.'

He sighed. 'This isn't the time or place for this debate, Eleanor. If you want to go on with it then we had better arrange something. In the meantime, don't you think you could speak with your fiancé and see whether he would agree to a blessing in the chapel here? It would mean so much to your aunt.'

'Suddenly you are concerned about my aunt's feelings. How do you think she would have felt if she'd known what you had been up to with me, an innocent and unworldly teenager? You seized your opportunity when she was away in Kridblikistan with the mission convent out there.'

'Events just conspired. I was only a young man. You were a very beautiful girl.'

'The world is full of beautiful girls,' she said bitterly. 'I waited for years, yes years, for you to come back. Nothing. Not even a paltry postcard. You stole my youth and spoiled me for somebody who might really love me.' The tears fell, ripping apart the curtain of stoicism that had sheltered her from emotional involvement down the years. She stood up, smacked her hand against the iron grill so that the priest recoiled and then strode out to the back of the chapel angrily. Sister Catherine had turned to see what the noise was but quickly went back to her prayers.

Eleanor genuflected and made her way to the kitchens with the box of figs. It was too early for the Filipino novices to be preparing tea so she sat on one of the bentwood chairs at the scrubbed table and covered her face with her hands. The sobs came long and choking. Years of passion, strangled in youth, saved for a man who wasn't worth it. Now it was too late. She loved Grant, of course she did, but it could never be the same. Oh, how handsome Father Guyler had been! So tall with fair hair and a kind and smiling face that had made her light up inside. His gentle voice when he spoke her name. The touch of his hand in hers. Their evenings in the old folly at the top of the slope in the convent grounds. It was gone forever, lost in the mists of time, vanished with her youth like the early morning dew.

'How could I have been so foolish?' she murmured to herself. 'Now Grant thinks he's my first love. If only he knew! Do I tell him? Does he have a right to know? Pull yourself together.' She got up and went to the deep sink and turned on the cold tap, splashing water over her blotchy face.

'Oh Miss Eleanor! I sorry. I not know you here.'
One of the novices had come in.

'I'm fine. I think I'm allergic to something,' Eleanor lied, dabbing at her eyes with a tissue.

'I help you?'

'No, no. It's alright now. Thank you. I have to go. There are some figs on the table. Bye-bye.' Eleanor made her way out of the kitchen, along the corridor past the chapel, up the stairs, across the oak-panelled hall and through the short corridor that led past the guest wing and then to the conservatory, blotting her eyes.

Sister Catherine was back in her usual place in the conservatory, fiddling around with her art and craft work.

'Ah, there you are, Eleanor.' She said, putting away some paintbrushes. 'Did you manage to make a good confession, my dear?'

'The same as usual. I saw you in there.'

'Well, I don't like to miss an opportunity. At my age you never know when the call may come.' She pointed knowingly towards the ceiling, 'and I do have a little spot of angina.'

'I'm sure you've got donkey's years in you yet, Sister Catherine. Now, please do show me what you've been working on.'

The nun pretended not to notice Eleanor's blotchy face and pulled out a box of duck eggshells.

'I've been doing up these blown shells in the style of the old *Fabergé* fancy eggs,' she said. 'Look! I've made a little crucifixion scene inside and bejewelled the rest of it. What do you think?'

'They are so lovely. Why, they've even got little hinges and clasps.'

'Certainly, they have. I intend to sell them to raise funds for the new minibus. We're having an Easter fair, you know, the week before your wedding.' She gave Eleanor a hard stare.

'Something up, my dear? Something upsetting you?'

'Oh nothing really, just bride stuff. The stress, you know.'

'You'll make a lovely bride. Such a shame we won't see you.' Eleanor bit on her tongue. She had to speak to Grant.

*

Next morning Eleanor was up bright and early at her own flat in *Isabel Avenue*. Pandora had advised her to dress casually for their first trip to the health farm so she was comfortably attired in brown stretch trews and a mushroom coloured acrylic sweater and slip-ons. Her future stepdaughter was on time and they set off in her car, out towards the countryside and the broads, arriving at the *Mansion Health Spa* at half past nine. They booked in and then went their separate ways. Was it Eleanor's imagination, or did Pandora wink at the pink-overalled attendant as she whisked her prey away.

'Where are we going?' Eleanor enquired civilly. The woman indicated the way forward and smiled.

'As it's your first time we'll do an assessment for your approval,' she said. 'In here, please, Miss Framp.'   It was a pleasant little salon reminiscent of an ice-cream parlour in its pastel shades of pink, peppermint green and pale blue.

'So, what happens first?'

'If you'd like to go behind that screen and put on one of those white towelling robes, Madam, then, we'll weigh and measure you and check your body mass index before calling in the specialists.'

'Specialists?' Eleanor wriggled her toes into the flip-flops.

'Oh, advisors, each for different aspects of your well being..
They are worth listening too,' she added, looking askance at the
fine, dark down on Eleanor's top lip. 'On the scales please,
Madam.' Then, out came the tape measure followed by height
against the wall. Everything was written down on a clipboard sheet.

'Would madam care for a cup of herbal tea or a mineral water?'

'Yes, please. A cup of camomile tea would be lovely.'

'I'll just go and see to that, madam. While I am doing so,
somebody will come in and take your medical particulars. Ah, here
she is now.' A small, young woman with a tight bandanna around
her head walked in like a ballerina and made herself comfortable in
a bucket chair opposite Eleanor. She too had a clipboard and, after
greeting her target, ploughed through two long lists of medical
questions all of which Eleanor repeatedly answered with a 'No'.

'Thank you, madam,' she said as she left handing the clipboard
to the Health Advisor who had just that moment arrived. Another
string of questions about Eleanor's bathing and exercise routines
and then diet. She too gave her thanks and left. In came the
Beauty Advisor. Eleanor started to feel as if she was on some sort
of conveyor belt as she sipped her tea during the inquisitions.

'So,' said the elegantly manicured, primped and poised Beauty
Advisor, 'I suggest we make a start on you today.' She smiled
widely with perfect teeth. 'Let's begin with a seaweed wrap and a
facial'

'You're in charge,' Eleanor half-smiled. Being brought up in a
convent hadn't exactly prepared her for such glamour routines.
She followed the Beauty Advisor along the corridor and into what
looked like a morgue. There were six, white, slabs with white
curtains pulled partly around them. Two were occupied by female
clients tightly wrapped in seaweed and plastic. Both had mud-
brown faces and slices of cucumber over their closed eyes. They
also had stereo headphones plugged into their ears and white
turbans over their hair. There was a slightly unpleasant smell of
rotting seaweed masked by perfume.

'Over here, please, Miss Framp.' Curtains were drawn around.
'Pop this elasticated turban over your hair and then strip off for me
and make yourself comfortable on the couch with this towel over

you.' Eleanor did as she was bade and stretched out ready for the onslaught. It was very humid. The beautician came back, now wearing waterproofs and white boots. Her extended nails were protected by rubber gloves.

'Does it have to be as warm as this in here?' Eleanor asked.

'Oh yes. We want you to get the full benefit. Please turn onto your side.' The bandaging and wrapping started. 'Arms down now, Madam.'

'No.'

'I'm sorry, Miss Framp, but you have to put your arms down for me.'

'What if there's a fire?'

'We would rescue you immediately.'

'I don't want my arms strapped to my sides. Please can you do it with them out?'

'Nobody's ever complained before.'

'Let's make this a first, shall we?' she wheedled.

'Very well but don't blame me if it isn't as good as it should be.' Eleanor's skin felt clammy and warm. The parcelling up took about ten minutes to achieve. Then it was mudpack time. There was a feint smell of rotten eggs.

'It comes from the slopes of a volcano where it goes into the sea,' the Beauty Advisor said, slapping it on with a plastic spatula. 'Here are your cucumber slices. Try not to move your face or speak. I'll be back in forty minutes.' With that she plugged two ear-pieces into Eleanor's ears and left her to the sound of waves breaking.

It was with a feeling of panic that the new client awoke to find that she couldn't open her eyelids, that her face was stiff and that when she moved her arms they slithered. Hot all over, she shook her head from side to side, dislodging the cucumber slices and flapping her heavy, soggy appendages about as she struggled to quell the deep sea swell assaulting her ear-drums.

'Aaagh!' she intoned through fixed lips, lifting her head and viewing her sludge-covered body while Atlantic rollers pounded in her ears, alone in her sulphur and seaweed stinking hell. She managed to wrench the ear-phones out.

'Yer-her! Is anybody there?' Silence. She tried more loudly. The other two victims had gone.

'Yer-her!' It was impossible to shout 'yoo-hoo' through caked, rigid lips.

'Here I am, Miss Framp. So sorry to keep you waiting. Shall we get you unwrapped now?'

'Yerse, plerse,' she replied grimly through clenched teeth. The whole unparcelling took place relatively quickly, although as the wrappings fell from Eleanor's body they revealed her long limbs and a torso that seemed to be embossed in seaweedy stencil shapes etched in brown and slime green.

'What abert the face mersk?'

'We'll take that off in a moment. Please try not to speak. Now, let's hose you down.' The Beauty Advisor, still in protective plastics, started sloshing warm water from a hose all over Eleanor's body, stroking away the putrid smelling application and rediscovering the pale, translucent skin, now blotchy and angry, invading her privacy in ways that Reverend Mother would surely have frowned upon.

'Kern't I do thert merself?' she pleaded, highly embarrassed.

'No need to worry. We do this all day long. I've seen bodies far worse than yours.' Eleanor swallowed with surprise at the insult. The woman went on, 'You wouldn't believe some of the shapes and sizes we get in here. Hush or you'll ruin your face mask.' The humiliation was unbearable. The perpetrator continued, 'Now, I'd like you to turn over.' She hosed on. 'Now please put this big towel around you and follow me in your flip-flops over to that cubicle in the corner.'

Once there, the towel came off and out came the long-handled scrubbing brush and fast-jet cool shower.

'Er! Er!' Eleanor danced about awkwardly.

'Nearly done. There. Close your eyes.' A slightly less powerful flow was directed at the naked lady's face. 'Gently massage the pack away with your hands,' the woman said. Then the hose was turned off and the fluffy, cotton dressing gown handed over. 'Pop that on, please, madam and follow me through to the hair-dressing and depilatory salon.'

By four o'clock, Eleanor was a shadow of her former self. She felt as if she had been thoroughly invaded. The look of disgust on the defuzzing assistant's face as she removed the middle-aged lady's upper lip fuzz, would stay with the future bride forever. Every hair on her legs had been ripped out and, to her great pain, she had learned precisely what a *Brazilian* was. In the hairdressing salon, the forty-year old side-parted bob had been vanquished. In its place sat a modern coiffure, raised at the crown, hanging longer at the cheeks and with streaks of blonde highlights over the new shade of warm brown that had replaced the salt and pepper.

The cosmetics expert had photographed her and then scrolled through possible 'looks' on the pc screen. Eleanor sat there in her bathrobe, hair stiff with lacquer, finger-nails extended, square-ended and scarlet-varnished, skin tingling, *Brazilian* burning and corn-removal sites throbbing as she chose her new face from a selection of digital visages thirty years her junior.

In the foyer of the health farm, Pandora relaxed as she flipped through a fashion magazine. She'd had a really lovely day. Just a massage, pedicure, hair-do and make-up. Her mobile buzzed.

'Hi Pops!' she said.

'How's it going?' Grant replied.

'Wait and see but I think you'll agree that the mission has been accomplished.'

'Is Eleanor alright?'

'Ask her yourself. Here she comes. Hold on a moment.'

Pandora beckoned to the slightly shaky-looking Eleanor who was sauntering awkwardly in a gingerly fashion across the marble floor, hoping she wasn't walking like a cowboy.

'Lover-boy is on the phone.' She handed it to her. 'You look great.'

'Hello? Grant?'

'Eleanor, my dear. Have you had a nice day?'

'Oh... oh yes. Very interesting.'

'What do you think of my *Mansion Health Spa*?'

'Amazing. I feel like a new woman.' She thought to herself that she might never be the same again

'Great. Well, can you meet up with me and we'll do dinner out somewhere?' Eleanor felt like bursting into tears and was probably in need of post-traumatic stress disorder counselling.

Pandora beamed encouragingly. Eleanor smiled back weakly.

'I'm not dressed for going out, Grant, darling,' she said, hoping that would get her off the hook.

'Well, my love, you just take a little detour back to your flat and find something ravishing in your wardrobe. There's somebody I want you to meet. I'll pick you up at seven-thirty. Love you.' Grant added that, having learned during his years courting the opposite sex that they needed to hear the words on a regular basis or trouble started brewing.

'You too. Bye.' Eleanor returned the mobile to Pandora.

'He wants me to go out to dinner tonight. I have to go home and change.'

'No time to lose then. Let's go.'

'What about paying for all our treatments?'

'Family perks. Come on. Here, take one of those free chiffon scarves from the box on the counter to keep your hair under control.' Eleanor did so, tying it loosely under her chin as Pandora did. Then the two primped and perfumed women turned out into the cold January afternoon car-park.

*

La Branche, an elegant, exclusive restaurant in the better part of Phillipstone, was the engaged couple's favourite night spot.

'I really enjoy coming here,' Grant remarked to Eleanor as the Maitre d'hôtel came forward to greet them. 'The ambience is just right.' She smiled nervously, still sore from the earlier beauty onslaught.

'You look stunning and I love you in that red satin dress,' he added admiringly, as they were relieved of their coats.

'Sir. Madam. Allow me to conduct you to your usual table.'

They followed across the carpeted area to their alcove away from the band. Was it Eleanor's imagination, or was there a lull in the buzz of conversation as they walked through?

The red satin dress was figure-hugging. She was tall and slim. She had always thought gawky. Now, she looked stunning and Grant held her hand and her gaze as they sat together. It was a table for six but they always preferred it. Grant's order of spring water was already in place, as were the menus.

Suddenly, he let go of her hand and rose to his feet in greeting.

'Teddy, good fellow. Swell to see you again!' Eleanor looked up to see a short, rotund man with black hair plastered to his head in a centre parting. He looked like something out of a nineteenth century barbershop band. He was in full evening dress with a purple bow tie.

'Delighted, old boy. Charmed. Is this your lovely lady?'

'Yes, Teddy, this is my wonderful Eleanor.'

'Utterly gorgeous!' he said, coming around to her side of the table, taking her hand and kissing the back of it with enthusiasm.

'Eleanor, meet Teddy Appleton-Smythe, an old school friend of mine. He came out to Texas for a year at my academy when we were fourteen and we've been in touch ever since.'

'I'm very pleased to meet you, Mr. Appleton-Smythe,' Eleanor said formally, keeping her chin down.

'Delighted, Eleanor. Please call me Teddy. I say, Grant, old fruit, you've landed yourself a real peach here.'

'Don't I know it,' he replied, giving Eleanor a wide smile. 'Take a seat, you rascal,' Grant added, beckoning the waiter over. 'Usual, Teddy?'

'Of course!'

Grant pushed the menu to one side. 'We're ready to order now. So, it will be bangers and mash for my associate here. My good lady will have a medium rare steak with sides and I'll have the roast beef.'

'Thank you sir.'

'Eleanor,' Grant said, waving his hand in the general direction of his plump friend, 'what do you think this young reprobate does to turn a coin?'

'I have no idea. I suppose he's in business of some kind? Do tell me.'

'That would spoil the fun. Go on! Have a little guess.'

She could see that he was wearing a big, gold watch. Otherwise there were no clues.

'Very well. Is he in import and export?'

'Nope.'

'Playing the Stock Market? Manufacturing? Media? Television?'

'Getting warmer, hotter actually.'

'A television actor?'

The old school chum rocked with laughter.

'Oh, I give up. Go on. Tell me, please.'

'Eleanor, my dear, you are sittin' at the same table as the head of *Sateevee Incorporated*, the biggest satellite television company in the world.' She didn't know how to respond so she leaned forward and said sincerely, 'Well done on being so successful.'

'Oh I like her style. I like it a lot,' Teddy chuckled.

'My darlin', do you have any idea how much power this man has?' Eleanor shook her head and looked suitably mystified.

'Tell her, Teddy.'

'Now, Grant my boy, I don't like waving my own flag.'

'OK. I'll do the commercial. My friend, Teddy here, has a string of satellites spinning around the Earth at various latitudes. He beams television, radio and telephone signals all over the planet. He is one of the wealthiest men you are ever likely to meet in your entire life.' Eleanor took a sharp intake of breath.

'Congratulations, Teddy. I am suitably impressed.'

'And,' said Grant, 'he saw you on that television broadcast you did for the Canadian programme from the UK airshow last year.'

'Did you really?' Eleanor said. 'They rather sprang that on me. I was standing on the Press Centre balcony and was suddenly on TV. I just sort of filled in until their satellite slot was finished.'

'You're a natural. You were very professional. I was over in Toronto on business when I saw the broadcast. Hey, Grant tells me you're going to be on an afternoon TV programme shortly to promote your magazine.'

'Yes,' she said with shy smile. 'It'll all be rather challenging.'

Grant took her hand. 'You'll be fine, Honey.'

'I hope so,' she sighed with a grimace as the food arrived.

Chapter 7

'Wow! You've made some progress but you'll be opening first.'

Celeste viewed Roland's photographic studio with approval as she took off her mac and hung it on an empty lamp stand. It was a miserable morning, rain tipping down in relentless sheets, traffic sitting steaming at the lights and the continual slooshing of tyres.

'Well, I thought I'd better make it as light as possible, hence the white everything.'

'It looks like a surgery. You did it jolly quickly.'

'You're going to laugh, but I had to take up all the carpet tiles that I put down.'

'I bet some of them were odd shapes to fit in.'

'I numbered them with chalk on the top so it was fairly easy-peasy to put them all back again.'

'You're so clever,' she mocked, rolling her eyes. 'I haven't put mine down yet.'

He strode about proudly demonstrating the white umbrellas, rolls of backing paper, floodlights on stands and piles of gel filters.

'Hey, you look like a Martian in here.' He viewed Celeste through a lime green gel. She grabbed a red one, declaring, 'and you look like the devil.' He pulled what he hoped was an evil face but she dismissed it with the flap of a hand.

'An improvement,' she said.

'You have no taste.'

'You can talk.'

'Oh yes?'

'Well, just look at the state of you.' He drew her to one side to look in a full-length mirror.

'Oh gosh!' she giggled. Her hair was tousled and messy.

'Why didn't you say when I first came in?' She stroked it down.

'I rather fancy you messed up a bit.'

'Oh Roland, do leave off. I know too much about you to ever get involved.'

'A fellow can change.'

She flapped her hand dismissively at him.

'Pigs may fly. I must have got this muck off the dress rails. I was putting together earlier.' She wiped her hands on a tissue.

'What are you doing about advertising?' he asked. 'Come through here and have a look. I've got myself a photocopier.' Next to it he had piled A5 sheets to be put through letterboxes. She viewed the colour with disdain. 'Fluorescent yellow. Are you sure?'

'Sure, I'm sure. Research shows that bright yellow is the best colour for advertising.'

'I'm going for bright pink.'

'Figures.'

'I know some mothers will have boys but pink is such a mumsy colour. I've got my pink and blue floor tiles anyway.'

'Speaking on behalf of red-blooded males, I object strongly to being lumped in with the girls. It could affect my development.'

'Too late. You've progressed as far as you're going to.'

'True,' he agreed with an air of fatalism. 'We are what we are, young, free, attractive...'

'Down to business, man!'

'Yes. We must.' He was suddenly serious. 'Do you want me to knock up some leaflets for you too?'

'Would you?'

'Let me have the copy and I'll see what I can do. When did you say you were opening?'

'The first of March.'

'I'm a month ahead of you. I'm opening on the first of February. I suppose you've got a plenty more to do in there.' He nodded towards the party wall. 'This place didn't have a lot in it really.' He clasped his hands together and blurted out, 'If I do your leaflets, would you help me with some photographs? I need some for the window.'

'Come on, Roland, we've had the conversation before. I don't want to do glamour pictures. I told you last year.'

'No, no, no!' he protested. 'I want pictures of your babies to display in my shop window. I'll do you some prints for free. They'll be a great crowd-puller, three pretty, little gurgling girls.'

'Mmmm,' she mused, folding her arms thoughtfully. 'Let me think about it. When do you need to know by?'

'Tomorrow?'

'OK. Let me sleep on it. Well, I'd better get back next door. I've been working out my labelling. It's going to be difficult doing new and quality used stuff.'

'So how will you do show the difference?'

'Pink for new. Green for recycled. There'll be notices up too.'

'Where will you get your stock from?'

'The problem is that nobody will give me credit until I've proved myself, so I'm having to pay up-front for everything and still wait for delivery until the cheques have cleared. I've got no bargaining power whatsoever.' She waved her hands about dejectedly. 'I never thought of that. However,' and she struck her finger in the air, 'there's plenty to be had from car boot sales, jumble sales and small ads.'

'What? You? Car boot sales and jumble sales? You're kidding. By the way, your pink paint's over there.'

'Thank-you. Roland, you have to understand that my life has changed beyond all recognition. Have you any idea what it is like to be an unmarried mother of triplets? Everything I was hoping to do with my airshow career has been scuppered. Rupert has gone...' There was a catch in her voice. 'And I've got to make this work. It's no time for being picky. If I can get a cot from a boot sale for ten pounds, clean it up and re-sell it for twenty-five, then I'm winning.'

'Yes, but by the time you've paid your rent, rates, insurance and repairs, not to mention your National Insurance, you're going to have to sell it at triple what you paid for it in order to survive. You'll have to brush up on your bargaining skills.'

'You're right,' she said grimly.

'I'm even wondering how I'm going to get on here,' he said by way of comfort, looking around his studio.

'We're survivors, Roland. You know we are. We both escaped that horrendous incident at the airshow last year. We have "luck" tattooed on our foreheads.' She picked up her paint, retrieved her mac, and went out into the downpour to her own shop next door.

Mums, Tums and Tots was crying out for a lick of paint. Celeste put the tins on the floor and looked up at the high ceiling. She was never going to be able to do such a huge area above her head, not after the Caesarean. Her muscles would never take it. Roland had enough to do. She couldn't ask him. The free local directory had a list of painters and decorators. January, not being a great month for interior refurbishments, meant that she had no less than three painters suing for business that very afternoon. She spread their appointments out and they turned up roughly on time, desperate for work. Two of them went away with the promise of a phone call soon to let them know but she decided that the father and son family duo looked the most reliable and engaged them on the spot. Starting on Monday they would put two coats of white on the ceiling and also provide that paint. The father looked askance at the cans of pretty pink that Roland had bought.

'Not industrial quality,' he commented, 'and there's not enough for two coats on all these walls. Do you want me to match it?'

'Yes please.'

'Leave it to me.' Then he gave her a quotation that took her breath away.

'Really?' she gasped.

'Look, my dear, we're going to bring in ladders, sheets, equipment and manpower. I've got overheads, like a van and insurance. If you think you can do it any cheaper, be my guest.'

'Oh no,' she added hastily. 'It's just more than I expected. It'll be fine.'

'We'll need a deposit. Say twenty-five percent, in cash, if you want us to start quickly.'

'When do you need it?'

'Now would be good. Then we can go and get your paint before the warehouse closes.'

Celeste dived into her purse and extracted the necessary notes. The man took them and shoved them in his back pocket and made as if to leave.

'Right,' he said, 'we'll see you on Monday.'

'What about a receipt?' she challenged.

'Oh we don't do receipts,' he replied with a wink. She stood her ground.

'I have to have a receipt.'

'Sorry, girly, we don't do 'em.'

'I'm not a "girly" and I do need a receipt.'

'New to this, are you?' he said patronisingly. 'Alright then. I'll make an exception but don't you go waving it about. Right?' He scribbled something on the back of a torn-off sheet of invoices and handed it to her. Then he picked up one of her cans of pink paint and joined his smirking son out in the unmarked van.

Celeste locked the shop door behind him, killed the nervous fluorescents and went up the front stairs to her flat. It smelled musty as she opened the door at the top of the flight and found herself on the little landing. Luckily, the outgoing tenants had left the carpets... not to her taste but better than nothing. In the through-lounge the heavily textured wallpaper reminded her of cheap pubs. She turned on the central light and sat on the floor with her back to the lukewarm radiator. The free local paper was full of furniture for sale. With a ballpoint pen she encircled three-piece suites, dining sets and coffee tables before getting busy with the mobile. Everybody she rang was out. Obviously they were all at work. So she went and bought some fish and chips and ate them upstairs with a cup of milk-less tea. There was something rather depressing about a solitary picnic in an empty room.

Next morning, Saturday, after a chilly night on some cushions in the upstairs front bedroom, she had a shower and got dressed. The previous evening's telephone calls had yielded some appointments to view. She rang Roland.

'Want to come furniture hunting with me?'

'I'm a bit busy,' he said. 'I've got to sort out some glitches with my computer.'

'I can help you with that.'

'What do you know about PCs?'

'Probably more than you. I happen to have an honours diploma in computer technology.'

'In that case, I'd be delighted to go furniture hunting.'

By lunchtime, they had earmarked a suite each, several coffee tables and one dining set and a divan bed that he agreed she could have. She left him to do the bargaining and fix up the van again. By teatime, the decrepit van had limped all over the borough and delivered its second-hand load to their shop forecourts.

There only remained the problem of how to carry all the stuff up the steep stairs. Celeste was obviously in no fit state to do so.

'I'll go and see if that guy from the chemist's will give us a hand,' Roland said confidently. 'He was helpful the other day, wasn't he?' He came back disappointed. 'He finishes early on Saturdays.'

Celeste, standing in her shop doorway, saw a group of yobs came along, pushing and shoving each other and shouting.

'Try them,' she urged.

'No way.'

'Then I will. We can't leave this stuff out here all night.' She stepped forward, diminutive Celeste, looking up at three youths wearing their baseball caps on backwards and wearing jeans that were more hole than material, complete with posterior cleavage. With an accent that her own mother would not have recognised, she said, 'Eh-oop fellas. Want ter earn a tenner?'

They stopped in their tracks and looked down at the short shopkeeper with amusement. One of them said, 'So, what are you offering us then, Missus?'

Without batting an eyelid and aware that Roland was trying to stop himself from laughing, she ploughed on.

'E're,' she said. 'Carry them things oop them flippin' stairs for us, will yah?'

'Tenner?'

'Tenner.'

'Come on lads.'

Roland was gob-smacked as the three burly youths hoisted the furniture shoulder-high and swung it up the stairs into Celeste's flat. They came down and the leader held out his hand for payment.

'Want to airn anoother?'

'You bet, lady.'

'Then tak me mate's gear oop 'is stairs for 'im. 'Poor fella's got an excrutiatin' hernia.'

If he didn't have one before, he was about to get one from laughing but he stood back and ushered his furniture upwards. The three lads went off mightily pleased with their unexpected earnings for ten minutes work.

Celeste stood with her hands on her hips and a look of smug superiority. Roland shook his head slowly in amazement.

'You really are something. Where did you learn that accent?'

'Amateur dramatics. I played the lead in many a school play. I always knew it would come in useful one day. Want a coffee?'

*

Gonzo enjoyed working at the beautiful *Villa Estancia*. The mild Millonchan climate suited his mixed parentage. The winters could be a little murky and damp but the early springs were full of the scent of almond blossom and, a little later, orange blossom. The summers burgeoned with bougainvillea and the autumns were gentle with generous harvests of nuts and olives.

He loved the history, the old buildings and the little wind turbine water pumps that scattered the countryside like flapping white moths. The tourists amused him as they willingly handed over their Euros for his guided weekend tours. When Grant Landscar was in residence, Gonzo's weekdays were spent ministering to his employer's whims at the villa. Gardening, pool maintenance, errands and odd-jobs all fell within his remit but he didn't mind because he mostly had the place to himself. Between visits he could do as he pleased.

However, Gonzo bore a grudge. The beautiful villa had once been his home. Of course it hadn't looked like that in his childhood days. Indeed, it had just been a *finca*, a small ranch with a lean-to stone and wood shack, but when his father had died, Gonzo's mother couldn't cope with the goat rearing and olive business and had handed the property back to the landlord, Grant Landscar. It broke her heart and she too died soon afterwards by her own hand.

Grant Landscar had kept her son on as a general purpose help about the place and, when all the renovations were in hand, it had been useful to have him there, bilingual and local. For Gonzo, it had been a bittersweet arrangement, his days peppered with the ghosts of his parents but his heart content in the countryside and climate. This was home.

However, of late, as his thirtieth birthday approached, he had thought of his future life being spent here as the lackey of this rich Texan. Yes, he had the use of a small cottage on the outskirts of the farm which was, by now, considerably larger than in his parents' day. Grant had bought up several surrounding *fincas* when land had been cheap and the estate was now of considerable size. He didn't farm it, however. The goats had long-gone and the olive terraces sub-contracted out. The fields had been turned over to grass which was made into hay by the travelling hay makers each summer. Even the almond trees were cared for by outsiders.

It was an idyllic life for Gonzo but it had to change and already he had a plan. He was going to be rich and to go to America to become even richer. He too was going to be wealthy and respected, not treated as a serf. He would find an American wife and start a dynasty, such as he had seen on the sub-titled television series from the States. They would not call him "Gonzo" in a derisory way, but he would be addressed as "Señor Gonzales" and highly respected.

As spring approached, he would start to put his plan into action. His tourism sideline had taken him to many parts of the islands, for not only did he know Milloncha like the back of his hand, but he was also intimately acquainted with its less known attributes. As well as taking tourists about on road tours in his open-top run-about that seated six, he was also the proud owner of a sea-going motor launch with which he thrilled his clients as it crossed the straits between the islands, leaving behind a creamy, foaming wake on the azure blue waves of the Mediterranean Sea.

The success of his plan would be in its simplicity. As he walked across the terrace at the rear of the *Villa Estancia*, he caught sight of his reflection in the patio windows and paused. Even though he said it himself, he was a fine-looking man, the sort that women fell in love with, the type that ladies of certain age found irresistible. He tossed his head with pride. Oh yes!

He jangled the keys hanging from his belt and found the one that opened the kitchen door. Even at this time of year, it was a sunny room. The refrigerator purred and the central heating was on low. The villa had to be kept in comfortable condition all the time and so it was here that Gonzo spent many hours, aping his boss, reclining on the expensive furniture in the lounge, eating micro-waved meals and watching satellite television. Sometimes he crashed out on the four-poster bed in the master bedroom.

The large satellite dish on the upper roof terrace picked up hundreds of stations but the evenings could be lonely and many a village girl enjoyed the luxurious lifestyle at his behest in return for a little housework. If only the lamb's wool rugs and white leather sofas could talk! He smiled with satisfaction.

He sauntered through into the sunroom and flopped out onto a chaise-long. Prickly pears stood in red-glazed pots on the wide terracotta window-ledges. Out through the plate glass windows he could see the evergreen holm oaks and remembered how he used to collect the acorns to feed the family's few pigs. In the distance, the almond blossom was out. The first batches of tourists would come this very weekend but before he decided on the route he would take them, he wanted to see what he needed to get for the carrying out of his grand plan. He took a pencil and a small note-pad out of the back pocket of his stone-washed jeans and started to make a list:

*Bottles of spring water, blankets, candles and matches,
small, blow-up dinghy and a hand-pump, nylon rope, duct
tape, can opener, tinned food, biscuits.*

He lifted his gaze to the holm oaks. Revenge would be good. He could almost see the ghosts of his parents... his mother driving the goats along the dusty lane to the small milking shed and carrying the pails of creamy milk into the tiny dairy room next door where she made the most wonderful cheese to sell at the market.

He imagined his father thrashing the olive trees until their firm, dark fruits fell in a patter onto the sheets below. Then, the young Gonzo would scoop them into the big wooden trailer, dragged by the donkey to the pressing mill in the old barn. The virgin oil oozed like liquid gold from the press into the wooden barrels. The bottled oil was sold to local hotels. Yes, revenge would be sweet. Oh yes!

Now, he would go and fill up his car with diesel. He would wash and polish the vehicle until it shone like one in a showroom. He had some visitors to conduct around the island tomorrow. He would smarten himself up, buy a new shirt, start using perfumed deodorant and practise his charm offensive and see if he could achieve his first lay of the spring. He rubbed his hands together gleefully. Oh, this was going to be a most interesting season!

Chapter 8

'It was quite a shock,' Eleanor remarked to Pandora as they sat at their respective workstations in the office of *Embroideryworld.*

'He just sprang it on me.'

'That's Pops.'

'I don't see how I could possibly go on television regularly. It's one thing to do the interview tomorrow for the magazine promotion, but being the "reasonable, middle-class, British face of caring for the planet" is quite something else.'

'Well, you knew my father was environment-mad when you met him.'

'True.'

'If you're going to be married to him, it'll be difficult to avoid all that stuff.'

'Yes, but don't you think I'll have enough to do, what with this magazine and the wedding and everything?'

'The wedding's just a passing phase.'

'It's quite important to me. I mean, he's done it a few times before but it's my first and, I hope, only.'

'Of course it is and we're going to make it really special for you. Once you get the Register Office thing over and done with this morning, you'll really believe it's going to happen.'

Eleanor looked down at her desk dejectedly. Pandora noticed.

'You're worried about your aunt at the convent. Yes?'

'I know she's terribly upset that it won't be a church wedding. Do you think there's any chance at all that Grant will change his mind and let us have, at least, a blessing in the convent chapel?'

'Knowing Dad, I'd say it was unlikely but,' and she waved her finger mysteriously in the air, 'you have a bargaining chip now.'

'I do?'

'You do. He wants you to front this environmental programme on the satellite for him.'

'...but I don't really want to.'

Eleanor looked at her nails nervously.

'Marriage is all about compromise. Why don't you say that you'll do it just for, say, ten programmes?'

'What about the magazine?'

'Oh, I'll be here to prop it up. It wouldn't take up all your time in any case.'

'He still wouldn't want the chapel ceremony, would he though?' Pandora picked up a pencil and tapped the side of her head.

'Leave it with Pandy,' she said. 'Now, about this free give-away cross-stitch set for the March issue. Look! I've got one here for you. They're inserting them into the magazine packaging at the printers.' She produced a small plastic bag containing a printed linen piece, a clutch of coloured threads, a needle, a threader and small booklet about the craft. 'They've made quite a good job of it, don't you think?' she remarked, taking out the contents and spreading them on the desk.

'How much are the sets costing us?'

'They've imported them from the far East so about ten pence each.'

'That seems very reasonable indeed.'

'Readers just love give-aways. Even if they just stick them in a drawer and never use them, they get this good and glowing feeling that the magazine cares about them.'

'I'm sure you're right. When will we get our stack of February issues?'

'They said they'd bring us over a hundred this afternoon. The rest are going out to the distributors and will go on sale the day after tomorrow on the tail of your television appearance.'

'You were right about the health farm.' Eleanor hesitated, biting her lower lip.

'It's part of the rich life-style. You will learn to love it. Trust me, Eleanor. You'll soon adapt.'

'The hairdresser is coming to my flat tomorrow before I go to the studio. I must say, I'd got used to the way I looked. This glamour image is far from how I feel.' She looked down at her chic sage suit with the ruffled blouse and then felt for the gold ear-clips and chain.

'You look lovely, Eleanor. Tastefully attired and quite the wife-to-be of a billionaire.'

'Oh gosh! Is he really?'

'You can bet on it.'

'I don't think about that side of things.'

'That's why he likes you. The others were gold-diggers.'

Eleanor hesitated. 'The others. What were they like?'

'Much younger. More my age. I can't say I took to any of them.'

'Any? I thought there were only two others, apart from your mother. Sorry. Perhaps you'd prefer that I didn't mention...'

'My mother got what she deserved. A plumber.'

'Your mother married a plumber?'

'Yes, after the divorce. A nice, simple man. Uncomplicated. She took a good settlement from my father and went off with her plumber to live in California. They're both as happy as two pigs in clover. I visit her once a year.'

'The others?'

'The girlfriends.'

'Were there many?'

'Don't ask.'

'Also young?'

'You'd better believe it.'

'Then why me?'

'He's ready to settle down.'

'Why now?'

'He hasn't mentioned anything to you, has he?'

'Please don't say there's something wrong...'

'Nothing much but I think he should tell you.'

'Oh dear. I hope it's nothing serious.'

'It's under control. Don't worry. I'm sure he would have got around to telling you. He's in denial but the medication is working.'

'He really should have said something to me.'

'Eleanor, there's one thing you have to understand about Pops. You will never know all of him. I've been around him for my entire life. He got custody of me. Even I don't know him.'

'I suppose I'll just have to trust my instinct.' Eleanor picked at the edges of her new nails. 'I'm not very experienced with men.'

'He's too old to fool around now. You two are going to be very happy and I'm more than pleased to have you as a stepmother.'

'Are you really?'

'Yes, of course I am. Charlie needs a granny-figure in his life too.'

'Thank you Pandora. I'll try and be a good granny to him. He's a delightful child.'

'He can be a handful but you and I are going to be good friends. Hey! Look at the time! Lover-boy will be here in a minute. You'd better freshen up.' She looked up as the door handle rattled. 'Too late!' Grant peered in without knocking, stetson clutched to his chest.

'Good morning ladies.'

*

'Well, that's over and done with, hopefully for the last time!' Grant declared as he and Eleanor sat in the Register Office car park after their interview. Taking his fiancée's hand in his, a broad smile creased his tanned face. Eleanor sat beside him in the front seat of his car, the leather interior trim smelling of newness and quality. She placed her other hand over their clasped fingers.

'Why didn't you tell me about your little health problem?'

'My lovely daughter's been spillin' the beans, has she? It just kind-a slipped my mind, my sweetie. I kept meaning to tell you but the moment was never right. It's nuthin'. I'm fine.'

Eleanor, although a woman in love, still had her own mind. She wouldn't have survived for fifty years without it. She took a deep breath.

'Grant, we have to be honest with each other,' she said. 'If we are going to be a real couple, to make a happy future together.'

'You're right, ma darlin'. I promise to be the picture of Texan light and truth from this day forward.' He laughed mischievously in that special way that made her heart turn over. 'Forgive me?'

'Yes, of course but what's wrong with you?'

'Diabetes and it's under control. Now,' he said seriously, his blue eyes twinkling, 'is there anything you want to declare?'

She felt palpitations start up as a hot flush spread through her body, making her want to tear off her warm coat and leap out into the fresh air. The menopause. Would it never end?

'It's just a bit warm in here,' she panted. He pressed the switch and the window wound smoothly down. She unbuttoned her coat.

'Better?'

'Yes, thank you. Whew!'

'As I was saying, do you have anything you want to tell me so that we have a clean slate, so to speak?'

'No. Nothing. Of course not. I'm just plain old Eleanor.'

'I will not allow you to besmirch the name of the woman I love. You are my beautiful, sensitive, kind, clever Eleanor and I will beat anybody around the ears with a wet lettuce who says otherwise.' They laughed together. The moment had passed.

'How do you feel about having a little look at a project of mine?' She checked her watch. 'Will it take long?'

'Ten minutes. It's just along the road here.' They fastened their seat-belts and he pulled out of the Register Office car park. The next time they would be there, would be on Easter Saturday, the big day. Traffic was busy on the dual carriageway, as usual, but Grant turned right at the lights and used the back doubles to bring the vehicle to a stop in the service road on the opposite side of the carriageway from his shopping parade.

'You wait there while I come and open your door for you.' She appreciated the courtesy. He conducted her to the bungalow's front gate. 'Come along in and see what I'm buying.' He guided her down the side passageway of the property and onto the rear terrace. She looked askance at the rubbish and broken windows.

'Take no notice of all that,' he said. 'It's irrelevant.'

'Why are you buying this?' she asked. 'It looks very run down. Are you going to do it up?'

'Shucks, no. I'm going to demolish the whole caboose.'

'Then what?' She shivered as she surveyed the enormous back garden with its oak trees, old tennis court and high hazel hedges.

'This, my lovely wife-to-be, is going to be the most modern, up-to-date, technologically innovative vehicle washing and electrical recharging facility in the county.'

'What about all the houses that back onto it? It's in a residential area. Won't there be problems?'

He stood with his feet firmly apart.

'Nope. My facility will be environmentally friendly in all respects, including noise and pollution minimisation.'

'Well, I must say, Grant, you're full of surprises.'

'What's life without a few of those? So, here's another one for you. Come on.' He took her arm through his and led her out of the garden and along the service road, crossing at the lights and then back along the other side to the terraced parade of four shops.

'Why are we over here?'

'I want to show you my new retail outlets. This parade is one of my little investments. The rental income will be very welcome, far better than leaving the money sitting in the bank.' They stood outside the photographic studio. The sign above it stated *Roland Dilger Photography*. Eleanor gave a little gasp of surprise. Signs in the window said that it would open the day after tomorrow, the first of February. Grant rapped on the glass shop door. Roland came through from the back room and immediately recognised the local entrepreneur who had refused to be photographed at last year's airshow.

'What the heck can he want?' he mumbled to himself. Then he spotted Eleanor who had been standing behind her fiancé. He unlocked the door and stepped out onto the tiled area in front of the doorway.

'Eleanor! Eleanor Framp, if I'm not mistaken! What on earth are you doing here?'

She minced forward and shook his hand.

'How very nice to see you again Roland.' Then she explained to Grant how she and the photographer had often bumped into each other at the airshows.

'A small world, then,' Grant said pointedly extending his hand to Roland. 'It seems that I am your landlord, just dropping by to get acquainted.'

'So,' Roland said, puzzled, 'why are you two together here?'

'Mr. Landscar and I are engaged to be married,' Eleanor said with a coy smile and then added, 'at Easter.'

Roland seized her hand again and pumped it enthusiastically.

'Congratulations! Congratulations!' Then he did the same to Grant who seemed rather taken a-back by the enthusiasm, considering that he and the photographer had not been on good terms at last year's airshow.

'Eleanor is launching her own magazine shortly,' Grant said.

'Well done you! What's it called? I'll buy a copy.'

'*Embroideryworld*,' Eleanor said.

'Excellent,' Roland replied amiably. He tipped his head towards the white-windowed shop next door. 'Of course, Mr. Landscar, you must be Celeste Blagden's landlord too.'

'Celeste Blagden?' Eleanor said and her face blanched.

'Yes, you remember Celeste. She was the Press Centre Manager at the airshow. Did you know she had triplets?'

'I knew she was expecting something,' Eleanor said, with a face like granite. She and Celeste had been at daggers drawn since day one at the airshow. How could she ever forget the humiliations that woman had inflicted on her? The rows, the altercations, the spite when Eleanor had been covering the event for the *Saturnian*, the local paper. Now that dreadful woman was Grant's tenant.

'Yes, I met her too,' Grant interjected. 'She sat at my table in the restaurant when the royals came to see that *ILEX* plane the week before the show started. I had no idea who it was opening this mother and baby shop until I popped in recently.'

'Indeed,' Eleanor remarked coldly.

Roland remembered only too well the ice wall between the two women. It had been the talk of the Press Centre.

'Ah well, ' he said with a hint of roguery, 'times change.'

'We'd better be going,' Eleanor said, linking her arm through Grant's. 'Goodbye for now, Roland. It was nice to see you.'

'Bye Eleanor, Mr. Landscar. Here, have one of my cards.'

Grant flashed him a quizzical look as he accepted it with a warm smile.

*

'Darling! How wonderful to see you!' Celeste's mother, in a cloud of perfume, crushed her daughter into her embrace the moment she opened the front door of the huge detached house on the outskirts of Phillipstone. 'Where have you been? You haven't seen the triplets for days.'

Celeste pulled away and put her bag and a bunch of flowers on the Louis XIV chiffonier in the hallway.

'Do mind the polish, dear,' her mother said, taking up the flowers. 'Lovely. Thank-you.' She sniffed at them. 'Freesias are so heavenly,' she enthused. Celeste hung her coat in the hall closet and tidied her hair in the mirror.

'Is Daddy home?'

'Golf. They have a foursome today. Since the frost has gone, they've allowed them back on the course.'

Celeste swept through to the lounge.

'You've changed the furniture around again,' she remarked.

'What did you say, dear?' her mother called from the hall as she buffed the chiffonier's surface with the sleeve of her Kashmir sweater. Then she appeared in the doorway.

'What do you think? It's better this way, isn't it?'

'Much,' Celeste said, knowing only too well that it was pointless to comment otherwise. She walked over to the patio doors and looked out at the garden. Two prams stood on the terrace. One was a twin and the other a single. The hoods were up. 'I see the babies are out getting their air.'

'Yes, Big Nanny is absolutely punctilious about it... that's head nanny, the one who came highly recommended from the stately home.'

Celeste had met the two women who were in daily charge of her triplets. The whole area of baby care was of little interest to her. The nurses' salaries, equipment and baby food were all being provided by the doting grandparents. There was a nervous tap at the open lounge door.

'Yes, Nanny?' Mrs. Blagden said imperiously.

A small, blousy blonde, who had been crammed into a nanny outfit clearly two sizes too small for her buxom figure, stood in the doorway.

'Excuse me for interrupting, Mrs. Blagden... oh good morning Miss Blagden... but we were wondering whether we should bring the babies in to see their mother.'

She deferred with a half-smile to Celeste who couldn't give two hoots for all this motherhood business.

'My daughter will come up to the nursery suite to see the children. Please tell head nanny that Miss Blagden will be up directly.'

'Very well Mrs. Blagden.' The girl exited backwards, oozing respect.

'We'll just give them a moment to get the triplets in and then we'll go up and have a look at them. They are dear little things.'

'You don't need to come up, Mother. I'll go on my own.'

'Nonsense dear. You need me to explain everything...'

'No thank you, Mother. You can tell me afterwards. While we're waiting, I need to speak to you about something else.'

'Yes, dear?'

'I have an ex-colleague from the airshow last year...'

'Oh, don't speak to me about that awful thing that happened...'

'That's history, Mother. We've all moved on. Now, this chap, Roland Dilger, is a professional photographer and I'd like him to come here and take some photographs of April, May and June.'

'I'm sure we could arrange that. Some time next week, perhaps?'

'No. Today.'

'Oh I couldn't possibly be ready in time.'

The doorbell sounded.

'Here he is now,' said Celeste, going to let him in.

Mrs. Blagden stood there, aghast. She hadn't had her hair set for two whole days. She heard her daughter greeting the newcomer.

'Come in Roland. We're expecting you.'

'Groovy pad,' he said with approval, casting his eyes around the sumptuous hall. He dumped his equipment on the Persian carpet.

'I'll just pop out to get a few more lights in.' He went to the car again and came back loaded with metal stands, boxes of bulbs and metal reflecting shades.

'OK. So where do you want me?' Then his mouth dropped open and he slowly took off his red baseball cap, folded it and stuffed it in his anorak pocket, all at time-lapse speed. Celeste followed his gaze. The younger of the two nannies, was carrying one of the babies through the hallway and was about to take her up the stairs to the nursery. The child was dressed entirely in pink. Big Nanny wasn't far behind, carrying the other two triplets, one on each arm. They were dressed in lemon and lilac respectively.

'Whatever are they wearing?' Celeste asked, astounded.

Big Nanny swung around to see who had spoken.

'Oh, good morning, Miss Blagden. We have to colour-code the girls. It saves confusion. If you would like to come up to the nursery, I can show you that we have done the same with all their other items.'

'They look like rainbow mix,' Celeste said, shaking her head in disbelief. She followed the nannies up the stairs, calling over her shoulder, 'Mother, please can you show Mr. Dilger into the lounge. I think we'd better do the pictures in there.'

Not at all keen to have an altercation with her daughter in the presence of strangers, Mrs. Blagden gushed, 'Good morning, Mr. Dilger. Please do come through.' Then she looked down at his trainers and nodded that he should remove them, which he duly did, staggering slightly under the weight of a large tripod as he eased them off without undoing the laces.

Once up in the well equipped nursery, Celeste felt strangely inadequate. Big Nanny surveyed her haughtily.

'What would you wish the children to be dressed in for their photographs, Madam?'

'Certainly not these things. Don't we have anything more tasteful in their wardrobes?'

The three babies were lying on their backs on their changing mats on a wide table. They were all still asleep. Celeste went over and peered at them. Little Nanny stood by.

'They look fine,' Celeste commented without touching them.

'Yes, they are,' the younger nanny said. 'I'll just unwrap and change them and then they'll probably wake up.'

'Good,' Celeste said. The girl gave her a sawny glance.

Over at the wardrobe, Big Nanny was riffling through dozens of baby hangers bearing a huge array of clothing. She held out a white satin dress with puffed sleeves.

'We have three of these,' she said, 'all identical but with a different coloured bow on the front of each.'

'They look suitable.'

'We have some white socks and white satin shoes to go with them.'

'Perfect,' Celeste approved. 'So, I'll leave you to get them changed and then perhaps you could bring them down to the lounge for their photographs, please.'

'Yes, Miss Blagden.' Celeste left the nursery with its plethora of baby ephemera and scent of baby oil. She left the walls papered with nursery characters, the dangling mobiles, window stickers and the three barred, white cots, each with a carrycot inside it, each with a coded ribbon attached. It felt like a baby factory. She couldn't wait to get out and was particularly annoyed that her breasts were tingling.

Downstairs in the lounge, Mrs. Blagden was launching a charm offensive on the middle-aged photographer.

'You must have met a large number of interesting people in your professional life,' she smarmed as he adjusted lamps and wing nuts.

'A few,' he replied.

'Do tell me about some of them. Have you met royalty?'

'Oh yes, and politicians and film stars.'

'How very interesting. Anybody in particular?'

'Most of the royal family.'

'Really?' she drawled. 'Of course, my father was equerry to a royal, you know, but we don't speak about it.'

Celeste came into the room. 'He was a footman at the Palace,' she corrected with raised eyebrows. 'They'll be down in a minute. Where are we going to put them, Roland?'

'That big sofa there with the damask cushions looks quite good. I shouldn't have to use direct flash because it's facing the window. I'll bounce some off the ceiling.'

The sound of the talking nannies coming down the stairs heralded the arrival of April, May and June. With their wobbly heads, sparse black hair and still wrinkly faces, they did bear a slight resemblance to monkeys. Celeste thought so but she said nothing.

'Ah, here are the little darlings,' gushed their grandmother rushing forward.

'Put them on the sofa, please, Nannies,' Celeste ordered, elbowing her mother out of the way.

'...but I haven't kissed them yet today...'

'Later, Mother. We haven't much time.' Then she looked down at the triplets with disapproval. 'Why are they flopping about like that? Can't they sit up a bit better?'

Big Nanny fixed her with a glare. 'They are only three and a half months old, Madam, and they were premature.' Celeste didn't know about the sitting up thing.

'Well, what do you suggest, Roland?'

'If we could sort of slope them on those cushions with their heads together, it would look quite good.'

The nannies shuffled the babies into position. April's face started to screw up like a lemon.

'Why's she pulling that face?' Celeste demanded.

'I think she's getting hungry. It's nearly their feed time.'

'Better hurry up, Roland.'

A clicking noise emanated from Mrs. Blagden. 'Here, here. Smile for Granny.' April's gummy mouth opened, her eyes shut tightly and she let out a heartbroken howl.'

'Can't you stop her?' Celeste said to Big Nanny who promptly stuck her little finger in the child's mouth, effectively silencing her. The other two triplets moved jerkily with excitement, kicking their little satin-clad feet and batting each other in their proximity. With her free hand, from her apron pocket, Big Nanny produced a bell-sounding rattle. That took all their attention for a moment. All three babies opened their eyes in amazement. The flash went off. Then there was a loud, gurgling noise and an unpleasant stench.

'My sofa!' exclaimed Mrs. Blagden, but it was too late.

Chapter 9

'My special guest this afternoon is a woman of some journalistic experience and one who is also tomorrow launching her very own specialist magazine. Ladies and gentlemen, please give a very warm welcome to Eleanor Framp.'

A young man with shoulder-length hair stood in front of the audience and to one side, holding up a big sign that read, 'THUNDEROUS APPLAUSE.' That's what Eleanor received as she came through the archway into the presentation area, quite overwhelmed by the strength of the welcome. She looked slightly taken aback. The presenter, a woman also of a certain age, rose to greet her, clapping enthusiastically.

'Eleanor, please come and join me.' She smiled broadly and ingratiatingly at her guest as she indicated a lime-green, easy chair the other side of a low, glass table from her own seat. The applause petered out and the lights bore down with unexpected heat. A hot flush was inevitable. Eleanor felt it sweep over her. She breathed through it as beads of perspiration broke apart the thick cake of make-up that had been plastered onto her face. A half-smile seemed to be the best way forward.

'Now,' said the programme hostess benevolently, 'here in the *Afternoons are Yours* studio, we have some very interesting guests each week but I believe this is the first time we have had the pleasure of meeting a woman who is starting up her own specialist magazine.' She quickly consulted her hand-held pile of cards. '*Embroideryworld* is a very tantalising name for a publication. Perhaps you would like to tell us how you came to choose it.' She looked up expectantly at Eleanor whose mouth had suddenly become so dry that the insides of her lips were sticking together. She interlocked her fingers tightly.

'Thank you for inviting me onto your show.' She paused. A red light lit up on the camera just behind the presenter. Eleanor looked into the lens as she had been instructed to do by a young women wearing head-phones and a microphone who had primed her in the green room beforehand. The girl was now waving her hand, encouraging Eleanor to speak. So she did. After taking a deep breath she launched into her diatribe.

'*Embroideryworld* seemed a very suitable name for my new publication because I hope to take my readers on a journey along the history and development of everything to do with the craft of embroidery in all its forms through all the continents and many countries.' The audience was deathly silent. She went on, 'To be honest, I trawled through the internet trying to find a magazine title that hadn't been used already.' She was getting into her stride now. 'All the obvious titles had gone so I had to be a little inventive. Actually,' she paused and said confidentially, 'sometimes it's good to be a little bit different. I hope my magazine will attract a wide variety of readers and craftspeople.'

'How interesting,' said the interviewer insincerely. She looked down at her cards. 'So, tell me, Eleanor, as you have up until recently only had a career in freelance journalism, you must have a financial backer for your magazine?'

'Yes, my business partner is my fiancé. I have his unstinting support with this project.'

'How very convenient for you.' The woman consulted her cards again. 'I'm right in thinking, I believe, that your fiancé is the environmentally inclined Texan, entrepreneur billionaire, Grant Landscar.'

'Yes, he is but...'

'... and that Mr. Landscar was involved last year in an unpleasant land dispute here in East Anglia.'

'Yes, but it was all a...'

'Yes, I'm sure it was, but let's move on, shall we?' The presenter had a knife gleam in her eye. 'So, when is the wedding to be?'

'I'm here to talk about *Embroideryworld*,' Eleanor said calmly. She didn't like bullies.

'Yes, of course you are but I'm sure our audience would love to hear about your wedding plans.' She turned to the rows of homely women who looked as if they had come in out of the rain. 'Wouldn't you, audience?'

The young man with the long hair appeared at the front, out of shot, and held up a placard stating, 'CHEER!' So they did.

Eleanor, in the mistaken belief that the baying crowd might actually come over onto her side, said, 'Very well. What would you like to know?'

The presenter leaned forward conspiratorially.

'When a woman reaches a certain age, would it be correct for her to wear white? I mean, surely, as this is your first marriage and you are, shall we say, not in the initial flush of youth, it would be difficult to imagine that there has never been anybody else,' she said archly and then looked meaningfully at the audience. They muttered amongst themselves. Eleanor felt embarrassed.

'I haven't decided what to wear,' she said adamantly, struggling for words.

'So, where will the ceremony take place?' The presenter ground on relentlessly. ' With a rich husband, I expect it will be a massive event... a cathedral perhaps?'

'No. The wedding will be in a register office.'

'Of course!' She looked down at her cards. 'Your fiancé has been married three times before. I expect he's being economical this time,' she chuckled, trying to draw the audience into the joke.

The woman was crucifying her. Then something else kicked in... years of journalism, a lifetime fighting causes. Eleanor tilted her head on one side.

'May I ask you something, please?'

'Indeed you may, Eleanor.'

'As you and I are obviously of a similar age, can I enquire where you had your face-lift done?'

The face in question dropped in anger and then promptly changed to a sickly smile as it turned towards camera three. 'We are going to a commercial break now. We'll be back in a couple of minutes.'

The commercials came on. The presenter stood up, ripped off her microphone and strode over to the producer. 'Get her off my set!'

'...but we haven't got anybody for the second half...'

'Get somebody out of the audience. They can't all be bozos.'

The producer walked across the painted, glossy floor and started to apologise to Eleanor who was already on her feet and who said, 'Don't worry, my dear. This was all a terrible mistake. Please help me to get these wires off.'

The audience was discussing the fracas loudly. Eleanor made her way past all the studio clutter to collect her things. She blinked back tears as she put on her coat in the dressing room.

On the set, the commercials were coming to a close. The silent countdown of fingers; five, four, three, two, one... and they were back on the air. The presenter was reinstalled in her seat and holding a hand microphone. She was ready to save herself. She held up her hand for silence.

'Ladies and gentlemen, I'm sorry to say that Eleanor Framp had to leave for an urgent appointment, but the show goes on and I'm coming out into the audience to talk to you about what sort of magazines you prefer to read.' She stepped down from the dais and climbed the steep central staircase. A woman in a tracksuit indicated that she had something to say. The microphone was poked under her chin. She took hold of it.

'I'm not from a wealthy background,' she said, 'but I do like to do embroidery. I'm looking forward to buying this new magazine.' The mic was snatched away with a cursory 'Thank-you.' Around the audience, the story was the same.

'My elderly mother enjoys cross-stitch.'

'My girls are into drawn thread-work.'

'I like to crochet on the edges of mats I've embroidered.'

'My aunty does Berlinwork. *Embroideryworld* sounds lovely.'

'I do beadwork. I'm going to buy the magazine.'

'We do gold thread-work for special events.'

The presenter appeared to become increasingly annoyed. Was there nobody who would help her to put that Framp woman in her place? This was her show, after all. She tried a burly man in the hope that he might balance the opinions of the others.

'I think you're onto a loser, love.'

The producer drew her finger slowly across her throat and the plug was pulled.

*

Next morning, Grant Landscar was alone in his king-size bed. Eleanor had stayed at her own flat last night, as usual. It was understandable that she was upset about the way the television interview had gone. Pandy had texted him earlier to say that the presenter had been spiteful. Grant munched on some toast and lime marmalade. The tray was on the bed beside him. The first of his daily newspapers was propped up on the Study Buddy® reading stand on his lap. He placed his half-spectacles on his nose and could hardly believe what he saw. He grabbed his mobile telephone and called Eleanor. She was eating breakfast at her kitchen table in her small flat.

'Mornin' my darling woman. How the heck did you pull that?'

'Hello Grant, dear. Pull what?'

'Haven't you seen the papers?'

'I don't have them delivered here any more because I'm hardly ever at home. Why?'

'Allow me to elucidate, my wonderful Eleanor.' He jerked the paper into submission and read aloud, '*Embroideryworld*, the brand new embroidery publication launched and on sale today throughout the country, is due to sell out by ten o'clock this morning due to the shenanigans of a malicious television presenter who made it her business to attempt to humiliate its editor, Miss Eleanor Framp.'

'What?' said Eleanor, incredulously.

Grant went on, 'As Miss Framp left the studio of *Afternoons are Yours* prematurely yesterday, an audience lash-back in the second half of the show made it clear that they had taken this middle-aged woman to their hearts and had every intention of supporting her new publication.'

'I don't believe this,' Eleanor gasped. She sipped her tea hastily. 'I thought they hated me.'

'Obviously not. I haven't seen the programme yet but I've got it on the digital recorder. As you know, I was at meetings all day and well into the evening yesterday. Why didn't you tell me about it? I was home by midnight.'

'Oh, I was fast asleep by then,' she said.

'Well, my darlin' woman, it's a coup. Let's see how the sales go and you may have to do a reprint for February.'

'I'm going over to the office in a minute. Pandora said she'd be in early.'

'My two favourite women. Well done you! Catch you later! Love and hugs.'

'To you too, my lovely man.' She smiled as she hung up.

Grant clicked off and then rang Pandora.

'Good morning darlin' daughter. Thank you for the SMS.'

'Hi Pops. You up yet?'

'Enjoying a leisurely breakfast in bed and reading the papers. It made the front page of all of them,' he said, riffling through the pile.

'It's in the blood.'

'What did it cost us to fix that presenter?'

'Five thousand pounds into her Swiss bank account.'

'...and to fill the audience with people from art and craft groups all over the country?'

'I got a good deal on the coaches and they'll all get a free copy of the magazine. It came to about the same. I paid for all the coaches up-front in cash. You can have the receipts next time I see you.'

'That's my girl. If my precious fiancée doesn't get the taste for television from this, there's no justice. How about that presenter?'

'She's as tough as old boots,' Pandora laughed. 'She'll publish an apology and do one on the main evening news as well. Eleanor will get some flowers and a contrite note from her.'

'Mission accomplished,' Grant said with satisfaction. 'Catch you later!

*

Over at the small parade of shops, Roland Dilger was in early to prepare for his photographic studio's opening day. It was a breezy morning but dry and grey. The tubs of purple winter pansies and primulas adorning the forecourt looked jolly.

'Morning,' said the man from the chemist's as he walked past on his way to work. Roland was up a stepladder hanging balloons above the fascia. They flapped about making a dull "bonk, bonk, bonk" on the plate glass, like distant drums.

'Morning,' he replied as the ladder wobbled. He came down, folded it and carried it back in through the shop. Next, he brought out the A-board and placed it on the forecourt. It stated:

Roland Dilger, Photographer.
Portraits, Weddings,
Parties and Pets.

Then he went inside and took away the paper sheeting that had covered the inside of the plate glass windows. He had been up until late into the evening before printing out A2 size photographs of the triplets. They were mounted on white easels that now stood in the right-hand window against a pale blue background. The left-hand window was full of photographs of beautiful views and flower arrangements. You couldn't actually see into the studio any more because he'd fitted a Venetian blind to the central glass front door. His opening hours were displayed on a substantial card dangling prominently.

Councillor Springstock, rumoured to be the next mayor, was due to perform the opening ceremony at twelve noon. He had promised to bring along a group of other councillors. Roland had also invited other influential people, such as the chairman of the local Residents' Association, the Chamber of Enterprise, the owner of the Sports and Social Club and various women's groups. The press would, of course, be in attendance, especially as there was a buffet lunch on offer.

Roland paused on the forecourt admiring his efforts. He went back in and came out with a large poster which he affixed to the shop door. It stated:

GRAND OPENING
12 NOON
BY INVITATION ONLY

Celeste drew up and parked outside her yet unfinished shop. She got out and wandered over to peer in Roland's windows. Amazed at the size of the photographs of the triplets, she stood and gazed. These were her children.

'Not bad, eh?' Roland said as he came out and stood beside her.

'Very good,' she had to agree. 'Do you want me to come in beforehand to help you set up inside?'

'No, ta. I've got some help.' He jerked his head towards the interior of the shop. 'The caterers will be here later and they'll do everything but come and have a look at what I've had done.' She followed him into the studio. He locked the door behind them.

A small reception counter had been constructed on the left and a staggered fibreboard wall made all across to cut off the rest of the shop area. There was a door behind the counter.

'Come through.' They went into the studio itself. Celeste was impressed. 'You've done a really good job, Roland,' she said. Within the 600 hundred square feet of space he had made specific areas for different kinds of portraiture. A large trestle table was laid out with a paper cloth for the buffet. He led her via a further door into his computer and laboratory room where he also had professionally sized photographic printers, walls of shelves bearing boxes of photographic paper and equipment and a curtained area in the corner.

'What's behind there?' she asked.

'Oh, just stuff,' he replied. 'See, I've incorporated the kitchenette into here as well so I can make drinks and heat things in the microwave.'

'A very good idea. What happens if they want to use your loo?'

'Ah. I'm glad you asked me that.'

'You haven't organised it yet, have you?'

'Well, not exactly. They are coming to re-fit it next week. Have a look. It's grim.'

She reluctantly followed him through the doorway at the end of the computer room and into a dark, little lobby with the back door leading off it.

'You can only get into it from outside.'

'You can't send people out there,' she remonstrated.

'It's worse. Cast your eyes over that.'

'Yuk!' she declared. It was spider heaven. It was also cold, smelled of damp and sported a rather cracked and crazed old white toilet without a seat but with an overhead chain steeped in rust. There was coconut matting on the floor and a dripping noise from somewhere. 'I see your problem.'

'Celeste...'

'No. Absolutely not!'

'Oh, go on! It'll only be until next week. Yours is so much cleaner and it's inside the back of your shop.'

'I can't have people trailing in and out while I'm setting up my business,' she retorted.

'I'll make it worth your while. They wouldn't have to come into your shop if we made a gap in the fencing out at the back and you gave me a back door key so they could just go into your loo. You could lock the inside lobby door. It really wouldn't interfere with you at all.'

'You will clean it and make it hygienic absolutely every single night?'

'I promise.'

'...and pay for the cleaning materials and lock it up properly before you go home?'

'Absolutely

'Very well then,' she said reluctantly. 'I'm doing this because we have to help each other at this time but don't push me!'

'You're a star!' he said happily, then looked at his watch. 'Heck! I must get on. The caterers will be here soon and I have one or two other things to see to.'

'So have I.' She wrenched the spare back door key from her ring. 'Here take this. I'll see you just before twelve.' She started to go back inside his shop. 'What are you doing?'

'Oh, just lifting away this section of fencing that I prepared earlier. I thought you'd agree to help me out. 'Owp!' he yelped, as she punched him on the arm.

They made their way back through into the studio.

'Where's that music coming from?' she asked. It seemed to emanate from the shop ceiling.

'Oh, just a friend upstairs,' he replied nonchalantly, walking ahead of her towards the studio front door and seeing her out. 'Well,' he said, 'I'll catch up with you later then at my reception.'

'Yes. I'm looking forward to it,' she called back over her shoulder as she walked across the forecourts to her own shop, wondering who was in Roland's flat.

He knew. She had been there all night and she greeted him at the top of the stairs with open arms and an open-fronted negligée to match.

'Nanny,' he whispered, as he folded the young, voluptuous, semi-clad nurse-maid of Celeste's triplets into his eager arms.

'Rolly...' she whispered breathily into his ear.

'What? Again?'

'Mmmm.'

'...But I've got the opening of my studio in a couple of hours.'

'It'll only take a little while.'

'That wasn't my experience last night,' he said, nuzzling her neck. He felt decidedly wobbly. Nanny sank to her knees in front of him.

'Oh crikey!' He felt the stirrings of passion yet again. She certainly knew what she was doing. He looked down and peeled back her negligée to reveal her milky white, plump, soft shoulders and matching accoutrements below them.

'Help me,' he muttered, struggling to unbutton his shirt. She reached up and tore at his shirt buttons. He sank down beside her on the floor of the landing and she placed her moist, full lips against his chest, pulling at the mixed grey hairs, teasing.

'Nanny, Nanny,' he groaned.

Suddenly, she pushed him away and got up and ran up the staircase, dropping the negligée as she went.

'Catch me if you can,' she called seductively.

He watched her rather plump rear disappear upwards around the curve of the treads.

'Wait! Wait!'

'Come and get me!' she called mischievously.

He staggered to his feet, clutching the newel post, dragging himself from step to step, hanging onto the banister.

'Rolly. Where are you? I'm getting impatient.'

'I'm coming, Nanny.'

'You're a very naughty boy to keep Nanny waiting.'

'Sorry Nanny,' he gasped, breathlessly, as he threw himself through the bedroom doorway to find her sitting up on the pillows with the portable radio aerial in her hand.

Somebody was hammering on the studio front door. Roland awoke with a start. Nanny slumbered sweetly beside him, her tousled blonde hair spread like candyfloss on the black satin pillow. He raised himself onto his elbows and looked at the clock on the dresser. Everything was blurry.

'What?' he exclaimed, leaping out of bed and nearly falling over. 'It can't be.'

'Can't be what?' she murmured, half-asleep.

'It's eleven-thirty. They'll all be here in a minute.'

'Mmmm.'

She half-opened her sleepy eyes and sighed contentedly as he struggled to get into his trousers, hopping about. Thank goodness he hadn't taken his socks off. He'd have to call out of the window. He flung it open.

'Yoo-hoo! Up here!' he yelled but the traffic was too loud. He could see the caterer's van parked in the service road below and the top of a white-clad head at his shop door.

'I'm up here!'

Nothing. In desperation he grabbed his hairbrush from the dressing table and flung it out of the window so that it landed on the forecourt. The caterer, surprised, looked up, a covered tray of canapés in his hands. He gave a broad grin.

'Be down in a minute,' Roland mouthed. The man nodded in acquiescence.

Little Nanny slept on.

'Let yourself out. I'll ring you on your mobile later,' the erstwhile lover said to the smiling, semi-sleeping woman.

Down the stairs he galloped, pulling on his shirt, running his fingers through his thinning hair, fumbling for the interior shop door keys in his trouser pocket. A jangle. A wrench. The door opened. He rushed to let the caterer in.

'Otherwise engaged and forgot the time, did we?' the man remarked, hiding a grin.

'Got a bit of a cold,' Roland returned. 'Feeling a bit under the weather. Thought a nap would do me good. Put them through there.' He indicated the trestle table in the studio. 'You get on with your unloading and I'll just nip upstairs and freshen up. Don't let anybody in.'

'Sure,' said the man, going out to the van again.

At ten to twelve, the first of the VIPS arrived. There was always somebody who wanted to be early.

'Please, help yourself to some fruit juice,' Roland said affably. 'The others will be here soon.' They were... piling into the studio, descending on the buffet like locusts, flipping through all his presentation books, talking loudly about council matters, leaving coffee cups all over the place and crumbs ground into the blue carpet-tiled floor. Women's voices chortled away in social laughter. Men guffawed at inane jokes.

Celeste arrived when it was all well underway.

'You look grim,' she remarked, selecting and nibbling a vol au vent stuffed with cream cheese and smoked salmon. 'These are nice.'

'I feel a bit tired,' Roland replied. 'I've done a lot lately.'

'A lot of what?' she said archly. Then, looking around, 'It seems to be going well.'

'You missed the press. They came and went in the first twenty minutes.'

'As long as they were here. One of your old cronies covering it?'

'You bet. Pulling strings is what it's all about. Hang on a mo.' He clutched at her. His knees suddenly felt weak.

'You want to watch it. You're not so young.'

'There's somebody I'd like you to meet.' He took Celeste by the arm and steered her across to a small, compact woman wearing a pair of long tan boots and a sparkling shimmy dress in dull gold. She was conversing avidly with two other women in a somewhat conspiratorial manner.

'Forgive me for interrupting,' Roland said. 'I'd like you to meet the chairwoman of Phillipstone naturalists, Mrs. Thackman.'

'Hello,' the woman said to Celeste. 'Are you a twitcher?'

Chapter 10

Eleanor Framp sat at her workstation in her office in *The Circle*. She couldn't stop fingering the heavy pendant that Grant had given her. 'The centre stone came from my grandmother in the States,' he'd said. 'It's a peridot, a kind of olivine. I want you to wear it always so that I am close to you where-ever I am. I've had it set around with diamonds for you. Do you like it?'

'It's so beautiful,' she'd replied, turning it this way and that so the diamonds sparkled. 'Thank you my darling fiancé.' She'd leaned across and kissed him on his stubbly cheek. His face had crinkled with pleasure In truth, she thought the stone was not to her taste and so heavy but how could she refuse? How could she refuse him anything? She was jolted back to the present.

'Hello, Roland. Is that you?'

'Eleanor?'

'Good afternoon to you. I'm just telephoning to say how sorry I was that I couldn't make it to the opening ceremony of your new photographic studio yesterday.'

'That's quite alright, Eleanor. I could see from the news that you had quite enough on your plate.'

'There hasn't been a moment. We've had to go for a re-print. Worse than that, we are getting orders from wholesalers all over Europe, the States and even Australia for *Embroideryworld*. It's been an absolute madhouse here. The telephones never stop ringing. We've had to put in five more lines and take on extra temporary staff in the office next door, which was empty, luckily for us. Never mind. How did your opening go?'

'Very well, thank you. The press came, which was the important thing, and I picked up quite a few commissions to get me started.'

'I'm very pleased for you Roland. You were always a hard worker. I'm sure you'll do very well.' She paused and took a deep breath. He could hear a telephone ringing in the background. 'Hold on a moment... yes, I'll call them back... sorry about that. Now, the other reason why I'm telephoning you is because I have your business card in my hand and it occurs to me that there is nobody I would like better to take my wedding photographs than you.'

Roland blinked with surprise. 'Well, Eleanor, that's really nice of you. I'd be delighted. When and where will it all be taking place?'

'Easter Saturday at Phillipstone Register Office. Two o'clock. The reception will be held at *Casslands* afterwards. It won't be a very large affair but one has to mark these occasions.'

'Absolutely. Will there be any bridesmaids?'

'My future stepdaughter, Pandora, will be my matron of honour and her son, Charlie, will be a rather old pageboy.'

'That's nice, including them.'

'He's going to present the wedding rings on a cushion. We wanted him to be part of the ceremony.'

'A very suitable touch,' Roland said.

'I will need a brochure from you. Would you be so kind as to drop one in the post to me at my flat in *Isabel Avenue*?'

'Yes, of course.'

'Number nine, *Glade House Mansions.*'

'...and a price.'

'I'll include my price list.'

'Thank you Roland. Goodbye.'

'Goodbye Eleanor.' He put down his pen, sat back on the high chair behind the reception counter and smiled to himself. Fancy that! Frumpy Eleanor. She had certainly smartened herself up when he saw her the other day with Grant Landscar. Perhaps all she had ever lacked was the love of a good man. He checked the appointments screen. This afternoon wasn't going to be very busy. Two sessions were booked.

He returned to the details of Eleanor's wedding. What would he charge her? After all, she was marrying a very rich man. Grant Landscar would probably be paying for everything. On the other hand, she was a most useful person to know. Because of her long history in freelance journalism, she was acquainted with everybody who was anybody and could well be his pass-card into the higher echelons of society.

If he was too cheap, they might not trust the quality. Yes, it was always better to err on the side of up-market. Possibly he should quote high and then do a generous discount. That would be the way to go. She was a very polite and proper woman who would appreciate a special price. His experience of wealthy people was that they always expected discount anyway and he didn't want to get into a hassle with the bridegroom.

The studio front door opened to the tinkle of a silver bell and a compact, little woman in a long, tan coat and boots came in. She was the first appointment of the afternoon. Roland went forward to greet her and take her through to the studio.

'Hello, Mrs. Thackman. Let me take your coat for you,' he said.

She relinquished it with a bit of a flourish and he hung it up very carefully. Then he turned to conduct her to the padded chair with the drape behind, and she held up one finger to stop him.

'I couldn't say on the telephone, but this is a rather special photograph I'll be wanting you to take today.'

'I'm sure I can set it up to show you to your best advantage.' He looked at her boxy shape. She was wearing a short, tailored jacket and a heavily pleated skirt in bottle green accompanied by long, tan boots. She looked down at her clothes and gave a look of mock despair.

'Oh, I won't be wearing these,' she announced. 'Just a moment. Could you look the other way, please?'

Roland's stomach pitched. He waited.

'Ready,' she said coyly.

He turned to face her. Her suit and boots were on the floor. She was standing wearing fishnet tights and a black bathing suit that made her look like a pile of rubber tyres.

Now there is always some point in a woman's life when it is injudicious, to say the least, to expose a body shape that has seen better days. Add to that the crêpe neck, jowls and upper arms like bat wings, and it is definitely time to throw in the towel. Roland stood, speechless.

'Look,' she said, 'I know I'm not gorgeous any more but I've got this boyfriend on the Internet. He lives abroad and we are never likely to meet. I want to send him a glamour picture that he can show to his friends. I've been widowed for rather a long time, you know.'

'Mmmm,' Roland pondered. 'Stay there a moment.' He dived into the back room and rummaged behind the curtain in the corner. He returned with lengths of chiffon, feathers and a wig.

'I see we are speaking the same language,' his client said with approval.

'Forget the chair. Come over here and let me place you on this satin couch.' After many years of attending airshows, mechanical handling exhibitions and car and caravan expositions, this was truly creative and he was really getting into the spirit of it.

'Do you charge extra for photo-editing?' she asked archly. He gave a cursory glance at her wrinkles and sags.

'As you are my first client, let's call it an introductory offer.'

The afternoon went from creative to boring in one dull dive. A pair of pensioners came in for a fiftieth wedding anniversary photograph for their family. They both had grey hair and eyebrows and clothes to match. Roland studied them seriously for a moment and then disappeared into his curtained corner in the back room again. They looked at each other in puzzlement as the sound of drawers opening and closing reached them. He reappeared and very tactfully suggested that the lady might like to wear these beautiful ear-clips and necklace that had once belonged to a famous actress. No, he couldn't say who as he had promised never to divulge. They were crystal pink and sparkled delightfully. Then, a matching pink handkerchief found its way into the husband's top front pocket together with a change of tie. The challenged photographer placed a large bunch of artificial, pink roses in the woman's arms.

That done, the next problem was to get the miserable pair to smile. No matter what he said or how he cavorted, they would not and sat with pursed lips. In desperation, he asked, 'Why won't you smile? Doesn't your family want to see you looking happy?'
The woman's eyes filled with tears. Her husband put his arm around her shoulders.

'There, there, love,' he said. Then he looked at Roland and announced, 'She's got no teeth.' The silence was palpable. Roland didn't know how he kept a straight face. His insides did a sort of convoluted slow motion tango.

'Never mind. I can paint some in for you.' The two of them broke into the biggest smiles he'd ever seen, the woman's being very gummy indeed.

'Really?' said the woman through her tears.

'Leave it to me,' the ambitious photographer said. His business was clearly destined to be built on vanity. He was going to become the local equivalent of a digitally active plastic surgeon. It couldn't be that difficult. If he could touch up the fuselage of an aeroplane in a photograph, then surely excising wrinkles and implanting a few teeth was a doddle. Ah yes, he was going into the happiness business!

*

'Please come in, Mr. Landscar... Grant,' Reverend Mother Veronica said as the tall, silver-haired entrepreneur removed his stetson and stepped into the oak-panelled hall of the convent. She closed the massive door and shot home the bolts. 'We can't be too careful,' she added. 'Let's go into the parlour. This way.'

He followed her meekly. With all his experience of the world, there was something about this convent that gave him the creeps. His hat was placed on the table and he hung his sheepskin jacket over a dining chair.

'Please do come and sit by the fire here. A log blaze is always so comforting, don't you think?'

'Indeed, Reverend Mother.' He sat in the winged chair opposite to hers.

'Tea? I was just having some. There's a spare cup here.'

'Yes please. No sugar or milk, thank you.' He hated tea but had long ago realised that it was necessary to go through the niceties sometimes.

'Now... may I call you Grant?'

'Yes, of course, Reverend Mother.'

'Grant.' She took up her cup and sipped and put it down again. 'I'm sure you know how dear Eleanor is to me.' He nodded. 'She is my most precious niece and I have cared for her since she was eight years old.'

'I gather her parents died out in Africa in a road crash.'

'Yes. It was a terrible shock. Her mother was my only relative. Naturally, I had to take over the care of Eleanor. She was a delightful child, you know. A little dreamy, always with her writing and drawing, but I believe she had a happy childhood here at the convent.'

'It was an unusual upbringing, I suppose,' Grant remarked.

'A strange situation all round. By their own choosing, nuns are not usually mothers but in some ways it was very good for the sisters to help me in her upbringing and by doing so to gain a great deal of joy themselves. Do take a biscuit. They are our own home-baked.'

Grant leaned over, helped himself to a flapjack and took a bite.

'Delicious,' he mumbled through the crumbs.

Reverend Mother folded her hands in her lap and started her pitch. He braced himself as she said, 'I do realise that Eleanor is a grown woman and must make her own decisions. I am very glad that she has found love and happiness with you... Grant.' She hesitated and looked up towards the statue of the Virgin Mary in the alcove as if for inspiration. 'You must see, however, how distressing it is for me to see her marrying without the blessing of the church. I know that she wants to please you and we both respect your views, but is there any chance that you might reconsider and allow a blessing here in the chapel at *St. Bede's*?'

He put his cup and saucer down and breathed in deeply, tilting his head thoughtfully to one side.

'Wouldn't that be rather hypocritical of me? I mean, I just don't believe in any of this...' He stopped as he saw the look of warning on her face.

'Sometimes... Grant... we have to bend a little for the happiness of others. If you don't believe, then I respect that, but if your marriage starts out with Eleanor feeling even the smallest bit resentful, is that a good thing? As you say, it is neither here nor there to you but it would give many of us, including all the sisters, a great deal of joy to see our dear Eleanor as a true bride receiving a blessing here in our very own chapel.'

Grant placed his hands on his knees. 'My daughter, Pandora, has been on at me too. Is it some kind of conspiracy?'

'I've never met your daughter but I look forward to doing so.' Reverend mother smiled with a glint of triumph.

'Will you do this small thing for us?'

'I'd hate to come up against you in business, Reverend Mother.' He slapped his thigh. 'O.K. Just to please you... and Eleanor.'

The old nun's face creased into a smile. 'A very good decision,' she said, nodding. 'It will bring its own rewards. Excuse me, for one moment please.' She raised herself unsteadily to her feet and toddled over towards the door. 'I'll be back shortly.' She was, but not alone.

'I'd like you to meet Father Guyler,' she said.

*

It was a beautiful early spring day at the *Villa Estancia* on the lovely Mediterranean island of Milloncha. Gonzo stretched out on a garden lounger on the patio beyond the sunroom. The scent of almond blossom was on the gentle breeze. Ah, it was good to feel the warmth of the sun on his face.

Last weekend's tours had gone very well. The visitors had tipped him handsomely on top of his usual fee as he had conducted them around the island's beauty spots in his open top vehicle. It had been fun hearing their panicked intakes of breath as he'd spun along the narrow roads through the mountains on the west coast. He had pushed the wheels of the car near to the rock-lined edges, threatening to tip his cargo down the precipitous, scrub-lined slopes, past the skittish, grazing goats and into the lush valley far below. How the ladies had squealed with a mixture of fear and delight! How they had admired his prowess at driving! One of them had admired his prowess in other areas afterwards. He smiled to himself. It was good here but it was going to get so very much better.

He took out the list from the pocket of his faded jeans. He'd bought everything on it except the dinghy. He wouldn't buy one of those expensive kinds from the marine supplier. Instead, he would get it from the tourist shop near one of the beaches. No point in paying out for something that was only going to be used a few times.

The other items were stored at home in his small cottage on this estate. He started to think about how he could arrange it all. The important thing was to be natural. Nothing should be different. He would behave as he always did, humble and obliging. They would never suspect him, Gonzo, of being clever enough to conceive and carry out such a daring and innovative plan. Yes, they would find out.

A ringing shook him out of his reverie. He got up and ambled through the sunroom and into the lounge.

'*Villa Estancia*. Gonzales speaking,' he answered in English. In truth, nobody but his boss, Grant Landscar, ever rang here. It was the same this time.

'Where were you? I've been ringing for ages.'

'I was in the garden doing some weeding, Señor Landscar.'

'Well, take the hands-free with you. Remember you work for me.'

'Yes, Señor Landscar.'

'Now, Gonzo, I have a special task for you. Over at the edge of the orchard, there's a small hen house where your parents used to keep chickens.'

Gonzo's mind flashed back to his childhood's early morning chore of collecting the warm brown eggs in a woven basket so that his mother could sell them in the market place.

'Are you listening to me, Gonzo?'

'I am here.'

'I want you to demolish that hen house and get rid of the wood. Then, on the exact spot, put down a hardcore base and concrete with some paving to match the terrace. Then construct an arbour. You know the sort of thing, wooden trellis with things climbing up it. You know what to do.'

'Yes, Señor.'

'Then when you've done that, I want you to put some patio roses in glazed pots around the edge and install a couple of nice wooden seats. It's to be a pleasant place for my new wife to sit out. Oh, and get a couple more of those sun umbrellas with heavy bases. Charge it all to me down at the garden centre. There shouldn't be a problem.'

'I'll get onto it right away, sir,' Gonzo replied. 'Is there anything else Señor?'

'That's all for now. Remember, I want everything in tip-top condition for my new wife's first visit to my Villa. Goodbye Gonzo.'

Gonzo put down the receiver. This latest order was a mixed blessing. Firstly, he had to do some work but on the other hand, it was an opportunity to make a little on the side. He sauntered out into the weak sunshine and strolled over to the far edge of the lawns where, behind a small olive spinney, stood the old chicken house. Around it were a few apple and plum trees, the remains of his parents' small orchard.

He opened the creaking plank door and looked inside. Something scuffled. Probably a rat. He gave the structure a kick. It shook and the rodent shot out of a gap in the timbers before scooting off into the long grass. Gonzo pushed his foot against the doorframe and it buckled. He walked around the little building and kicked each side with increasing anger. Slowly, like a film of a skyscraper falling, the sides caved in and the roof collapsed in a cloud of dust and mould spores. Some birds flew off in fright from the apple trees. He would get one of the local lads to chop up the wood and sell it for kindling.

Back on the terrace, he sat down on the sun lounger, took out his own mobile phone and called up the garden centre to order everything that he needed for the new arbour, plus a few little extras, like a couple more pairs of garden shears, some new garden forks and spades and a wheelbarrow. While he was at it, he ordered twice as many patio roses as required and an extra bench. Then he kicked off his trainers, put his feet up on the lounger and called a friend who specialised in odd jobs.

'Hey, I want you to do some work for me up at the villa,' he said. 'I can pay you in the usual way. I need you for two days, starting the day after tomorrow. Send one of your boys up in the morning to chop up some wood and take it away for me.'

The friend never argued. He was kept in high quality tools and equipment by Gonzo, the man who worked for the billionaire Texan. The *Villa Estancia* estate was very highly thought of locally. Businesses around were pleased to supply it.

A certain mystique surrounded billionaire Grant Landscar. He had smothered the roof of the villa in black, shining, solar panels to provide hot water for the house and to heat the large, heart-shaped swimming pool. He had installed six wind turbines over on the hill to give the villa its own electricity supply. They turned slowly, a reminder of his power. What Grant Landscar wanted, he got and the area's officials were the beneficiaries, no matter how much the locals objected. The Texan commanded respect.

He had swept into the island as a stranger about ten years ago, full of grandiose plans for the extension to the *finca*. Some say he had greased the palms of the planners so that alterations were done quickly. The islanders knew him as an absentee landlord, one who had pressed Gonzo's parents for their annual rent.

After their deaths, the place had been a-buzz with the news that Grant Landscar was coming to live there. The tradesmen rubbed their hands in glee but it was a false hope. He only came for holidays but he did employ Gonzo and occasional help from the village.

Gonzo thought about how this would be his last summer at the villa. He would be sad to leave it but when he had his own ranch in America, with horses, cattle and sheep, he would be as grand as his boss. He smiled smugly to himself. They would find out. They shouldn't underestimate him, Señor Gonzales.

Chapter 11

Celeste Blagden was ready on Monday morning for the arrival of her decorators. While she waited, she busied herself in *Mums, Tums and Tots* by sitting at her laptop in the stockroom designing leaflets. She was going to follow Roland's example and make them A5 size, just right for slipping through letterboxes. She racked her brains. The name of the shop had to be on there prominently, of course, but she needed another "hook" to get the customers in.

"Try us First! New and Quality Pre-owned Mother, Baby and Children's clothes, toys and equipment," she wrote. "Open 1st March". Then she made some balloon shapes and a fancy border. Having grouped all the items together she printed and pasted two leaflets on an A4 sheet and saved the design onto a stick. She would take that to Roland later.

'Morning! Yoo-hoo! Anybody there?' The decorator and his smirking son had arrived. Celeste hastily turned off the laptop and threw her coat over it.

'Coming! she said, as they humped their ladders and dust sheets into the shop. She'd forgotten to lock the shop door. Not good.

'Get that kettle on, darling,' the father said. Although resentful of his style of address, she went back into the stockroom without protest and did as he had requested.

'Strong, two sugars and milk, both,' he called out.

'Yes, sir,' she replied, taking some mugs down from the shelf.

'...and a biscuit wouldn't go amiss,' he added.

Was it going to be like this all week, at the beck and call of workmen? The surly son came and peered in at her. He was chubby, sun-tanned and heavy with gold jewellery that hung around his neck, dragged on his pierced ears and culminated in a watch of gargantuan proportions. His hair was gelled up into a sort of pyramid that curled over into a wave and he stank of cheap aftershave. She put his age at about sixteen.

'Watcha darling,' he simpered at her.

'I'll bring your tea out to you,' she said with a forced smile.

'Stop chasing that girl and come and stir this paint,' his father yelled.

'See you later,' the lad said with a knowing wink.

'First, get them sheets down. Don't want paint all over that chipboard flooring, do we?'

'Yes Dad. No Dad.'

Celeste stirred the mugs, spinning the tea-bags around until the brew looked dark and evil. She added milk and sugar and put the mugs on a tin tray with some biscuits.

'Here we are,' she said cheerfully, setting the tray down on the floor in the corner of the shop. 'Let me know if you want any more.'

'We always want more, don't we Dad?' the lad said with meaning.

'Belt up!'

'Yes Dad.'

Now Celeste had a dilemma. Should she stay here and look as if she didn't trust them or should she go and risk losing control of the situation? She decided to take her laptop and go.

'See you later,' she said, making for the shop door. It was at that precise moment that a delivery man with a pen behind his ear appeared in her path.

'Sign 'ere, please.'

'What for?' she queried.

'This is *Mums, Tums and Tots*, ain't it?'

'Yes.' She took the pen from him and put her moniker on the delivery note. He tore off the top copy and handed it to her.

'Want the stuff in 'ere?'

'Yes. I suppose so.' She shrugged and walked through to the stockroom to put her things down again. She could hear thumping noises coming from outside. It was only when she went and peeked through the penny-hole she had made in the whited-out window that she grasped the problem. Six massive boxes were piled on a flatbed trolley and they were heading from a panting delivery lorry and towards her shop door.

Cots! In huge boxes! Paying up front must have some advantages. She rushed forward to try and avert disaster.

'I don't have room for them yet,' she pleaded.

'You've signed for them, Miss. They're yours. Now, where do you want 'em?'

Celeste looked imploringly at the decorators who pretended they didn't know what was going on. The lad was straightening dustsheets and the father sipping tea as he gazed up at the ceiling. In desperation, she said, 'Oh well, just put them there in the middle of the floor.' The delivery man did so and went out whistling.

'You expect us to work around that mountain of boxes?' the father asked.

'I'll get it sorted,' she said. 'Just give me a moment, please.'

She went and sat down at her little table in the stockroom and put her head in her hands. How on earth was she going to get the cots through and into one of the sheds? A loud knocking came and she realised it was coming from the shop door so she rushed out to it again.

'Delivery for *Mums, Tums and Tots*,' the young man said.

'What?'

'*Brindlestint Buggies*. Delivery. Think I've got ten for you. Sign 'ere please.' He thrust the clipboard and pen into her trembling hand and hummed his way out to the van. More thumping noises and another trolley came in. At least these items weren't in boxes, just stout polythene wrappers.

'Please put them there,' she said as the painter made a sort of whooshing noise of disbelief. By lunchtime, she had four delivery notes. Added to the pile of cots and buggies, were boxes of baby garments and three baby car seats. Dreams of leaving the decorators to get on with it had evaporated. She dared not quit the shop in case something else turned up. The men had worked on nonchalantly throughout all the chaos, brushing down the ceiling and walls so that each new stock delivery bore a light dusting of what looked like icing sugar.

'We're off for lunch now,' the father said, 'so, if you could just shift that lot, we can get on with it this afternoon. See you later.' They were gone, leaving behind them a miniature mountain and air so thick with choking dust that Celeste was coughing.

'What am I going to do?' she wailed to herself.' Roland. He has to help me.' She locked up and went next door. She rang the little bell on the reception desk and he appeared, looking rather dishevelled.

'Roland,' she hissed. 'You have to help me.'

'I can't. I'm working.' He sucked at his wrist.

'What have you done?'

'Got bitten.'

'By a customer?'

'A dog,' he murmured with a jerk of his head.

'Oh dear! Mind it doesn't go septic. When will you be finished?'

'About twenty minutes, hopefully.'

'Please come and help me to move some things.'

'OK. Got to go.' He disappeared through the partition doorway to the sound of a low-throated growl. Celeste couldn't help giggling to herself as she made her way back to her shop.

*

As Eleanor approached Grant's library, she could hear the gentle tones of a Spanish guitar music. She tapped gently on the door and the music stopped.

'Come in! Ah, Eleanor, my dear.' He putting the remote on the table. 'How was it at the office today?' He stood up to kiss her on the cheek.

'Frantic but we're coping. It's going really well,' she added with a smile. 'I never dreamed it would take off like this.'

'Come and sit on the sofa and tell me all your news.'

As they settled down on the low, black leather three-seater, he took her hand and squeezed it. 'I'm so pleased for you. You deserve it.'

'When I think of all those years when I half flogged myself to death with the freelance journalism... '

'The time was right. That's all. So,' he paused, 'they've gone for a fourth run at the printers?'

'Yes, and that may not be the last of it.'

'What else then?'

'Australia's wanting to put it on the internet and America wants a special version just for over there because of their heritage.'

'Dandy!' he said, smiling broadly. 'That's my girl!'

'I couldn't have done it all without your backing.' He knew that but said, 'Nonsense. Big success was always within your grasp.' He squeezed her hand again. 'Now, about this satellite television channel...' He felt her try to withdraw her hand but he held onto it.

'It would mean so much to me if you would front it, Eleanor dear... oh, I've got some news for you... you're going to be surprised...' He waited for maximum effect. 'I went to see your aunt over at the convent today. She invited me for tea.'

Eleanor looked at him coolly. 'Why did she want to see you?'

'Your Aunty Rev is a very tough cookie. She coerced me into a wedding blessing in the convent chapel.'

'Oh! Oh! How wonderful of you! Grant! Oh!' She threw her arms around his neck and he hugged her in return. Then she peppered his cheek with kisses like a woodpecker.

'Hold on! Steady!' he laughed. 'She made me see the error of my ways. After all, if it makes you happy, it's worth it, as long as you realise that for me it is just a charade.'

She calmed down immediately. 'Really?'

'Eleanor,' he said, 'I love you. Truly I do but I don't go with all this religious stuff. However, I realise that if your aunt is unhappy then you would be too and I don't want us to start off on the wrong foot.'

She was less excited now and said, 'I appreciate it so much, Grant. Thank you.'

'My pleasure.' After a decent pause, he went on, '...and now, about this television thing...'

Eleanor recalled Pandora's words about compromise.

'Yes, of course I'll do it for you but please could I try it just for ten episodes and see how I get on?'

'I'm sure Teddy will go with that. You'll be ideal. Oh, by the way, that nice Father Guyler will do our convent chapel ceremony.'

*

Even the unflappable Pandora Brand seemed slightly flustered when Eleanor appeared in the office the next morning.

'Thank goodness you're here,' she whispered, hand across the mouthpiece of the telephone. 'Canada wants a special edition too. They emailed overnight. I've replied and said you'll call them this afternoon because of the time difference... yes, hello. Is that the print room? It's *Embroideryworld* magazine here. We're going to need another run of fourteen thousand.' She raised her eyebrows dramatically at Eleanor. 'When? No. We must have them by tomorrow. They need to go to the wholesalers in Derby. It seems we have a big following in that area. OK. I'll hold.' She turned and indicated the corner of the office. Piled up against the giant Swiss Cheese plant's tub were several mailbags. 'Those,' she said, 'are just the tip of the iceberg. There are at least ten more in the office next door. I've taken two of the girls off the telephones to just sit and open them.'

Eleanor put her bag and briefcase on the desk and peeled off her coat. She stood there clutching it. This was all too much.

'Be a dear and fetch me some biscuits,' Pandora said. 'I've been talking since seven o'clock this morning and I'm starving.'

'Shall I send out for some sandwiches?' Eleanor asked as she hung up her coat and disappeared into the kitchenette.

'Good idea. Ham and tomato for me, please,' she called out. Then to her telephone, 'Yes? You can? Brilliant! Add it to the multiple invoice. Thank you.' She hung up but as soon as the receiver hit the cradle, it rang again. '*Embroideryworld*,' she said. 'One moment. I'll see if she's free.' She pointed to the receiver and mimed to Eleanor as she emerged with a packet of digestive biscuits, "R-A-D-I-O".

Eleanor went to her workstation and sat down. 'I'm putting you through now,' Pandora said.

It went on like that continually. If Eleanor had thought she was going to run a cosy, little two-person magazine for a handful of UK embroidery enthusiasts, she had been badly mistaken. Her long cherished ambition had burgeoned into a monster but there was something rather thrilling about the sweet smell of success and she quite liked it.

By lunchtime, the pair of them were utterly exhausted. By the end of the day they were like a couple of limp rags. In the end, one of the temps from their office next door had been sent out several times for the sandwiches that had sustained them.

'Put it on voicemail now,' Pandora suggested. 'We really have to have a break. All the girls next door have gone home. Our office hours are clearly stated in the front of the magazine for future reference so people will soon learn. Did you ring Canada?'

'I never dreamed it would be like this,' Eleanor said, leaning back in her executive chair. She pushed her spectacles on top of her head and closed her eyes. 'Yes, I rang Toronto.'

'... and we have to do it all again tomorrow,' Pandora replied with a wry smile. 'Let's go and have a look next door.' Reluctantly, Eleanor got up and followed her future step-daughter out into the corridor and through a door with a piece of paper taped to it stating, *Embroideryworld. Office No.2.*

A scene of orderly chaos greeted them. The place smelled of perfume, hairspray and salt and vinegar crisps. There were cola cans and empty water bottles everywhere. The four workstations that had been hastily set up were piled high with letters with their envelopes stapled to them. The stacks were so tall that big bundles of mail held in elastic bands had been placed on top to stabilise them. The girls had clearly done their best to get through the workload but there was still much to do.

Pandora said, 'I gave them their instructions to open the letters and list the telephone messages, making sure they got the return numbers, nothing more. They are here in a fire-fighting capacity but this just isn't going to be enough.'

Eleanor shook her head in slow disbelief. There were still mailbags unopened and more would arrive tomorrow. 'What are we going to do?'

'Well, in my experience, I think we have a winner on our hands. We're going to need a lot more staff. If I were you, Eleanor, I'd take over this whole floor of offices. *Embroideryworld* is going into the big time.'

*

'Celeste! Open this door!' Roland stood pounding on the front door of the baby shop flat. The roar of the early morning traffic drowned out the sound of Celeste coming down the stairs in her shorty dressing gown. She threw open the door, fully expecting it to be another delivery but, instead, Roland stood there, agitated, with a sheet of paper in his hand. 'Have you seen this?' She half-sleepily took it from him and blinked to get the print into focus.

'What is it? I'm still half asleep.'

'Look at it! I found it pinned on the gate of that broken down bungalow over the road. It's a planning application for a major change of use.'

'I don't expect it will affect us,' she yawned.

'Celeste, can't you see what it says? They're going to knock that house down, bulldoze the site and put in a twenty-four hour washing facility and electric recharging place for vehicles. There'll be noise day and night, all week. Worse than that, they are going to widen the dual carriageway to make an additional entry into the place and that means taking away our forecourts and service road on this side. We'll be ruined.'

'What?' She clicked into awake mode. Her Saturday morning lie-in had now been ruined anyway. 'Come in and have a coffee.' He stepped over the threshold and found himself standing on the small square of hallway at the bottom of the steep, high staircase that led up to the flat, a mirror image of his own premises. 'Shut the door behind you,' she called over her shoulder as she climbed the treads, giving him a bird's eye-view of the back of her rather scrumptious thighs.

Upstairs in the lounge, they sat by the plug-in electric fire and discussed the implications of the planning application.

'I was counting on my forecourt for displaying my quality used prams and pushchairs,' she said.

'...and I want mine so that I can put boards out with photographs and special offers on,' he replied.

'Well, it's only an application. It has to go through a lot of... hang on a moment... that Landscar chappie was over there the other day snooping about. I bet he's behind it.'

'First thing Monday, you'll have to go up to the Town Hall and look at the plans. I can't. I'm up to my ears with loads of long appointments.'

'My painters have finished now so I don't have to be here apart from goods arriving. It's all pink and blue in there and looks very smart, by the way. If you could take in any deliveries it will only be small boxes now. I could go to the Planning Department and suss it all out. By the way, thanks for all your help shifting the stock out of the shop the other day when the painters were in.'

'Don't mention it. Are you pleased with your leaflets?'

'Brilliant! Thanks a million. I'm going out to deliver some this weekend. It's only just over a week until I open so I've got to drum up trade.'

'I can do any other photo-copying you need and thanks for the use of your shop loo for my customers. The plumber's coming first thing on Monday to put in the new toilet and a hand basin. Give me a couple of evenings to paint it out and then we won't be using your facilities any more.'

'That's coincidence. Mine's coming on Monday too, but in the afternoon, to start installing the central heating in the shop and stockroom. I must say, you've kept my loo nice and clean so it hasn't been a problem,' she said.

'Good, but getting back to this planning issue, we need to fight it from the start.'

'Do we have a Chamber of Commercial Enterprise here?' she queried.

'There ought to be. If not, we're going to have to start one. It'll affect the other shops along here too. I mean, where will our customers park? As sure as eggs are eggs, they'll still have a double yellow line along the main road.'

'All those lovely oak trees on the verge and in the bungalow garden will go. I like looking out on them,' she said whistfully.

'Say, Celeste, you've got really nice legs.'

'Roland!' She took a rug from the arm of the chair and wrapped it around her lower half.

'Worth a try,' he observed with a grin. 'Well, I'd better get back to work. No peace for the self-employed. Dead cheeky of the council to put that notice up last thing on Friday, though.'

'Why?'

'They've saved themselves a whole two days of complaints.'

'Hang on. I'll just let you out, then I'm going to shower and get dressed. I want to distribute those leaflets. Say, why don't I take some of yours to distribute too?'

'Good idea. I'll leave them on the shop doorstep for you. Catch you later.'

*

There was something about the hot, dry atmosphere in Phillipstone Town Hall Planning Department that was conducive to sleep. Councillor Percival Springstock had found himself a snug corner table and randomly spread out the official drawings for the redevelopment of his bungalow site by the dual carriageway. It was mid-morning and a watery February sun was filtering in between the vertical blinds. 'Ting!' went the bell on the reception counter. He blearily forced himself to look and see who it was. A young, attractive but rather short woman with shoulder-length, dark hair, stood there repeatedly pinging the bell.

'I was on my way,' the receptionist remarked curtly. ' How can I help you?'

Celeste unfolded the planning notice and handed it to her.

'Where did you get that from? That's one of the ones we affix to the property in question. You shouldn't have that.'

'Somebody gave it to me. It's irrelevant how I got it. The important thing is that I wish to see the plans for the development and I want them now.'

'Well,' said the receptionist laconically, 'you're out of luck, Miss. They're already out.'

'You mean you only have one set?' Celeste retorted.

'Council cuts, you know,' the woman replied with an air of satisfaction. It was a Monday morning and she was heartily fed up with her job.

'Who's got them?'

'I'm afraid I can't divulge that.'

'When will they be returned?'

'I simply cannot say.'

'Today?'

'They have to be back in the file by five o'clock.'

'I'm not trailing all the way over here again tomorrow. Isn't there any other way I can see them?'

'You can buy a copy.'

'Why didn't you say so before? How much?'

'Five pounds for the drawings and another five pounds for the extract.'

'How long will it take to have them copied?'

'About an hour. Would you care to wait?'

'This is outrageous. I want to see the Planning Department manager.'

'I'm sorry, Miss, but he's away today and I'm in charge.'

'Then I want to see the Chief Executive.'

'I regret, Miss, that he doesn't see the public without an appointment. Would you still care to wait?'

'Can't you do the copying a little quicker?'

'I'm very busy. As I said, my manager's away today and I have such a lot to...'

'This is intolerable. Yes please. I'll wait.'

'That will be ten pounds please.'

Celeste handed over the money and received a receipt. Then she went and sat at one of the tables and took out her mobile phone.

'I'm afraid you can't use that in here,' the woman whispered. Celeste switched it off and put it in her bag. There was a pile of magazines on a side table so she went over and took one. On her way back, she was just passing an old gentleman snoozing at the corner table and noticed that he had a large plan spread out before him. She paused and tilted her head to see what he had been studying. The plan of the dual carriage way looked familiar. She gently slid it away from him and rotated it. Everything Roland had said was true. Utter devastation and rebuilding of the area opposite to her shop. Somebody somewhere had it in for them. Who was behind all this?

'Your plans are ready now, Miss,' the woman called across to her as she folded and slid them into a large envelope. It had been an utterly boring hour. The snoring, elderly man had slept through it but now the sound of the receptionist's voice had woken him.

'Where? What?' he muttered, straightening up in his seat and putting his slipped spectacles back into position. Then he realised where he was and looked embarrassed as Celeste rose from her table and walked over to the reception desk.

'Who's he?' she asked, indicating the Councillor.

'I'm afraid I can't say,' the woman replied cagily as she handed over the envelope and beat a retreat into the back office. Celeste was not so easily put off. She strode over to him with her hand extended.

'How lovely to see you again,' she said with an ingratiating smile. He stood up rather shakily and took her hand. It was then that she remembered seeing him at Roland's photographic studio launch party.

'Delighted to meet you again too.' It was clear that he had no idea who she was.

'How are you keeping?'

'Not too bad. A bit of rheumatism, but that's to be expected at my age,' he said, and made that strange chuckling that most older people seem to incorporate into their conversations, as if life has been one long joke but they can't quite remember the punch line.

'I'm so sorry, but I can't recall your name,' Celeste said apologetically.

'Councillor Springstock,' he replied.

'Of course, Councillor Springstock,' she repeated. 'The one and only. Aren't you going to be our new Mayor in the spring?'

'Well, it's pretty well in the bag and next week they will announce that I am the Mayor Elect but don't say anything,' he chortled again.

'Your secret's safe with me, Councillor. Goodbye for now.'

She left the Planning Department wondering what his interest was in a dilapidated bungalow on the busy dual carriageway opposite her shop.

Chapter 12

'I can't believe they're really going to do this. It's outrageous!' Celeste said angrily, looking at the plan spread out on the table in Roland's studio one evening.

'It's only a planning application,' Roland replied. 'There's no guarantee that they'll get it.'

'Where that Grant Landscar's concerned, it's probably a done deal. Well, he's not going to win this one. We need to set up an action committee.'

'Oh yes? Who do you think is going to be on it?'

'You and I, for a start.'

'Aw, Celeste, I'm not a committee kind of person.'

'Now, listen here, you wimp...'

'Steady on...'

'I mean it, Roland. This is no time to be lily-livered. Do you want your business wiped out before it starts and do you want to have to put up with all that activity, day and night, over the road? There will be huge lorries and tankers, floodlights, the sound of engines, water gushing, people shouting, the stink of diesel...'

'I take your point but aren't they going to build an electric fuel recharging facility over there, not a petrol station?'

'So, Mr. Big Brain, how many tankers do you think will be running on electricity? The whole concept of electric-powered vehicles is in its infancy. It's alright for little vans and local cars but not for long-haul vehicles. Take my word for it, the whole plan is designed to be hell for the people who live and work here.' She sat back on the swivel chair with her arms folded.

'I suppose while it's being built it will be pretty grim for the residents over the road and backing onto the site. We could get them involved.' He paused in thought. 'As a matter of interest, who owns the bungalow and who's put in the application?'

Celeste riffled through the papers. 'Typical!' she said. 'The form's been filled in by an agent but I bet it's on Landscar's behalf. Who owns the place anyway?'

'Anybody can send in a planning application for a project. They don't have to own the premises,' he said sagely.

'That's easy enough to find out,' she replied. 'We just have to look at the register of electors.'

'The person registered to vote at that address may not be the owner of the bungalow. They could be renting it.'

'Nobody's living there. You can see that. I went over and had a look earlier.'

'Well then, who pays the rates?'

'The person who lives there would be but there's nobody there so I expect no rates are being paid by anybody.' She gnawed at the edge of her fingernail. 'There's only one thing for it. We have to do a search at the Land Registry.'

'Won't that take ages and cost us a bit into the bargain?'

'Not if one of us goes up there in person and does a search.' She slapped the pile of documents down. 'It can't be me. I'm opening on the first and I've still got tons to do. Anyway, it's your turn. I got the plans from the Town Hall.'

Roland sucked at his lips, wrinkled his nose and blinked. Then he shook his head slowly. 'My diary is full. I'm not cancelling any photographic appointments. We'll have to get somebody else to do it for us, somebody with a lot of time on their hands and who owes me a favour. Leave it with me.'

*

The following evening, Roland knocked on Celeste's shop flat door and she came galloping down the stairs, eager to hear his news.

'Come on up. I'm having dinner but it doesn't matter.'

'You're not going to believe this,' he said, waving a large envelope about. He followed her up to the through-lounge.

'Grab a chair and sit with me while I finish this salad. I'm famished. Who went and got that for you?'

'Oh, some little lady who thinks I'm wonderful. Look!' He fished out the contents of the envelope and spread them on the table.

'Just look! The crafty bunch of twisters and rogues!'

Celeste, munching on some celery, leaned over and her eyes grew wide in amazement. She swallowed in haste and gulped some water.

'I saw him yesterday in the Planning Department. He was looking at a plan identical to the one we've got. Mr. Percival Archibald Springstock is Councillor Springstock and he's going to be Phillipstone's next mayor. He's the owner. The devious little rat!'

'If this got out, it wouldn't make him very popular with the voters, would it? There's a local election in April. No wonder he's keeping very quiet about it.'

'I don't know about you, Roland, but I think we need the help of the local Chamber of Commercial Enterprise.'

'If there is one, won't they be on the side of big business?'

'Hold on a mo. I've got a telephone book here.' Celeste got up and went and picked up the local directory from the floor in the corner. She riffled through and found what she wanted. 'I'm going to ring them right now,' she announced, only to get a voicemail service so she hung up. 'Nobody's there until the morning.'

*

'You have a truly beautiful home, Mr. Landscar,' Father Guyler said appreciatively, his eyes scanning the opulent lounge at Casslands on the sunny Saturday afternoon. 'Where shall I sit?'

'Anywhere. Please make yourself comfortable.' He walked over to the fireplace and snapped his fingers next to a small microphone embedded in the wall.

'Tea for three now, please, Synth,' he said.

'Certainly Mr. Landscar. It's all ready. I'll bring it through.'

'Thank you, Synth.' He snapped his fingers twice.

The priest opened his eyes wide in surprise.

'That's neat,' he remarked.

'This is a very big house and it saves a lot of time.'

Father Guyler settled back in the uncut moquette sofa and pulled up the knees of his black, ecclesiastical trousers before adjusting the white priest's collar that perched like icing around his crinkled neck. Wearing his trademark outfit, he felt secure and important.

'So,' he said pompously, 'was Eleanor surprised at your change of heart?'

'A little, but very pleased. She'll be joining us in a minute.'

'She knew how disappointed Reverend Mother was at the thought of her only and favourite niece tying the knot without the benefit of at least a blessing.'

'Yes.'

'You've been married before, I understand.'

'Yes. Three times.'

'Going to get it right this time?' The priest joked.

'Eleanor is an extraordinary woman. If I'd met her first, then perhaps the others wouldn't have had a look in, but then you know that, having been acquainted with her since she was young and being brought up by Reverend Mother Veronica.'

'Yes, indeed.'

'So, what was she like back in those days?'

The priest shifted awkwardly in his chair. 'Like all young women, I suppose. Full of hopes and dreams.'

'Attractive?'

'Oh, that's not for me to say, Mr. Landscar. I'm a priest. Those things tend to pass me by.'

'Come on, Father. Surely you can still identify a pretty girl when you see one.'

'Yes, I suppose she had a sort of fresh-faced charm about her.' He paused. 'Of course, until recently I hadn't seen her since... oh let me think... since she was in her teenage years. I went to India, you know, to do missionary work in an orphanage.'

'Very noble, I'm sure but what has brought you back to England now?'

'Early retirement is approaching and I have been given one last job, assessing the estates of church property.'

'A kind-a touring religious surveyor,' Grant joked.

'You could put it like that.'

The door handle rattled and Eleanor appeared. She was wearing a light blue, polo-necked sweater, with calf-length cream skirt. The tea trolley was close on her heels.

'Come in Synth. Just park it over there, please,' Grant said, his attention on Eleanor. He walked across the deep pile carpet to plant a tender kiss on his fiancée's peachy cheek. She smiled demurely and blushed. A surprising sexual thrill ran through her.

Father Guyler rose to his feet and came across to extend a warm handshake to Eleanor, aware of her high colour.

'Hello... Father...' she said. 'How very good of you to come all the way out here from the convent.'

'It was a very pleasant drive. I have a hire car, you know. Your Aunt sends her love and hopes you'll be over to see them all again soon.'

'Yes, yes I will. I've been very busy with the magazine, you know.'

'Will you pour, dear?' Grant said. Both the men sat down.

'Of course. It's milk but no sugar for you Father, I seem to remember.'

'You have a good memory, Eleanor,' he replied.

'Oh yes, indeed I do.' She added the milk and carried the bone china cup and saucer over to him.

'Thank you, my dear.' He took a sip. 'Perfect.'

'I have a memory for such details,' she replied with a hint of a smile.

'So,' said Grant, 'what is it you need to talk to us about, Father Guyler?' Grant was punctilious in addressing the priest in full for using just the title of "Father" somehow suggested that he was within the church clan. He wasn't and never would be.

'I have a sort of cosy chat with all my engaged couples,' the priest said. 'Even out in India, our orphans grew up and married within the church, so I'm an old hand at this.'

'I'm sure you are,' Grant said. 'Fire away!' He took his cup of tea gratefully from Eleanor. 'Thank you, darling.' She poured one for herself and sat next to him on the sofa.

'Marriage is an honourable estate...' the priest began.

About an hour later, Synth tapped on the door and came into the lounge to see if she could clear away the crockery. The room was empty so she set to, piling things onto the trolley.

'Ah,' a voice said.

She looked up and saw that the priest had entered.

'I just returned to collect my jacket. Don't let me disturb you.'

'You don't remember me, do you, Father?' she said.

'I can't say that I do,' he replied, as he put on his jacket. 'I meet a lot of people in my work and it is a matter of some regret to me that it is impossible to retain all of their names. Please remind me.'

'My name is Synth Hunt.'

'Sorry, my dear, but it doesn't ring any bells.'

'I was quite a little girl but I'll never forget you.'

'I'm sorry, young lady, but I don't think that we've ever met.'

'Ah, there you are, Father Guyler,' Grant said, breezing into the room. 'I thought you might have got lost in our maze of staircases and corridors. Before you go,' and he slapped the priest amicably on the arm, 'why don't you come along to my library and take a look at my rare books collection?'

'That would be grand,' the priest said, and then to Synth, 'It was a pleasure to meet you. The tea was lovely.' Then he turned and followed Grant out of the room.

'Evil slimeball!' Synth said to the closing door in a low voice laced with venom.

*

Celeste balanced precariously on the raised staging in the shop window of *Mums, Tums and Tots*. It was a couple of feet off the ground and carpeted in pale pink. The backcloth was in rouched forget-me-not blue satin and above that, pink drapes.

The *pièce de résistance* was a full-sized mannequin that Roland had nick-named "Boompsy" for reasons best known to himself, as he had brought it in from the van on that momentous rainy day. The shop accoutrements recycling centre had come up trumps on that score. The pair of them had saved a lot of expenditure by picking up used fitments for their shops

Boompsy was very tall, and there was something slightly disproportionate about her arms that had probably come from another shop window dummy. There was a certain ape-like quality as they dangled next to her bump.

'You look gorgeous,' Celeste murmured to the towering, bald figure looking down at her with glassy eyes and a *retroussè* nose. The plaster mouth had something of a sneer about it so the amateur window dresser got to work with a lip brush and painted in a little smile at the corners of the pouting lips. She had picked up a couple of wigs from the charity shop. One had spiky black hair and the other golden ringlets. She tried the first on the dummy but the effect was rather intimidating so Boompsy ended up looking like a pregnant country and western singer. However, the flowing maternity dress was very fetching and the bump, alias a scatter cushion, taped into place beneath it, was very convincing. A touch of blusher to the mum-to-be's plaster cheeks and it all looked very authentic.

Celeste had intended to put a smart little pram in the window but it was too heavy for her to lift single-handed and she didn't want to disturb Roland's Sunday. So she had opened up a foldaway buggy and installed a large baby doll in it. This she had dressed in a snowsuit, a little out of keeping with its mother's flowing summer dress, but needs must. All she had to do now, was place the mannequin's hard, cold hands onto the buggy handles. They just kept slipping off. In the end, she stuck them into place with some double-sided carpet tape and hoped nobody would notice. That was the grand centrepiece of the right-hand shop window. She scattered some odds and ends on the carpet, things like harnesses, feeding bottles and potties, before addressing the left-hand window.

This, she had decided, was going to be her good-as-new display. Into it she heaved a baby bath, a basket of plastic toys, some teddy bears, and a baby walker. On the hooks at the side, she hung little hangers bearing toddler clothes. It was time to wipe the big shop windows clean of their coating of whitening. She was still working in the shop at midnight but all was ready for her to start trading the next day.

When Celeste opened the shop door at eight o'clock the following morning, to put the prams and pushchairs out on the forecourt, a queue was already forming and she had to summon up all her P.R. skills to prevent the over-eager band of mums from forcing their way past her and into *Mums, Tums and Tots*. She smiled sweetly and apologised but there was grumbling in the ranks. In she went. Out she came, this time brandishing a very long chain that she then proceeded to thread through the wheels of her baby carriages and secure with a heavy padlock. This had been Roland's idea. After all, she didn't want anybody wheeling away her stock.

Inside the shop, she put the float in the till and hoped it would be enough. She felt like a goldfish in a bowl as her audience outside commented to each other on everything she did. What the members of the queue didn't realise was that as they shouted above the noise of the traffic, everything they said could be heard clearly inside the shop.

'Fancy keeping us waiting like this. She can see we're here.'

'Don't think much of that dummy in the window. Looks like Goldilocks got tubbed!' Shrieks of laughter. 'How much is that dummy in the window?' one of them chanted. So it went on. In the end, Celeste went into the stockroom and had a cup of tea. At ten to nine, she couldn't stand the suspense any longer and opened up the shop. The crowd had now grown to about fifteen women in "let me in and at it" mode. They charged through the doorway and started riffling through the racks of baby's and children's clothes, rummaging in the bargain tubs, checking that toys squeaked, jingled and whistled, that cot sides went up and down, that pram brakes and hoods worked and that their pre-school offspring ground as many jelly sweets into the chequered carpet tiles as possible. It was a scrum.

If Celeste had, in her wildest dreams, thought that a mother and baby shop was going to bear any relation to her formerly high-powered managerial post with the airshow, she was swiftly crash-landed in the real world of motherhood. Here was a genre of women with whom she did not remotely relate. They all seemed to be on the edge of hysteria, rushed off their feet and with hairstyles resembling haystacks.

The till rang continuously all morning. As one shoal of customers left, another swarmed in. The leaflets had done their job and every purchaser took another little advertisement away with them. The only other advertising Celeste had done, was to take a large box advert in the local paper. It had paid off. Word had gone around like wildfire. The system of new and second-hand labelling was working well.

No fewer than seven customers had asked if she would be interested in selling their no longer needed prams and pushchairs for them. Thinking on her feet, she agreed to do so on a one third commission but that the goods had to be in scrupulously clean and serviceable condition.

The lunch-hour came and Celeste locked up and went up to her flat for a snack and to put her feet up. She'd scarcely taken a bite out of her sandwich when the front door bell of the flat entrance door was rung again and again. Reluctantly she slipped her shoes on and went downstairs to find two irate women on the doorstep.

'Why are you closed?' One of them barked.

'It's the lunch hour.'

'I've come all the way over here on the bus and I've got to get back to work. I want that buggy out of the window.'

Business was business, so Celeste opened up, peeled Boompsy's hands from the handles and made the sale. When other people saw that she was in the shop, they came in too and her lunch hour was gone. By half past five, the till was full of notes, the stock decimated and she was nearly on her knees. She locked the door and pulled down the blind. She flicked the shop window lights on and limped upstairs, exhausted, leaving Boopsy looking like a bereaved orang-u-tang in drag. The phone rang. It was her mother.

'Hello, Darling. How did your first day go?'

'I've just come upstairs. Very busy. I'm so tired. Can I ring you back later?'

'I just thought I'd better tell you that April and May have both got a snuffle. Nanny says it's nothing to worry about but I thought you should know. I expect June will get it too.'

'Thank you for telling me. I'm sure they'll be fine. I'll call you back later...'

'Oh, and Daddy says please could we have some of those photographs that your nice photographer friend took of the triplets here?'

'I'll see what I can do. Bye for now.' She hung up and flopped out on the sofa and was instantly asleep, only to wake with a start at one in the morning to the sound of dripping water. Befuddled, she swung her legs around and sat up, peering at her watch, unable to believe how long she had slept. It was too late to ring her mother now. She stood up, stretching and yawning and meandered through to the kitchen at the back of the flat. The sound of trickling water became louder. The cold tap was running gently into the washing up bowl which was blocking the plug-hole. For some reason, the overflow wasn't working and the excess water was trickling gently over the side of the stainless steel sink and onto the plastic flooring. From there it seemed to disappear down a crack next to the unit. She turned the tap off but it kept on flowing from the neck of it. Once the washing up bowl was emptied, the water could go down the plug-hole.

'The stockroom!' she exclaimed and ran back into the lounge to get her shoes on. Down the stairs she rushed, unlocking the communicating door into the shop, hitting the light switches, crashing past the counter, unlocking the stockroom door and flicking the light on in there. There was a flash and a bang and all the lights went out. The carpet beneath her feet felt squelchy. She was lucky not to have been electrocuted. She found the water main under the sink and struggled to turn it off.

Tentatively, she felt her way through the darkened shop. Amber coloured streetlights outside shone through the top of the shop windows, illuminating the stock around her in an eerie orange glow. She couldn't deal with this. Roland was her only hope so she went out onto the forecourts, shivering, and rang his flat doorbell. No response. Nothing. So she started to hammer and ring at the same time. Silence. She shouted through the letterbox, 'Roland! It's me! Celeste! I need your help. Please come down!' The traffic lights on the corner cycled through their colours as the thinning traffic filtered through and somebody cycled along the service road on a clanking bicycle. She heard the bolts being drawn back.

'This had better be good,' Roland said grumpily. She tried not to look down at his sky blue briefs, for that was all he was wearing. The hairs on his legs were sandy coloured in contrast to the grey ones on his chest.

'Some water came through into the stock-room and fused all the lights.'

'What? Even the ones upstairs?'

She bit her lip. 'I don't know.'

'Well stand back over there on the pavement and look up.'

Her lounge lights were still on.

'They seem to be alright,' she said.

'Then it can wait until the morning. Call an electrician, Celeste. I'm going back to bed.'

'Who is it?' a woman's voice called from above.

'Nobody important.' Celeste bristled at the insult but he called, 'I'm coming back up now,' as he softly shut the front door and left the miserable shop proprietress standing out on the cold, March pavement. She walked past her dismally dark shop windows and let herself in again. After locking up, she mounted the stairs wearily and got ready for bed. So, Roland had a girl in. Well, it was to be expected really. His track record spoke for itself. Somehow, though, it was something she would rather not have known. She set the alarm for seven a.m. and settled down on the cushions in the cheerless top, front bedroom. Suddenly, she felt very lonely.

Next morning, she hit the alarm clock so hard that it fell on the floor and lay looking up at her. 'I know how you feel,' she said, picking it up and putting it back on the box beside her. Getting up in this miserable flat was no fun. She thought about her luxurious en suite bedroom at her parents' house as she pottered downstairs to the first floor. The kitchen tap was dry. She made her way into the yellow bathroom and then remembered that the water was off. There was enough left in the kettle though. Toast and then another gruelling day lay ahead. The home she had shared with Rupert, poor dead Rupert, had at least been more comfortable than this place. She got dressed in front of the electric fire in the lounge and ran a comb through her hair, grabbed her handbag and the telephone book and went down into the shop.

It was a dull, grey morning and, as the shop fluorescents were all out, the remaining stock looked very forlorn in the cold light of day. Without even bothering to go into the stock room to assess the damage properly, she dialled up the electrician who had wired in some sockets for her a couple of weeks ago. Although sympathetic, he said he couldn't come out until the afternoon.

'...but my till won't work either. It's electric.'

'I'll be there as soon as I can after lunch.'

'Thank you, ' she said, wondering whether to stay closed until the lights were fixed or to try and make the best of it. She decided to open. At nine o'clock, she did so. There wasn't a soul in sight and one of Boompsy's arms had fallen off.

Chapter 13

'Eleanor, my dear. How good to see you!' Reverend Mother Veronica embraced her niece.

'You're looking well, Aunty Rev. I'm sorry it's been such a long time but the magazine has been incredibly busy.' She rummaged in her bag. 'Here. I've brought you a copy.'

'Thank you dear. The sisters will enjoy that. You know they're always sewing things. Pop it on the shelf there and come along through to the conservatory to see Sister Catherine. She's been looking forward to your visit. So have I.'

Eleanor put her coat on the settle in the oak-panelled hall and followed her aunt along the corridor, past the guest suite and into the sunlit conservatory. Sister Catherine was sitting in her art corner painting away at Easter mugs. She put down her brush immediately when the two women came in.

'Reverend Mother,' and she nodded her head as she stood up in acknowledgement of her superior. 'Eleanor.' She walked across and took the bride-to-be's hands in greeting. 'You truly are looking radiant. I see that you have a new hairstyle. It's very becoming.'

Eleanor patted the coiffure and giggled slightly. 'They're trying to glamorise me for the media and for the wedding,' she said conspiratorially. 'I have a meeting tomorrow for the satellite television channel so I really can't stay for very long. I hope you understand.'

'Of course we do but we want to talk to you about the wedding,' Reverend Mother said with a meaningful look. 'I know you appreciate it when I say that we consider the real wedding to be taking place in our chapel here and that the register office is just a legal one.'

'Of course, Aunty Rev. I must say I was surprised that Grant changed his mind about all this. You must have been extremely persuasive.'

'Nonsense dear. He only wants to make you happy. So, shall we go through and look at the chapel and make some plans?'

'Do you want me to come too?' Sister Catherine asked, with a gleam of hope in her eyes. Eleanor was quick to reply.

'You have been part of my life since I was a little girl, Sister, so you have to come and help with this... that's as long as it doesn't interfere with your work there.'

'I can put the brush in a plastic bag and it won't dry out. You go on ahead and I'll catch you up in a minute.'

The chapel was a beautiful and peaceful room and very ornate. Previous wealthy occupants, many decades before, had lavished time and money on creating an exquisite place of worship. There was even a stained glass window that had been endowed by the grateful parents of one of the pupils. St. Bede, at his lectern, surrounded by books and flowers, gazed benevolently down, the sunlight streaming through the cerulean sky above him.

Eleanor and her aunt both genuflected and then stood gazing up at the rococo plasterwork with its gold leaf embellishments. The carved stations of the cross, pulpit and statues were all draped in Lent purple. The embroidered velvet kneelers, made by sisters down the years, graced the pews. The altar too was in Lent colours laid over the crisp, white cloths. Even the monstrance, that large, gold crucifix with the portal for displaying the holy wafer, had a purple ribbon tied around its solid gold stand in the tabernacle. The traditional, small, red glass, oil lamp hung to one side. It was never extinguished apart from between Good Friday and Easter Sunday.

'I love it in here,' Eleanor whispered. 'It has never changed.'

'Let's kneel and say a quick prayer while we wait for Sister,' her aunt replied. So they did. No sound, save for the chirping of some house sparrows in the eves. A timeless moment.

Then the chapel door opened quietly and Sister Catherine came in and genuflected with difficulty. The other two women rose and all three went and sat in the last pew, Eleanor in the middle of them.

'So,' asked Reverend Mother, 'who is going to give you away?' Eleanor felt a little awkward.

'I don't know,' she admitted. 'I don't have any male relatives.' Reverend Mother looked down at her hands.

'It doesn't have to be a man.'

'You're right, Aunty.' Then, as if she had thought of it herself, she blurted out, 'You could do it. You could give me away.'
Her aunt flushed with delight.

'If you're sure...'

'It would be perfect. You have been a parent to me all my life. It has to be you.'

'I'll check with the Mother House, but I'm sure it would be alright in the circumstances. Thank you, dear. I should be delighted.' She beamed. Sister Catherine leaned forward slightly and spoke across Eleanor.

'Our nice Father Guyler is going to perform the ceremony, isn't he?' Reverend Mother nodded.

'I believe so.' She looked at Eleanor.

'Yes, he is. He came to see us at *Casslands* last Saturday.' Reverend Mother already knew.

'So, how would you like the chapel to be decorated for the event?'

'Well, as the convent ceremony is on Easter Monday, I think we should have spring flowers. What do you think?'

'Excellent. We can do those ourselves, can't we Sister?'

'Oh yes we can. We'll have plenty of flowers in the grounds and I believe there might even be a few more exotic ones lurking about.' She gave a knowing smile.

Reverend Mother said, 'I understand that you will be having Grant's daughter as your matron of honour at the register office but will you be repeating that here?'

'No, I don't think so but she will be here and so will her son Charlie.' She bit her lip and hesitated. 'Aunty Rev...'

'Yes, dear?'

'How would you feel about the novices being my bridesmaids? How many have you got in training at the moment?'

'We have the four Filipino girls. Oh, that's a lovely idea! Again, I will check with the Mother House and also with the novices but I think they would be thrilled.'

'You'll be in white, of course, won't you Eleanor dear?' Sister Catherine asked. There was a moment of awkwardness. Eleanor hesitated.

'Now, now, Sister, let Eleanor surprise us,' Reverend Mother said. Sister Catherine put her hand to her mouth. 'Ooh. It's so exciting. We've never had a wedding in the chapel before.'

'Yes, Sister. It will be splendid, a wonderful day.'

Eleanor was very touched by the goodwill and happiness that the forthcoming chapel wedding was engendering.

'Thank you so much. I'm really looking forward to having my wedding here.'

'Technically, it's a blessing but we all know what you mean.' Reverend Mother stood up. 'Come along ladies. Let's go down to the sitting room and discuss the buffet. We have lots of ideas.'

'Oh no. You mustn't do all that. We can get some caterers in.'

'It will be our honour and our pleasure to do that for you and Grant, Eleanor.'

'Very well, Aunty, I'll let you do the food but the costs must not come out of convent funds. I'll cover those. I can afford it.'

'Agreed. Come along. I love discussing food, don't you?'

*

The limousine approached the grand headquarters of *Sateevee Incorporated* via a tree-lined drive interspersed with statues in the modern art style. Eleanor sat in the back seat of the car, eyes wide with surprise as they passed convoluted stone representations of human beings in bizarre poses with organs misplaced and hardly to scale. Some even had holes right through their middles. She would never understand this kind of art.

The car drew up outside the glass fronted reception area of the main building and a concierge came forward to assist Eleanor out. It was another pleasant, early spring day but the wind was chilly and still held the promise of winter's encores.

She presented herself at reception, only to be informed that Mr. Appleton-Smythe was already on his way down.

The receptionist indicated a slightly narrower lift to the side of the four main ones. The indicator lights above it scrolled sideways from fifteen down to zero and the doors opened quietly. Her host stepped forward to greet her.

'Eleanor. How delightful to see you again.'

'Thank you for inviting me. You have a beautiful building here.'

'We've extended it several times but there's never enough room as the company grows. We may end up moving yet again.' He took her by the elbow, steered her into his private lift and spirited her up to the top floor and his personal suite of offices.

'What can I offer you to drink? Please come and sit down over here on the sofa. It's so much more comfortable.'

'I think I'd just like a glass of plain water, please, Mr. Appleton-Smythe.'

'Do please call me Teddy.' He pressed a button on his desk and his personal assistant came in. 'A glass of plain water for Miss Framp, please, and I'll have one too.' The smart woman nodded and smiled as she withdrew.

It was a very large office with panoramic windows giving a view of the parkland in which the buildings were situated. Mr. Appleton-Smythe liked to have plenty of plants around him and Eleanor smiled at the plethora of greenery dotted everywhere in white ceramic tubs, some of the specimens reaching nearly to the ceiling.

'I see you like your foliage... Teddy...' she said by way of conversation.

'Yes, I find that they make the air so much fresher indoors. No amount of air conditioning can make up for a lack of real air and greenery.' He strode across to the ceiling-height windows and touched a button on the edge of the frame, causing the massive pane to slide effortlessly across, opening the office out onto a wide balcony with tables, chairs and folded down sun umbrellas in shades of blue and white.

Eleanor looked across with admiration.

'That's lovely,' she commented as the glasses of water arrived on a tray with tongs and dish of lemon slices and ice-cubes.

'Please help yourself,' he indicated but she took it plain.

'Now then, Eleanor, I expect Grant has explained to you that I would like you to front a series of television programmes on environmental issues to be broadcast via my company's satellite system worldwide.'

'Yes, he has. It all sounds very big and important. Are you sure that I'm the right person for this? I have little television experience, although I have spoken on the radio quite a few times.'

'You'll be perfect, Eleanor, and I'll tell you why. The public is, in my opinion, becoming a little tired of this youth culture. Nearly all of the female television broadcasters, from weather girls to news-readers, are in the lower age bracket. This really doesn't reflect the make-up of the population. In my opinion, these bimbos tend to get the jobs because they are selected by men in the hierarchy. It wouldn't be any better if women were in the higher echelons because they would probably be jealous of any other woman trying to climb the ladder. The result is that Mrs. Viewing Average, is not seeing herself reflected in the areas of media presentation and that's not fair.'

Eleanor couldn't believe what she was hearing. After all her years in journalism, she had met little in the way of support for older women in the business. If he wanted to smarm her, then he was certainly on the right path but she was wary. She was too long in the tooth to be taken for a ride.

'That's a very radical view, er, Teddy,' she said. 'I suspect that most men would not agree with it.'

He breathed in deeply and took a sip from his glass, placing it back on the onyx coffee table. 'Look,' he said, 'as the developing countries take their lead from us, the women... and I'm talking here about those over thirty years of age... are going to see that we dump our older ladies when they still have many years of work and experience to offer. What sort of an example is that, especially as their own daughters will one day face the same fate? As their life expectancy is extended to catch up with that in the west, will they also look forward to being put on the scrap heap at the peak of their lives?'

'You make a very strong case,' Eleanor said, cradling her ice-cold glass of water and sipping from it, 'but, to be frank, I don't consider myself to be much of an oil painting...'

'Stop it right there, my lady!' he barked at her laughing. 'My friend Grant thinks you're the best thing since sliced bread and I have to agree with him.'

'I mean, I have wrinkles and things...'

'So do a lot of male broadcasters but that doesn't stop them working well into old age. Anyway, I don't see wrinkles...'

'Now you're just being nice...'

'Laughter traces,' he said.

'Whatever you say,' she smiled back at him. She really liked this old friend of Grant's.

'O.K. Then we are agreed that you are the woman for the job. The series is going to be called, *A World of Difference*, and you will introduce and finish each episode and record all the voice-overs for the camera-work. Those will be put on afterwards. You just have to read the script into a microphone.'

'When will they take the films?'

'Already done. We just need you to come into the studio as soon as possible and get recording.'

'How long would it take?'

'I reckon that with re-takes, if we worked full-time for a week, we could cover the whole ten episodes within that time-scale. You'd need to start early in the mornings and record on into the evenings but I know you're a hard worker.' He slapped his thigh. 'By the way, congratulations on the success of your magazine. Grant tells me it's going great guns.'

'Yes, it's doing well but it's early days.' She paused. 'I'm not sure I can take an entire week off because I have to get the March issue put to bed and then the wedding is coming up over the Easter weekend.'

'Five thousand pounds per episode.'

She was gob-smacked. 'You're willing to pay me fifty thousand pounds for ten episodes?'

'Yes, I am because you are the face of the mature, intelligent woman that I want to front my series on the environment. What do you say?'

Eleanor knocked back a gulp of cold water as she felt a hot flush coming on. She took a couple of slow, deep breaths. 'Just a moment, please,' she said.

'Take your time. Why don't you walk out onto the balcony for a moment while you think about it?'

'Yes, thank you. I will.' She got up and did so. He remained on the sofa, watching his friend's fiancée as she placed her hands on the balcony rail and let the early spring breeze ruffle her hair as she weighed up the offer.

Would she do it? He had no fewer than twelve satellites up there, passing around the world, covering every latitude and longitude, twenty-four hours a day. After about five minutes, she came back into the office and sat down beside him.

'It's a very attractive offer, Teddy, but I think I have to talk it over with Grant. I also have to see what arrangements I could make for office cover for my magazine. We are pretty snowed under at present. What with the wedding and everything, it's come at a pretty difficult time.'

'I understand,' he said. 'How about sleeping on it and you can let me know in the morning?' He got to his feet as his P.A. came in. The interview was over. 'Let me take you down to the foyer.' He led her to the lift entrance but before he got in, he nodded to his P.A. By the time the concierge had opened the big, glass door out of reception, the limousine was purring in readiness. Eleanor climbed in and was whisked away from *Sateevee Incorporated* with her head buzzing.

*

The Phillipstone Chamber of Commercial Enterprise met regularly on the first Thursday evening of the month in the back room of a restaurant and hotel next to the golf links. The Minutes and Membership secretary, a buxom woman of uncertain age, whose fore and aft were note-worthy, greeted Celeste and Roland as they presented themselves on the breezy March evening in the golf-themed salon.

'Welcome,' she gushed. 'The committee has approved your membership, so you are entitled to attend tonight's Annual General Meeting. Here are your window stickers and cards. The latter will entitle you to ten percent discount in any of the retail outlets owned by the members. Quite a perk, don't you think?'

The woman placed the items in the new members' hands.

'Thank you,' Celeste said, accepting hers together with the knowledge that she too would have to give discount, as would Roland.' The musty smelling room was sparsely filled with serious looking individuals muttering in groups.

'Come this way and meet the Treasurer and Chamber Secretary. The Chairman should be along shortly.' They followed the woman obediently and spent ten minutes discussing the country's economic situation, Sunday trading and whether we should pull out of Europe, with a trio of bespectacled and suited men who might as well have had *BOREDOM* tattooed on their foreheads. On the pretext of circulating, Celeste and Roland broke away for a quick sub-conference.

'Is this really our sort of thing?' Roland queried, looking askance at the forty or so assembled business people.

'We need them,' Celeste hissed back. 'Anyway, we're members now and can stick the badges in our windows.'

'I suppose it might lead to a little extra work. You never know. Wheels within wheels and all that.'

'Ah, there you are,' gushed Mrs. Fore and Aft in a cloud of *Eau de Violet*. We're all going to sit down now, so do come over and find a place at one of the tables.' The wall clock showed eight o'clock. Sounds of merriment could be heard filtering through from a party in an adjacent amenity room.

The sombre gathering of white, middle-class males took their seats. Celeste realised that she was one of only two women in the room... until the door opened and Eleanor Framp came in accompanied by Grant Landscar.

'Ah here's the chairman and his fiancée now,' the Minutes Secretary said, taking up her shorthand pad.

'You look like a goldfish,' Roland whispered to Celeste. She was speechless and her face had gone white.

'We should have guessed he'd have his finger in this pie,' she groaned. 'Talk about bearding the lion in his den...' She was full of despair.

Grant Landscar stopped in his tracks as he spotted his tenants sitting there as bold as brass. Celeste lifted her pretty little hand and gave him a smile and a tentative wave. He turned to say something to Eleanor but she looked the other way and greeted somebody else. They both sat down, he in the centre seat of the main table and she next to him.

'There's only one way to deal with those two,' Celeste said grimly, 'we have to get onto the committee.'

'You are joking,' Roland hissed.

Somebody tapped a pen on the main table.

'Order,' appealed Mrs. Fore and Aft. Then the AGM began and proceeded in all its traditional tedium. The members of the PCCE, gave every word their absolute, undivided attention whilst the two newcomers fought to stay awake, their glazed expressions a reflection of their self-employed exhaustion.

'Now!' said the Chamber Secretary, a bearded man of swarthy appearance with a voice like a deep drain. Everybody sat up a little straighter. 'It is time to elect our new committee. The Chairman, Treasurer, Minutes and Membership Secretary and myself are willing to stand again and are allowed to do so within the rules of this chamber but we need five new committee members to cover the areas of Publicity and Recruitment, Police joint sub-committee, Council Liaison Officer, Special Projects and, of course, General Purposes.'

'He means dogsbody,' Roland muttered.

'Sounds like the perfect job for you.'

'Get lost.'

Celeste raised her hand.

'Would you like to introduce yourself to the members, Miss Blagden?'

'Yes, certainly,' she replied, switching on that ingratiating smile that she had honed to perfection in her years with the airshow. 'I am Celeste Blagden and I am a local trader with a retail outlet called *Mums, Tums and Tots*.'

The male members looked at each other with raised eyebrows and a touch of distaste. She didn't care. Life had thrown too much at her in the past year for the disdain of a handful of narrow-minded suburbanites to push her off kilter.

'I would like to stand as Council Liaison Officer.'

'Is there a seconder?' the Company Secretary asked.

Celeste pressed her neat little foot against Roland's ankle. His hand shot up.

'...and you are?'

'Roland Dilger, Photographer. My company is *Roland Dilger Photography*. I would like to second Miss Blagden.'

'Anybody else wish to stand?' Nobody did.

'Any objections?' None. She was in.

'... and I would like to stand as Publicity and Recruitment Officer,' Roland said, striking while the iron was hot. Celeste seconded him and as nobody else wanted the job he also was in.

A miserable man with a hair drape volunteered to be Police Liaison Officer. There were no other contenders.

'Special Projects?'

Grant Landscar spoke for the first time. 'I would like to propose my future wife, Miss Eleanor Framp, soon to be Mrs. Grant Landscar, for this post.'

Eleanor's head whipped around so quickly in astonishment that you could hear the vertebrae crack. She'd clearly had this sprung upon her. A flush crept up her face. She felt breathless. If there was one thing that wasn't needed right now it was more work and her future husband had dropped her right in it. She placed her hand on his forearm but he turned to her with that fixed smile that implied, "Don't mess with me. This is a *fait accompli*. Don't rock the boat.'

Everybody clapped. She put on a brave smile. He put his arm around her shoulders and gave her a firm hug. She was furious but nothing could be done.

Nobody wanted the job of General Purposes Officer, so Mrs. Fore and Aft reluctantly said she would take it on in addition to her other duties as she had done every year since time immemorial. The new committee was ready for action.

No member was keener to get started than its new Council Liaison Officer, Miss Celeste Blagden.

'Any other business?' the Company Secretary asked. Celeste raised her hand. The assembled gathering smelled trouble and bristled somewhat, clearing throats and feeling in pockets. She was up and away.

'I would like to ask what the committee's feelings, and indeed the general membership's feelings, are about the proposed lorry cleaning facility and electric vehicle recharging premises planned for the dual carriage site opposite my shop on Phillipstone Road?'

A stunned silence pervaded the room.

'Do we know anything about this?' asked the Chamber Secretary.

Grant Landscar said, 'As a matter of fact, I do. It's my venture.' There wasn't exactly a gasp but people were surprised and looked at each other. Celeste had her audience though and pitched in with a vengeance, outlining everything she had said to Roland the other night.

'So,' she said, 'I am asking this Chamber to back me in a campaign to prevent this facility being built.' It was more than a little embarrassing for the members. The newcomer was throwing her weight about in a most unseemly fashion. How could they possibly go against their all-powerful chairman?

Grant Landscar, who had habitually handed over the running of the monthly meetings to the Chamber Secretary, he of the Neanderthal appearance, looked at Celeste in a pitying kind of way. Was this young woman stupid? Didn't she realise how difficult he could make her life? For goodness sakes! He was her landlord. He could give her notice! He could implement every minute detail of the *Put and Keep* lease.

Eleanor, not entirely enamoured with her fiancée's behaviour in manipulating her this evening, raised her hand. 'I'm wondering,' she said in a measured tone, 'whether perhaps we should discuss this matter at the regular committee meeting, whenever that may be.' Hands went up. The Chamber Secretary looked at Grant and said, 'Agreed. This matter to be decided at the regular committee. Meeting closed at ten p.m.'

Outside, Celeste got into Roland's car.

'Well,' she said. 'That should set off a few fireworks.'
He started the engine and rattled the gear lever into reverse.

'I hope we don't live to regret it.'
He pulled away and the engine stalled.

Chapter 14

'Hiya, boss lady,' Pandora said, phone clamped to her ear in waiting mode. Eleanor placed her brown briefcase onto her desk and waved her hands about in a theatrical fashion, indicating exhaustion. She sank into her executive chair.

'Who's on the line?'

'Hong Kong. Printers for the Far East. They say they can do us a good deal. He's gone off to get me some more figures. It's taken me ages to get him so I didn't want to risk a call back.'

'Very wise. I see they've opened up the other offices for us.'

'Yes. The telephone and Internet people will be in this morning. The galleys for the April issue are here, by the way, and I'm doing interviews this afternoon. Want to join me?'

'I'll leave it to you, Pandora. There's so much to tidy up. I'm in the satellite television studios all next week...'

'What?'

'I'm really sorry to spring it on you but it's just too good a deal to turn down and Grant's very keen for me to do it.'

'Hello. Yes. Please email me those figures urgently. Thank you. Goodbye.' She hung up and flicked a switch on the small control box to divert all incoming calls to the office next door before giving Eleanor her full attention.

'All week?'

'Yes, I'm afraid so.'

'I suppose I can manage, but a bit more notice would have been nice.'

'I spoke to Grant about it last night and he is adamant that it's the right thing for me to do. They are going to record the voice-overs and top and tailers for the entire ten programmes. Once those are completed, things should get back to normal, apart from the wedding, that is.'

'Ah!' Pandora got up, walked across the room and opened the closet. 'This came earlier.' She hauled out a large, white box and lifted it lightly onto the top of an Eleanor's workstation. 'I think it must be your outfit.'

'Oooh. That is exciting. Please, help me to open it.'

The pair of them wrestled with it and then Pandora lifted out the gown, peeling away the tissue paper.

'That's very nice indeed,' she commented. 'Excellent. You'll look lovely.'

'Do you think it will suit me?'

'You bet. You'll look ravishing.'

'I'll take it home to the flat with me today and try it on but it should fit perfectly. They were only small alterations.'

'You have a nice figure, Eleanor, but then you haven't gone all saggy with child bearing, like some of us.' She looked down at her stomach and grimaced.

'I was always skinny.'

'I wish I was. After Charlie was born, I never seemed to be able to get my shape back,' she sighed.

'You look fine to me. Scrawny can be a bit unflattering as we mature.'

They both began to pack the dress away again, arranging the tissue paper carefully. Eleanor stroked the material and said, 'I can't believe it's only three weeks to the wedding. I don't know where time is going. What about your matron of honour dress?'

'I've tucked it away at my house and Dad won't see it, so don't worry. You and I can have a dress show if you'd like?'

'Yes, we must, but first let me get this satellite television thing over and done with.' She tucked in the box flaps and then looked up. 'What about young Charlie?'

'Since he went back to boarding school, he's been quite a good chap. Grant gave him a good telling off for going walk-about from his friend's house that time. Children just don't seem to realise what a dangerous place the world it.'

'I suppose boys are more adventurous.'

'Don't talk to me about it. Grant gave Charlie a mini-motor-cycle for his birthday and he's been haring about my paddocks like a grand prix hopeful, scaring the life out of my horses.'

'Were you a hyper child?'

'You should ask Grant about me when I was a kid. I gave him a few frights. I expect you had a quiet sort of life at the convent.'

'Rather,' Eleanor said, 'but it had advantages.'

'Such as?'

'Lots of space to roam the grounds and kindly nuns.'

'It wouldn't have suited me. I'd have been in trouble all the time.'

'I suppose we're all different. It was a good childhood, different, but secure.'

'I hope you don't mind me asking, but the nuns live a sort of poor life, don't they? What happened when you wanted things like the other children? I mean, Charlie is always after the latest trainers or gizmo.' She lifted the dress box and put it away.

''Oh, we had a sort of arrangement. Children are quite quick to pick up on what is possible. My parents had left a kitty of money in the bank for me and small, regular, pocket money was doled out from there with bigger sums for my birthday or Christmas. I could choose things up to a certain amount. There was quite a debate when I asked for a bicycle, I seem to recall.'

'Did you get it?'

'A compromise. The father of one of the other pupils renovated a second-hand one for me. It was really very well done, with a new white saddle and all the trimmings. I loved that bike and rode it everywhere.'

'You'll never guess what else Grant gave Charlie for his thirteenth birthday.'

'I can't imagine. Go on, tell me.'

'His own digital video-camera.'

'I expect that was expensive.'

'Top of the range. I think it's ridiculous spending that much on a present for a child, but he enjoyed making a documentary about football with the school's camera and has been bitten by the movie bug. I expect it will pass like all his other crazes... the boots with wheels on the heels, the walkie-talkie, the magic goo and all those things that kids find fascinating.'

The telephone rang. Pandora picked up. 'Very well. Put them on, please.' She put her hand over the mouthpiece. 'Calls are backing up next door, so I'd better help them for a while. Go and look at the extra offices. You'll be pleased... Good morning, *Embroideryworld* Editorial. How can I help you? Yes, it's Pandora Brand, the Managing Editor, here.'

Eleanor looked up sharply. That was news to her.

Along the corridor the building still smelt very new. Eleanor felt like an intruder as she opened the other doors and peered into the new offices. Quite a little empire! She imagined that it was like looking around somebody's house after they had died, a feeling that you were being watched and had no right to be there. On the way back, she paid the temps a visit in their answering centre and mail receiving room. They all stood up with their earphones still on as she came in.

'Don't get up, ladies,' Eleanor said with a smile. They all unhitched one ear to hear her and said to their callers, 'One moment please.'

'I've just popped in to say how much I appreciate all your hard work.'

The one nearest the door took her headset off and came over to shake Eleanor's hand. 'We're hearing some very complimentary remarks about the magazine. People are really enjoying the March issue with the free cross-stitch kit.'

'Any other feedback?'

''Yes,' the woman said, 'they all seem to like the celebrity stitchers.'

'Oh, I am pleased. Are we getting much for the letter page?'

'We've put them in a stack over there, Miss Framp. About five thousand letters. Mrs. Brand said she would go through them and select some for publication.'

'Excellent. Is there anything the customers don't like?'

'Well, there are always a few strange ones, I suppose.'

'Like what?'

'Some lady wanted to know if we were going to do a piece about embroidering fruit and somebody else rang up and said that crewel needles were hard to find and wanted us to recommend a supplier.'

'Did you?'

'I pointed her towards one in the back of the magazine. She only had to look.'

Eleanor glanced askance at the pile of full mailbags over by the door. 'Still struggling to keep up?'

'Yes, but Mrs. Brand said we will be getting more help next week while you're away.'

'News travels fast. I only just told her.'

'Oh, she told us the other day that you were going to be recording for satellite television next week.'

'Did she now?'

'Yes, she did, and she also said that I am being promoted to Office Manager after Easter.'

'It seems that Mrs. Brand has things well organised. I'll leave you to get on now. Thank you again for all your hard work.'

Eleanor took her leave and stood in the corridor to regain her composure. Why did she have this feeling that *Embroideryworld* was slipping away from her? The cosy little magazine that she had envisaged was turning into a tail wagging the dog. It was all growing too fast and she was losing control. Pandora seemed to have her hand on everything and surely Grant couldn't have told his daughter about next week before it was even decided? Had they all thought her so malleable and gullible that she couldn't turn down the *Sateevee* offer? Why did she feel that things were going on behind her back all the time?

Her office door opened and Pandora looked out. 'There you are! I've got a call for you from Milloncha.'

'For me? I don't know anybody over there.'

'It's the gardener-handyman, Gonzo. He says he can't get hold of Dad and that Synth gave him this number.'

'Grant's in a meeting up in town all day today, something very important and not to be disturbed. I'll see what I can do.'

She took up the receiver. 'Miss Framp speaking.'

'Good morning, lady. Here is Gonzales from the *Villa Estancia.*'

'Good morning. What can I do for you, Gonzales?'

'I need permission from Señor Landscar to pay somebody to take away the débris from the small wooden building he asked me to demolish for him.'

'How much money is involved?'

'The contractor would like five hundred Euros.'

'Mr. Landscar is in a meeting all day today. Are you sure it can't it wait until tomorrow?'

'No, Miss Framp, I cannot wait because the cement is coming in the morning.'

'Very well. I'd better give you permission then. Go ahead and pay the contractor and I'll tell Mr. Landscar that you will need to be reimbursed. Have you got enough cash?'

'Yes, I think so, lady, but I will need to be repaid pronto.'

'Don't worry. I'll see to it.'

'Gracias and goodbye.' The line went dead. Eleanor looked quizzically at the receiver and put it down. 'I hope I did the right thing.'

'I'm sure you did. Dad will be pleased that you sorted it out.'

'Mmmm.' She paused and put her finger to her temple. 'Now, what was it I wanted to ask you?' She sat down. 'I know. The flowers for the register office. Cream roses. What's happening?'

'I placed the order the other day. The florist will go in early on Easter Saturday and put the displays in place. Of course, the people getting married earlier in the day will get the benefit of them too, but at least you will have some lovely fresh flowers for your ceremony.'

'That's good. I don't have to worry about that then. What about my bouquet?'

'They'll deliver it to your flat in good time on the wedding day. The cream rose lapel sprigs for the gentlemen guests will be handed out in the reception area at the register office as they go in.' She tapped her fingers on the receiver as the phone rang again. 'By the way, who's going to give you away?'

Eleanor sensed a loaded question.

'I haven't got anybody for the register office. I don't have any other men in my life.'

'No male relatives or friends?' She picked up the receiver. 'Editorial. No, you need the customer feedback line. Hold on one moment please and I'll put you through.' She hung up.

'None.' Eleanor said.

'That's a pity.'

'It certainly needs some thought because time is running. Oh, while we're talking, I gather you are promoting that girl next door to be Manager of the telephone and mail inwards room.'

'Yes, she's very organised and capable. The others look up to her. It will happen after Easter. I mean, you'll be away on your fabulous honeymoon in Dad's wonderful villa on the magical island of Milloncha and I'll need her to take some responsibility. Add to that the new personnel that I'll be recruiting this afternoon, and we should be able to manage while you are away for a month.'

'A month?'

'Oh yes. You have to have a decent honeymoon.'

'I can't possibly leave *Embroideryworld* for a whole month,' the bride-to-be exclaimed.

'Don't worry. It'll run like clockwork. Just tell me what you want done and I'll get onto it. I've already written the editor's page for the next three months. Do you want to look at it?'

Eleanor was speechless with a mixture of astonishment and disappointment. The rug was slowly but surely being pulled from beneath her feet. She felt a hot flush creeping up her neck and into her face together with panicky breathlessness.

'I'm just going to slip out for some sandwiches. Shall I get you a pack too?' She collected her coat from the closet.

'Yes, please. If you could get me some beef and tomato on rye as usual. Thanks Eleanor.' Pandora picked up the phone after one ring. '*Embroideryworld*,' she said, 'Managing Editor speaking.'

Eleanor closed the door quietly behind her, gritting her teeth.

*

On Monday morning, Eleanor stepped out of the limousine at *Sateevee Incorporated.* The smiling concierge came forward to greet her.

'Good morning, madam,' he said, as he opened the car door..

'Good morning. Would you be kind enough to retrieve my clothes portmanteau from the boot for me?'

'Yes, of course, madam.' He lifted the foldaway case and led the way to reception, walking behind her as she carried her brief case and shoulder-bag. Once there, a smart young man in grey slacks and a pale yellow sweater stepped forward to shake hands and introduce himself as the director of *A World of Difference*.

'Delighted to meet you, Miss Framp. Let me carry your case for you.' He took it from the concierge. 'I expect this is your wardrobe of different outfits for each episode. We'll store it safely for you.'

'Thank you. It is rather heavy,' she replied.

'I'm afraid it's a bit of a hike,' he said but it is a very big building and the studios are at the rear. Would you prefer me to take you around the outside in one of our golf buggies?

'No, don't worry. I'm good at walking and you have some interesting pieces of art along these walls.'

'Yes. We're pretty lucky to work here. Appleton-Smythe looks after the staff very well too. He's a bit of an art collector, you know. I expect you saw the statues along the drive.'

'Yes. Most interesting,' she said.

'Quite!' Their opinions appeared to coincide and they smiled knowingly at one another.

Walking together along seemingly endless corridors, through sets of swing doors, up and down ramps, passing other staff who nodded affably, they finally entered Studio Two.

'Here's your chair, Miss Framp.' The director pointed at a studio foldaway with her name on the back.

'Just like the real movies,' she laughed.

The studio was only partially lit but her gaze upwards found gantries and metal beams laden with spotlights and cables, above which the deep darkness of the high ceiling hung like a night sky.

'Will we be filming in here today?' she asked.

'No. We'll be going into the sound studio next door for some voice tests and rehearsals but I thought you'd like to see in here first. That's the green screen over there.' He indicated the far wall where the huge oblong hung in the gloom. 'We'll be standing you against that for your openers and enders and then we'll insert the background electronically afterwards.'

'It's all very exciting. I can't wait to get started.'

'Come along then and meet the sound crew.'

She picked up her briefcase and went with him.

'Guys, this is Miss Eleanor Framp.'

The crew put down their cups and got up to greet her. There were two men and a girl with cascading brown curls.

The director placed the portmanteau on a stand.

'So, I'll leave you in the capable hands of my sound team,' he said. 'I'll be over in Studio Three if you need me. Otherwise, I'll come and collect you for lunch at one o'clock, Miss Framp.'

'I'll see you later then.' She turned to the crew and asked, 'Now, what would you like me to do?'

The girl took her coat and then escorted Eleanor to a sound booth and shut the door. Once seated, she looked around at the stippled walls and felt the dead feel of the place. It was about the size of a telephone box. Although she would never have admitted to claustrophobia, she wasn't very keen on confined spaces but, calling on the techniques learned from a self-help book about panic, she breathed slowly and her heart gradually slowed down, the pulsing in her temples fading. Her hand felt for the familiar briefcase at her feet. It was her comfort rag, somehow.

She looked out of the glass pane in front where one of the men was waving his arms, miming that she should put on the headphones. They were on a hook to one side so she took them and placed them over her elegant coiffure. Immediately she could hear him speaking and see his lips moving beyond the pane.

'Miss Framp, can you hear me clearly?'

'Yes, I can, thank you,' she said into the microphone.

'I'd like you to read to me from that sheet of paper on the ledge in front of you.'

'Just a moment. I need my glasses.' She took out her bottle of water and then fumbled for her spectacles in the front compartment of the briefcase putting them on, pushing the arms under the earphones. It wasn't very comfortable. Then she took up the sheet of paper and started to read.

'I am Eleanor Framp and I am going to be your guide through the fascinating and fragile world of renewable energy and energy conservation...'

'Hold it there!'

'Did I do something wrong?'

'No. You're fine. A bit "essy" and your p is popping.'

It all sounded like mumbo-jumbo to her but this was a new experience and she was up for it.

'Carry on, please,' the engineer said, and so she did, for three long hours, reciting nursery rhymes, counting, pausing, repeating and learning to breathe in quietly. It was quite an education. She couldn't wait to tell Grant all about it that night.

*

'Hello, my lovely, darling woman,' Grant said, looking up from his newspaper as Eleanor walked into the lounge at *Casslands* that evening. 'Long day? Gracious me! It's after ten o'clock.'

'I'm utterly exhausted,' she said, dropping a kiss on the top of his silver hair before falling into the arms of a comfortable sofa, kicking off her shoes and putting her feet up on the black, velvet pouffe.

'I'm fed up with the sound of my own voice. Nobody warned me it would be such hard work.'

'Teddy said you did really well. The technicians were pleased with you and said you were a fast learner.'

'He rang you about me?'

'Your progress was mentioned while we were discussing other matters. We have business interests, you know.'

'Yes, of course.' She stretched and yawned. 'Have you dined yet?'

'No. I waited for you. Synth's gone to her quarters for the night but she brought something on trays for us up here. Do you want to eat now? There's some juice on the table there for you.'

'I'll just go and wash my hands and then I need feeding. We had a very good lunch at the studios but I'm starving now.'

'Your wish is my command.' He put down his newspaper and went over to collect her supper tray and place it on a low table for her. He took his own tray and sat with it on his lap on the sofa. When he removed the silver cover, there was smoked salmon, brown bread and butter, a salad, and a dessert of freshly made strawberry mousse. He was nibbling at a slice of bread when she returned.

'Come along. Dig in! This is lovely. Synth's a good girl.'

Eleanor made herself comfortable beside him and took her tray.

'This looks delicious. Scottish smoked salmon?'

'Of course.'

They both tucked in. After a couple of minutes of silence, she turned to him and said, 'I was talking to Pandora the other day. She's expecting me to be away on honeymoon for a whole month.'

'Oh, she's spoiled my surprise! I didn't want you to know yet. That daughter of mine! What am I going to do with her?'

'Grant, that's an awful long time for me to be away from the magazine. I mean, *Embroideryworld* is my brainchild and I rather want to keep my hand on the tiller.'

'Come now, Eleanor, honey, Pandy will look after it for you. The magazine's doing really well and you should be proud of it.'

'...But,'

'No buts. You deserve a lovely, long honeymoon. You'll adore my *Villa Estancia* and the island of Milloncha. We can relax and really get to know each other, as a married couple. You know what I mean.' He placed his hand on her knee and a quiver ran up her insides.

It was a done deal. She swallowed a mouthful of lettuce and took a sip from the glass of juice beside her. There was no point in arguing. She changed the subject.

'Pandy says that Charlie's really very pleased with his birthday present from you. Apparently he's roaring all over her fields and having a great time.'

'Well, he's a wonderful kid, full of energy and real bright. I can see him taking over from me one day. He deserves the best... shame he has no father.'

Eleanor paused. Should she ask?

'What happened there?'

'We don't talk about it much.'

'It doesn't matter. I didn't mean to pry.' She stabbed at a piece of tomato. Grant put down his fork and rocked his head from side to side as if debating something with himself.

'O.K. I'll tell you but don't say anything to Pandy.'

'Of course.'

Grant took a deep breath. Eleanor waited, toying with her food, tense with anticipation. She put down her knife and fork.

'Pandora was always a bit of a challenge,' he said. 'Don't get me wrong, but she was one of those kids that just couldn't be contained. She was thrown out of no less than three schools and, as I had custody of her after the divorce, it reflected mighty badly on me.' He sighed deeply. 'So,' he said, 'I sent her to one of those outward bound residential academies and that's when she really found herself. It was there that she realised what a leader she was. She went on a business course, started her own import and export business.. early into the far East market... and has made me real proud of her. Now she freelances and makes a packet.'

'What about Charlie?'

'The product of some spur of the moment marriage in the Seychelles while she was on holiday.'

'The father?'

'An adventurer techno-whizz who disappeared soon after. His name was Xavier Brand. After seven years and no contact, she had him declared dead officially so she is, by law, a widow.'

'How awful for her.'

'Well, she's come to terms with it now, although she was nuts about Xavier at the time. The love of her life, you might say. She came back to England and had baby Charlie here. If you go over to her house, you'll see a framed photo of her and Xavier on her sideboard. She's never quite let him go.'

'Thank you for telling me. I won't say anything.'
She smiled brightly. 'So, tell me about the honeymoon.'

'We'll have a terrific time out there in Milloncha,' he said. 'We'll go in the pool, walk, go out in the boat, relax in the gardens. You'll love it.'

'It sounds idyllic. Very well. You win. A long honeymoon it is. I'm sure it'll be lovely.'

'That's my girl.' He gave her that disarming smile that always made her heart melt. She was so lucky but niggled. She picked up her knife and fork again.

'Hey! Did I tell you that we have a situation developing over my plans for the heavy vehicle cleaning station and electric vehicle recharging centre?'

'Oh dear! What now?'

'Those wretched tenants of mine have ganged up on me. You know, that Roland Dilger and Miss Blagden?'

'Yes, I know who they are. What have they done?'

'Only put in an objection to my planning application.'

'That's rather unfortunate on several counts.'

'You bet it is. Apart from the fact that I've already bought the bungalow on the dual carriageway from the vendor and ordered the cleaning equipment from the U.S. and got my friend on the council to agree to change all the council run-about vehicles to electric in the new financial year, there's the bad publicity.'

'You'll find a way around it, won't you?'

'I have a fallback plan to build a children's play area on the park nearby and to re-roof the local library. I hope that will be enough to sweeten the planners. You should have heard those two back-stabbers at the Chamber committee earlier this evening. By the way, I made apologies for your absence... but they really went for me.'

'What did they say?'

'They were banging on about twenty-four hour noise from vehicles coming and going, about it attracting more heavy traffic to the area, about the loss of the trees, the disturbance to the residential neighbours during the building... you should have heard them...'

'They have a point.'

'You're not on their side, surely?'

'Well, you have to see it from their view.' Eleanor, as a former journalist, was well versed in the art of seeing things from every angle. 'They've just started up their businesses and suddenly there's going to be all that noise and mess opposite and, if I understand it from the application, they stand to lose their shop forecourts and customer parking in the service road.'

'How did you know about that?'

'I looked up the application on the web last night.'

'Humph!' he said grumpily, digging into his smoked salmon and lifting a wafer-thin slice onto his bread and butter.

'Oh Grant,' she said, putting down her fork, 'of course I'm on your side. It's just that other people may see it differently.'

'It will be one helluva goldmine,' he said. 'Do you have any idea how many lorries and transporters are on the roads of this country? They cover some four billion road miles a year.

'Four Billion? Really? As much as that?' She was surprised.

'With the new port opening on the east coast and the M212 link...'

'Yes, I can see that it would only be a short detour off the motorway for them to come and have their vehicles cleaned before they catch the ferry to Europe,' she said.

'I'll let you into a little secret,' he leaned towards her. 'I'm going to add a snack bar to the plans too so that while the vehicles are being seen to, the drivers can eat. What do you think of that?'

'On the residential side of the carriageway? I think you'll have trouble.'

'I've got the ministry with me on this one. Guess what?'

'You're going to tell me.'

'They are concerned that heavy vehicle drivers are eating junk food that gives them a high followed by a low and a drop in driving ability. They've actually done tests to show that.'

'So, what are you going to feed them? Bird seed?'

'Don't jest with me, Eleanor. I'm going to provide proper balanced meals, meat and two vegetables, that sort of thing.'

'Then it will be more than a snack bar. Rather a restaurant.'

'What's in a name?'

'I take my hat off to you, my darling,' she said, 'you truly are an entrepreneur.'

'You'd better believe it!' He grinned in triumph, running his hand up under her skirt.

Chapter 15

'Come in, Pandora. Please, let me take your coat.' Eleanor welcomed her future daughter-in-law into her spinsterish, little flat in *Isabel Avenue.*

'This is cosy,' the visitor remarked, making her way through to the sitting room, the door of which stood open. 'My goodness! You do like your embroidery, don't you?' She called over her shoulder before surveying in amazement the walls of the compact room that were smothered in framed embroideries.

'It's always been a hobby of mine, ever since convent days. The nuns taught me how to do cross-stitch and other thread-work. I find it very soothing.'

'No wonder you wanted to start a magazine about it. What a lovely room,' she said, not really believing it. 'How long have you been here?'

'Let me think.' Eleanor paused. 'Oh, about twenty-five years. I bought it in my mid-twenties after living in various rented places while I was working as a young journalist. I made the effort to leave the convent when I was nineteen, using the remains of my parents' bequest. It was hard to live alone at first but you get used to it.'

'Shall I park myself here?' Pandora indicated the sofa.

'Yes, anywhere. I'll go and put the kettle on.'

Pandora put her handbag on the round glass table beside her and took in the ambience of this small sitting room where Eleanor had spent so many lonely days and evenings. Marrying Grant really was going to be a huge change for her. There was an atmosphere of maiden aunt about the place, exacerbated by the plants on the window sill, the rouched net curtains, scatter rugs and cushions dating from the sixties.

The room was fairly devoid of knick-knacks though and there was no evidence of a pet of any kind.

'Tea?' Eleanor called from the kitchen.

'Milk. No sugar, ta,' Pandora replied. 'So, how's the recording going?'

Eleanor came back into the room, the sound of the grumbling kettle in the background.

'We're finished but I'm going to pop in next week to watch highlights from the final edited version. Grant's coming with me.'

'I bet you're glad that's over and done with.'

'I most certainly am. It was a lot of pressure what with all the re-takes and changes. The magazine is calling me, though. How are things?'

'We've had a good week. There's been plenty of reader response, especially after your chat show.'

'Oh, that was awful. That dreadful woman was determined to put me down.'

'Eleanor, I've only known you for a short while, but I should think you're quite difficult to put down,' she laughed. The kettle clicked off and the hostess disappeared into the kitchen again.

Pandora leaned back on the plump cushions and gazed at the plethora of embroidered pictures. Flowers, birds, views, a few religious scenes and one glorious masterpiece hanging over the mock coal, flickering electric fire. She wondered what had inspired it. Eleanor came back in bearing the tea tray and set it down on the little table.

'I love that tapestry above the fireplace,' Pandora remarked with a nod towards it. 'Glorious colours. Did you do it over a transfer?'

'No. It's my own design.'

'All those clouds, the sunset, the blossom trees...'   She got up and walked over to it. 'What's that building?'

'It's the old ruin in the convent gardens. Haven't you seen it?'

'No. It looks very Gothic.'

'It's a folly, built by past owners of St. Bede's Convent. I'm rather fond of it.' She looked down at the teacups and hastily added, 'I used to go up there quite a lot in my youth. It holds special memories for me.' She bent over and poured the tea, a flush flooding her face.

'Are you OK, Eleanor?'

'Just these wretched hot flushes. I hope they abate soon.'

'Sit down. I'll finish the pouring.'

'Thank you, Pandora. I keep thinking they're stopping but they catch me unawares.'

'Can't you get something for them?'

'I'm not keen on doctors. I expect nature will take its course.'

'Here.' Pandora handed the tea to Eleanor. 'Get that down you.' Eleanor took it gratefully.

'Well,' said the guest, beaming, 'I'm really looking forward to our clothes try-on in a minute. Let's do the register office dresses first. '

'Yes, it'll be fun to see us both all rigged out.'

'I think white was the choice for you for the chapel, Eleanor.'

'I agree. Much as I detested that woman on the chat show, she did have a point. Nobody's going to expect a woman of my age to wear white. Then I thought how much it would please Aunty Rev.'

'It's your day. Go for it! Are you wearing a veil?''

'You bet,' Eleanor giggled, 'I'm going the whole hog.'

She reached down beside the chair and lifted a small, cardboard box with a see-through lid. 'A fascinator for the register office,' she declared, taking it out and holding against her hair.

'Oh, that is so pretty and very flattering! Not too much, just enough. Forget-me-not blue really is your colour I like it. Well done! It'll pick up on the blue of my matron of honour dress.'

'Do you really think it will look alright?'

'Perfect.' She smiled approvingly and Eleanor put it on the arm of the chair.

'Are you happy with your blue and white posy?'

Pandora half-laughed. 'Yes, of course, and you'll be carrying Dutch irises too, so we shall be nicely co-ordinated. Weren't you keen to have some of that white, fluffy gypsophela stuff in your bouquet?'

'Oh yes. I really like it. There's something ethereal and floaty about those tiny little white flowers sort of hovering on very thin stems.'

'Mmm,' agreed Pandora. 'It's important to have something you really like on your special day. I can't wait to see us both done up with our pearly blue shoes and everything. Gold jewellery, wasn't it?'

'I think so, don't you? Something plain and tasteful.'

'Agreed. We've got to look the part.' She finished her tea and put the bone china cup down on the table. 'So, let's get to it!'

Eleanor rose, conducting Pandora into the spinster bedroom.

The visitor didn't know quite what she was expecting but the room certainly came as something of a surprise. If she had expected a nun-like cell, she was pleasantly surprised.

'Wow! This is lovely!' Pandora exclaimed. The whole theme of the room was lilac and white. If that wasn't enough, all the furniture was white with rococo embellishments touched with gold leaf. A pale lilac carpet covered the floor and above the bed hung white, frilly drapes with gold swags and tassels. Deep violet, velvet curtains hung at the windows beside crisp white, frilly drapes tied back with bows.

'This certainly wasn't what I expected,' Pandora gasped. 'Quite a change from the convent!'

'The furniture belonged to my mother. She was quite a different person from my aunt, Reverend Mother Veronica. She loved pretty things. I have vague memories of our house when I was a little girl. It was full of beauty and embellishments. When I'm in here, I remember her. I was only eight, you know.' She sat on the bed and kicked off her shoes.

'I'm so sorry, Eleanor.' Pandora sat and kicked off hers as well.

'No need. I've come to terms with it all long ago but I do find myself thinking about her on special occasions particularly. I wonder what she would have thought of me?'

Pandora paused, looking for a moment at their feet.

'She would have been very proud, I'm sure.' Pandora touched Eleanor comfortingly on the arm. 'Come on! Let's get dolled up!'

*

'My dear lady,' said Teddy Appleton-Smythe, kissing the back of Eleanor's hand and bowing as far as his portly figure would allow. 'Welcome again to *Sateevee*.' He slapped Grant Landscar on the arm. 'And as for you, you old reprobate... ha ha ha!' Grant half-heartedly pretended to shadow-box with him. Then both the men remembered Eleanor. Teddy coughed with embarrassment. 'Forgot ladies present,' he said deferentially. 'Please follow me through into the viewing room both of you. So good to come on a Sunday.'

Eleanor had seen Hollywood movies where the directors and actors sat in comfortable armchairs and looked at the film rushes.

Stories of how a little Miss Nobody suddenly shot to stardom were the basis of many a celluloid extravaganza. So Eleanor wasn't quite prepared for what had happened behind the scenes since her recording week incarcerated in the sound booth or standing in front of green screens.

The lights dimmed as beautiful orchestral music swelled and filled the sumptuous viewing theatre. The screen faded up to pan across gloriously snow-covered mountains against a blue sky. Then she heard her own voice-over.

'We only have one planet. Ours is the generation that must save it. Too much has been invested in the exploitation of our natural resources and not enough in the preservation of our global environment.'

Then the view dissolved into Eleanor, standing on a balcony with the azure sea behind her. The sight of this much younger version of herself made her turn in astonishment to look at Grant beside her but he was transfixed, eyes glued to the screen. The make-up people had certainly done a great job. Indeed, even Eleanor smiled to herself at the loss of some ten years from her life-worn face.

'Here in Venzuela...' her alter-ego continued as the trio sat viewing the first episode in the luxurious, viewing theatre. So the film went on, amazing backgrounds digitally inserted behind the understated script delivery of a middle-aged woman who seemed to look straight through the camera lens and into the eyes of the viewer, imbuing the words with meaning and true sincerity. Yes, Eleanor Framp was the new face on the environmental block.

After a while she whispered to Grant, 'I just need to pop out to the ladies' room.' He nodded, only half paying attention. She got up quietly but Teddy saw her move and gestured whether he should stop the show. She waved her hands in a negative response and pointed to the exit. He realised and gave a quick nod in response before turning his eyes back to the screen.

Once outside in the silent, carpeted corridor, Eleanor looked to left and right. Now, which way had they come in? She didn't remember passing a cloakroom as the security man had led them along the seemingly endless, dim passages and walkways, so she walked, scanning the gold names and numbers on the teak-finish doors of rooms for all kinds of people and purposes, deathly quiet.

At last she came to a large alcove containing a relaxation area. She was pleased to see the object of her search, the cloakroom. It was with relief that she emerged a few minutes later, and set off back to the film viewing theatre. Now, which way was it? Surely it was...? Or was it..? In no time at all she found herself totally lost. Then she thought she saw a turn in the corridor with a notice board. Yes, she was sure she had seen that on the way... but weren't the notices different from just now? Perhaps it was another one. Eleanor looked around and saw a door with the sign,

NAVSATU
RECEPTION

She pressed the handle and went in. The room immediately lit up with wildly flashing lights as a deafening siren sounded. The door had somehow slam-locked behind her and no matter how much she rattled the handle it was hopeless, so standing there with her eyes shut and her ears in pain, she rummaged in her shoulder bag for her mobile phone. With half-opened eyes in the flickering light, she called Grant but he had dutifully turned his mobile off on entering the building.

Hammering on the door, achieved nothing so she briskly walked over to the business side of the reception desk. Perhaps there was a telephone there. Yes. She picked up the receiver. Just as she put it to her ear, the door burst open and two security guards rushed in with a large Alsation that tore towards her, barking furiously.

'Stop! Stop!' she shouted hysterically, dropping her bag and trying to put the typist's chair between her and the dog.

'Heel, Rex!' said the taller of the security guards. 'Turn that flipping alarm off!' he indicated to his partner who duly strode over to a box on the wall, inserted a key, tapped in a code and restored silence and normal lighting. 'So,' said the tall one, 'what do you think you are doing in here in this restricted area?'

*

Celeste hammered on Roland's flat door. No reply. She did it again.

'Alright, alright. I'm coming,' he said, flinging the door open and struggling to do up his trousers at the same time. 'Can't a fellow get up in the morning without all this hassle?'

She waved a sheet of paper at him. 'Have you had one of these too? Have you opened your mail yet?'

'No. Of course I haven't. There isn't any, unless that postman's put it into the studio instead of the flat. Hang on.' He took the keys out of his pocket and unlocked the communicating door. There was mail.

'Open it. Go on!' she urged, jumping about with arms folded as he picked up the long, white, official-looking envelope from the floor.

'Oh, for goodness sake come in. You're making a spectacle of yourself,' he said, moving aside.

She stepped over the threshold and they both adjourned to his studio where he ripped open the sole envelope with his key.

'Have you got one too,' she asked anxiously.

'Hang on a mo. What's this all about?'

'It's from our landlord, that lousy Grant Landscar.'

'I told you we were making trouble,' he grumbled, unfolding a letter. A cheque fell out. He blinked and looked puzzled. Celeste continued, 'I've had a letter from Landscar about the *Put and Keep* clause of my lease. He's sending an agent to inspect the premises and instruct me about anything that needs putting in order or repairing under the terms of the lease. Haven't you got one?"

He looked up. 'No, just an account settlement from a client.'
Celeste flapped, 'They're coming on Friday, my busiest day. Well,' she stormed, 'if he wants a fight, then he's got one.'

'What do you intend to do? You've got to let them carry out the inspection.'

'Hell knoweth no fury...' she said ignominiously as she flounced out onto his studio forecourt and made her way back to her flat, red-faced and fuming.

*

Gonzo stood out on the lawn in the early springtime sun in the garden of the *Villa Estancia*. He stretched his arms in contentment, viewing with smug satisfaction two Millonchan labourers laying concrete for the new area that his boss, Grant Landscar, had ordered. The trellises were there, and the bench as well as the roses and glazed flower pots. Mr. Landscar would congratulate him on his good work, never dreaming that a spade had not touched his hands and that he could already feel the wad of bank-notes in his jeans pocket, the kickback from his friend who had sent the workmen up to the villa in exchange for another consignment of top quality free tools and equipment from Gonzo, purchased with the unknowing Landscar's money.

It had been a very successful week. The almond blossom tours had gone well and he had taken a party of eight out in his launch for a trip around the islands. All that would have to stop when the boss arrived.

Gonzo sauntered away to the front of the villa and got into his open-top transporter. Five minutes drive found him down by the beach, purchasing the rubber dingy from the holiday-makers' shop. He chose a red one. Fifty Euros well spent. In two weeks time Mr. Landscar and his new wife would arrive for their honeymoon. He would give them a honeymoon never to be forgotten.

*

'It's so nice to have an afternoon off,' Synth said to Reverend Mother Veronica, looking out through the parlour window at the convent grounds, fresh with early spring grass.

'Does Mr. Landscar give you enough free time at *Casslands*?'

'Oh yes, but the problem is what to do with it and where to go.'

'Ah. I see,' said the elderly nun wisely. 'You don't want to fall into old ways.'

'You've helped me so much to lead a better life, Reverend Mother, that I'd feel terrible if I let you down.'

'You won't. You wouldn't let either of us down.' She smiled. 'Do have another cookie... I think that's what the novices call them.'

'They are a bit more-ish,' Synth said, helping herself.

'So, how is your mother? You've just come from the care home, haven't you?'

'She's fine, thank you. The cat is permanently on her lap so she's happy, although Mum's been a bit naughty again.'

'Oh?'

"Well you know how absent-minded she is...'

'Indeed.'

'She smuggled the cat into her bedroom, accidently shut it in the en suite for the night and slept right through its yowling to get out. In the morning the cleaning woman went in and this sopping wet cat threw itself past her like a bat out of... well, you know.'

'Deary me.'

'The poor animal had been trying to drink from the toilet and fell in.'

Reverend Mother rocked with mirth. 'We shouldn't laugh.' She put her hand across her mouth. 'Poor cat.'

'It's none the worse but the care home manager gave Mum a firm talking to, for all the good that will do. You should have heard Mum imitating her: "This simply will not do, Mrs. Hunt. Pussy may not go into the bedrooms." I cannot repeat what Mum replied to that.'

'Old age isn't easy,' Reverend Mother said reflectively, 'but what can we do to make your social life more interesting? We'll have to think of some things.'

The parlour door opened.

'Father Guyler. Do come in and join us. I have a guest. This is Synth Hunt, a friend of the convent.'

'We met briefly up at *Casslands*,' he said, going over to shake the younger woman's hand. Synth looked up at him with those bewitching green eyes of hers.

'I think we met before that, long ago,' she said.

'I'm afraid I don't recall...' said the priest.

'I was a little girl. I think you knew my mother, Maud Hunt.'

'Mmmm,' he mused. 'Maud Hunt. The name doesn't ring any bells with me, but then you must appreciate that in my job I get to meet literally thousands of people...' Then he realised he'd said that to her before.

'...and don't forget,' added the nun, 'Father has been out of the country for over thirty years, running a missionary station for orphans in India.'

'Yes, I answered that calling,' he said pompously.

'It must have been very worthwhile,' Synth said.

'You have no idea of the enormity of the problem,' he replied, putting the tips of his fingers together and launching forth into a diatribe on his good works. 'We used to go out in the night and collect these poor little waifs from the pavements where they were at such risk. We started with a few and by the time I had been there for five years, we had five hundred and our dilapidated, old orphanage had so many shanty-style extensions that it looked like a small village on its own. However, fate took a hand.'

'How was that?' enquired Reverend Mother.

'There was a flood and the whole complex was washed away.. Luckily there were no casualties but we were left with all these orphans, nowhere to put them and the monsoon raging.'

'So what did you do?' asked Synth.

'Polythene sheeting and bamboo sticks. The children thought it was great fun.'

'Not very permanent though,' said Reverend Mother.

'You're right. So I appealed in the market place. I stood on a box with a big placard asking for alms for the orphans.'

'Did you get much?' Synth said.

'No, but a man with a fruit export business offered me the use of an empty warehouse and we moved in there. That became our headquarters for many years, especially as he was very generous with fruit.'

'People can be very kind in a crisis,' Synth said quietly, looking across at the nun who raised her hand just a little to try and stay what she knew was about to come from the younger woman. Synth continued, 'When our rented cottage here in the convent grounds burned down last year during the airshow, Reverend Mother kindly put is up here in the convent guest rooms until the brand new prefabricated bungalow was built.'

'That's the sort of gesture I would have expected from Reverend Mother,' he said, nodding and smiling at her.

'Now, now,' the nun said a trifle brusquely, anxious to move on, but Synth wasn't having any of it. 'The sisters were so kind to us. I had employment problems...' She looked meaningfully at the nun. '...and Reverend Mother sent me on a cookery training course and found me a job at *Casslands*.'

Reverend Mother saw that it was useless to protest so added, 'The intention was for Synth to take over in due course from our cook in the convent school but the other opportunity came up and we seized it, didn't we dear?'

Synth smiled in agreement. The nun slapped her hand down on her own knee decisively.

'So, Father, tell Synth why you have come back to England after all your years abroad.'

'I came back reluctantly but the bishop insisted. There's no need to talk about it. Just the passage of time. The climate and the burden of work was getting too much for me. Don't forget I can see sixty on the horizon. So they've kindly given me this part-time job going around the country looking at convents and churches, assessing their land, property and possibilities for making the most of their assets.'

'This order, however,' Reverend Mother said, 'owns the entire property due to the forethought of one of our previous reverend mothers. Father knows that he is here solely in an advisory capacity... and we are very pleased to welcome him back.'

'You've been here before then?' Synth asked archly.

'Yes, when I was a young priest, before I went to India.'

'Father was suddenly called away to serve near Glyderabad and I regret that we lost touch,' said the nun.

Now it was the priest's turn to change the subject.

'Synth. That's an unusual name. How do you spell it?'

'S-y-n-t-h.'

'I'm guessing that it's short for something... Cynthia?'

'Synthesiser,' she said.

'Do you play the piano?'

'Yes I do... well... the electronic one.

'I thought it was short for Cynthia too,' said Reverend Mother. 'You know there's a patron saint by that name, a martyr.'

'Just plain Synth,' the young woman said.

'That can't have been your birth name,' said the priest. 'What's your real name?'

'O.K. I give in. My birth name is Cynthia but I hate it so I changed the spelling as soon as I could and it fitted in well with the music.' She hesitated. 'I used to play the piano and sing to earn a living.'

'Ah,' said the priest. 'We got you!' All three laughed and he added, 'A rose by any other name...'

Synth got to her feet. 'Well, I'd better be going now. I have to get back and prepare Mr. Landscar's evening meal.'

'You stay there, Reverend Mother. I'll see the young lady out,' said Father Guyler, also getting up. Synth took her leave of the nun and went out into the oak panelled hall to put on her coat.

'Here, let me help you.'

'You haven't changed much,' she said.

'Sorry?' he said quizzically.

'Your voice. It's still the same.'

'I don't know what you mean.'

'You may have lost some of your nice blond hair and you've put on a bit of weight but I'd know the sound of your voice anywhere. I remember you from when I was a little girl.'

He froze. Maud Hunt. It all come flooding back. Synth turned to face him.

'You were one of my mother's customers when she ran her brothel in Argmening Street,' she said, drawing back the bolt on the big front door.

Chapter 16

'How could you have done such a foolish thing, Eleanor?' Grant stood and ranted at his fiancée as she sat on his sofa snivelling and dabbing at her eyes with a tissue.

'I'm so sorry Grant.' She gave a huge sniff. 'I didn't mean to embarrass you at *Sateevee.*'

'Embarrassment is an under-statement. I've known Teddy for over fifty years. It looked as if I had sent you to poke around in his company. What must he have thought?'

'Oh Grant, don't say that...'

'Security guards rushing about, alarms going off everywhere...'

'I got lost...'

'You sure did, honey.' He sat down heavily beside her. 'Don't you realise that Teddy and I have real major business interests together, that trust means everything?'

'I didn't get lost on purpose. I was only trying to find my way back from the ladies' room.'

'Are you sure about that Eleanor? Isn't it quite possible that the journalist in you got just a little bit nosy?'

She stood up angrily. 'Grant! How can you say such a thing?'

'Well,' he drawled, 'it's possible.' He looked up at her. 'You've sent him an email apologising?'

'Yes, of course.'

'Did he reply?'

'No. Not yet.'

'Shucks. That's not a good sign.' He stood up. 'I'd better go over and see him.'

'No,' said Eleanor firmly. 'It was my mistake and I'll put it right. You didn't need to shout at me like that.'

'Gee, I'm sorry, lovely, but you must see what damage it has done.'

'It was an honest mistake but I must admit he seemed a little bit cross.' She gave a deep sniff and looked out of the window.

'Well, of course he was. His company is at the cutting edge of satellite technology. They don't want some goofer poking around purloining trade secrets.'

'I'm not a goofer!' Eleanor retorted, body bristling with rage. 'I'm going home. Perhaps this marriage isn't such a good idea after all.' She grabbed her handbag and made for the door.

'Eleanor... honey...' but she was gone, running along the hallway, out through the double front doors and into her car before he could catch up with her. He followed her out onto the drive but she had locked the car doors and sped off, leaving his window-tapping knuckles suspended in mid-air.

*

A crowd had gathered around one of Celeste's shop windows. Roland stepped out of his studio on his way to buy a paper and heard the babble of voices. So he sauntered over to have a look. A large, yellow notice, stuck on the inside of the glass, was the source of the attraction.

NO TO VEHICLE SERVICE CENTRE PLANS!
Sign the Petition here!

It then went on to list what was on the cards for the plot opposite the shops. Celeste had put it in the window late last night, not expecting such an immediate response. For the rest of the day, a stream of people came in to add their names to the petition.

'Disgraceful! Outrageous! Bad for the local residents!' were the comments. The local paper soon caught on and a reporter duly arrived.

'And what seem to be the main objections, Miss Blagden?' he enquired of Celeste in between her serving customers.

'If planning permission is granted, we're going to lose all those lovely oak trees over there, the residents close to the site will have to put up with months of dirt and noise followed by a twenty-four hours a day disturbance once the centre is up and running, and to cap it all we, the shopkeepers, will lose our display forecourts and our convenient service road parking for our customers.'

'So, you're not best pleased then,' commented the cub reporter glibly. She glared at him. He looked scared and scribbled away.

'I am also a member of the Chamber of Commercial Enterprise,' she added with dignity. 'You can see the sticker on the shop door.' He put that in his notes. 'Anything else you want mentioned?'

'Yes, you can say that I'm the mother of triplet baby girls and I want my children to have a better future.'

'Triplets? That's interesting. Where are they?'

'Well, I obviously can't bring them to work with me, so they are cared for elsewhere,' she said as if her inquisitor was on the stupid side.

'No. No. Of course not. Of course you can't but can I send our photographer over to take a snap of you with them?'

'There's no need. If you go next-door, Roland Dilger has some excellent pictures of me with my babies. Now I really must get on. Forgive me.' The queue of people waiting to be served was growing.

'One last thing... he persevered, 'will you be in the public gallery when the planning committee makes its decision on Friday?'

Without a second thought Celeste said, 'Yes, of course, together with a lot of other people.'

*

'Are you mad?' Roland asked, exasperated. 'Friday's the day when the agent's coming to look around your premises for the *Put and Keep* leases' inspection.' He surveyed his studio. 'Thank goodness they're not doing me too. It's a tip upstairs.'

Celeste pulled a face. 'Ugh. I'd forgotten about him coming.' She ran her hands through her shoulder-length, dark hair. 'Why me and not you? I'm still clearing up the mess from the flood through my stockroom ceiling the other night,' she said. 'I had to drag the carpet out and it didn't do my stitches' scars any good.'

'You should have asked me.'

'I nearly did but saw that your bedroom light was the only one on in your entire building.'

'I was having an early night.'

'I'll bet,' she retorted in a flash.

'Give a fella a break, Celeste. I'm a red-blooded male.'

'You won't be red-blooded for much longer if you go on like this.'

He changed the subject. 'Did the man come to fix your electrics?'

'Yes, but charged an arm and a leg. It seems to be one thing after another. There's an awful water mark on the stockroom ceiling.'

'The agent will be sure to pick that out,' he remarked sagely.

'I know. He'll probably notice a load of other things too. It would have been worse if Rupert hadn't remembered me in his will.'

'I didn't know he'd done that.'

'Neither did I but the money came through the other day.' She choked a little as she spoke.

'Come on, old thing. Don't start going blubby. Remember, onwards and upwards.'

She forced a smile. 'Absolutely. The past is over.' She paused and then said, 'I'll put another notice in the window telling them to bring placards to the planning committee at the Town Hall on Friday. We can march around the car park first and then fill out the public gallery.'

'Sounds as if you're going to be on twenty-seven hour days this week,' Roland replied, putting covers over his cameras. 'Oh, and by the way, I had that reporter round today wanting photos of you and your brood. I emailed them to the paper. Was that right?'

'Yes, fine. Ta. I'm off to have some dinner now. See you.' Celeste let herself out and walked back to her own shop next door and took out the key. She had just poked it into the lock when somebody tapped her on the shoulder making her jump with surprise. 'What the...?'

'Sorry, didn't mean spook you.' It was a short, plump lady. 'We met at Roland's launch,' she said. 'Don't you remember me? I'm Mrs. Thackman. He's doing some pictures of me for a friend.'
Celeste looked puzzled and viewed the woman with suspicion. Then she suddenly remembered those ghastly tan boots crammed over thick shins.

'Ah yes, I do. I'm afraid I'm very busy just now...'

'I'm sure you are, dear, but I think five minutes with me might be time well spent. You want to scupper those beastly plans for opposite, don't you?' She nodded towards the bungalow across the road.

'Yes, of course, but how can you help? You haven't even signed the petition.'

'Not yet, I agree, but I will. I've been running around doing other things to help, like going up to London to get a copy of the deeds of that place...' she jerked her thumb in the direction of the bungalow.

'Oh, it was you, was it?' Celeste said, surprised.

'Roland's a good egg and I wanted to do something useful. However,' and she paused for dramatic effect, 'I can do even better. Spare a minute?'

'You'd better come in,' Celeste said.

*

'My dear Eleanor, whatever's the matter?'

'It's all off, Aunty Rev. How could I ever have thought I could be married?'

'Dear girl, come and sit in the conservatory and tell me all about it. Sister Catherine has finished in there for the day. I always find that the presence of plants is very calming.'

Eleanor followed her through the oak-panelled hallway, along the passage and into the conservatory at the side of *St. Bede's Convent*. In the dusk of the March afternoon the air was pleasantly moist. Spring flowers burgeoned in tubs and troughs and the old vine crept in its meandering way into the rafters, many side shoots full of the promise of fruit later in the year.

'Now, tell me all about it.' So Eleanor did and had just reached the part where Grant had shouted at her when Father Guyler appeared, obviously having overheard the last few words.

'Am I intruding?' he ventured. The two women looked at each other.

'Eleanor has a little problem,' Reverend Mother said quietly.

'Can I help? There's not much we priests haven't come across before.'

If there was one person in the entire world that the dejected woman would choose not to share her problems with, it had to be this man, the one who had enchanted the young Eleanor, stolen her heart and then abandoned her.

'There's nothing anyone can do,' she said miserably looking down at her hands. He noted that she had removed the expensive emerald and diamond engagement ring and said, 'Why don't we go for a little walk in the grounds. Some fresh air might clear your head.'

Eleanor looked at Reverend Mother, somehow pleading with her to prevent the inevitable but she smiled benevolently back and concurred that it might be a good idea. So the middle-aged woman and the slightly older priest, let themselves out of the side door of the conservatory and made their way across the lawn and up the gentle slope that led to the folly on the little hill. With a heavy heart Reverend Mother watched them go until their silhouettes merged with the folly against the setting sun and a sudden breeze whipped up the early leaves on the trees, disturbing the roosting birds.

'This talk is long overdue,' Father Guyler said, pausing to face Eleanor as soon as they were out of sight of the convent building. She made more distance between them. He stepped forward.

'Please don't stand so near to me.' She could smell his soap. He still used the same soap. For goodness sake! What sort of a man uses the same soap for thirty years?

'What's the matter?' The daffodils around them nodded, waiting.

'The scent. You still use the same soap.'

'Do I? It's just a plain old olive oil soap. I suppose we get into habits.'

Didn't he realise? That perfume transported her back to a time when she was young and vulnerable and he was so utterly gorgeous that her heart still skipped a beat at the memory of those days, summer evenings spent in the old folly while the nuns were at vespers. The couple had lain on their backs in the lush grass that grew in the centre of the open-topped folly, watching the aircraft take off from the nearby airport. They had torn off grass stalks and sucked the sweet juice, teasing each other with the lazy wipe of a grass stem across the cheek or her bare arm.

They had laughed and loved, the seventeen year-old and the young priest, she believing that he would leave the priesthood to be her husband and he knowing that the wrong he was doing was worth every second of his stabbing conscience. He loved her and he told her so. She said that she would love him forever but then, one day, when she came back from college, he had gone.

'Where's Father Guyler?' she had asked Reverend Mother.

'The Bishop had an urgent job for him,' she had replied.

'When's he coming back?'

'He's going abroad.'

'But he didn't say goodbye.'

'There was no time. He said to say goodbye to you. I'm just off to the chapel. I'll see you at teatime, Eleanor.' Then her aunt, the nun, had walked away, her rosary swinging at her waist, her veil floating serenely behind her and her lips pressed together in firm resolve, her telephone conversation with the Bishop two days before still ringing in her ears.

A middle-aged Eleanor stood in the folly's shadow by her former sweetheart, he with thinning, blond hair, flabby jowls and a figure that spoke of myriad chapattis, but still those piercing blue eyes.

'I wasted my youth waiting for you to come back,' she said.

'I'm sorry Eleanor. Truly sorry. I loved you so dearly.'

'But not enough to even have the courage to say goodbye or visit me again,' she said with a whispered air of reproach.

'I was young, my dear. It was very cowardly. Forgive me.'

Eleanor looked at him hard and long. She pushed a tendril of hair away from her cheek and turned her back on him, not wanting him to see the tears brimming, tears for all the lost years, the lost loving, the lost family life.

He stepped quietly forward and slid his arms around her waist, pulling her towards him. She could smell that soap again, that wretched soap.

'No!' she shouted, swinging her elbows backwards as they had taught her at the self-defence classes. 'No!' The blows caught him in the ribs and he went flying to the ground, landing with a thud, catching his temple on a small stone so that blood trickled down.

She stood over him, the anger of decades expiated at last, draining from her, relieving her of the guilt, pent-up passion and resentment. It was finished.

*

Grant had followed Eleanor to the convent. His Hercedix arrived simultaneously with the ambulance at the door of St. Bede's. The paramedics leapt out in their greens and ran up the slope in the dusk, guided by one of the Filipino novices.

In the ruins of the folly, accompanied by Reverend Mother, Eleanor knelt on the damp grass beside Father Guyler, cradling his head in one hand whilst, with the other, she applied pressure with a tissue to the wound on his temple. He was out cold.

'He looks so pale,' she said to the paramedics as they took over. 'He slipped and fell.' Her aunt stood there, eyes closed, hands clasped, in silent prayer.

Grant said, 'So this is where you went.'

'What did you say?' Eleanor looked up it him, distress on her face. She seemed hardly aware of his presence. He had followed the paramedics up the slope.

Once stabilised, the priest was carried on a stretcher down to the ambulance that stood with open doors, surrounded by nuns like a flock of penguins.

'Does somebody want to come with him?'

'I will,' Eleanor said.

'I will,' echoed Grant, and then they looked at each other in a moment of mutual realisation that they had said their wedding vows.

'We will,' Grant corrected. 'We'll follow in my car.'

*

The hospital car-park was full as visiting time was approaching but Grant found a good space and turned off the engine. They had driven in silence behind the ambulance. He touched Eleanor on the wrist.

'He'll be fine.'

'He looked dreadful.'

'Come on. Let's go and find out,' Grant said, unclipping his seat belt and getting out. He walked around the Hercedix and opened the door for Eleanor. She stayed in her seat.

'It's all my fault, she said. 'If I hadn't ruined things at *Sateevee* and we hadn't had a row, I wouldn't even have been with him.'

'Don't blame yourself. He just tripped and fell, didn't he? It was getting towards dark. What were you doing up there by the folly anyhow?'

'Just talking.'

'Well, I'm not a religious guy, as you well know, but it sounds like an act of God to me,' and he laughed as he pulled on the sleeve of her coat. 'Come on my lady. Stop psychologically flagellating yourself and let's go and look-see.'

She gave him a rueful smile and accepted his hand as he helped her out of the car.

'I'm really sorry about *Sateevee*,' she said.

'Forget it. Teddy rang me earlier. No harm done. He's torn a strip off security though for not keeping doors locked. I mean, it was only you but it could have been somebody really on the look-out for sensitive information.'

She waited while he locked the car and then they fell into step, she with her arm linked through his in the familiar and comforting fashion.

'I'm sorry too, Eleanor... that I shouted at you. It's just that I've got millions invested in Teddy's geostatic satellites.'

'I'm not used to being yelled at,' she said. 'My father died when I was young and I don't recall him ever raising his voice to me. Although,' she added, 'those horrid men who got into the convent last year shouted a fair bit. That was awful.'

'Don't talk about it. That was dreadful for you and the nuns.'

'I honestly thought we were going to die...'

'Come on. Forget it. Let's go and see how that priest is.'

He steered her through the hospital's entrance foyer and they presented themselves at reception.

'Are you family?' the receptionist asked.

'No, long-term friends.'

'He's still in Casualty. If you'd like to go along there and follow the signs you can wait there.'

'Thank you,' they said in unison.

The Casualty department was crowded out with people sitting in rows on plastic chairs. Black eyes, arms in slings, crying children and sleeping pensioners... it was all there.

'Eleanor joined the queue at the desk.

'A priest, you say?'

'Yes. Father Guyler. He had a fall up at *St. Bede's Convent* this evening.'

'And who might you be?'

'A close friend. He's staying at my aunt's convent.'

The woman looked at Eleanor, noting the red-rimmed eyes and dishevelled hair.

'Please wait over there and I'll see if there's any news.'

She continued dealing with people until the queue dwindled to two or three. Then she disappeared into one of the curtained cubicles for a minute. When she came out, she walked briskly over to Eleanor and Grant.

'The doctor's still with him. He'll come and have a word with you shortly.'

'Thank you...' but she had gone back to her duties processing the relatives, directing the minor injuries to triage and making cow's eyes at a young male nurse who was riffling through a box of files behind her.

'A great way to spend an evening,' Grant said looking around.

'So, let's not waste the time. How are our wedding preparations getting along?'

'You still want to marry me?'

He removed his stetson from his lap and held it up in front of his face, whispering behind it, 'I can't wait to rip your bodice off.'

Eleanor gave a muffled squeak and hunched her shoulders in paroxysms of laughter. She leaned against him affectionately. They were back to being themselves again.

'You're dreadful,' she remonstrated with mock severity. He put his hat back on his knees and grinned at her, his white teeth gleaming against his suntanned face.

'Go on. Tell me all the latest news about our wedding. It's your department. I'm just paying the bills.'

She dimpled as she launched forth into a list of minor details about flowers and dresses, cars and ribbons, Charlie and the rings on a cushion and the reception afterwards.

'I've booked the musicians too,' she said.

'Have you now?' He was surprised. 'What sort?'

'It's a surprise. Wait and see.'

'Okey-dokey. I await being surprised. Now I have some other news, a bit annoying, but I would appreciate your take on it.'

'Go on.'

That tenant of mine, you know, the one with the baby shop, what's her name...?'

'Celeste. Celeste Blagden.'

'She's started up some petition to stop my refuelling and lorry-cleaning centre opposite the shopping parade getting planning permission.'

'Really?' Eleanor said. 'I never liked her but I didn't think she was stupid, going to war with her landlord.'

'I'll have the last laugh though,' Grant replied grimly.

'Yes? What do you have in mind? Nothing naughty or illegal, I hope.'

'Quite the opposite. I'm using my lawful position as landlord to enforce the *Put and Keep* clause of the tenancy agreement. My agent is going in on Friday to give *Mums, Tums and Tots* and the flat above it, and the yard, a very good critical appraisal.'

'That should take the wind out of her sales,.'

'You bet, and what's more, I thought I wouldn't do the same to that photographer next to her because you said he's doing our wedding photographs. They are no doubt in cahoots over this but I think she's the brains behind it. That should shove a wedge between them!'

'Oh?' said Eleanor, trying not to show the delight she felt at the thought of her old enemy being upset. 'I'm glad you spared Roland. He gave me a very good quotation for the work.'

'Hey, here comes the medic.'

The doctor appeared beside them, restoring seriousness to the moment. Eleanor and Grant stood up and introduced themselves.

'Well,' said the houseman, 'there's good news and there's some bad news.'

Eleanor clutched Grant's arm. The doctor continued, 'We think Father Guyler has fractured a couple of ribs and he certainly has a concussion and a temple abrasion. '

'Is he still unconscious?' Eleanor enquired.

'He's got his eyes shut but he is awake. However, there is something else.'

Eleanor and Grant exchanged a look.

'He seems to be a little bit confused so as soon as his X-rays are done we will be admitting him to be on the safe side.'

'How long will he have to stay in here?' Grant asked.

'It's hard to say. Let's get the tests done and then we'll be in a better position to judge. We'd like to keep an eye on him.'

'Father Guyler is supposed to be marrying us in a couple of weeks,' Grant said.

'Congratulations but I should have a back-up in place just in case he hasn't recovered enough. O.K.?'

If Eleanor felt a slight surge of relief, she hid it well. She had never wanted him to marry them in the first place. Maybe fate was being kind to her.

'Please can I see him?' Eleanor asked.

'I don't see why not. Come with me. He won't be going down to X-ray for a few minutes.'

So Eleanor followed the young doctor into the cubicle where Father Guyler lay looking like an effigy on a tomb. His eyes were closed and there was a dressing on his forehead.

'Father Guyler, it's me, Eleanor.'

His eyes flickered open.

'Who?' he said. 'Who are you?'

Chapter 17

'Is my hair tidy, Pandy?'

'You look fabulous.'

'Has my lipstick smudged? Is my fascinator on alright?'

'No. Yes. You're perfect. Now, will you stop worrying and let's get inside and marry you off to that old reprobate of a father of mine.' She gave Eleanor a gentle nudge in the back and then whispered, 'He's absolutely besotted with you. Make the most of it.'

The bride turned and looked at her matron of honour. 'Oh Pandy, I'm so lucky.'

'No, he's the lucky one. Go get him!'

They went in giggling together, bride Eleanor in her pale blue brocade two-piece with the floor length skirt, followed by Pandora wearing a darker shade of blue in the same style but with a calf-length skirt. Both carried small posies of cream roses and Dutch iris. Pandy wore a single matching rose in the side of their hair.

The registrar was waiting for them. So was Roland Dilger.

'Welcome to Phillipstone Register Office,' the woman said in warm greeting. 'Would you like to just step in here for a moment, ladies?'

'Smile,' said Roland, and they did as the camera flashed.

The registrar took the women into a side-room. 'I do this for all my brides,' she said. 'It just gives you a moment to catch your breath and prepare yourself. There's a full-length mirror there if you want to just do a final check.'

'Thank-you.' Eleanor turned and looked at her reflection. Pandy came and stood beside her.

'You look gorgeous,' she said.

Eleanor dimpled. 'So do you. We're very glamorous.'

'Ready now?' asked the registrar. 'Please follow me. I'll go in first. Just wait a moment by the door while your music starts up and then come in slowly. Don't rush. Let the guests enjoy seeing you arrive.'

Eleanor nodded in acquiescence.

Grant Landscar and his best man, the redoubtable Teddy Appleton-Smythe, were standing waiting in front of the huge desk.

Young Charlie Brand, with hair smarmed down to a gleaming sheen, swayed about in an impatient kind of way, balancing a red, velvet cushion on which rested two gold wedding rings. Teddy turned and gave Eleanor a wink as the music started up and bride and matron of honour paraded elegantly across the parquet flooring to the strains of a Bach *Prelude* to take their places.

Grant heard the rustle of Eleanor's skirt and then, suddenly, she was beside him. He turned to rest his eyes upon her, breathed in the heady scent of the cream roses and whispered huskily, 'Oh, my Eleanor.' It was as if a force field existed between them holding their mutual gaze. The world stood still. The registrar coughed and broke the spell. The music faded. Pandy extricated the flowers from the bride's hand.

The room was packed with Grant's business associates sitting in neat rows, the men in smart suits and the ladies in their finery. At the back, feeling out of place, Synth clutched her snappy camera.

'Can you keep an eye on this lot for me?' Roland said to her, with a meaningful look down at his hold-all of accessories.

'Yes, of course.' Synth replied as he left her to creep up the Register Office aisle in a hunched and silent style reminiscent of guerrilla warfare. He was here. He was there, popping up and melting away to reappear from another angle, never intruding, no flash and not even the sound of his breathing as he floated like the spirit of photography around the happy couple.

'Who has the rings, please?' the Registrar asked, knowing full well that it was Charlie.

'I do,' said the boy proudly, stepping forward and proffering the velvet cushion. Eleanor and Grant smiled down at his cheeky enthusiasm and his wide grin.

'Repeat after me,' said the Registrar. 'With this ring...'

It was such a simple ceremony, legal and binding, terribly disappointing in its brevity and tinged with sadness for Eleanor as she had nobody to give her away. Grant saw the tears glistening in her eyes and presumed they were tears of joy, not dreaming for a moment that his bride ached with sadness at lack of family.

'Here,' he said, taking out a handkerchief. 'I always seem to be waving this about near your eyes.'

'Sorry,' she smiled. 'It's all rather much for me.'

How could she say that she wanted her parents to be there and her aunt and all the nuns? The Landscar clan were her new family and she had to learn to live with it as it dawned on her at that moment that you don't just take on a husband, you take on his circle of friends, family and business acquaintances. She had nothing similar with which to reciprocate. Acquiring affection for a group of strangers was going to be a struggle.

'To me,' said Roland.

*

The reception was being held at *Casslands*. Synth had slipped away from the Register Office at the earliest opportunity so that she could be back at the house before the guests arrived. The caterers were in so she had nothing to do. On this occasion she was a low ranking guest but she wanted to check that all was in order. She climbed into her little *Verva* and pulled away, seeing in the rear view mirror the happy crowd on the civic offices patio, throwing confetti and laughing as Eleanor and Grant basked in the glow of a temporary spotlight. Some people had all the luck.

The sun had come out after a showery morning. The brilliance of the afternoon beams lit up *Casslands* and its extensive grounds burgeoning with spring blooms and very green willows. Synth pulled into the drive and parked at the side of the house on her allotted space. She went in through the kitchen door to find a hive of activity.

'Ah, Miss Hunt,' said the catering manager. 'How did it go?'

'Fine, fine,' she replied, taking off her coat and unpinning the small, feather fascinator from her hair. 'Let me just put these in the cupboard here for a moment and then I'll be all yours. They'll be here in a minute,' she said over her shoulder.

He followed her, saying, 'Everything's been done according to Miss Framp's specifications. Staff are in the main hall to take the coats. Welcoming drinks and canapés are ready to be served in the front reception salon.'

'That all sounds good,' Synth said.

' We are aiming for the sit-down meal in the main dining room at four o'clock.'

'Is that going to pan out?'

'It's all running to time,' he replied. 'Oh, and the wedding cake is set up in the corner by the bay window.'

'I'll just go and have a look,' Synth said.

The large, formal dining room was a stunning eclectic vision of seventeenth century powder blue and white elegance, enhanced by crystal chandeliers, huge gold-framed rococo mirrors, Chinese washed and sculpted aqua carpets and a mock Adams fireplace. The walls were enhanced by genuine old masters in gilt frames.

Synth stood in the doorway and surveyed the scene. After the welcoming drinks in the salon it would be heaving with over-perfumed and coiffured guests, chortling away as they forgot all about the bride and groom, intent only on a jolly good chat and a great meal. They would not be disappointed.

She walked back into the hall and, through the half-glazed double front doors, she could see Roland Dilger already in place awaiting Grant Landscar's car, festooned in white ribbons, cruising up the long tree-lined avenue, accompanied by the sound of rattling tin cans. Traditions die hard. Synth went out to join Roland just in time to see the gardener turned chauffeur opening the limousine door. Grant stepped out, put on his white stetson and then strode around the vehicle to assist a nervously smiling Eleanor from her seat where she sat clutching her cream roses.

'Smile,' said Roland as the couple paused before starting to go inside.

'Congratulations Mr. and Mrs. Landscar,' Synth said as they strolled past her into the house.

'Thank you, Synth,' Eleanor said, clutching at Grant's arm. This was going to be difficult, meeting all those strangers in what was now to be her home. Pandora's car had also arrived and she and Charlie came in and joined them in the entrance hall.

'Can I go and play on my games console?' Charlie asked patting his bulging jacket pocket.

'Certainly not,' Pandy replied. 'Go and tidy your hair'

'I'm going to freshen up too,' Eleanor said to Pandy. ' Coming?'

Her new daughter-in-law nodded and whispered, 'Let's touch up your make-up.' Then to Grant, 'We're just going to smarten ourselves up. Be five minutes, Dad.'

'You're taking my bride away from me already?' he pretended to look anguished.

Eleanor simpered at him. 'Bride. Me a bride. I still don't believe it.'

'You'd better, my lady. I've got you now.' He pulled her towards him. 'And I'm gonna keep you.'

'Oh stop all that smarmy stuff, you two,' Pandy jibed. 'There'll be plenty of time for that when you get away.' Then she was off up the wide rose and ivy entwined staircase that curved away into two parts at the top. In the broad gallery to the right a string quartet, already seated, had been playing quietly. Now they swung into full volume as the guests' cars started to arrive before the women had made it to the top of the stairs.

Grant walked briskly along the carpeted corridor on the ground floor into the south part of the house and his study. The bathroom leading from it was his aim. Charlie tagged along.

'Did I do alright, Grand-dad?'

'You were swell.'

'I didn't drop the rings.'

'Nope. You sure didn't.'

'Can I play with my gamer now?'

'No. Didn't you hear what your mother said?'

'I'm bored.'

They reached the study door and went in.

'D'you wanna use the facilities?'

Charlie shook his head. Grant said, 'Well I do. You wait here and don't touch anything. Then you need to wash your hands. I think I know who tied those noisy tin cans to my lovely auto.' He gave the boy a knowing smile.

The boy sat down at his Grand-dad's desk and ran his grubby finger around the rim of the onyx pen-holder. He swivelled around in the brown leather executive chair until it rose in the air and he could look down at the huge desk. He felt grand. The telephone rang. Should he pick it up? It rang three times and then the voicemail kicked in.

A woman's voice said, 'Hello there, Grant. It's Debbie. Just to wish you both luck on your special day. Give me a ring when you arrive and we'll set up a meeting.' There was a click. Grant came out of the bathroom. He clearly hadn't heard the phone. He looked at Charlie perched on the executive chair.

' Go on then, fella-me-lad. Get those grubby paws clean.'
The boy climbed down reluctantly. Should he tell him about the woman who rang? No. Probably better to keep quiet.

'O.K.' he mumbled.
Grant standing and winding down the chair to its proper height, noticed that the voicemail was flashing its red light. He pressed the button and heard Debbie's voice. It was a long time since he'd seen her.

'All clean,' said Charlie, reappearing.

'Great. Let's go and greet the guests,' Grant said, feigning a punch at his grandson who dodged and grinned. They returned to the hall as Eleanor and Pandora came down the stairs.

'My darlin' woman,' Grant said, going forward to take his wife's hand. 'Come and meet our friends. Hey, Teddy, old boy!'

People were still arriving in crowds but as the newly married couple appeared in the front reception salon a ripple of applause broke out. Guests in the hall were divested of their coats. The staff spirited away cashmere designer wear into the well-appointed cloaks room to the side where coats and wraps were slipped carefully onto padded hangers and protected by plastic covers bearing the owner's name.

In the salon a bearded man said loudly 'What, no booze?' .
'Shhh!'
'Why shush me? This is a wedding isn't it? Where's the booze?'
'Keep it down, old man. This is a dry house.'
'What? Nothing at all? Why for goodness sake? He looks as if he can afford it.'
His wife whispered something in his ear. His expression changed.

'Really? I never realised.' Subdued and with a look of abject despair, he helped himself to a pineapple juice from the trolley.

*

'Well, that went splendidly,' Grant said to Eleanor as the last of the guests departed and the couple wandered into the lounge to relax on the sofa. Synth appeared and paused in the doorway.

'Mr. Landscar, Mrs. Landscar, can I get you anything before I go up to my flat? A warm beverage perhaps?'

The newly-weds looked at each other.

'No thank-you, Synth,' Eleanor said. 'You get away to bed now. It's been a long day for you'

'Yes, I will, Miss El... I mean, Mrs. Landscar.'

'You're off later tomorrow but you'll be back good and early for Monday morning won't you for our chapel ceremony?' Grant said.

'Yes, I'll be back. I'll finish the Malloncha packing too.'

'Going somewhere nice tomorrow?' Eleanor asked.

'Not really. I'm going to visit my mother in the home. She's been playing up a bit lately. I'll take her out somewhere for the day and then spend the night in their guest room.'

'Well we both sure appreciate all you've done these past weeks with all the preparations, don't we Eleanor?'

'Yes, we do. Thanks for everything. Enjoy yourself tomorrow.'

'Goodnight and congratulations again to you both again.'

'O.K. Goodnight. Sleep well,' Grant said with a dismissive wave of his hand. The door closed quietly and they were alone. He slid his arm around Eleanor's shoulders and nuzzled her hair.

'You look stunning in that outfit. My princess.'

'You really like it?'

'Gorgeous!.'

'You were very debonair in your rig-out too.'

'You don't think the cream waistcoat with the gold watch chain was too much?'

'Very wild west with the bootlace tie. I loved it... and the jacket and trousers were cut just beautifully. Your usual tailor?'

'Yep. He knows what I like. He kind-a tried to talk me out of the cream shade... said it would get grubby... but it was fine.'

'Weren't we the elegant pair!'

'We sure were!'

'Did you see the way Pandy did that rugby tackle to try and catch my little bouquet?'

'That's my girl, never letting an opportunity go by. She gets it from her Dad.' He pulled Eleanor gently towards him.

'So, my cute, little honey-bun, how d'you want to play it tonight?' Eleanor blushed. 'You're going to laugh at me when I tell you that I don't feel properly married yet.'

He reached into his jacket inside pocket and unfolded the marriage certificate. 'It says here that you are, legal and final.'

'Yes, but it won't feel right until Monday when we do the chapel service at the convent.'

'You mean you're going to deprive me of my marital rights tonight?' He pinched the side of her face playfully. 'Come on, lady. Live dangerously. Let me have my wicked way with you.'

She lowered her head and closed her eyes bashfully.

'You're shy. Shucks! You're shy.'

She nodded.

'Look at me, Eleanor.' With one finger under her chin, he tenderly tipped her face towards him. 'Do I seem like a monster?'

She shook her head very slightly, looking away.

'I'm not very experienced...'

'Well, I am, enough for both of us... and, in case you're worried, I have a clean bill of health in that department,' he added, looking southwards.

'That's a comfort,' she giggled.

He stood up and took her hand, pulling her to her feet.

'Let's go up. The staff have all left and we have the house to ourselves. Synth looked wacked. She'll be in the Land of Nod by now.'

So the pair quit the lounge, turning out the lights as they left to cross the hall and climb the big staircase. Along the wide gallery they tip-toed like a pair of naughty school-children, holding hands, as if on an adventure. Well, they were, in a way.

When they reached Grant's bedroom door, he turned the crystal handle silently and led his bride inside. There were candles burning in glass holders everywhere and a wistful CD played faintly in the background. On the double bed lay the beautiful, flimsy night-dress that Pandora had bought for Eleanor. She caught her breath. She was actually expected to put it on.

Eleanor stood in her bare feet clutching her vanity bag on the cold, glossy marble floor of one of the ensuite bathrooms. The air was scented with lavender. Subdued lighting had come on as she'd entered and it shone with subtle elegance from concealed sources. The room was comfortably warm. She hung her nightie on a hook and helped herself to two luxuriously fluffy white towels and hung them on the rail by the walk-through, multi-jet shower.

'There's a shower cap in the left-hand cupboard,' someone said. She started and looked around. Nobody was there. That was Grant's voice. It came from a gold-plated grille above the door. She went over and looked out. He was perched on the side of the bed grinning.

'How did you do that?'

He indicated one of the studs on the white velvet headboard.

'Concealed microphone. See if you can find the one in there.' She shook her head in disbelief.

'Why? Why do you need this communication?'

'You never know. Just snap your fingers to activate it.'

Eleanor withdrew and scanned the bathroom walls. Her eyes searched warily. She found it embedded in a convoluted rose-style stud above the basin and snapped her fingers.

'Can you hear me?'

'Loud and clear.'

'How do I turn it off?'

'Snap your fingers twice.' She did so, puzzled. There was clearly a lot she didn't know about her new husband's home.

She peeled off her wedding dress and hung it on a hanger on the back of the door. Then she took off her underwear and turned the gold-plated turret fitting that selected the water temperature. Shampoo and shower gel glinted in cut-glass dispensers on the wall next to a full-length, heated mirror. Her reflection looked back at her. How could Grant possibly find her desirable? She was tall and skinny. The first etchings of menopausal wrinkles were crawling around her eyes like the rivulets of a delta. Her curves sagged ever so slightly downwards, a sad record of a fulfilled but somehow disappointing life. This was a body that ached for love before it was too late. She put on a shower cap.

The spray beckoned her in and she submitted to its caress, lathering herself liberally with the *Charibe Number Nine* perfumed gel, sliding her fingers sensuously through the foam. Then she rinsed it all off, turned the jets up to the cool setting and felt the sting of watery needles pounding against her skin, stimulating the nerve endings until she wanted to throw her arms upwards and scream with delight.

How different, how very different from Friday night bathtimes in the convent! She cast her mind back to the beige, slit-sided linen shifts that she and the rest of the pupils had worn in their two inches of tepid bath water, a precaution against vanity and temptation. The carbolic soap, rough towels, green linoleum and chill atmosphere would be always with her.

She turned off the shower and stepped out onto a soft, pink mat. Taking the large, white towel she draped it around herself, tucking the edge in to hold it in place. She swivelled from side to side, smiling at herself in the mirrored wall.

It was as if the scales had dropped from her eyes. Endless years of modesty and self-denial had been stripped away by Grant's love. She felt girlish and skittish and somehow relieved of the pressure with which a life-time of convent rules had constrained her. Was it a sin to admire your own body? To want to feel the closeness and strength of a man? Was it so wicked to admit to womanly needs? How could her aunt, Reverend Mother Veronica, ever have thought that her niece, Eleanor, shared her desire for a life of purity and chastity? Somehow, though, she had convinced the child that the life of a nun could still be lived in the secular world. Not any more. There are some doorways through which there is no return.

Eleanor patted herself dry and slipped into the see-through nightie. She gasped but then reappraised herself. It really didn't look too bad, especially once she had taken the shower cap off. Full of devilment, she snapped her fingers in front of the microphone.

'Hello, Grant.'

Back came the reply. 'Hello, Eleanor.'

'Are you in bed yet?'

'Ready and waiting.'

Eleanor snapped her fingers twice to turn the microphone off. Well, this was it. She reached up to the glass shelf and took down her favourite perfume. Then she opened her vanity bag and took out her hairbrush. One hundred strokes. That's what Aunty Rev had taught her to do. She brushed and brushed until the hair stylist's crisp laquer had yielded to soft waves. Then it was time for night cream, followed by hand cream. She put on the white, towelling slippers and came back into the bedroom.

'Grant,' she said, but he was asleep.

*

'You mean, you've never done it before?'

'Never.'

'You must be joking,' he replied in his Texan drawl, his eyes wide in disbelief.

Grant threw himself back onto the feather pillows, closed his eyes and slowly shook his head in amazement. His new wife, the middle-aged former spinster Eleanor Framp, drew the pale blue satin sheet up nervously over her nightie-clad body and blinked away a tear.

'Grant,' she said, through trembling lips, 'I'm so terribly, terribly sorry.'

He patted her shoulder. 'Well, I should have realised.'

'What? That I was so ugly and undesirable that nobody ever wanted me until now?'

'No, no, Eleanor. Not that. I meant with your background and everything.' He ran fingers through his silver hair in despair as she brought her hands out from under the covers and played with the wedding and engagement rings on her third finger.

'Being brought up in a convent by an aunt who was the reverend mother wasn't much of a preparation for real life, I suppose.'

'That's very likely but if what I've heard about convent girls is true, you must be the one that got away.'

'Don't make fun of me.'

He rolled onto his side and drew her to him. 'I care about you far too much to ever do that.' He looked down into her grey eyes and, instead of seeing desire, saw only fear.

'Well, eternal virgin Eleanor, what are we going to do with you?'

She rested her head against his shoulder and giggled like a schoolgirl. 'What would Aunty Rev say if she could see me?'

'Don't ask. The poor woman would probably have hysterics. Her pure and good-as-gold niece in bed with a wicked, evil, three times married and equally divorced man.'

'A lovely, kind and very patient man,' she remonstrated gently, 'whose wives didn't understand him.'

'Well, yes, that's as may be but unfortunately they probably wouldn't see it that way.' He released her slightly and then drew her to him again in a bear hug.

'If only they'd been like you.' He took a deep breath.

'It was a lovely wedding reception,' she said, playing for time.

There was a knock at the door.

'Enter!' Grant said before Eleanor could protest.

The door swung open to reveal Synth in her black maid's outfit, wearing a frilly white apron. Her red hair was swept up in a severe chignon and she carried a bed-tray with an air of experience.

'Good morning, Mr. Landscar, Miss Eleanor... I mean, Mrs. Landscar,' she said formally. They both sat up, Eleanor scarlet in the face with embarrassment, scrabbling to keep the sheet over her.

'Pass it to me here, Synth. Thank you.'

'Will there be anything else, Mr. Landscar? Another tray for your wife, perhaps?'

'No. That'll be all. We'll share this one.' He paused. 'Oh, bring the papers up, will you?'

'Yes, sir.'

Then she was gone, quietly closing the crystal-handled door and leaving Eleanor gasping for composure. The glance that had passed between the two women had been completely unnoticed by Grant.

'Does she always do that? Just turn up with breakfast?'

'Generally.'

Eleanor looked warily around the large, white bedroom, taking in the lacy, four-poster drapes, the chandelier, objects d'art and velvet curtains that were still not drawn from last night. Was this a regular occurrence? How many ghosts of women past lingered in the fitted wardrobes and the double bathroom?

'She didn't seem concerned... that I was in your bed.'

'Well, we're all adults and we're married so why should she be?'

He poked at the scrambled egg with a fork.

'Here. Have a bit,' and tried to feed it to her.

'No. No thank you, Grant. I'll just have some juice.' She picked up the cut glass beaker from the tray and sipped while he tucked into the repast.

'It was a bit awkward for me.'

'You'll soon get used to the staff.'

'I used to know her slightly before when she stayed at the convent. Aunty Rev used to rent her the cottage in the convent grounds... well, the rebuilt one... you know the old building was destroyed by fire last year.'

'Yes, I remember but your aunt recommended her for this job..'

Eleanor sipped the juice, gulping it down.

'I thought she might have had a hand in it,' she smiled.

'It seemed a mutually convenient arrangement,' he said.

'Synth stayed in the convent with Maud, her mother, for quite a few months last year.'

He swallowed, took a sip from his coffee and commented, 'Yes, she said your Aunty Rev was good to them.'

'She's a very kind woman.'

She bit her lower lip and blinked rapidly. He patted her hand.

'I know you're very fond of her.'

Eleanor tried to change the subject. 'Shall we always have breakfast in bed like this?' she asked.

'That depends. You know that I travel quite a lot so it's up to you as to how you want to arrange things while I'm away. You're the lady of the house now.'

'I don't know whether to give up my flat in Isabel Avenue,' she said wistfully.

'How about renting it out?'

For Grant, sentimentality about money was anathema. What was the point in leaving property sitting about earning nothing? If he'd had his way, Eleanor would have got rid of the place and moved in with him months ago.

'Possibly,' she said.

Eleanor had never been one for burning her boats. Selling off her little flat or even renting it out would somehow ruin her memories of the tens of years of independence, the nights sitting embroidering and cross-stitching in front of documentaries on the television. The decades kaleidoscoped into one long moment of loneliness, of an aching heart that had forever yearned for the return of Father Guyler. As the years had passed, the hope had diminished but never gone away completely. She had imagined sitting across the breakfast table from him, hearing the sound of their children playing and fantasised about lying in his arms at night. Now he had come back, too late, and in denial.

Grant had moved on to toast. 'Well, your holy aunt will be very happy when we do the necessary in the convent chapel tomorrow,' he said between munches.

'Easter's such a lovely time for it,' Eleanor said. 'She wasn't too pleased about the register office. Thank you so much for...'

'Shucks, lady, you know I'll do anythin' to make you happy. It'll all be alright tomorrow. You'll see.' He considered for a moment. 'Well, I suppose it was a lot to ask of her considering everything, like three ex-wives,' he replied with chagrin and a wry smile.

'I was trying to be delicate,' she said with a look askance at him.

'Facts are facts. I've been through the matrimonial machine so many times they're thinking of givin' me a season ticket.' He grinned. 'By the way, I was real taken with that tie-pin you gave me to remember our special day. I shall wear it tomorrow. Thank you kindly for that.'

He put down the toast and turned to look at her with a long, lingering look that conveyed his feelings far better than any words.

'Happy Easter, wife.'

'Oh! I'd forgotten it was Easter Sunday today.'

She leaned over and kissed him on his grey-stubbled cheek, feeling the thrilling roughness touching her lips. 'Happy Easter.'

'Well I hadn't forgotten. Now, you go ahead and unwrap my little gift. He fumbled in his bedside cabinet and hauled out a big, black plastic carrier bag. She took it and plunged her hand into its depths.

'Goodness me! It's the biggest one I've ever seen!'

There was a loud crash, muttering and then a tap on the door.

'Enter!' Grant called, sipping his coffee. Synth came in.

'Thank you, dear,' he said, taking the papers from her. 'What was that terrible noise outside?'

She fumbled nervously with her apron. He perused the front page thoughtfully.

'I'm really sorry, Mr. Landscar. My elbow just sort of caught it.'

'Caught what?'

'That statue on the landing.'

'Jeepers! Not my priceless *Du Pintzi Michael dela Troubedour?*'

'If you mean the one with the turban on, sir? Yes, I'm afraid so.'

'Synth! Have you any idea how much that cost?'

'You could stop it out of my wages, sir.'

'You'd be working for three hundred years to pay for it.'

Eleanor kept her grey eyes down firmly on Grant's gift while this interchange took place. He put the newspaper down. 'I'll come and look at it in a minute and survey the damage when I've finished my breakfast.'

'The head came off, sir.' Synth said, with a surprised glance at what Eleanor clutched in her hands.

'You're lucky your head isn't coming off, young lady.'

'Sorry, Mr. Landscar. Really sorry, sir.'

'Get away with you and try to be more careful in future.'

Synth backed out of the room. Grant turned sharply to Eleanor and observed, 'That'll have to be an insurance claim, I'm afraid.'

'I suppose having so many extraordinary valuables about is a bit of a nightmare in some respects. I mean, it's wonderful to have lovely things about the place, but... '

'You're not wrong, my dear.' Then, 'What do you think of that?'

'It's enormous,' she said admiringly.

He picked up the paper again. 'Now, I suggest that you get yourself up while I have a little look at this and then I'll be busy with a telephone conference to the States for a while but we can go visit your aunt before lunch. What do you say?'

She was aware that there was no option but to make herself scarce. He watched her as she placed the giant chocolate, gold-foil wrapped Easter Egg on her bedside cabinet before getting out to walk across the white carpet, struggling to preserve her modesty with the negligée. He'd have to do something about that.

Chapter 18

The sound of the chapel organ meandering through Sister Catherine's variations sounded vaguely spooky to Eleanor as she stood outside the door on the landing that smelled of floor polish and old incense on Easter Monday morning. Reverend Mother Veronica was at her elbow. Behind her the four, diminutive, Filipino postulants waited patiently, suppressing smiles. They were thrilled to be bridesmaids, the only acknowledgement of which was their posies of primroses.

'Are you alright, my dear?' Reverend Mother looked up at her anxiously who responded with a tight-lipped half-smile, a nod and a deep breath. The white, silk wedding gown rustled. Why not white? Half the brides weren't virgins. Eleanor raised her hand tentatively to stop the veil from tickling her face.

The music stopped. One of the other nuns opened the heavy, oak chapel door from the inside and Eleanor had her first glance of Grant's grey-suited figure with Charlie standing beside him, grinning back at her. Father Guyler looked at her steadily from his place in the wheelchair in front of the daffodil-adorned altar. She had warned Grant not to turn around.

'That's nonsense,' he'd said. 'Just a superstition.'

'Let's not take any risks,' she'd joked.

An audible sigh followed Eleanor's progress as the sisters smiled in approval but the bridegroom didn't turn to see the love of his life proceed slowly down the short aisle to the strains of Handel's *Largo*, to stand beside him. It was only then that he gave a little glance to his left and caught his breath. A man of several marriages, this was going to be the one that touched him deeply. Non-religious though he was, there was something special about the chapel atmosphere on this spring morning. Eleanor turned to hand her bouquet of spring flowers to one of the novices who helped her to lift the bridal veil away.

Eleanor and Grant looked at each other. Both had tears in their eyes, as did the priest, Father Guyler, sitting before them waiting.

Charlie, hair smarmed down again, was doubling as best man and ring-bearer today. He stood to attention holding a small, silver salver bearing the rings which the couple had relinquished to his care earlier via Pandy.

The sisters had bedecked the entire convent chapel with a plethora of spring blooms, the frilled speciality narcissi filling the air with a heady perfume. The ends of the pews bore big white bows and the entire room was a-glow with candle-light that glinted from the gold-embellished ceiling and glanced off the tiny crystals on Eleanor's gown.

Father Guyler cleared his throat. It was only then that Eleanor became fully aware of him. She gazed down at the man seated before her, the very one who had stolen her innocence, broken her heart and left her to grieve alone for decades. Now he was going to perform her wedding ceremony in front of her aunt and all the sisters in the chapel where she had worshipped as a girl.

Did she imagine it or was there a beseeching look on his face? Was he asking her, 'Are you sure?' or was he saying, 'Please forgive me.' She lowered her shoulders and cast her eyes to the floor, glad not to be feeling the burden of guilt that had followed her down the years. He couldn't touch her now.

The priest raised the slim book in his hand and read, 'Who giveth this woman to be married to this man?'

'I do,' said Reverend Mother proudly.

*

With a cacophony like the chatter of magpies, the sisters clustered around the happy couple in the convent dining room, feeling the white guipure lace on the edge of the bride's sleeves, tipping their heads on one side in a mêlée of admiration and joy. The massive buffet was spread out on pristine, starched, white cloths, commandeered from the altar trappings. Garlands of ivy and primroses scalloped their way along the front of the long table in the centre of which stood a large display of pink apple blossom.

Roland was chatting with Father Guyler. 'I'll be off in a mo. They only wanted that one outside picture of them all together.'

Eleanor turned to her aunt, her face alive with happiness. 'You've done it all so beautifully.'

'We did our best for you,' said Reverend Mother, 'and I think it's turned out rather well.' Then she whispered, 'Thank you so much, dear, for allowing me to give you away. Your mother would have liked that.'

Eleanor gave her aunt a long hug. 'There was nobody to give me away at the register office. I'm so glad you stood in today. You know, I've thought about Mummy and Daddy a lot during the past weeks. They would have been so proud and pleased about how you brought me up and cared for me and did the honours today.'

'Nonsense, dear. We turned the tragedy of their loss into a real joy. It was wonderful having you in the convent for all those years. All the sisters and I loved it. As for today, I couldn't be more happy for you.' Then, gesturing to her right, 'Of course, you have to thank Sister Catherine. She's the artistic brain behind all this and the chapel.'

'Did somebody mention my name?

'Oh, Sister Catherine, it's all so lovely. Isn't it, Grant?'

'Sure is,' said the bridegroom, lightly placing his arm around Eleanor's shoulders and taking her hand. 'You ladies have made a real, fine spread here too.' He glanced at the feast. "When do we get to start on it?' His new wife tapped him on the wrist.

'You're terrible,' she laughed.

Reverend Mother laughed too and then turned away to clap her hands.

'Bride and bridegroom, Father Guyler, ladies and gentlemen, fruit drinks, coffees and teas are on the sideboard and I declare the buffet well and truly open.'

'Hoorah for that,' said Grant affably. 'Come on, little wife, I'm starving. What'll you have?' He picked up a plain, white plate, the sort that the nuns dined from every day. The simplicity was refreshing after the extravagant reception that had taken place at *Casslands* only a couple of days before.

'Gosh, we're spoiled for choice. I think I'll have a little of that smoked salmon and cold chicken with some salad.' Eleanor turned to him. 'What do you fancy?'

'You,' he said with a naughty grin.

'Grant,' she remonstrated under her breath. 'Behave!'

'I've got you now,' he said equally quietly. 'Just you wait until I get you home. You may have wriggled out of my clutches so far, but I don't give up easy.'

Eleanor's heart lurched. In the midst of all the chapel wedding excitement she had forgotten about that, the wedding night that still had to be conquered. It just hadn't happened over the weekend because she had feigned tiredness and played for time. The transition from proverbial spinster to sexually active wife was something she would have to come to terms with. Roland came over to take his leave, then she heard a tyre squeak and saw that Father Guyler had wheeled himself to her side.

'Father,' she said, 'thank you for a beautiful ceremony.'

'Your aunt is pleased. That's the important thing.'

Grant had placed the plate of food in Eleanor's hand, taken another for himself and drifted away to the end of the table. She fumbled for a fork from the pile on the white cloth. She was somehow lost for words. If only the priest would go away.

'It wasn't only for Aunty,' she said. 'It was somehow for my parents too. They would have liked to have seen me have a white wedding, even though...'

'It's right that you were married in white,' he said firmly.

She gave him an ironic look.

'How are you getting on with the wheelchair?'

'It's an acquired art. The hospital stipulated it.'

'Are you still officially a patient?'

'I certainly am. I had to sign a declaration before they would let me out. I'm still rather unsteady. The fall seems to have affected my balance but my memory's mostly come back. I gather that I didn't recognise you when I was in A & E.'

'I'm so sorry...'

'About what? I simply tripped and fell.'

'You don't remember?'

'What, Eleanor? What don't I remember?'

So that was how he was going to play it. Deceit or genuine amnesia? Would she ever know?

'Look at me, please, Eleanor,' young Charlie said, interrupting at just the right moment. She found herself being videoed.

'Be interesting!' he commanded, zooming in on her face.

'Hey, young man, not too close, if you don't mind.'

'I'm going to interview you. Have you enjoyed getting married to my Grand-dad?'

Eleanor smiled. 'Yes, of course I have and I've married him twice so we are well and truly hitched.'

Charlie started to walk around her. 'Keep looking at me,' he insisted. 'This is a very special technique. I like to do things from unusual angles.'

Father Guyler smiled, amused, and reached up and took a plate which he put on his lap, wheeling himself away to survey the food.

'Well, why don't you take some footage of Grand-dad and me together?' She beckoned to Grant who sauntered back to join her.

'Kiss her!' Charlie directed.

The two looked at each other, raised their eyebrows and then leaned forward, holding their food plates aside, and did so. The couple laughed. Some of the nuns had spotted the moment and giggled, hands to their mouths. It was a long time since they had seen such a thing. Charlie, however, hadn't finished yet.

'I need more passion.'

'Charlie, my lad, that's all you're getting, so why don't you turn that thing off and have something to eat?' Grant said.

'I'm an artist. Food can wait.'

'There won't be any left if you don't get in there.'

The boy lowered the video-cam and reluctantly agreed, 'OK.'

'What would you like? Eleanor asked. 'There are some nice, flaky sausage rolls over there.'

'What's all this snogging in public then?' Pandora whispered in Eleanor's ear, startling her.

'Oh! I didn't hear you coming.'

'What's my daughter up to now?' Grant enquired.

'Commenting on our public show of affection.'

'You ain't seen nothin' yet,' Grant quipped.

*

'I need you for a moment, Eleanor,' Pandy said conspiratorially. The bride looked up from her slice of wedding cake. 'Now?'

'If you don't mind.'

'Can't whatever it is be done here?'

'Absolutely not. It has to be before you go away on honeymoon.' Eleanor's heart sank. From what she had learned about Pandy, it wasn't beyond her sense of humour to endow her new step-mother with a kit of sex toys to take away.

'It's nothing... embarrassing...?'

'Not if we handle it right. Come on. The men are talking. They won't notice us slip away. Where can we go where it's private? You know this place.'

'I suppose the chapel will be empty.' She quietly put her plate down and followed Pandy out of the room, smiling kindly at Sister Catherine as she passed her.

Along the polished parquet corridor they rustled, Eleanor's white veil flying behind her as had the veils for generations of nuns who had paced these floors before. All was quiet. They found a pew on the right hand side of the flower bedecked chapel.

'Now, Pandy, what's this all about?'

Pandora played with her finger nail tips. Now the moment was here, it was all a bit awkward.

'Do you remember when I came over to your flat to try on our wedding outfits?'

'Yes, of course I do.'

'And how we tried on our new shoes in your bedroom?'

'Yes.' Where was this all going?

'I noticed your feet.'

'Well, they're hard to miss!' Eleanor joked.

'They are a bit... special.'

'Oh, you mean my toes?'

Yes.'

'I know they're rather strange but I'm so used to them I don't even notice.'

'You don't mind me mentioning them?'

'Pandy, why would you be interested in my feet?'

'Because they are the same as Charlie's. The second and third toes are joined together up to half way'

'I know it's unusual but it does happen.'

Pandora took Eleanor's hand in hers and turned to look into her face. 'Why, Eleanor, do you have a photograph of my ex-husband on your bedside cabinet?'

Eleanor snatched her hand back and pulled away, blanching so that her face matched the veil.

'It's nothing to do with you...I don't want to talk about it... I, I...'

She burst into tears, sobbing as if her heart would break. Pandora put her arm around the shaking shoulders.

'There, Eleanor. I didn't mean to upset you. It's OK. We'll sort it all out. Please tell me about it.' She handed over a tissue. The bride, blotchy and snivelling, dabbed at her nose and eyes, streaking the mascara as it filled her laughter lines.

'What am I going to do?' Eleanor wailed. 'So many people are involved. They'll never forgive me.'

'It can't be that bad...'

'It is. It's dreadful. I've deceived them all, Aunty Rev, the nuns, Grant... Oh Grant!' she cried, collapsing into paroxysms of sobs again.

'Eleanor,' Pandora said. 'What did you do? I'll help you fix things and make them right.'

'Some things just can't be undone,' she sobbed hopelessly.

'You've got to tell me, Eleanor. I need to know what the heck the connection is between you and my ex-husband, Xavier. Now, take a deep breath, calm down and spill the beans. It's time to make a clean breast of it.'

The bride did as she was told. It was all going to come out now. Grant would annul their marriage, Aunty Rev would disown her and the scandal would have repercussions that would kill her magazine stone dead and ruin her life. She began.

'The man in the photograph is my son.'

Pandy's sharp intake of breath was not lost on her.

'Yes, my son. I gave birth to him in Italy, far away from the convent so my aunt wouldn't find out. I got pregnant when she was away in on a mission. I took a job in Italy and had my baby over there. I gave him up for adoption but I didn't call my child Xavier. I named him after my father.'

'What was his birth name?' Pandy asked gently.

'Paul.'

Pandy said in a low voice, 'My husband was adopted. He grew up in Italy. He spoke English with an Italian accent.'

'I know.'

'You had contact with him when he was an adult? You met him? How?' Pandy quizzed.

'Yes, I met him.'

'Where? When? How did you get the photograph?' Pandy demanded enthusiastically.

'He gave it to me. I had to find out what happened to him, whether he had a happy life, so I used an agency to trace him.'

'How long ago?'

'Oh, about ten years. He was living in Rome, working for some software company.'

'But where did you meet? It must have been difficult.'

'He came over to the airshow. We had lunch together. He had the toes thing too, you know. It was all a bit formal. He forgave me for giving him up but he wanted to know who his real father was.'

'Did you tell him?'

'No .I wouldn't tell him. He was very angry with me. We never met or spoke again. Then he just disappeared.'

'Tell me about it! He vanished out of my life too when I was pregnant with Charlie. You know I had the deserting rat certified as dead after seven years?'

'Grant told me. I didn't like to say anything to you. I'm sorry you were abandoned. I had no idea...'

'Probably good riddance... oh I shouldn't say that... he was your son...'

'No. I just gave birth to him. He was somebody else's son.'

'Eleanor, I'm so sorry.'

The bride suddenly smiled through her smeared make-up. 'That means Charlie really is my grandson.'

'And you are not only my new step-mother, but my former mother-in-law too!'

Suddenly they were both laughing hysterically, clinging to each other.

'How the hell are we going to tell Dad?'

Eleanor stopped in mid-smile and looked down coyly.

'Pandy, you're a woman of the world.'

'Yes, I suppose I am.'

Eleanor laboured on, 'After childbirth our bodies are never quite the same, are they?'

'I suppose not.'

'I mean, there are stretch marks and...'

'OK. I get your drift.'

'I'm ashamed to say that I have been putting off the wedding night because of what Grant might find out.'

Pandy clasped her hand over her mouth and giggled. 'He thinks you're a virgin?'

Eleanor nodded dumbly and then looked up with a hint of mischief in her eyes. 'Apart from one unfortunate incident, I am!'

They rocked with laughter again. This roller-coaster of emotions couldn't go on.

'We've got to get a grip on ourselves,' Pandy said soberly, 'and we have to fix your make-up again. Just so that I am totally up to speed on this news-breaking story, please tell me Eleanor, and I promise to take the secret to my grave, who was Xavier's father?'

'I'm not telling,' Eleanor replied stony-faced.

*

'How did it go yesterday?' Celeste asked Roland congenially as she mashed the tea bags in the mugs on Easter Tuesday.

'It was quite a different ballgame from the register office on Saturday. They didn't want any pictures taken in the chapel so I just did a couple outside the front of the convent with all the nuns and the happy couple. It looked like a penguin convention! All a bit weird. I wouldn't say they were keen to get rid of me but I felt like an intruder really. So I shot off as soon as I could.'

'Well, nobody really wants to work on a bank holiday anyway, do they?'

'Apart from the self-employed!'

'Too true. I was actually sorting stock yesterday.'

'Didn't you get to see your gorgeous babies over the long weekend?'

'I popped down on Sunday and took them some Easter eggs. Big Nanny said that babies shouldn't eat chocolate eggs so I told her she should share them with Little Nanny.'

'Little Nanny?'

'Oh, I can't remember their names.'

'If "Little Nanny" is who I think she is, she's far from little.'

'You know her?'

'Er, rather. Yes.'

'Oh Roland, you didn't!'

He gave her a devil may care grin and shrugged. 'Only young once!'

'You are not going to make it to old if you go on at this rate you lascivious reprobate.'

'That's a bit strong, madam! The solution is in your own hands.'

'What? Me? And you? You're kidding.'

He got up from the chair and sidled up next to her on her sofa.

'Don't you miss it?'

'Give it a rest, Roland. I don't even have time to think about it.'

He traced his finger over her wrist. She shook him away. 'The tea will be stewed.' She fished out the tea bags and put them, dripping, on the tray before adding a dash of milk to the mugs. 'Here, drink your tea. I've put some bromide in for you.'

He wasn't giving up so easily. Little Nanny's charms were wearing thin. She was too much of a good thing and it was very pleasant to spend evenings like this with Celeste, and so very handy, being only next door.

'If I promise to be a good boy will you let me take some nice photos of you?'

'Why?'

'For practice. I'm used to doing aircraft and trains and factory machinery and all that sort of thing. People snapping isn't really my forte. It would be a great help. I need to hone my lighting skills,' he lied.

'I'll think about it but there's something else I want to tell you. It's important. It's why I invited you round this evening. I had a visit from that woman with the orange boots... what's her name?'

'Mrs Thackman, the local naturalist? What did she want?'

'You may well ask. She door-stepped me the other day and I had to invite her in. She was keen to tell me all about some endangered species that's living in the garden of that bungalow opposite, you know, the one Landscar wants to develop.'

'Go on.'

'Well you can see from upstairs over here that the garden has got huge hedges all around at the back.'

'Yes, it does and they look overgrown.'

'She says they are hazel hedges.'

'And what's the significance of that?'

'Dormice.'

'Dormice?'

'Yes. She's a bit of a busybody, you know, and she had a look around the back garden and found their nests in the hedge.'

'So?'

'She managed to identify one of the dormice as... hang on... I wrote it down...'

Celeste got up and went over to the mantelpiece to pick up a scrap of paper. She read out slowly, *'Muscardinus samdinus.'*

'Give it here.'

Roland scrutinised the paper. 'And what does *Site of Extraordinary Scientific Interest* mean?'

'She said this particular dormouse is an endangered species and that we should try and get the garden designated as what it says on there and it will be protected and Landscar won't be able to build on it and...'

'Slow down. You mean a ruddy dormouse could save the day?'

'Yes. She says its related to another one, something beginning with avell... but this *sam* one is rare.'

'Mmm.'

'And,' she added with emphasis, 'it likes to sleep in oak trees.'

'Bingo!' Roland declared.

*

'Welcome to the *Villa Estancia*!' declared Gonzo with a smile smarmed all over his face. 'Congrrratulations on your marriage, Señor Landscar, Señorrra Landscar!' He rolled his r dramatically. Grant ignored the greeting. Eleanor looked puzzled.

'Put these in the trunk room for now, Gonzo,' Grant said grumpily, indicating the pile of suitcases that the airport chauffeur had humped into the marble hallway. Synth went through to the kitchen and started to clatter about. Eleanor heard the sound of cupboards and drawers being checked. Back in the lounge, Grant was in high dudgeon.

'Gonzo, where the hell were you?' Grant demanded. 'You were supposed to meet us off the plane.'

'Forrgive me, Señor Landscar...'

'It doesn't matter. I told you to be ready for us at three o'clock. We've had an awful flight. Turbulance. Delays. I should have used my own plane.' Eleanor looked up sharply. Gonzo went on, waving his arms about convincingly.

'Issa the time differrence, Señor Landscar. It-a confuse me.' From his tousled appearance he had clearly been enjoying a siesta.

'Take my wife's hand luggage up to her room,' he ordered. 'I've just got to make an important phone call.'

Eleanor froze. Her room? She looked towards Grant but he was striding through to the lounge. 'Come and tell me what you think of this, Eleanor.'

She did as she was bade, her shoes clattering across the marble floor and into the huge room furnished with white sofas, a massive television screen and agave plants in terracotta pots. Panoramic windows gave out onto a substantial, well stocked conservatory and thence to a terrace and grounds that stretched forth in a canvas of fruit blossom and bright green fields against a cerulean sky. She walked slowly to the window, her steady grey eyes taking in the scene before her.

'Grant, this is absolutely beautiful.' She gazed out awe-struck at what she could see of the vast estate.

'You enjoy it, my dear. Synth's organising some tea for you and I just need to make this call.'

Eleanor alone in the vast lounge, sounds of clattering coming from Synth in the kitchen. Grant's voice floated to her ears.

'Hello, Teddy? Yes, we're here. All set. When will you do it? O.K. Keep me posted, old man.'

Eleanor put her handbag on a side-table but kept her suede jacket on. It was cool in here despite the warm spring sunshine outside. So this was Grant's Milloncha estate. She could see low hills on the horizon, starlings flying in great clouds above the fields and tubs full of flowering plants on the patio beyond the conservatory.

So this was to be her life now, one of privilege and luxury. After years living alone in her modest flat in *Isabel Avenue*, she was now to be the lady of not just one house but several with staff at her beck and call. Would she ever get used to it? Anything she wanted, anything at all, was hers to command. Sweet peas in December? No problem. Did she fancy a spur of the moment trip to their chalet in Switzerland? Just summon up the private plane. How about a few weeks on Grant's cattle ranch in Texas? Or his flat in Venice? It was all too much to take in. Should she use her own money to buy things for herself or would he give her an allowance? Such matters hadn't been discussed beyond him saying, 'My darlin' Eleanor, you can have any darned thing you like. Just name it and it's yours. Come on! Choose something!'

At that moment, she had been unable think of anything apart from her Aunty Rev and the other nuns, wearing their scratchy habits, sleeping at night in their cold cells and living on a diet that contained an inordinate amount of cabbage and potatoes.

'Some thicker duvets for the sisters for next winter,' she'd said. How he had laughed, but he had bought them.

Now she turned and surveyed the white, leather sofas and the giant television screen, taking in the pale walls with just a hint of light green and the ornate central ceiling lamp. Silk embroidered cushions in glowing shades were scattered on the seating.

'I show-a you to-a your room now. Yes?' Gonzo had appeared, interrupting her reverie.

As not much else was going on, Eleanor nodded and followed the grinning, fawning fellow up the polished wooden staircase to a neatly appointed bedroom on the first floor. He opened the door for her.

'Here-a we are, lady. You like it?'

Eleanor surveyed the pink and white salon with its rouched nets, velvet drapes and circular double bed strewn with tasselled, satin cushions.

'Er, very nice,' she replied, a trifle take a-back by the bordello-style ambience.

'My dear Señorrra Landscar, I am here to serve you. Anything at all that I can do to make your honeymoon special, then please-a do not hesitate to call me.' He indicated a heavily embroidered sash hanging next to the bed. 'Just pull on that gentle,' he said, 'and I will appear to fulfil your every wish.'

Was it her imagination, or was there a sexual undertone in his words? The handsome and sparkling young man then proceeded to back out of the room nodding his head extremely slowly, leaving behind only his wide, ingratiating smile, like a the Cheshire cat disappearing. She vowed never to pull the sash.

Chapter 19

Eleanor Landscar sat alone in the conservatory of the *Villa Estancia* eating croissants and drinking coffee at a white, wrought-iron, glass-topped table. So this was married life! Grant had kissed her tenderly on the forehead before he'd left for a business meeting on the other side of the island.

'I promise not to be too long and I'll do my best to be back for tea.'

'But it's the first real day of our honeymoon. Can't we spend it together?'

He had pressed his hand firmly on her wrist.

'My sweet, I promise you this is a one-off. Then I'll be all yours.'

She'd smiled in resignation. This was not the time to start nagging. He was a billionaire businessman. Deals were what drove him. Without them he was an empty shell.

'I'll see you later then.'

He had blown her a kiss from the doorway.

'Will there be anything else, Mrs. Landscar?' Synth enquired.

'No. No thank you. The croissants were very nice.'

'I baked them fresh first thing specially for you. I know you like them.'

'Did you really do them yourself? You are a clever lady.'

Synth wasn't often addressed as a lady and was rather tickled that the upmarket Eleanor had bestowed such a compliment on her.

'I'm just nipping into the village for some provisions,' she smiled. 'It's OK. Mr. Landscar told me that he has an account in the little *supermercado*. I can choose what we need and they'll deliver it later. Is there anything special I can get for you?'

Eleanor thought for a moment. 'Yes, there is, actually. Please could you pick me up a tube of hand-cream? I seem to have forgotten to pack mine.'

'No problem,' said Synth. 'I'm off then. Mr. Landscar said it's only a ten minute cycle ride down the hill and there's a bike I can use at the side of the villa. Bye for now.' Then she was gone.

Eleanor finished her breakfast and took the crockery into the smart, shiny kitchen. So here she was, alone on the first day of their honeymoon. Grant had gone to his own room last night and she to hers.

'It's been a tiring few days,' he'd said, 'and we'll be refreshed for a proper wedding night tomorrow night in my bedroom suite. So, my darling wife, have a nice rest and prepare to be ravaged by your husband.'

The thought of dear, kind Grant ravaging her didn't sound likely or appealing but she had sensed there was something not quite right when they'd arrived yesterday. He had behaved like a child after the party, bawling out Gonzo.

She opened the kitchen door and wandered onto a shady, paved patio with a grape vine meandering above it on a latticed support. The tendrils were wafting about in the gentle breeze, entwining where they could.

'Ello, Mrs. Landscar,' said a voice behind her. She started.

'Oh, it's you, Gonzo. I didn't hear you. What a lovely day!'

'Yes, indeed.'

There was an awkward silence. She felt uncomfortable near him.

'May I respectfully ask-you, Mrs. Landscar, what-a you would like me to do for you today?'

She was rather surprised. Surely it wasn't up to her to now direct Grant's staff?

'I don't think there is anything at all that you can do for me, thank you, Gonzo.'

'Ah, but I think there is.'

She took a step away from him, raised her eyebrows and gave him one of her disapproving stares that had always held her in good stead when she had been a journalist and somebody was coming on too strongly.

He took a step forward. 'Pleass, Mrs. Landscar, I know that your husband is away today and that perhaps you would like to have some joy. So, why don't you allow me to drive you around for a small tour of our beautiful island of Milloncha?'

It was so lovely today. The man had worked for Grant for years so she thought he must be trustworthy.

'Very well then, Gonzo. That's very kind of you. I'll just go and write a note for my husband and get my jacket. I'll see you by the front door in ten minutes.'

'Very good, Madam,' he said in an unctuous tone.

> *'My Darling Grant,*
> *This is just to let you know that Gonzo is taking me for a little tour of the island in his car as I have nothing else to do today but I expect I'll be back before you anyway.*
>
> *Love Eleanor x'*

She planted a kiss on it and left it on the side table in the marble entrance hall. Out she rushed, into the open-topped four-by-four that Gonzo had washed and polished in her honour, if she all but knew it. The motor was running. She strapped herself in and pulled her favourite lilac beanie hat on firmly.

'Let's go!' said Gonzo as he roared away, throwing her back sharply in the warm leather seat. 'We will have fun!'

'Not too fast, please,' she entreated.

'You no want to be thrilled?'

No, she certainly didn't. 'I like to be driven steadily,' she said.

'And there was I thinking you wassa a kind of lady wot liked-a for adventure!'

'No, Gonzo. No adventure. Just a nice, gentle tour. OK?'

'Whatever you say, Madam,' he smirked.

*

'Hi! Is that you, Eleanor?'

'Hello, Pandy. Good to hear your voice. How are you? How are things at *Embroideryworld*?'

'Don't you worry. It's all going swimmingly. The next issue is in the bag, we've got loads of advertisers and a big fan-base of readers growing. Now, tell me what you think of *Villa Estancia*.'

'Oh, it's beautiful here, only...'

'Only what?'

'I haven't seen much of your father.'

'What? On your honeymoon?'

'He's been so busy.'

'That is utterly unforgivable. I'll give him a right rollicking when I speak to him...'

'No. No. Please don't. He has to do his business deals. It's what makes him happy.'

'Yes, but on your honeymoon...'

'It's only been yesterday and today... but we'll have the weekend. He's promised me he'll be back tonight.'

'I could smack him sometimes, I really could,' Pandy hissed. Then she took a deep breath and asked what Eleanor had been doing to entertain herself.'

'Well,' said the bride, 'it's actually not been too bad. The man, Gonzo, has been taking me out in his open-top four-by-four touring the island. It is so pretty here, Pandy.'

'Gonzo. Oh yes, the local glamour boy. He should know it like the back of his hand. He was born there, you know. His parents used to rent the *finca* from Dad before they died.'

'I didn't know that.'

'Oh yes. Dad kept him on out of kindness. Well, that's what he'd like people to think.'

'Now, now, Pandy...'

'Eleanor, if there's one thing you must learn about Dad, it's that he always has an ulterior motive. With Gonzo it's guilt.'

'Guilt?'

'Yes, he drove the man's parents to an early grave with his excessive rent demands.'

'No. I can't believe that.'

'Yes. He did and Gonzo is a smarmy little git who rips Dad off at every turn.'

'Oh dear,' Eleanor said, perplexed. She was learning a lot about her new husband and his estate manager.

'Just don't leave your handbag lying around unattended!' Pandy said with a laugh. 'Well, I'd really better get back to work. The galleys have just come in. You enjoy your "me time".'

'I will,' Eleanor said. 'Gonzo's taking me out in his boat later.'

'Well make sure you have a life jacket!' Pandy said. 'Bye-eee.'

Eleanor had hardly put down the phone when it rang again.

'Hello,' she said tentatively, thinking it was Pandora ringing her back about something she'd forgotten.

'My darling wife! How are you? I crept out this morning not to wake you.'

'Missing you. How are the negotiations going?'

'Pretty good but that's not why I rang you. I just wanted to say how sorry I am about last night.'

'There's no need, Grant. These things happen.'

'I feel dreadful, letting you down like that...'

'Grant, it really doesn't matter. We have time to get everything right.'

'Yes, but to have a flop-out on our first night...'

'Please stop. I love you. We'll sort it out.' There was a pause.

'I have to be honest with you, Eleanor. It may be the diabetes.'

'I thought you said it was under control.'

'It is. Yes, it is but loss of "you know" can be a side effect of it.'

Eleanor stood up, taking the phone with her to the window, gazing out over the lovely estate, listening to the chirping of a pair of mating starlings through the open window. Was fulfilment ever going to be hers?

'Surely something can be done?' she said.

'I'll go back and see my specialist when we're home.'

Disappointment was sinking through her like a stone. The lovely night-gown, the expectation, the foreplay... all leading to nothing. He had pleased her, of course he had, but not in the way she had longed for. She summoned up a bright tone.

'Well, don't worry about it,' she said. 'I had such a great time last night. I'm only sorry you didn't.'

'To hold you naked in my arms for the first time was wonderful, Eleanor. To feel the softness of your skin against mine...'

There was a click on the line. She hoped nobody was listening in to their conversation.

'Did you hear that click, Grant?' Silence.

'Grant?'

He had gone. She put the phone down. After a millisecond there was a "ting". Then it rang again and she picked up the receiver.

'I think we got cut off,' Grant said.

'Yes.'

'These phone lines can be very unreliable. It's nonsense to be driving back and forth across the island. I'll get my head down here tonight, finish by the afternoon and then I should be with you for dinner tomorrow night.'

'Oh Grant. I can hardly wait. I just want you with me.'

'Mmmah!' came a kiss down the line in response.

'Mmmah! to you too, my darling man.'

*

Synth rushed into the villa lounge.

'Mrs. Landscar!'

Eleanor looked up from her newspaper, surprised to see the woman in such a state.

'Mrs. Landscar,' Synth repeated breathlessly. 'I have to go.'

'Go where?' Eleanor enquired, putting down her paper and standing up. 'What's the matter?'

'My mother, Maud. She's very poorly. They think it might be a stroke. The home rang me on my mobile while I was down in the village.'

Eleanor was quick to take command. 'Have you booked a flight yet?'

'No, nothing…'

'Leave that to me. You go and put some things in a bag and I'll round up Gonzo to take you to the airport. There's bound to be something on the midday flight in business class.'

Synth was in floods of tears. 'Thank you, thank you. I'll just go…'

Eleanor was already on the phone, punching in the number for the local airport that was displayed prominently on the telephone table. This was turning out to be some honeymoon.

*

Eleanor stood beside Synth at check-in.

'Window seat?' the *Millonchan Airways* clerk enquired.

'Yes, yes please.' Synth replied.

'Any luggage?'

'Just hand luggage.'

'That's seat C1,' the girl said as she handed Synth her boarding card. 'Have a pleasant flight.'

Gonzo was waiting for Eleanor in the airport car-park. 'All OK?'

'She's very upset but the flight was supposed to be leaving on time, Eleanor replied.'

'Good. Good. Then we can go straight to my boat. It is down in *Puerto Nacarado'*

'I should go back to the villa first,' Eleanor said.

'What-a for? You have-a your bag and a cardigan and your-a pretty hat. What-a more do you want-a?'

Eleanor felt her bare neck. She'd forgotten to put on her pendant. Oh well.

'You're right,' she said. Grant was away. Synth had gone. It was a lovely, warm day. A cruise along the Mediterranean island coast this afternoon would be perfect.

'I know you enjoy it,' Gonzo replied, flashing her a charming smile and jamming the vehicle into first. 'I have picnic for you.'

*

'That's right,' Roland said. 'Just push your shoulder a bit further forward.'

Celeste did so, clutching the lilac chiffon to her chest in his icy cold studio.

'Now, head down. Look up and smoulder.'

'For goodness sake, Roland, how can I smoulder. I'm freezing to death here.'

'Think of me in my boxer shorts.'

'Perish the thought!' She struggled to obey his commands. 'Will the goose-bumps show?'

'It's not that bad in here.'

'A single bar electric fire is totally inadequate for keeping me toasty.'

'Well, get up off the couch for a minute and jump up and down a bit.' He licked his lips lasciviously. He couldn't wait to see all her bouncy bits jiggling about.

Celeste got to her feet, held onto her breasts and ran on the spot until she was breathless and her shoulder-length, dark hair fluffed up in a wanton, hedge-dragged fashion.

'Better now?'

'Better,' she replied huskily, settling down onto the satin again. He stepped forward. 'Let me rearrange you.'

'Hands off, you perve!' she warned. 'Why I ever agreed to this I don't know.'

He fiddled around with the camera and then one of the lamps and mused, 'I wonder what Eleanor Framp wore on her wedding night.'

'Roland! Have you no decency? I don't like the woman but...' She paused. 'Probably a brushed cotton nightie and a pair of grey, woolly bed-socks,' she tittered.

'And a chastity belt,' he guffawed.

'And her hair in rollers,'

'And half an inch thick of face cream!' Then his face took on a sober expression. 'We shouldn't be unkind. She's landed herself nicely there, though.'

'What? Getting hitched to a Texan billionaire? I'll say!'

'Shame he's such a toe-rag with his plans for opposite,' Roland observed. Then, 'To me! Look away! Back again! Touch your hair! Good. Good.'

'How long's this going on for?' Celeste whined. 'It's late and I've got to be up early. My shop floor's filthy. Some kid's trodden jelly sweets into the carpet and there are smear marks all over the window again.'

'Nearly done. Just swing your legs over the back of the couch and lean across with one finger in your mouth.'

'Absolutely not. You are sliding from glamour into naughty stuff and I just will not do it.'

'Aw. Go on, Celeste. Put the sparkly veil over your eyes and nobody will recognise you.'

She wearily swung her legs into the required position and posed as required, draping the material so that only her eyes showed above the edge of it.

'Click! Click! Whizz!'

'That's it,' she said, regaining a decent position. 'I'm wacked.'

'You're a star.'

'My twinkle's fading with exhaustion.' She got up and retrieved her black velvet coat and slipped her well manicured toes into her shoes.

'I've got to be up early in the morning too,' Roland said as he tidied away things. 'The environment woman, Mrs. Thackman, is taking me into the bungalow garden to show me where the dormice nests are. With luck, we might catch a pic of one of them snoozing. We've got to pick up a copy of the daily paper first though so that the date can be in the shot.'

'Don't talk to me about papers. I hear them being delivered every morning at five o'clock to the supermarket. Doesn't it wake you?'

'Nope. I sleep the sleep of the just.'

'The just awful,' she said with her hand on the door latch.

'BANG!' The door swung open and a frenzied woman burst in. Celeste leapt back. It took them a moment to realise who it was. Little Nanny, and she was raging, furious and dangerous.

'Ha!' she yelled. 'Got you!'

Celeste backed away towards Roland. 'It's one of the Nannies,' she said tremulously.

'I know who it is,' he hissed back, 'and she's not happy.'

'You two! I thought something was going on! You filthy rotter!'

She charged across the room, knocking Celeste sideways as she pummelled Roland on the chest.

'Steady on, Nanny. What's all this about?'

'You! And her! Double-timing!'

'No, no, Nanny. You've got it all wrong.' He wrestled her away but she was in for vengeance. Grabbing a lamp-stand she swept it in an arc around her, yanking the plug out of its socket, shattering the bulb and sweeping a selection of framed photographs off the shelf together with a couple of expensive, digital cameras.

'Beast! Two-timing rat!'

'But Nanny, we haven't been... hey! Mind what you're doing! Celeste's just been helping me with some portraiture.'

'Rubbish!' she said, letting the lamp-stand go with a crash onto the floor as she lunged at Celeste and ripped apart her black velvet coat to show, well, not a lot in the way of clothing. 'See! I was right!'

'They're only glamour photos, Nanny. Celeste and I are just good friends.'

The marauding woman wouldn't be appeased. In a frenzy she tore down the drapes behind the couch, heaved the couch over onto its face, kicked the waste-bin and then looked around for more carnage opportunities.

'Thwack!' Nanny was face down on the floor in a half-Nelson with Celeste sitting on her back.

'Celeste! How did you do that?'

'Self defence, evening classes. Very useful, don't you think?' Roland scratched his head. 'You could have killed her.'

'Here, you take over. I'm going home. You decide what you're going to do with her.' Celeste left, slamming the door as she went.

Little Nanny drummed her feet on the floor. 'Let me up!'

'Only if you behave. Come on,' said Roland. 'I'll drive you home.' He extended a hand. 'By the way, you'll be paying for all this and I think you can consider yourself fired.'

She picked lump of carpet fluff out of her mouth. 'Fancy a shag?'

*

Reverend Mother came out of the vestry leading off the little convent chapel of St. Bede's after benediction on the Thursday afternoon. She was carrying the still smouldering thurible. The stench of incense got onto her chest and she was coughing discreetly behind one hand when she came across Father Guyler sitting in his wheelchair in silent prayer next to one of the front pews. He glanced up, taking in her expression of distaste at the pungent smoke emitting from the censer. He made no attempt to get up out of the chair.

'Here, let me help you with that, Reverend Mother.'

She gratefully handed it over to him and whispered, 'Thank you, Father. I can't abide the smell of the stuff.'

'It's only a matter of time before they ban it,' he said confidentially, 'what with all this anti-smoking legislation.'

'It can't be soon enough for me,' she nodded.

'Do you want me to extinguish it?'

'Oh, yes please, if you would be so kind, Father.'

He fiddled with the gold-plated chains and the lid came down with a clang, cutting out the air and vanquishing the clouds of stinking fumes.

'There! That's killed it!' he declared in a triumphant whisper, returning it to Reverend Mother.

'I'll put it back in the vestry,' she said.

She hobbled across the parquet floor and then came back to make a deep and creaky genuflection to the altar. The wedding flowers were starting to fade now. The elderly nun replayed in her head the beauty of dear Eleanor's wedding. It had been a truly lovely day.

Father Guyler and Reverend Mother left the chapel together. As she walked slowly along the corridor next to his wheelchair, their conversation turned to this afternoon's forthcoming tea party.

'I'm looking forward to a nice piece of cake,' he said.

'I was going to let the event slip past but Sister Catherine is such a terror when it comes to birthdays, anniversaries and saints' days. She's already planning St. Emilia's Feast Day in May.'

'At the risk if being indelicate, I gather that this is a rather special birthday for you?'

'Nuns can't be vain, Father. I'm eighty today.'

'Congratulations, Reverend Mother. To have reached this age and spent your life in the service of God must be very gratifying.'

'I was called. When one is called, there is no alternative.'

'Precisely. I have spent my life similarly but the years abroad have taken their toll, hence my forthcoming early retirement. I suspect that the bishop has given me this post of assessing St. Bede's assets as my last job before putting me out to grass.'

'Come now, Father, you have more years of work in you, surely?'

'I'm afraid not, Reverend Mother. I think my card is marked.'

'Oh, they won't pension you off yet, Father.'

Considerate as she was, she was aware of his fragility. His fall had really affected him. She paused outside the door of the front parlour.

'I'm so happy that you were able to officiate at Eleanor's wedding ceremony here in the chapel.'

'My pleasure. Your niece is a wonderful person, Reverend Mother. I have always admired her.'

'I know.'

'I sincerely hope that she'll be very happy with Mr. Landscar.'

'It's not quite what I envisaged for her, I must confess, but she's a grown woman and she has to make her own choices.'

'True. True, but you must have had hopes and dreams for her.'

'Only those aspirations that any parent would have. I was a nun first, Father, and then Eleanor's guardian.'

'I sometimes wondered how she was getting along when I was out in India.'

'I'm sure you did, Father.'

'Was she happy, as a young woman?'

'She had a teenage crush on you...'

'Did she?' He feigned surprise. 'That's unfortunate. I was never aware...'

'It didn't go unobserved.'

'We priests are like doctors and teachers, you know. Young women can get fixations. We're trained to deal with it though.'

'That's a good thing. When I returned from the mission in Kridblikistan back then and found you gone, I was a trifle surprised. I thought you enjoyed being our pastor... mind you... we were a far bigger community then. Do you realise that we had ninety-two nuns here? Ninety-two! Now look at us!' she mused.

If the young Father Guyler had realised that his flirtation with Eleanor was under observation he would have taken his exit sooner. After all, he had planned a comfortable career in the priesthood and no shenanigans with a love-sick teenager was going to get in the way of that. Still, Eleanor had been very sweet and compliant. It had been a charming interlude for him.

Reverend Mother rambled on. 'Yes, it was just as well that you went to India to do your good work in the orphanage.' She looked down and rearranged the beads of the rosary hanging from her waist. 'Well, Father,' she said,' why don't you go in and have a nice rest before tea? Benediction was very good today and you must be tired coping with it all from the wheelchair.'

'Yes, you're right. I'm still a bit unsteady. The hospital says that will improve. I'll see you later then. What time?'

'My birthday tea will be at half past six in here. We thought we'd have it on our laps after the news on the radio.'

*

'Happy Birthday, dear Reverend Mother, Happy Birthday to you!' The eight cake candles flickered, lighting up the old nun's creased features as she beamed at the sea of happy faces around her. St. Bede's was a small community, of thirteen nuns, four of whom were postulants.

'Thank you, sisters, Father. What a lovely cake! Who baked it?' Nobody owned up. The postulants giggled.

'She bake it,' said the youngest of the Filipinos, pointing at one of the others who hung her head shyly.

'Well done, sister. We shall all enjoy this.'

'Blow out the candles now!'
Reverend Mother took a deep breath and blew with all her might. All went out and the sisters clapped.

'Make a wish!'
Reverend Mother closed her eyes and wished that Eleanor would be very happy. She opened her eyes.

'There! Now, would somebody please be mother and cut this up for us?' The postulant who had baked the cake stood up and came forward to do the honours. Then one of the others said, 'We have gift for you.'

"Oh, my dears, I can't accept presents. My vow of poverty forbids it.'

'No, Reverend Mother. Not really for you. For garden.'
Then from behind the sofa a *Photinia* shrub in a pot appeared.

'How did you afford that?' Reverend Mother was amazed.

'Man in market give it to me when I say it your birthday.'

'How very kind of him! Thank you!'

'They have lovely red leaves,' said Father Guyler.

'You like cake, Father?'

'Oh yes please, I like cake.'

They all laughed. The phone rang. Reverend Mother got up and shuffled through to the hall, saying as she went, 'That'll be Eleanor.'

She came back a couple of minutes later, her face ashen.

'It was Grant Landscar. Eleanor's gone missing.'

Chapter 20

'What the flaming heck to you mean when you say you don't know where she is?' Grant stormed at Gonzo who just shrugged. 'For goodness sake, man, she's my wife. You were supposed to keep an eye on her.' He slammed his leather document case down on the coffee table and threw his stetson onto one of the white sofas in the lounge of *Villa Estancia*. 'And where's Synth? Has she seen Eleanor?' He'd found Eleanor's note in the hall and waved it.

'Synth has-a gone to England. Herrr mother iss ill.'
Grant paced about, running his hands through his white hair.

'So when did you last see Mrs. Landscar?'

'We take-a Synth to *aeropuerto* for midday flight to London.'

'Yes. Yes, and then what?' Grant demanded urgently.
Gonzo plunged his hands into the pockets of his jeans and rolled his eyes in an expression of abject despair.

'I dunno-a. Mrs. Landscar say she want to go look at shops in town so I let her out from car.'

'Where? Where? Tell me, man! Where did you drop her off?'

'Traffic busy so I put her out at corner of *piazza*... near ice-a cream-a *tienda*.'

'What time?'

Gonzo looked at the ceiling and hummed a little. 'I think-a about half-a past midday.'
Grant glanced at his watch. 'It's eight thirty. She's been gone for eight hours.'

The doorbell rang. With no Synth to answer it, Gonzo lazily made his way there.

'Is-a *policia*,' he called, but Grant was already behind him.

*

Dawn next morning was damp and misty as Roland Dilger and the orange-booted Mrs. Thackman made their way quietly along the garden path of the bungalow opposite his studio. Through the side gate they walked and into the overgrown back garden that was a haven for wildlife.

'I can smell fox,' she declared.

'Thought it was cats,' Roland replied, waving the newspaper about as if to dispel the pong. His companion pointed across to that part of the hazel hedge growing thickly next to one of the giant oak trees.

'That's where the nests are.'

Their feet left footprints in the early morning dew of the overgrown lawn.

'Approach quietly,' Mrs. Thackman said. 'They are extremely sensitive creatures and we don't want to scare them. Here. Look here!' She placed a gloved hand gently into the thicket, parting the twigs and leaves to reveal a nest. Roland peered over her shoulder. There, curled up in deepest slumber, lay the saviour of their neighbourhood.

'It's important to have the front of the newspaper in the picture,' she said. Roland slipped the rolled up publication past her hand and propped it up behind the nest. The date was clearly visible. Then, using his small, digital camera, he took his close-up pictures. The dormouse didn't stir, just its sensitive whiskers twitching in deepest sleep.

'Better do some establishing shots too,' he murmured, moving slightly away. 'Can you get the newspaper out and hold it in front of you?' She did. Then the pair of them crept away again, across the dew-bedecked lawn, past the pea-soup swimming pool and the crazed tennis court, along the path and onto the suburban pavement.

*

'Reverend Mother, she's disappeared without trace. The police have been out all night looking for her. What am I going to do?'

Reverend Mother stayed calm, clutching the telephone firmly.

'Grant, she said, 'wherever Eleanor is she will be fine. She has great inner strength. Did she take anything with her?'

'I don't know but I've looked through her wardrobe and there seem to be plenty of clothes in there. Her favourite lilac beanie hat isn't in the hall. Has she ever gone off like this before?'

'No. It's not in her nature to cause everybody so much worry.'

'The police have searched all the lock-ups and garages and warehouses. They're still interviewing shopkeepers around the piazza in case anybody saw her and looking at security videos. The hospitals have been checked too. Nothing.'

Swallowing her own fear for her niece's situation, Reverend Mother took a deep breath and said, 'Grant, my dear, we will be praying for Eleanor's safe return.'

His anger bubbled over. 'What good's that going to do?'

Reverend Mother replied, 'There is great power in prayer. You should try it.'

'I don't hold with all that. I'm sorry, Reverend Mother, and I don't mean any disrespect, but why would your God let this happen in the first place? I mean, what harm has Eleanor ever done to anybody?'

An old hand at handling sceptics, Reverend Mother replied, 'it's not for us to know the reasoning of the Almighty.'

'I have to go,' he said. 'I'll let you know of any developments.'

'God bless you,' said Reverend Mother as Grant's phone clicked off sharply.

There was a tap on her open study door and Father Guyler put his head round. He was walking with a stick. 'Any news?'

'Nothing. They've been looking in all sorts of places for her. Poor Eleanor.' She bit her lip and shook her head slowly and woefully. 'Anything could have happened to her, an accident ... she could be lying in a ditch somewhere...'

'Does she speak the language?'

'Not as far as I know.' She twisted her hands anxiously together in distress. Father Guyler limped further into the room. 'Would you like me to fly out and see if I can help with the search?'

Reverend Mother looked up sharply. 'You're not well enough, Father, but thank you for offering.' She smiled. 'In any case, Grant Landscar has plenty of help at his disposal. He'll be leaving no stone unturned in the search for my niece... and I know that he, at least, does speak a little of the language.' She sorted some papers on her desk and then looked up again.' Are you comfortable in the guest suite, Father?'

'Yes, thank-you. Excellent.' He shuffled over to the window.

'St. Bede's is a fine piece of property, Reverend Mother.'

'We're very lucky to have it, thanks to old Reverend Mother who got it for us under a legal loophole years ago. It makes us feel very secure, especially after that ridiculous misunderstanding last year with Mr. Landscar about the wind farm.'

'That all sounds rather interesting.' He turned towards her. 'What happened?'

'Oh, a storm in a teacup but worrying at the time. It's all sorted now and the airport pays us a substantial rent for part of our land, as you no doubt have seen from the accounts.'

'Yes.' He stroked his chin and gazed down across the fields. 'I suppose, though, that you're rather under-occupying this place nowadays, with the reduction in the size of the community.'

'Maybe but we live in hope of new vocations.'

'It must be a lot of work for the sisters, managing the crops and orchard.'

'It keeps them fit, although I suppose time is marching on for all of us... but we do have some machinery to help us. The postulants enjoy driving the mini-tractor you know.'

'I can't imagine that.'

'Yes, you should see them. Don't forget they come from farming communities in their homeland.'

'Still with so few of you to run the place...'

Reverend Mother lifted her chin and gave him a hard stare. 'Father, I thought you were on our side.'

'Of course I am,' he said, slowly making for the door, nearly bumping into Sister Catherine as she came in.

'Oh!' she said.

'I'll see you later, Sisters,' he said.

'Is everything alright, Sister Catherine?' Reverend Mother enquired.

'Well, no, actually. I've got Synth Hunt downstairs. Her mother's been taken ill. Synth's just flown back from Milloncha. She doesn't know about Eleanor. Will you tell her?'

'Yes, of course. I'll come down. It seems to be one thing after another at the moment.' Reverend Mother replied, getting rather creakily to her feet, using the desk for support.

Downstairs in the panelled hallway Synth stood anxiously waiting with her hand-luggage bag on the floor beside her.

'Oh Reverend Mother, what am I going to do? They think my mother's had a stroke.'

'Come through into the parlour, my dear. Here, come in.' She opened the door and ushered the distressed woman into the comfort of the sitting room. 'Sister Catherine, please can you ask one of the postulants to make some tea for Synth? Why don't we all have a cup?' Sister Catherine nodded as she left, smiling encouragingly at Synth who was now sitting by the unlit fire.

'Now then, what can we do to help?'

'I didn't know where else to go. I spent last night at *Casslands* alone but it was a bit scary.'

'You can stay here, my dear. No need to go anywhere else.'

'Can I really? Are you sure?'

'Yes but the guest suite is already occupied by Father Guyler. Could you manage in one of the empty cells?'

'That would be fine,' Synth said. 'All I need is a bed for the night.'

'That's settled then. Now, tell me about your mother.'

Synth picked at the edges of her finger nails, fighting back tears.

'They found her on the floor of her en suite. She was completely unconscious. She still is.'

'You've seen her, of course.'

'Yes, I took a taxi from the airport to the hospital. Eleanor gave me some cash before I left. She and Gonzo took me to the airport and...' She stopped. Something was wrong.

Reverend Mother leaned across from her chair opposite Synth and touched her lightly on the wrist.

'I'm sorry to be the bearer of still more bad tidings, my dear, but Mrs. Landscar, Eleanor, is missing.'

'Wh... what?'

'When Mr. Landscar got back from his business trip on the other side of the island later yesterday, she had disappeared during a shopping trip in town.'

Synth's hands flew to her face. 'Oh no! How dreadful! How long has she been gone?'

'As far as we can work out, a good twenty-four hours now. They're doing everything they can to find her.'

*

'Did you see the lunchtime news?' Roland asked impatiently.

'No. Too busy. Why?' Celeste replied disinterested.

'Eleanor Framp, I mean Landscar. She's gone missing on the island of Milloncha.'

Celeste looked up. 'Really? Good!'

'Aw, come on, Celeste! She's on her honeymoon for goodness sake!'

'Perhaps she decided that being an old maid suited her better after all.' She folded up some baby vests and added them to the pile on the counter. 'Do you think these striped ones will sell?'

Roland slapped his hand down. 'Celeste! Listen to me!'

'I'm listening.'

'If she's gone AWOL then it's a really good time to pull the rug out from under her hubby's feet with this dormouse thing.'

Now he had her full attention. 'You're right,' she said, 'what do you think we should do?'

'We've got the photographs.'

'And?'

'I suggest you write a nice piece for one of the daily papers to go with them.'

'What? Me?'

'Yes, you. I know you can write because you did all the copy for the airshow. You must have some connections in Fleet Street.'

'Yes...'

'Do you want to lose your forecourt and service road and to have that noisy, smelly development opposite?'

'No, of course not.'

'Then will you do it?'

'Yes, yes. OK. When do you need it by?'

'Tomorrow morning so it hits the Monday papers.'

'I'll see what strings I can pull. Leave it with me.'

*

'Mum. It's me, Synth.' No response.

Synth looked around the ward. In the midst of her personal crisis life still went on. Nurses bustled back and forth doing all the things that nurses do. Patients slept or read newspapers or sat out next to their beds with expressions of blank resignation. An odour of old cooking and stale urine hung in the over-heated air while various monitoring machines hummed and blipped.

The long, blue curtains were partly pulled around Maud Hunt's bed where she lay back, an oxygen mask over her face and a shunt in her wrist. She snored in a gurgling kind of way.

At times like this Synth wished she had somebody to support her, to hold her and say that everything was going to be alright. In the old days, before Reverend Mother had stepped into her life, she would have hit the town, picked up a client or two and gone home at dawn with a handbag full of bank-notes. Did she miss all that? Yes and no. It had been a life that she had fallen into without much thought for the consequences.

She remembered the first man who had taken her body for money. After that, they all seemed the same somehow. She looked at her mother, the former brothel owner who had introduced her daughter into the dark side of morality. What sort of a mother was that? An unmarried one who only did what she knew. Synth shuddered. To have been in the middle of that kind of life had somehow blinkered her to other possibilities. Thank goodness for Reverend Mother.

'Eurgh!'

'Mum! Are you awake?'

Maud moved her head from side to side trying to shift the oxygen mask away.

'Mwrsmapoosie?'

'What, Mum? What are you trying to say?'

'Mwrsmupsy?'

Synth let go of Maud's hand and waved to a nurse carrying a bed-pan.

'She's awake.'

The nurse signalled to hold on a moment and then joined her once she had disposed of the pan and removed her gloves.

'Hello, Mrs. Hunt,' she said.

Maud groaned and again tried to shift the oxygen mask.

'Here, let me take that away for a moment. Good to see you back with us.'

Maud continued to mumble incoherently. The nurse said, 'These left-brain strokes always seem to affect the speech but I think she can understand you. Talk to her. She's probably very frightened.

'Hello, Mum.'

'Nnnnnn.'

'I know you can't talk much, You've had a stroke. You're in the hospital but you're going to be alright.'

Maud became agitated, struggling to look around. 'Whersh Mwrsmapoosie?'

Synth racked her brains. What the heck was her mother trying to say? Something about a poosie. Ah! 'You're asking about pussy?'

'Yersh.'

The younger woman smiled. 'The cat's just fine. I saw her earlier when I went to the home to get your things.'

Maud nodded contentedly and then fell asleep promptly. The nurse returned and said, 'She's drifted off again.'

'My mother's a fighter, you know.'

'I'm sure she is. It's going to be a long road to recovery but as long as she doesn't have any more strokes for now...'

'I'll keep my fingers crossed.'

'Come in any time you like. We have open visiting on this ward all afternoon and evening.'

'I'll be here,' Synth said.

*

Pandy swivelled her chair in the offices of *Embroideryworld,* the phone held against her ear with a hunched shoulder as she told her assistant, 'yes, ring them back and say we need to double the print run for next month. Hello? Is that marketing? We've found a space for you. A whole page? You're in luck.'

Pandy loved running the magazine without Eleanor. Decision making was second nature to her. She wasn't some dreamer but a pragmatic, street-wise entrepreneuse cast in the mould of her father. Mail came in by the bagful. Advertisers were vying for space. Designers begged for work. Special offers abounded. The thrill of building a business never left her. The phone rang again.

Embroideryworld.'

'Pandy, it's Dad.'

'Any news?'

'Nothin'. She seems to have disappeared into thin air. I'm going berserk with worry.'

'What are the police doing?'

'All the usual. Shucks, Pandy, anythin' could've happened to my Eleanor. I thought Milloncha was a safe place.'

'No-where's completely safe nowadays, Dad. Were things OK between you?'

'Of course they were. Why are you asking?'

'Well,' she hesitated, 'when I spoke to Eleanor before, she said she hadn't seen a lot of you...'

'Business. She understood that.'

'Yes, but Dad, it was supposed to be your honeymoon.'

'Eleanor was fine with it.'

'With what, exactly?'

'The hotel enterprise with that woman from the airshow, you know, the pilot lady.'

'Oh, last summer's fling.'

'Now, now Pandy. It was strictly business. She needs my investment.'

'Did I hear the sound of the marines marching this way?'

'Sarcasm is out of place right now, darlin' daughter.'

Pandy sighed. Would he ever change? 'Look, Dad, Eleanor's disappearance is all over the papers here.' She picked up the copy of *Daily News Expression* from her desk. 'Hear this:

TEXAN BILLIONAIRE'S WIFE DISAPPEARS

Wife of Texan billionaire entrepreneur Grant Landscar has disappeared during their honeymoon on the Mediterranean island of Milloncha. Mrs. Landscar, the former journalist Eleanor Framp and now head of the recently launched specialist craft magazine,

Embroideryworld, hasn't been seen since last Tuesday when she was spotted on security cameras at Milloncha Airport. There is much speculation about what may have happened to her. Nearly a week later there is no trace of the billionaire's wife. As no ransom note has been received, it's possible that she has suffered some kind of accident or simply decided that the rich life is not for her after all. Grant Landscar is offering $50,000 reward for the safe return of his wife.'

'It's on the front page, Dad.'

'Do you think $50,000 is enough?'

'It's not for me to say. Your decision. What's a wife worth?'

'Good question. Eleanor is priceless to me.'

'Well, see how it goes. I just hope she's alright. Keep me posted.'

'Will do.'

'...Hang on a mo. There's something else here...'

'What?'

'In a small box at the bottom. Hold on. It says to go to page nineteen, their environment section.'

Grant heard the sound of rustling paper as Pandy thumbed through.

'Ah, here it is...

RARE DORMOUSE FOUND

The exceedingly rare dormouse, 'Muscardinus samdinus, has been discovered in the overgrown garden of a property on the outskirts of Phillipstone in East Anglia. The dormouse which is closely related to the hazel dormouse, Muscardinus avellanarious, is almost extinct with very few breeding pairs surviving in this country. Mr. Landscar, the renowned environmentalist whose wind farm application on Phillipstone Airport land failed last year, has applied for planning permission to build the UK's first mulit-purpose electric vehicle recharging and cleaning centre on the site.'

'What? A dormouse? In the bungalow garden?'

'Yes, and there's a picture of it all sort of curled up in a nest, well, sleeping.'

'Who's behind this?'
'I'll tell you. There's more:

Phillipstone local environmental group leader, Mrs. Monica Thackman who discovered the dormouse, said that it is extremely important that Muscardinus samdinus is left undisturbed and that her group will be objecting strongly to Mr. Landscar's planning application. They are also hoping to get the site designated a Site of Extraordinary Scientific Interest (SESI).'

'I don't believe this. I'll get my lawyers onto it straight away. I'm not putting up with this.'

'I've seen you take on a lot of opponents, Dad, but never a dormouse.' Pandy couldn't help laughing.

'It's not funny. I've got all the state of the art cleaning equipment coming from the U.S. and I've bought the perishing property, and had to bung a sweetener to that pillock Springstock into the bargain.'

'I'll leave you to it, Dad. You've fished yourself out of worse situations than this. Got to get on. Let me know if you hear anything about poor Eleanor.'

Grant put down the phone. Was nothing going his way right now? First Eleanor gone, then the discovery of the flaming dormouse, nobody to do the cooking and housekeeping in the villa with Synth away and to cap it all problems with his hotel business deal. Was he getting too old for all this? He sat down on one of the white sofas and rubbed his eyes. He put his head back onto the down cushion and, before he knew it, was deeply asleep, mouth open, snoring.

*

'Señor Landscar! 'Señor Landscar!'
Grant jolted awake.
'Wake up! Wake up!'
'What is it, Gonzo. Can't you see I was takin' a nap?'
'Importante! Here! See!' He thrust an envelope into Grant's hand.

'What the heck...?' Grant ripped it open.

**5 MILLION EUROS
YOU WANT SEE
WIFE ALIVE AGAIN.
NO POLICE.
WAIT INSTRUCTIONS**

Grant sat bolt upright.

'Who delivered this?'

'I dunno-a, 'Señor Landscar. I find it on outside step by front door... I hear motor cycle.'

Throwing down the ransom note, Grant got to his feet and rushed through the marble hall, flinging open the door to be greeted by the scent of spring flowers mixed with a feint whiff of two-stroke. He strode out angrily onto the gravel forecourt, scrutinising it for tyre marks, temporarily silencing the tranquil chirping of birds on the villa's red tiled roof. A deep channel was cut in the gravel. It came in an arc from the long drive, had clearly skidded to pile up the shingle and had then curved off and away back down the drive again. He looked about him wildly. Somebody had been here and that person knew where Eleanor was being held. So she was still alive.

He walked back inside. No police. Should he ring them? He looked at his reflection in the ornate hall mirror. A wild-eyed, tousle-haired, grey-faced man gazed back at him. He checked his watch. It was time for his diabetes medication. No wonder he looked rough. He went into the kitchen and took the tablets with a glass of water. Now he had to wait. How much longer before the kidnappers got in touch again?

Gonzo had followed him out and in again. 'Iss good news, yes? She still alive.'

Grant nodded gravely and walked thoughtfully through to the lounge again. He sat down, heart pounding, and retrieved the note. Logic, that's what was needed.

He examined the writing. It was large and scrawling, done with a red marker pen that showed through the thin quality paper to the other side. The paper itself was rather like grease-proof, having a slightly translucent quality. He sniffed it. There was a slight smell of oil. He stared at the words again. Something was missing. It was like shorthand, as if the writer was either being very economical or didn't speak the language well. It was child-like in the construction.

He looked at the torn open envelope. Just a plain manilla A5 size stuck down with sticky tape. The dry glue seal had not been licked so there was no chance of a DNA match. The kidnappers had clearly thought that through.

'Eleanor, oh Eleanor,' he muttered to himself.

'Pleass?' Gonzo enquired.

Grant looked up. 'Where were you when this arrived? Did you see anybody?'

'I out in greenhouse, watering tomatoes. I see nobody. They very good, strong plants this year...'

'I'm not interested in tomato plants. Who has a motor bike around here.'

'Many, many people, Señor Landscar. Half-a of the men on the island.' Gonzo stood, hands dangling by his side. 'Señor, forgive-a me but I must-a ask you... what we do about food? Synth she gone and I no cook.'

'Food? Who cares about food? Some vile people have got my lovely wife captive and you expect me to think about something as mundane as eating?'

'Yessir. Iss importante to be strong.'

'What have we got?'

'I look in fridge. May I respectful offer services of my friend Valeria? She good cook and clean.'

'Is she reliable?'

'Oh yes, Señor. She do for the shops in village. She iss verrry hygienic.'

'How much an hour?'

'I think she take ten Euros for one hour.'

'Very well, Gonzo. Please ask her.' Grant didn't have the emotional strength haggle.

'Certainly, Sirrr. I will do so without hesitation.'

Grant waved him away and Gonzo backed out of the room nodding obsequiously.

The Mediterranean spring sun sank gracefully over the blue horizon leaving behind a pink glow that shone with magical effervescence on the smooth surface of the sea. A few wispy clouds took up the rose hue and held it tentatively as a gentle breeze sprang up, relinquishing it at last as the moon appeared and shone with calmness onto the scene. Grant Landscar stood on one of the *Villa Estancia's* top terraces, a glass of sugar-free lime juice in his hand, watching as day turned to night.

Where was Eleanor? Was she afraid? Was it his fault? If he'd been with her would she perhaps not have gone shopping? Why had nobody seen her? She was so recognisable, tall and slim with a dignity and presence to be admired. His beautiful Eleanor, possibly bound and gagged somewhere in some filthy place, terrified and alone. He stifled a sob.

Chapter 21

Eleanor shivered. It was cold and damp. A thin sliver of light shone in from high up and dappled the surface of the water. How could she have been so stupid? So trusting? 'Let me show you beautiful caves of *Adroncia*,' Gonzo had said. It had all seemed so innocent, first a pleasant trip along the coast of Milloncha and then a turn into a secluded bay where he had dropped anchor. She'd wondered why he had been towing a small, red inflatable behind them. 'We need go into little boat,' he had said. 'Big boat no good for caves. You like caves. So beautiful, nice *stalagmita*.'

Eleanor, never very confident around water, wasn't keen to transfer to the blow-up dinghy but she was suddenly afraid that if she hurt his feelings he might not be so nice.

'Very well,' she had said, 'but not for long. I have to get back for Mr. Landscar.' She had hitched her shoulder bag across her body.

'No worry, lady. We only ten minutes in there.'

Gonzo had produced a battery-driven lantern and fixed it to the front of the dinghy. Then, with steady strokes he had rowed her in through the large mouth of the cave, along increasingly narrow tunnels which suddenly opened out into a huge internal cavern, massive as a cathedral with soaring pillars where stalagmites and stalactites had met, its glittering walls stained in streaks of red.

'It's wonderful,' Eleanor had said as he had stowed the oars and unfixed the lamp. He shone it around to show rocks draped with glistening black seaweed, luminous algae floating on the water's surface and crystalline forms from a fairytale. 'Where are we?'

'We call-a it *Carmesi Profundi... Crimson Deeps*. You look. The water iss red and verrry, verrry deep.' He shone the lamp down to show her. 'I told you it beautiful,' he said, 'but no touch. Come, I show you grotto. You hold-a lamp.' He took up the oars again and rowed to a shallow ledge, crafted by nature as a landing point.

'We get out. Iss O.K. Grotto very nice.'

Clutching her shoulder-bag, Eleanor had nervously climbed out onto the moist ledge. This was a once-in-a-lifetime experience.

'Look over here, Señora Landscar.' He beckoned her forward into a wide crevasse. It was slippery underfoot. 'I take-a your hand.' There, sparkling in the lamp-light was the most exquisite, crystalline grotto Eleanor had ever seen. Water trickled down through it from some unknown source and small flower-like crystals clung to the walls reflecting rainbow-coloured sparks.

'Iss rainwater,' he'd said. 'Can drink it.'

She'd turned to ask him how he knew about this place but he had moved away, taking the lamp with him, stepping into the dinghy, pushing off from the ledge.

'Wait!' she had said. 'Wait for me!'

He had laughed at her, his voice echoing up through the void above. 'You make joke, yes? No, my lady. You stay here. You my pass-a-port-a to good time.'

'Gonzo, please stop. Don't leave me here.' Her voice rose to a wail. 'Gonzo! I beseech you!' Some disturbed bats fluttered above.

'You no call me Gonzo. You call me Señor Gonzales now.'

Eleanor struggled to steady her voice. 'Please... Señor Gonzales... we can work this out. I can give you money. I've my own money.'

'Your money? Peanuts!' he said, steadily pulling away. 'You find provisions in box next to grotto. Enjoy your stay!'

She shrieked in panic, finally acknowledging that he really was going to leave her alone in this cold, slimy place and that nobody knew where she was. As his boat disappeared through the exit into the tunnel, leaving her with only the shining, floating algae lit by a solitary beam of light from above, he called out, 'and don't touch red water. Iss poisonous from aluminium works.'

If she had even been able to swim there was no way she could cross the crimson lake. She'd dropped to all fours and scrabbled her way back to the grotto in the semi-darkness, scraping her hands, feeling about until she'd found the big, plastic storage box and pulled the lid off, rummaging around inside, sensing tins, candles, a polythene bag that seemed to have boxes of matches in it and, finally, a torch which she clicked on. Then she had wept uncontrollably as hot flush after hot flush had swept over her.

*

'Theess is my friend-a Valeria,' Gonzo said to Grant.

A diminutive woman with dark, curly hair gave a half-curtsey to her new boss, somewhat awkwardly as she was wearing frayed jeans and plimsolls.

'Take her into town, Gonzo, and get her properly dressed. Then she can have the job. Does she speak English?'

'Not one word, Señor.'

Grant nodded to the woman.

'*Bienvenida*,'

She smiled and nodded back at him. Gonzo took her by the arm and led her out of the room, gabbling away in the vernacular. Grant heard them leave in the four-by-four and then he returned to his paper as he reclined on the sun-lounger in the conservatory of *Villa Estancia.*

Life without Eleanor was so empty. He put down his paper and looked out towards the distant fruit blossom trees. The petals were coming down in pink and white clouds, floating away on the spring breeze against the vivid blue sky. Over a week now. As every day passed and the police and media interest faded, he struggled to keep up his hopes. They told him that most kidnap victims were dead within two days. He had not disclosed the ransom note to the police. There had been no further contact from the kidnappers. The thought crossed his mind that if Eleanor was indeed dead, then he was glad he had insured her life heavily. Every cloud had a silver lining. No, no, he mustn't think like that.

The phone rang. He took it from the table beside him and said, 'Landscar.'

'Ah, is that you Mr. Landscar? It's me, Percival Springstock. Councillor Springstock.'

'Hi.'

There was an awkward silence.

'What can I do for you Councillor Springstock?'

'Dreadful news. Dreadful... about your wife. Please accept my condolences.'

'I hope that's not necessary. She may still be alive.'

'Of course. Of course. Worrying business for you. It's all over the papers here and on the news.'

'Is it now?' Grant said, feigning surprise. 'But what do you really want?'

'Oh, oh... well... I was wondering whether I might come out and use the flat in Milloncha. You said I could visit it for holidays. Although no documents have come through from your solicitor, I'm hoping you're a man of your word.'

The fact that he had given the man carte blanche to use the luxury flat in Milloncha had somehow slipped Grant's mind with everything else going on.

'And... and...' Councillor Springstock hurried on breathlessly, 'it's a pity about the bungalow.'

'What about it?'

'Oh, didn't you hear? Your planning application failed to get through the other night at the council meeting. There's some endangered rodent in the bungalow garden... I never knew about that, of course, when I sold the place to you... it was all done in good faith. I had no idea about the little furry creature in the back garden.'

'I know about the dormice. Want to buy the property back?'

'Indeed, no. No thank-you. I did my best to get the application through for you but the local environmental group have got some SESI slapped on it.'

'And what would that be?'

'Site of Extraordinary Scientific Interest. The grounds must not be disturbed.'

Grant gave a long sigh of exasperation. Councillor Springstock continued, 'The flat?'

'It's being redecorated at present.'

'When will it be ready for me?'

'I can't say.'

'That's a pity. I rather fancy a spring break in Milloncha.'

'Sorry about that,' Grant said with thinly veiled insincerity.

'Will I get the legal document soon?'

There was a moment's silence.

'I regret that I have to go now, Councillor. Pressing business. Goodbye.'

*

Eleanor took out her notebook, perched it on her knees and began to write by candlelight. She drew her thin cardigan around her shoulders. The steady trickling of crystal clear water in the grotto was a background to her every hour in this dismal place.

> _Monday_. I've been here for over a week. My food
> is running out. I've eaten cold things from the tins,
> rationed the biscuits and drunk water from the sparkling
> grotto. I've managed to keep myself reasonably clean by
> using my neckscarf as a flannel. Nights are cold
> and damp as I lie on the inflatable that I found
> stashed in the corner with two blankets. I'm sitting
> on that now. I only have a couple of candles left.
> Gonzo hasn't been back since he left me. I use an
> empty beans can as a loo and tip it into the lake
> at the end of the flat shelf on which I'm stranded.
> The lake smells bad anyway. Next to the grotto is
> a sort of internal rock chimney and I can feel fresh
> air drifting down it. I've shone the torch up there but
> it's far too narrow for a person to climb up. If I stand
> beneath it I can see a little porthole at the top and
> a few stars by night and a tiny patch of blue sky by day.

Eleanor had wept tears until she was dry. The ache in her heart was so heavy that she thought it would rise up and choke her. She put her notebook in her shoulder-bag and prepared to settled down for the night, wearing her lilac beanie hat, pulling the blankets over her. The shaft of light that peered in from high up in the cavern's roof was fading. Night came quickly in the Mediterranean and she didn't want to waste the candles or torch.

She was deeply asleep when she was woken by something brushing past her face. Did she dream it? She sat up, hastily turning on the torch, shining its beam about her. There was a scuffling sound from the corner away from the grotto and then two green eyes shone back at her.

'Oh!' she squeaked, drawing up her legs.

'Meow.'

'A cat!' she exclaimed with delight. 'Oh, you beautiful thing. Come here.' She extended her hand. The animal came towards her and pushed its firm, furry head against her fingers, purring loudly. 'You are gorgeous,' she said, lifting it onto her lap and stroking its thick, black fur. 'How did you get in here?'

This first sign of life in a bleak week was so heartening. Hope. Hope at last. Here was a contact with the outside world. She was not abandoned after all to die in this grim place. She looked at her watch. It was three a.m. The cat felt warm. Would it stay? It would, settling down on her lap, imparting its gentle heat to her chilled body. She sat like that until the glimmer of dawn came through the cavern roof, then she gently lifted the sleeping animal onto the blankets and went to open her last tin of sardines.

As soon as the animal smelt the fish, it was awake, winding itself in and out of her legs as she stood peeling back the can lid with the key. 'Yes, yes. You'll have some,' she said. Together the pair shared their fishy breakfast. Then the cat sat in the half-light as it would in front of a fire in its own home and fastidiously cleaned its paws and licked its back. Lick, lick, lick. That was strange. The sound was echoing. It wasn't. It was the rhythmic plop of oars dipping into water. Gonzo was coming back. He was coming back! The cat paused in mid-lick and then stood up and walked firmly away, showing the keyhole that denoted a female. A sound of scrabbling, and she was gone, leaving Eleanor sitting on the lilo straining her eyes for the boat that she knew was coming.

*

'Hey! Look at this, Celeste!'

'What?' She was deep in her accounts at her dining table.

'There's a tremendous bit in the local rag about Landscar's project opposite being scuppered.'

'We knew it was.'

'Yes, but it's in the public domain now.'

'Roland, I'm trying to see if I have to pay VAT or not.'

'Show me your threshold.'

'No. My business accounts are not your concern.'

'Well, look in your new business handbook or check it on the internet.'

'I will.'

'Want to come round to mine tonight? We can have a take-away.'

She looked up. 'Why should I come into your pad of seduction and debauchery?'

'A bit of friendly companionship. Anyway, I thought you'd like to see Eleanor Framp's wedding pictures. I've printed up a set. Mind you, she may never get to see them. They said they're giving up the search.'

'Good. If I never see the woman again it'll be too soon. By the way, I'm resigning from the Chamber of Commercial Enterprise. I haven't got time for all that stuff and we've won now anyway.'

'I will too. Bunch of old fuddy-duddies and back-scratchers. We'll take the independent route to commercial success! Knickers to them all!'

He looked around her flat. She'd made it quite pleasant and cosy with a log effect electric fire, recycled furniture and a shaggy rug on the floor. He looked down at it, imagining her naked body stretched out seductively before the fire's flickering warmth. Failing that, skidding about on his black satin sheets upstairs next door in his bachelor flat.

Celeste closed her books and stretched.

'It's only nine o'clock and I'm bushed.'

'Let's have an early night... together.'

'Roland, have you looked at yourself lately? You may think you're Rudolph Valentino but with your paunch and bald patch you are nearer to a his dad.'

'Cruel, cruel woman. It's not about the physical.' He waved his hands in the air. 'See these? These are magic fingers. I can thrill you to your spine with just the merest touch.'

'Well, get them to do my washing up for me. It's piled up through there in the kitchen.'

'Blow the washing up! Come and put your head on my shoulder and let's sit and watch the news together like some old married couple.'

'You're incorrigible! It only seems like yesterday you were being attacked by Little Nanny, flailing around in your studio. If I hadn't grounded her you would have been mince-meat.'

'True. I need a strong woman to look after me.'

'I don't do looking after. Surely you've worked that one out.'

'You're not the mumsy type then?'

'You'd better believe it.'

'When did you last see the triplets?'

'Sunday.'

'Well, how are they?'

'Teething. Grizzling all the time. I picked one of them up and she puked all over me. I handed her back to Big Nanny sharpish.'

'I saw Little Nanny the other day...'

'That's not still going on?'

'No, of course not but she said you definitely sacked her.'

'Of course. I can't possibly have somebody like that around my children. My mother's organising a replacement.'

'She paid me for the damage, you know.'

'And so she should have.' Celeste heaved the books onto the fitted sideboard.

Roland got up from the sofa and came towards her.

'You stink of curry,' she said, turning to him.

He grabbed her and pulled her to him, plunging his lips onto hers. To his amazement, she responded, taking her hand up behind his head, pulling on his hair, lifting her leg to wrap it around his waist. This was indeed a surprise but hay-making while the sun shone was his speciality. Before they knew it, clothes littered the floor, the centre light was off and the shaggy rug lived up to its name.

'Condom!' she commanded.

'Aw, Celeste...'

'In the jar on the mantelpiece,' she panted.

'You expected this?' he asked with amazement as he reached up to get the jar, the electric firelight flickering on the curly hair of his chest.

'Planning is my speciality,' she said, pulling him down onto her.

*

'More toast, Synth?' Reverend mother held the rack out.

'Mmm. Yes please. I'm starving today. I couldn't eat much yesterday because I was so worried about Mum.'

'Well, it's good that she's regained consciousness.'

Synth spread a thin layer of margarine and then some marmalade.

'Yes, but it'll be a long job to get her fit again.'

'She's full of spirit. Sister Catherine and I thought we might go and see her one afternoon after our grand silence.'

'That would be nice for her. She always liked you, you know.'

'We oldies have to stick together.'

'Good morning, ladies,' Father Guyler said, taking his place at the end of the long table in the dining room. A chorus of reciprocal "Good Mornings" greeted him. 'Sorry I'm a bit late. It was such a lovely morning that I took a gentle walk up to the folly. The daffodils have all finished now, you know.'

'Yes, spring is soon over,' Reverend Mother said regretfully. 'We have to enjoy each one.' The unspoken words that she didn't know how many more she would see were not lost on the priest.

'Did you hear on the news, Reverend Mother, that they are scaling down the search for Eleanor?' he said.

'No. I heard it from Grant. He telephoned yesterday. I would have thought they would have gone on looking for a bit longer.'

'They seem to have exhausted all possible places on the island,' Father Guyler commented, tucking into his cereal.

'Poor Eleanor,' Reverend Mother said sadly. 'What a tragedy so soon after her lovely wedding here.'

'We're all remembering her in our prayers,' Sister Catherine said. 'I wonder if we will ever see her again.'

'Now, now, sisters. Don't think negatively.'

Reverend Mother suddenly rose to her feet, a handkerchief in her hand. 'Excuse me,' she muttered, shuffling out of the dining room before emotions overwhelmed her.

'She's taking it badly, Father,' Sister Catherine said. 'Eleanor is like a daughter to her.'

'We're all very shaken by events,' the priest replied.

One by one the nuns left the dining room, smiling and nodding, taking their crockery to the dirty crocks trolley as they went outside.

They were anxious to get on with their day's work.

'Well,' said Father Guyler to Synth when they were finally alone. She went to get up, not wanting to be on her own with the priest.

'No, no,' he said, 'stay for a little chat about old times.'

'I want to forget that. I have a new life now,' she gabbled.

'Oh, I don't think you ever forget all those little tricks that you learned at your mother's knee. You did follow her into the profession, didn't you? I'm sure you must have.'

She flushed. 'No. Yes. Let it go, Father Guyler. It's in the past.'

'Ah,' he said, 'but it's that past that makes us the people we are today. Why don't you pay me a little visit in the guest suite later tonight? I'll make it worth your while.'

'You disgust me!' she said, starting to pick up her plate. He leaned across and pinned her wrist to the table.

'No doubt,' he said pompously, 'but I think your position as housekeeper to Grant Landscar would be in jeopardy if he really knew what was living under his roof... and what about dear old Reverend Mother? Does she suspect you're a former hooker.'

'Don't use that word.'

'Well, that's what you were.'

'And you were one of my mother's clients.'

'Who's going to believe it? Me, a respectable man of the cloth and you throwing around wild accusations because I rebuffed your advances. Come now, Synth. Be realistic. You only have to be nice to me a little.' He leaned back in his dining chair and took a long, deep sip from his coffee cup. 'Mmm... and I will remain silent.'

She watched his throat pulsate as the liquid glugged down. How she hated him, and her past. She got up unhindered and took her crockery to the trolley.

'Your mother had a nice little business going back then in Argmening Street,' he said laconically. 'Oh I could tell you stories of folk coming to confession relating to me all the naughty things they did in your mother's brothel. You wouldn't believe what they got up to. She used to let me in by the back door of course, you know. Shall we say about midnight?' he said.

*

Ha! You still here?' Gonzo laughed as he rowed across the lake towards his hostage. The lamp was lashed to the front of the dinghy. Eleanor rose to her feet and stood, arms folded, waiting.

'Gonzo, I mean, Señor Gonzales...' her voice was shaky. 'Please take me away from here. I can't bear it any longer. Please... there are bats in here.'

'Stand back. Go next to the grotto. I have supplies for you.'
She did as she was bade. 'People will be missing me. They will be searching.'

'Oh, they are, lady. They are.' He brought the dinghy up next to the ledge and slung a rope around a large rock to stop it drifting away. Then he unloaded a box of provisions.

'I need fresh fruit and vegetables,' Eleanor said, aware that her mouth was feeling sore. I can't live on tinned stuff.'

'You complain-a about this hotel?' he scoffed callously.

She took a step forward. Could she rush him? Push him into the contaminated red water?

'Stay there! Don't move or I leave you to die!'

Eleanor burst into tears, hiccupping as she tried to control her speech. The she shouted, 'Señor Gonzales! This really will not do. You have to let me go.' He ignored her so she bent down and picked up a rock the size of a cricket ball, pitching it towards his head as he bent to lift the cardboard box tied with string but he saw her movement from the corner of his eye at the last moment and ducked. The rock plopped into the red water.

'So, you play-a nasty with me! Perhaps I must tie you up. Yes, I will do that.'
She shrank against the rock-face. 'No. Please don't tie me up.'

'I think a lady like-a you enjoy being tied up. Yes?'

He came towards her, unsheathing a long-bladed knife from his belt. 'Don't-a move or I slash-a your prrretty face.' She froze. He brought the blade up close to her cheek. She slowly lifted her chin, looking down onto his swarthy, tanned features, smelling his sweat, taking in the pattern on the bandanna he wore around his head.

'You behave good?'
She was trembling.

'Yes. I'll behave.' With his other hand, he slapped her cheek almost playfully and lowered the knife.

'Then we have-a nice relationship. You find-a yummy food and more candles. I bringed you big juice for your health. See!' He pointed to the landing place. There were two large plastic containers of orange juice.

'Th-thank-you,' she stammered.

'See! I not so bad fellow.'

She summoned up a weak smile and nodded gratefully.

'When I return to *Villa Estancia*, your rich-a husband will have had visitor.'

'Don't hurt Grant,' she begged.

'Stay back. I go now.'

'When will you come again?'

'You find out,' he laughed, pulling away, the plish-plash of his oars fading as the dinghy was swallowed into the dark exit tunnels that led out to the secluded cove.

*

'Where the heck've you been, Gonzo?'

'I go visit my *dentista*. I have-a tooth pain.'

'Look, it's six o'clock and I've had to drive home right across the island to find no meal ready. Where's that Valeria friend of yours? She's supposed to be cooking for us.'

'I not know, Señor.'

The doorbell rang. Gonzo answered it. The stench of fish and chips pervaded the air. Grant was on his feet, outraged. He joined Gonzo by the front door where Valeria stood, her arms full of packages of cod and chips. She smiled broadly, clearly expecting her arrival to be greeted with delight.

'Fish and chips?' Grant gasped.

'Very nice. Best on island,' Gonzo said.

'Then you eat them. I'm going out.' He stormed past the pair, out onto the tiled porch, then stopped in his tracks.

'Who put this thing here?' he pointed down to a flower pot containing a bougainvillea and festooned with a big red bow.

'I not know, Señor.'

Grant stooped to pick it up, noticing the greetings tag attached to it.
'What's this...?'

I MISS YOU MUCH.
LOVE ELEANOR. X

He strode forward looking around, holding the pot loosely in one
hand, his feet crunching on the gravel. Eleanor? Could she have
been here? No. Surely not. Who delivered it? If she missed him so
much, she would have entered. Why would she come here and
leave a message. No. the grammar was all wrong. This was from
the kidnappers.

'I didn't hear anybody deliver this. How did it get here?' he
demanded. Nobody knew. He stood, vacantly, broken. His staff
were frozen like dummies too. Grant turned and went back into the
house carrying the plant and leaving the fading afternoon sun
behind him, his stomach rumbling.

'Let's eat the fish and chips,' he said over his shoulder. 'Have
we got any vinegar?'

'We look, Sirrr.'

Gonzo hustled Valeria into the kitchen. She was now clad in a
navy blue school skirt and white blouse but still wore plimsolls. Her
curly, black hair was scraped back under a white hair-band.
Dangley earrings hung from her lobes, swinging about as she
moved.

Two minutes later she handed a tray to Grant in the
conservatory. The fish and chips had been tipped out from the
paper and arranged on a bone china plate edged with gold. The
gold-plated knife and fork were rolled in a blue paper serviette to
the side and a vinegar shaker and salt cellar completed the exotic
presentation.

Grant took it and placed it on the glass-topped, white, wrought
iron table where only ten days ago he had bade farewell to Eleanor
as she'd eaten her croissants. How times changed! He plunged the
knife into the batter and a swirl of steamy fish vapour shot up his
nostrils. He stabbed a chip with his gold-plated fork and then a
sense of the ridiculous came over him and he couldn't eat for
laughing. A wild kind of hysteria had set in. Here he was, a

billionaire entrepreneur, sitting in state in one of his many homes, having accidentally mislaid his fourth wife on their honeymoon and reduced to eating very greasy fish and chips.

He looked across at the ribbon-swathed plant pot bearing the bogus note from his dear Eleanor. His mobile phone rang. He hurriedly put down the cutlery, composed himself and answered it. A man's muffled voice said in very precise English, 'Did you receive the plant?'

Chapter 22

'Come on, Mum. Try and eat some of this puréed stuff. It really looks very tasty.'

'Shan't'

'It'll do you good.'

'I want cornflakesh.'

'Look, they've made it all nice in the shapes of the things it's supposed to be.' Synth looked down sceptically at the blobs of potato, cauliflower and lamb, all carefully sculpted on the plate. 'It must have taken them ages to do it.'

Suddenly, Maud started wailing. 'Ow! Ow!'

Synth pulled the bed-table away. 'What's the matter?'

Her mother was gesturing frantically to the floor with her good arm.

'Ooooh!' she cried, drawing up her knees.

Synth got up and went around to the other side of the bed to have a look. The urine bag was brim full. The catheter was working well, too well.

'Hang on, Mum. I'll get the nurse.'

Other patients in the six-bed ward were looking at each other and silently shaking their heads. They'd all had more than enough of Maud's shenanigans. They'd suffered everything from night-time shouting to things being thrown across the room.

When Synth returned with the Staff Nurse, Maud had pulled the bed-table back and had her hands plunged into the dinner, mixing it all together in swirls.

'Now, now, Mrs. Hunt,' the nurse said, trying to remove the old lady's hands from the mess. Maud was too quick though and deliberately slapped a hand-print in the middle of the bib-front of the starched, white apron. She received no response, which disappointed her because what she wanted was a reaction. A second attempt was foiled, however, as Staff Nurse grabbed both wrists and held them in the air.

'Fetch one of the auxiliaries for me, would you please, Miss Hunt?'

Hugely embarrassed by her mother's behaviour, Synth did as she was bade. Then the two nursing staff took control of the situation, cleaning up and restoring order while Maud protested loudly with shouts of, "Moleshting me. Help!'

The curtains were drawn around the bed. As Synth was retreating to the corridor waiting area she was beckoned over by a lady in the bed near the door.

'Do you have a minute?' she whispered.

Synth went to her. 'I'm really sorry about my mother... she has dementia...'

'I guessed so, that's why I hate to complain but none of us is getting any sleep. We've asked for your mother to be moved into another room but they say there aren't any free, only the private ones. I'm really sorry... I thought you should know...'

'Thanks for telling me. I'll see what can be done.'

Maud's desperate daughter sat on the chair outside and wanted to burst into tears. She loved her mother, of course she did, but coping with her dementia was always going to be challenging. Staff nurse came out and joined her.

'Do you have a minute?'

Synth followed her into the office and took a seat. Staff Nurse produced Maud's notes and studied them for a moment. Then she looked up.

'It's going to be several months before your mother will be fit enough to return to her residential home. Indeed, there is a possibility that they may not wish to take her back as it isn't geared up there to deal with severe stroke victims who are also suffering from dementia.'

Synth twisted her fingers together in anxiety, shaking her head and pursing her lips. 'I don't know what'll happen to her. I kept her at home for as long as I could but I have to work to keep us both and she couldn't be trusted alone in the house. She set fire to one place we lived in.'

'Miss Hunt, I gather you've had to fly back urgently from the Mediterranean to be here with your mother.'

She nodded. 'I had to abandon my job. I hope they keep it open for me.'

'It must all be very worrying for you. Look, what I'm going to do is to suggest that you try and raise the finance to have her moved into one of our private rooms. She's very disruptive, you know. The alternative is to keep her permanently under sedation and that's not only expensive but makes it more difficult to care for her.'

'How much do the private rooms cost?'

'Two thousand pounds a week.'

Synth gasped. 'I couldn't possibly pay for that.'

'Then,' said the Staff Nurse, 'I'm going to suggest that we sedate your mother as a temporary measure until some more suitable arrangement can be made for her. Do you agree to that?'

'Can I see her first?'

'Yes, of course. Her bed-sheets are just being changed, again. She keeps pulling the catheter out, you know.'

'That's because the bag was full. It was hurting her.'

'Miss Hunt, we're very short-staffed here. You can see there are only two fully qualified nursing staff and two auxiliaries on this very large hub of wards. Regrettably, we can't always check the urine bags as often as we would like.'

'Could she be moved to another hospital where they have amenity rooms on the health service?'

The staff nurse suppressed a smile and rather condescendingly said, 'We have an ageing population, Miss Hunt. Strokes are big business for the elderly. Few hospitals want to take in old people from outside, especially with several medical conditions going on and a not very bright prognosis.'

Synth rose. 'Thank you for being so clear about Mum's future.'

Staff Nurse got to her feet too. 'It wouldn't be fair of me to give you false hopes, Miss Hunt. Your mother really is getting on in years and now has multiple problems. You are going to have to address these. Is there any possibility that you could become her full-time carer again?'

'Not a hope in hell,' Synth said. 'I deserve a life too!' She left without a backward glance, deciding not to say farewell to Maud. She could hear her shouting in the background as she went.

*

'How was your mother today, Synth, dear,' Reverend Mother enquired, looking up from her wicker seat in the warm conservatory where she was reading a lives of the saints book.

'Not good. Very awkward and distressed. Staff Nurse said they can't keep her on the ward because she's so disruptive and they don't have a separate room free for her. I don't know what I'm going to do.' Tears brimmed over as she sat down beside the nun.

'Now, now, don't upset yourself. We'll work something out.' She patted Synth on the shoulder. 'Shall I go and see her?'

'It wouldn't be worth it. They're going to sedate her. I can see their point of view.' She threw her hands out, fingers spread. 'Do you know, the Staff Nurse even had the cheek to ask me if I would consider being Mum's full-time carer again?'

'Would you?'

'I couldn't. I'm too angry with her.'

'Why? What's she done?'

'It was all a long time ago, Reverend Mother, but she ruined my life for me.'

'Do you want to tell me about it?'

'I'd rather not.'

'Something to do with the night-work you were doing when you lived in the old cottage here on the convent estate?'

'Maybe.'

'Synth, dear, I didn't fall out of a tree yesterday. I may be a nun, and believe me I have been a nun for a very long time, but I do know about the world.'

Synth's face flooded red with embarrassment. It was the elephant in the room. Reverend Mother knew about her sleazy past and Synth knew that. Neither spoke of it but both understood that it was a life she didn't want to return to. Reverend Mother took the woman's hand. Synth was a grown woman but this elderly nun made her feel like a school-girl.

'So,' she said, 'how have you left it with Mr. Landscar?'

'I just had to get on a plane. Miss Eleanor was going to tell him... I mean, Mrs. Landscar, but then she disappeared so I think Gonzo, the villa manager must have.'

'Mmmm,' said the nun. 'I think you'd better ring your employer.'

'You're right. I must. He's been very good to me. I like working for him. Do you know, I broke a valuable statue and he didn't stop it out of my wages?'

Reverend Mother smiled. Of course it would have been insured. Men like Grant Landscar always had insurance. The garden door opened and Father Guyler came in.

'Reverend Mother. Synth. How are you both?' He shut the door behind him and the window panes rattled.

Synth gave him a hard stare. Reverend Mother put her book on the window-ledge and said, 'We're fine, thank you Father. What have you been up to, then?'

'Oh just taking some photographs of the grounds.' He waved a small digital camera about. 'I'm getting much stronger on my legs now and my balance is better so it's good to get out and look at the convent estate. I must say, you have a lot of land here. Rather impressive.'

'Yes,' said Reverend Mother, 'and we'd quite like to keep it.'

She pursed her lips in a determined smile. He looked down on Synth and raised his eyebrows, his eyes twinkling as if he shared a secret with her.

'And how's your mother, Synth?'

'Not too good. They're going to sedate her.'

'I'm sorry to hear that.'

She shrugged. 'Not much I can do about it. It's only a matter of time. Her quality of life is poor anyway. Mum was dotty as a polka-dot dress before the stroke but now she's frustrated and angry. She's confused and won't eat.'

Father Guyler looked at Reverend Mother for inspiration as to how this awkward conversation should go. As usual, her diplomacy triumphed. 'Have you seen Sister Catherine's lovely earrings?' she said, indicating a table on the far side of the conservatory. Synth got up to have a look.

'They're really lovely,' she said. 'What'll she do with them all?'

'Oh she sells them on our market stall in Phillipstone town square,' she replied.

'I didn't know you had a stall there,' Father Guyler said, surprised.

'We sell our surplus fruit and vegetables once a month. The sisters knit things from donated yarn and, of course Sister Catherine sells her paintings as well. Oh yes, it's a great little earner,' she laughed. 'Sometimes the postulants make sweets and sell them too. We're very commercial!'

Synth looked at the jewellery. 'They're really pretty,' she said picking up a pair of dangly earrings on a blue card. 'I'm going to ask her to show me how to make them.'

'I'm sure she'll be delighted. There's nothing Sister Catherine likes more than passing on her talents to others. She does an art class at our school on Thursday afternoons, you know.'

'Does she really?' said Father Guyler with feigned interest. He strode about slowly, looking at the tubs of plants and burgeoning grapevine. 'I always feel it's very important for people to pass on their skills. Don't you agree, Synth?'

She glared at him. 'Depends what they are,' she said. 'Some skills are not worth a penny.'

'Ah,' said the priest. 'That's where you're wrong. All our gifts and talents are equal in the eyes of the Lord.'

If Synth could have got up and strangled him she would have. What a hypocrite! The man who had subjected her to pleasuring him in the guest suite of the convent only last night now stood there pompously pontificating.

Did Reverend Mother smell a rat? She looked from one to the other. What was going on?

'Well,' she said, 'I think I'll just pop down to the kitchens and see how the bread and buttering is going on. I like to keep my hand in.'

'Yes,' said the priest, 'it's very important to keep your hand in.'

'I'll come and help you,' Synth said hastily.

*

Eleanor stabbed at her mobile phone again. Nothing. The thick walls of the cavern made sure of that. She stood on the wide ledge looking out across *Crimson Deeps*. The surface of the water was as smooth as glass except where an occasional bubble burst. She looked up at the small slit in the ceiling where the shaft of light was creating a pool of silver in the centre of the lake. The red-stained cavern walls looked like hell. What was outside? Did people ever walk up there? She had shouted and shouted during the first week but only her own voice had echoed back to her, ricocheting off the walls, diminishing in volume, '**HELP!** HELP! Help!' Then the eerie silence, punctuated solely by the trickle of pure water in the grotto behind her. She also tried shouting up the rock chimney next to the grotto. It sounded muffled. Her cries only brought visits from the beautiful, black cat who somehow scrambled down the tube to share her food on a daily basis.

'Yes, please,' she had told Gonzo. 'I love tinned fish. Please bring me lots of it... tuna, sardines, pilchards. I don't mind. Anything.'

'Strange-a lady,' he had sneered. 'You turn-a into a merrrmaid, ha?'

She'd smiled demurely. 'I've always liked fish.' Strangely enough, the cat invariably took off when she heard Eleanor's captor approaching in the red dinghy.

Gonzo and Eleanor had settled into a cordial routine, jailor and victim. She kept her distance and he brought her provisions. Living on cold food was somehow dispiriting though and she begged him for a hot meal. 'It's very chilly in here. Please couldn't I have a little spirit stove or a mini gas cylinder? I could at least make myself a hot drink.'

'What you gotta for me if I do-a this favorrr for you?'

'You can have my gold and diamond pendant. It was a gift from my husband... it's very valuable...' her voice tailed off. 'Oh, I seem to have left it at home...' she fumbled around her neckline. 'Silly me.'

'You one stupid lady, yes?'

'Yes,' she agreed humbly. Anything to keep on the right side of him.

'Well, what else-a?'

She rolled back the sleeve of her cardigan. 'Would you like this bracelet?'

'I like-a your diamond watch better.' His eyes glinted with avarice. 'And your nice-a emerald ring?'

She rolled back her other sleeve and said innocently, 'Oh, I'm sorry. Because of the rush to see Synth off at the airport, I seem to have forgotten to put on my watch and ring too.

'O.K. I take-a the bracelet. Give it here.'

He grabbed the silver-link bracelet roughly. She backed away. 'My engagement ring's at home.'

He grunted. He would steal the ring later from Eleanor's bedroom.

'One, more thing, Señor Gonzales, that orange juice was very refreshing. Is it possible to have some more please?'

'You drunk-a it already?'

'I do so like my fruit juice,' she'd lied. In truth, she detested orange juice and had poured it into the lake at the end of the ledge.

'No more. That's it. I go now,' he said pompously.

'Safe journey!' Eleanor had called after him, enjoying a moment of levity. She knew her survival depended on him. The lapping of the oars faded into the distance and she was alone again.

'Meow.'

'Hello, Kitty,' she said, bending to pick up the cat. 'We have new supplies now and I have a little job for you.'

As the cat lapped up the mashed tuna, Eleanor fondled its neck and carefully tied a short piece of string around it. Gonzo had been careless and left the string on his delivery boxes. Attached to the string collar, Eleanor tied a note encased in a rolled up crisp packet. It read,

To the finder of this note.
Please help me. I am trapped in a big cave.
I don't know where it is but I think it's near the aluminium works.
Tell my husband that I'm alive.
                              Eleanor Landscar

She had dated it and hoped she had counted the days correctly. The cat finished its meal and settled down on her lap for some pampering. After a while it got up and gave a mew of farewell before scrambling up the rock chimney again. Maybe it was somebody's pet. Perhaps they would read the note. She hoped they spoke English.

She took her diamond watch out of her bra cup and checked the time. It was five o-clock in the afternoon. Thank goodness she had out-smarted Gonzo on that one. She wrote her journal:

I can't believe I've been here for three weeks. I expect
they've all given up on me. It's grim in here, a bit humid
and weird but a sort of daily routine has evolved. My clothes
are pretty dirty but there's not much I can do about that. I
wash out my panties in the grotto water, wring them out and
put them on again. They dry quicker on me than if I drape
them on a rock. Gonzo keeps me well supplied with food and
my mouth has cleared up now. I clean my teeth with the
corner of my headscarf and floss them with a thin bit of
string that I unwound from the hairy string he left here.
I've washed my hair a couple of times in the grotto water but
it's very cold. It's grown rather and looks a mess from what
I can see in my small compact mirror. Gonzo rifled through
my handbag when I first came here. He took the cash from
it but left me my notebook, make-up and comb. He must
have planned my kidnap well in advance. I wonder whether
Grant has received a ransom note yet? I sing. Yes, I sing, all
alone in here. The acoustics are very good actually. I do my
scales and then work through all the songs I know. After that, I
do a bit of exercise. Don't want to get a thrombosis or piles
from sitting. There's not a lot of room here. The ledge is about
six metres long by three metres wide. Behind me is a sort of
lobby in the rock with the grotto and the rock chimney that
Kitty comes down. The worst time is waking up in the morning,
that moment before my eyes open and think my world is
fine... then I open my eyes and hear the trickle of the grotto
and know that I am stuck here for another day..

Anybody walking on the cliffs above the cavern might have heard the sad voice of Eleanor Landscar as she sang the Latin mass, followed by a few hymns and then songs from the shows.

*

'Qué?' Valeria stood before Grant Landscar in the lounge of *Villa Estancia.*

'What do you mean? Don't you know where he is?' Grant asked her in the Millonchan dialect, as far as he could manage it, but she seemed not to understand. He waved her away. Then he heard the front door open.

'I am home, Señor Landscar,' Gonzo called out ingratiatingly.

'Where the heck have you been?'

'Dentista. More pain. So sorry.' He put his hand to his cheek.

'I thought it was the other side.'

'Both sides-a,' he added hastily. 'O.K. now.'

'Will you tell this girl that I want feeding?'

'Yes, Señor, right away.'

'Before you go, where did you put the four-by-four keys?'

'Oh, I forgetta. They in my room. I fetch-a them. I took-a my own little runabout to go to dentist. I not use your car for pleasure.'

'Well if you think going to the dentist is a pleasure, you're a funnier fellow than I thought.'

'Ha ha, Señor Landscar. Very amusing.'

Grant took his mobile phone out of his trouser pocket and speed-dialled Teddy Appleton-Smythe.

'Hello, old boy, ' his former school chum said with bonhomie.

'Hi there, Teddy.'

'Any news of poor Eleanor? You must be worried to death.'

'Nope. Nothin' new.' He hadn't told Teddy about the kidnappers' notes. 'We live in hope, though.'

' I was a bit surprised that the experiment didn't work. It was supposed to transmit at noon yesterday.'

'Gee!' Grant said, sitting more upright. 'I'd clean forgotten. Of course! The pendant! Eleanor promised to always wear it.'

'Well, nothing came through. As the satellite was immediately above Milloncha at noon your time, we should have picked up a signal. Nothing came in. That's rather disappointing as the technicians are supposed to have perfected it. The warmth of her skin should have kept it activated.'

Grant closed his eyes. The pendant should have saved his Eleanor.

'Well,' said Teddy, 'I'm off to Oz tomorrow but the guys here will monitor the pendant for a signal every day at noon. We'll keep you informed, Grant my old chum.'

'Thanks, Teddy. Have a good trip!' They both hung up.

'Gonzo! Gonzo? Where's my dinner?'

'Here-a Señor Landscar. You like calamari, yes?'

'Yes, thanks, Gonzo. Put it here. I'll watch the weather on the UK channel.' He clicked on the tv and took the tray on his lap.

'We're expecting a few fine days here in the UK with temperatures into the upper twenties, perhaps making the lower thirties.. However, for those of you about to go on holiday to the Mediterranean, we're keeping an eye on Tropical storm Petunia which is moving up the west coast of Africa and tracking in towards the Mediterranean. It's expected to hit the islands later tomorrow.'

Grant chewed on the calamari. It was rubbery. He didn't want a tropical storm. He was planning an up-river fishing trip tomorrow. His kit was already stashed in the hall. Fishing in the sparkling waters of the local river was one of his great pleasures on Milloncha. Then a thought struck him. What if Eleanor hadn't worn the transmitter pendant after all? He put down his tray and wandered upstairs to her room.

The pink boudoir was neat and tidy. Her hairbrush lay on the dressing table. No clothes were draped about and no shoes kicked off carelessly to rest on the thick carpet. His Eleanor was a tidy person. He felt like an intruder. They respected boundaries. In normal circumstances he wouldn't have pried in her room. Of course he had checked her wardrobe as the police had requested but, to be honest, he had no idea what should have been in there since his darling Eleanor and Pandy had been on several shopping expeditions in the weeks before the wedding.

Now he walked over to the dressing table and opened the top drawer. The leather-bound jewel box was there, nestling amidst her silk underwear. He picked up a pair of her panties and sniffed them. Too clean. No scent of Eleanor. He opened the jewel box. The pendant was there, glinting at him with the engagement ring.

*

'Good morning, Mrs. Thackman.'

'Good morning to you too, Mr. Dilger.'

Roland stood at the counter in the small reception area at the front of his photographic studio. "Tan Boots" hadn't conceded her fashion statement to the warm weather.

'I've come to thank you for those lovely photos you took of me. My friend on the internet's very pleased with them.'

'Great!' he said, grinning. 'We like a happy customer.'

'There's more.' She leaned across the counter conspiratorially. Roland leaned towards her.

'More?'

'Yes. I want to enter for a competition.'

'What sort of a competition?'

'Oh, glamour,' she said nonchalantly.

He swallowed. 'Are there categories?'

'Just the one. Larger ladies. The winner will get a contract to model underwear for an outsize catalogue. It could be the start of a new career for me,' she beamed.

During their photographic session, Roland had gone overboard to present the client in the best possible light with carefully draped fabrics followed by some post-op artwork.

'I need to be photographed in some glamorous underwear,' she announced.

Roland, for all his experiences with the female form, had tended towards enjoying the slightly less ripe end of the market.

'Hmmm.'

'Can you do it?'

Did he fancy it? That was the point.

'Mrs. Thackman... I don't really do that sort of work...'

'Oh go on! Be a devil! You owe me, you know. I got the bungalow redevelopment stopped with my dormouse discovery.'

She had, of course. What the hell!

'Alright, Mrs. Thackman but you will have to provide your own garments.'

She reached down to the floor and picked up a bag. She was about to empty the lot onto the counter when the shop door swung opened and Celeste came in.

She stopped on the threshold. 'I'll come back later.'

'No, no, my dear. You come in now. Good about the dormice wasn't it?'

'Excellent,' Celeste replied. 'Thank you for your help, Mrs. Thackman.'

Tan Boots turned back to Roland. 'Now, when shall we make that appointment for?'

He consulted the diary. 'I can see you on Thursday at 2pm. Is that alright?'

'Perfect,' she said, gathering up her bag. 'See you then.' She swept out of the studio, smiling.

'Another happy customer,' Celeste remarked.

'Come on through.' He took her by the hand but she snatched it away.

'No,' she hissed, 'it would be bad for business.'

He opened the door into the studio and flicked on the lights.

'Come here!' She did. After all the time they had known each other, all the rows they'd had at the airshows down the years, all the highly charged debates and mild flirtations, she had rather come to like the man. He was a bit of a rascal with women. She knew that but their relationship hadn't looked back since that night on her shaggy rug. He really knew his stuff and, to be honest, Celeste enjoyed it more than anything that her former partner had come up with. He might have been the father of her triplets but he had been pretty dull in the bedroom. Since the births she had been celibate, needing time to come to terms with the loss of her high-powered post at the airshow, the sudden death of Rupert and the responsibility of motherhood. This last item was low on her list of priorities, however, as her mother seemed to be relishing the role that should have been hers. Never mind, she was enjoying running her own business with all its challenges and minor successes.

'Come round to me tonight, Celeste.'

'I'd rather not. I can't quite face being in the same bed as the one you romanced Little Nanny in.'

'I've changed the sheets.'

'Oh Roland! Sometimes I think you know nothing about women at all.'

'We never did it here in the studio,' he said like a naughty boy.

'My place, after dinner. See you about eight,' she said firmly, disentangling herself from his fondling. 'Can you keep yourself in check until then?'

'Oooh. I don't know. I'm feeling rather rampant at the moment.' She pulled his mouth down onto hers. 'Contain it, tiger!'

Chapter 23

'Synth,' said Sister Catherine knocking on the cell door that Grant's housekeeper now occupied. 'There's a telephone call for you.'

'Coming, Sister.' She came out of the small, white room with a crucifix on the wall and the wooden prie-dieu in the corner to find Sister Catherine with one hand on the door-frame and the other on her chest.

'Are you alright, Sister Catherine?'

'Just a touch of angina. Don't worry. It'll pass in a moment. It's the hospital on the phone about your mother. You'd better go.'

'If you're sure I can't do anything...' The nun shook her head. Synth hurried along the corridor and down the stairs to the wall telephone in the hall. She picked the receiver up from the ledge.

'Synth Hunt. Who's calling please?'

'It's Staff Nurse here. We wondered whether you would like to come in and accompany your mother to the nursing home.'

'I don't understand. Why's she being moved?'

'The funds have come through and the ambulance will take her this afternoon to the new purpose-built nursing home over by The Broads.'

'I didn't arrange any of this. What's going on?'

There was the sound of rustling paper. 'We just need you to sign the consent form and you can do that if you come in after lunch. The ambulance is ordered for three o'clock.' Synth was puzzled.

'Is it a National Health home?'

'Oh no, Miss Hunt. It's a top of the range private one. We'll see you later then, shall we?'

'Yes,' Synth said as she put the receiver down.

'Good news?' enquired Reverend Mother coming out of the small convent library.

'I don't understand. They're moving Mum to a nice nursing home, a private one.'

'I'm very pleased for both of you.'

'But who's paying for it? I don't have that kind of money.'

'We know somebody who does. I think you really ought to telephone him again right away.'

'Mr. Landscar?'

'Who else?'

Then it dawned on Synth. 'You rang him?'

'Guilty as charged.'

Unable to contain her gratitude, Synth threw her arms around Reverend Mother.

'Steady on, young lady,' the nun said, laughing and holding her away slightly.

'How... how did you do it?'

'Oh, just a little comforting chat with him. I did happen to mention that unless somewhere suitable was found for Maud, he'd be losing his very good housekeeper. It seems he's really missed your efficiency and home cooking.'

Synth went to hug the nun again.

'Enough!' commanded Reverend Mother. She took the phone off the hook and handed it to Synth. Then she waddled off along the hallway and through the narrow passage to the conservatory where Sister Catherine had resumed her earring-making. She looked up.

'Mission accomplished?'

'Game, set and match,' replied Reverend Mother with a nod.

*

'Byeeee! I shall mish you all!' shouted Maud, waving her good arm about and smiling at her fellow patients as the orderlies propelled her out of the ward. Synth walked along beside her, carrying her vanity bag and dressing gown, throwing apologetic glances at the occupants of the beds.

An hour later, Maud was established in her private room with en-suite in the new nursing home. It was more of a bed-sitting room with walking-rails around all the walls, a large television, a view of the gardens and one wall of thick glass from where the duty nurse could look in at all times, not only on Maud but on five other patients in similar suites.

'This is lovely, Mum. You are very lucky.'

'I desherve it,' Maud said pompously, looking around.

'You've got to behave yourself. Do you understand?'

'Wheresh me cornflakes?' demanded Maud.

Synth looked at the ceiling in exasperation.

'Would your mother like some cornflakes?' The nurse put her head around the heavy, glass door.

'That would be very nice. Thank you. I'll help her with them.'

The nurse smiled.

As Synth left an hour later, the nurse reassured her. 'Your mother will be very happy here. Don't worry. By the way, she's not the only patient who has a wish for a special food. We mix a supplement into the milk, so she'll get all her nutritional needs.'

Through the glass, Synth could see Maud now propped up on pillows, dozing in the comfortable bed.

'She's exhausted. It's been a long day for her but she's full of fight and I think you might be surprised at how she recovers here.' She smiled. 'The doctor and the physiotherapist will see her in the morning and you can come in any time you feel like it. We'll ring you immediately if we have concerns.'

'Thank you so much.'

'Our pleasure.'

*

Eleanor became aware of a hollow howling in the rock chimney next to the grotto. At first it was a gentle moaning and then, as the hours of that long night passed, it rose to frightening *whoomphs*. If she'd been in a house she would have feared the roof flying away but here, encased in the solid rock of the cavern, the sound of the gale only increased her feelings of isolation and loneliness.

Kitty hadn't visited her today. Maybe the cat had sensed the coming storm. She'd missed sharing a tin with her. Huddled in her blankets, sitting up on the blow-up bed, wearing some track-suit bottoms and socks that Gonzo had brought in for her, she contemplated her fate.

Never plump, she was aware that the flesh was falling away from her bones. The diet was scarcely adequate. If she complained to her captor he just sneered. There had recently been a turn in events that had worsened her relationship with Gonzo. She still shook when she thought about it.

Yesterday, he'd arrived with a plastic bag containing some notepaper and an envelope. He'd handed it to her.

'You take-a it out. I no touch.' Clearly he was worried about his finger-prints being found.

It was Grant's own headed paper bearing the address of *Casslands.*

'How did you get this?'

'I take it. He have plenty.'

'Why?'

'For you to write your beloved hussband nice letter. I think time come for a leetle bit-a heart strings, yes? Here is English magazine for you to lean on.'

Eleanor took the ball-point pen that he offered and placed the paper on the journal. She was about to write.

'No, no!' Gonzo commanded. 'I tell you what-a to say.'

Eleanor, with pen poised, had looked up at him. 'Well?'

Gonzo had started to dictate.

My Darling husband of few weeks, I am missing from your bed. I am in dreadful place. Please pay ransom money so I come home to you. I embrace you. Eleanor.

'He's never going to believe those are my words.'

'Doesn'a matter. Iss yourrr hand-writing I want.'

'Then you won't get it,' she said, suddenly angry at the whole situation, screwing up the paper and throwing it out as far as she could into the crimson water.

'You verry stupid woman. You no do as I say, I can kill you.'

Full of false bravado, Eleanor shrieked, 'Go on then! I don't care! Look! I'll save you the trouble! I'll jump into the lake myself!' She'd stood up. He'd leaped across and pulled her back from the edge, pushing her down onto the cold stoniness of the rock shelf. His breath stank of garlic and beer.

'You want die?' His body was on top of her, pinning her down.

No, of course she didn't. He was right though. He could kill her at any time, either directly or by just leaving her to starve. The desperation of her situation terrified her.

Through gritted teeth she hissed, ' How do I know you won't kill me anyway?'

'You don't, lady. However,' and he sounded very pompous, 'I quite like-a you. Yes, in other times I take you for my woman. Perhaps, we try a little bit now, yes?'

She spat at him and wriggled, digging her long nails into his face dragging them down so they left long slashes in his unshaven cheeks.

'Get off!' She shrieked. With one enormous effort, and trying to summon up all she had learned at the self-defence classes, she drew up her knees and then straightened her legs with all her might, propelling him away from her through the air so that he hit the rocks behind them and slithered to the floor, winded.

The red dinghy... yes! While he had groaned away, wheezing, she'd stepped into it gingerly and unhitched the rope from the rock, pushing herself away, taking up the oars and awkwardly trying to manoeuvre it further out onto the crimson lake, panicking, catching short gasps of breath.

He had staggered to his feet, cursing. 'Come-a back here, you stupid woman!'

'Never!' Eleanor had yelled, applying all her might to a job she had not attempted before.

'Then you die in the *Crimson Deeps*!'

She saw the knife glinting in his hand. 'Come back, or I throw and puncture dinghy!'

A quick look at the dinghy confirmed that it only appeared to have two compartments. A puncture anywhere would deflate half of it and she would drown and be poisoned as she did so in the deep, red, contaminated water. Tears streamed down her face. She gulped. There was no choice. Floundering around with the oars, she slowly took the little dinghy back to the landing shelf.

Gonzo, rubbing his back, grabbed the rope and hooked it over the rock again, having placed the evil-looking knife back into its holster on his belt.

'Get out! Give me!' he commanded. He pulled her out and swiped her across the face with the back of his other hand.

'Oh!' Her fingers flew to her face as he flung her away like a rag doll.

'You no play games-a with ME!' he shouted.

'Sorry, Gonzo... I mean Señor Gonzales. It won't happen again.'

'You bet-a it won't! This time I tie you up good!'

She submitted to the rough, hairy string being laced around her wrists and ankles, forcing her hands behind her back. She sobbed all the time.

'I no trust you. You no write letter? I bring just little food. I want you suffer but not die because you nice lady with spirit. I like that I bet you hot in bed.'

She was disgusted at his thoughts. Through the bitter tears she thought of how near she had come to death. Maybe she would die in this dreadful place that smelled of damp and chemicals and the remains of rancid fish tins that lay in a heap in the corner with old packaging and plastic fruit juice containers.

Angrily, Gonzo cast off. 'You learn-a a lesson, lady. You no mess with Señor Gonzales!'

Eleanor had hung her head in misery, listening to the fading plopping of the oars and the trickle of the water in the grotto.

As soon as he was out of sight, she had shuffled across on her bottom and set to rubbing her string-encased wrists against an outcrop of rock at the back of the ledge. Back forth, back and forth. She felt the scratching of the rock as abrasions took hold but she went on. Sobbing with the effort but determined to get the use of her hands and legs back, she'd given a cry of delight as the string had given out and her sore wrists were waved in the air to restore the circulation. Then she'd untied her ankles, tentatively standing up to get movement back. This triumph deserved a biscuit! She'd staggered to her box and treated herself to a digestive. Then she'd wrapped her shivering body in the blankets and sat down on the inflatable to listen to the howling of the wind in the rock chimney.

*

Pops! You've got to hear this!'

'What, honey. What's goin' on. You sound kinda excited.'

'The kidnappers. Eleanor's kidnappers!'

'What about them?' Grant replied.

'They've contacted me.'

He sat bolt upright in his study in the *Villa Estancia*.

'When? How?'

'Just now. I was going to lunch and the phone rang and this man said, 'Pay attention!' in a very cultured English voice.'

'Did it sound like anybody we know?'

'No. Didn't ring any bells... and then he said, 'Do you want to see Eleanor Landscar alive again?'

'I asked him who he was and he said he was the guardian of Eleanor's life. He sounded really creepy and threatening. Then I asked him why he was ringing me and he said just to make sure I told you that he knows where I am too.'

'Oh shucks, Pandy. Get out-a that office pronto!'

'I don't much like being bullied,' she said firmly.

'Honey, my new wife's in their hands. I don't know who these people are but it's been nearly a month. We don't know where the heck poor Eleanor is or in what conditions she's being kept. I sure as hell don't want you taken too.'

'Pops, you should know that I intend to put some precautions in place, like hiring a body-guard.'

'Good. Good. What about Charlie?'

'I don't want to alarm him. He's upset enough about Eleanor's disappearance. He's been having nightmares, you know. He woke me up at two o'clock the other morning when he was home for the weekend, saying he'd dreamed she was calling to him for help and he couldn't find her.'

'Poor kid.' He hesitated. 'Did you try to check back and find out the number of whoever rang you?'

'Number withheld. Of course, if I got onto the police, they could...

'No,' said Grant. No more police involvement.'

Pandy smelt a rat. 'Pops, are you telling me everything?'

'Sure, I am.'

She sensed there was something else.

'Have the kidnappers been in touch with you?'

'I'd rather not talk about it any more. It's too distressin' for me.'

'Pops, you've got to tell me.'

He sighed. 'O.K. Pandy. 'There've been a couple of notes and a phone call. They want five million dollars.'

'Do they say where and when?'

'Nope. They're just keepin' me dangling.'

'Don't you think you should tell the police?'

'They told me not to. I don't want to risk Eleanor's life.' He broke down. 'My poor Eleanor... if only she'd worn...' Then he stopped.

'Worn what, Pops?'

He was at the bottom of his emotional strength. He needed to talk.

'The pendant.'

'What, that heavy, ugly thing with the diamonds around that you gave her? I never understood why she always wore it... to please you I suppose.'

'It has a hidden transmitter in it, powered by body heat.'

'What? Why would you do that?'

'It was a sort of wager with Teddy Appleton-Smythe.'

'Your old satellite entrepreneur chum.'

'The very one.'

'So why involve poor Eleanor in your schoolboy games?'

Grant overcame his feelings of shame. 'Well, honey, Teddy has this chain of geostatic satellites circling the Earth. Well, I say geostatic but they can actually be moved up and down in their positions or from side to side, sort of hunting for a transmitter. The government's very interested in his technology, especially since the transmitters are so minute. Just think of the possibilities for tagging people and items as they go off around the world. Imagine the scope of it. It works to within 100 metres, then you can use a hand-held tracking device. Teddy's left one with me.'

'Oh, Pops. You're a disgrace.'

'Well, there was no risk whatsoever to Eleanor and, to be honest, sweetheart, it gave me some comfort to know that if ever she was lost we could track her down real easy.'

'Letting her in on it would have been the decent thing to do.'

'I guess so. Too late now. She went out without the pendant that day. If she'd worn it we might know where she is. Oh Eleanor, my...'

Pandy cut in, stood up and said, 'I'm going to ring a security firm now and get myself a nice, hunky bodyguard.'

'You do that, honey.'

'Then, I'm going to drive down and pick up Charlie from boarding school. I'll keep him with me until this is all sorted out and Eleanor comes home. She will come home safe and well. You've got to hold onto that thought.'

'I'll try. Bye, Pandy.' He clicked off the phone and, on a whim, thought he would go for a drive up into the hills for a little fresh air and to raise his spirits. He'd hung around the villa, waiting for more contact from the kidnappers, but he was getting a good dose of cabin fever since he'd cancelled his fishing trip due to the storm.

In the hall the big, blue, glass bowl that usually contained the four-by-four keys was empty. Gonzo had said he was going to have lunch with some *amigos* in the pizzeria in town and had taken off in his own vehicle.

'Heck! Would that man ever remember to put the keys back in the dish?' Without them, Grant would have to call a taxi. No, he'd have a look upstairs.

Gonzo's quarters, were in an incredible mess. Clothes were strewn everywhere, and there was a big cardboard box of snacks on top of the chest of drawers. Grant peeked in and found crisps, biscuits, bananas and some cans of cola. He looked around. Where would he have dumped the four-by-four keys? The bedside cabinets yielded nothing but soft porn magazines and chewing gum.

He got down on all fours and peered under the double bed. It was pretty dusty and there was dirty washing stuffed under there. He rummaged through the clothes in the wardrobe, never thinking for a moment that he was invading his staff's privacy. It was his home, the keys belonged to his car and the staff were his employees. That gave him total rights. There was an old radio/tape-player on the window ledge. The en-suite yielded yet more dirty laundry. He came downstairs, furious. The keys were nowhere to be found in Gonzo's room. Where had the idiot fellow put them? On the kitchen side.

Grant grabbed them and strode out to the four-by-four. Revving up the engine he skidded out across the gravel and took the road up into the hills to the west of the island. One of the great things about Milloncha was that once on the top of the central heights, you could see the sea on all sides. Never were you so aware that you were on an island as then, but today he wanted the green hills and took the road west.

Last night's tropical storm had soaked the landscape. The streams were cascading down the hillsides, bouncing off rocks and splashing to throw up instant mini-rainbows. The air was clear. He stopped the car and got out to breathe it in. It felt so good.

'Eleanor. Where are you?' he thought.

Then his mobile rang.

'Hello. Is that you Grant? Teddy here. Not a very good line. Can you hear me?'

'Teddy, old chum. How are you?' Grant got out of the vehicle.

'Rather pleased, actually,' he replied.

'I'm glad somebody is,' Grant said with chagrin.

'I've just had a call from England,' Teddy said. 'Our Satellite FOUSC32 picked up a signal from Eleanor's transmitter at noon today.' Grant leaned against the car, his heart thumping. 'The pendant's at home. Eleanor's not wearing it. I saw it in her drawer.'

'Then somebody else has it,' Teddy said, 'because you know it needs body heat to activate it. You've got the hand-held tracker device, haven't you?'

Grant was so shaking with emotion that he couldn't speak. When he did, his voice cracked.

'Yes, I have it.'

'Then get busy, old fruit!'

Grant got into the car and drove back to the villa at full pelt. Panting, he climbed the stairs and went into Eleanor's bedroom. He strode over to the dressing table and opened the drawer. The jewellery case lay open. The emerald and diamond engagement ring was still in its small box but the pendant had gone.

Chapter 24

'To me, Mrs. Thackman. And again. One more.' Roland gave instructions to his client who, thrilled to be before the camera in her exotic lingerie, revelled in the star treatment.

'I want to look as glamorous as possible for the competition,' she said. 'It could be a life-changing experience for me.'

'What do your children think about all this?' he asked, triggering the remote. Flash. Flash.

'Oh I'm not telling them,' she replied as if the very thought of her adult offspring knowing about her private life was anathema. 'It's none of their business. Do you know, Mr. Dilger, that I spent all of my marriage just trying to please them and my dead husband... rest his soul, but now I do what I like. I don't criticise their lives and I expect them to leave me to mine,' she declared with her chin up.

'Good for you! You look rather attractive feisty,' he said approvingly. She stuck her ample chest out above the bustier.

'Do you think you could stretch your neck up a bit and look down at me all haughty?'

'Is that haughty enough?' She fixed him with a snooty glare.

'Too terrifying,' he laughed. 'A bit less severe please.'
She softened the glare from scary to mild disapproval.

'That's better. Now, I think that's all I can do with the black lace lingerie. Would you like to slip through the curtain there into the little room and change into the pink set?'

She swung her legs down from the couch, today swathed in white satin, and walked softly across the carpet tiles and into the back room on her neat little feet. While she was gone, Roland had a quick look through the shots. Not bad. The woman had a kind of vibrancy about her. He could see her appeal to some men.

'Are you nearly ready?'

'Just coming.' She reappeared. The ample pink, silk French knickers trimmed with white lace, the suspenders, white stockings and incredibly fancy bra made her look like a delicious iced cake.

'You look amazing, Mrs. Thackman,' he said, genuinely gob-smacked by her stunning appearance.

'Do you really like it?' she asked coyly. 'Is the frilly garter too much?'

'You'll knock 'em dead in the aisles,' he said.

So the Thursday afternoon passed in a welter of glorious under-garments as the joyful pair lost themselves in the creation of beauty in an unusual form. Roland admitted to himself after she had gone that he had thoroughly enjoyed the work, not only from an artistic and photographic point of view, but because he quite liked the lady herself. There was something wholesome and uncomplicated about her. He hoped his efforts behind the camera would do her justice.

*

Eleanor Landscar drew up her legs and watched the water lapping only inches away around her blow-up bed on the rock shelf in the cavern. Last night's storm had increased the flow of water into the crystal grotto so that it overflowed and cascaded across the rock platform. Worse still, water was flowing down the walls of the huge cavern, bringing more red poison into the *Crimson Deeps* which were rising and spilling over the rocks around her. For the first time she saw the surface disturbed by ripples.

Where was Gonzo? Since their row the other day he hadn't been back. Food supplies were seriously low. She heard a light bonking sound and turned to see that one of the big, empty orange juice containers was bobbing around in the shallow water behind her. Sitting isolated on the blow-up mattress, she was becoming surrounded by water.

She had watched the bats fly out last night as they did every evening and heard them come back before dawn, squeaking and fluttering high above her as their guano plopped into the red water below.

Now, suddenly, she heard a turbulent splashing and strained her eyes to see. The surface of the crimson lake was disturbed into a creamy, tinted foam as a family of sea otters approached and then cajoled and romped around only a few metres away from her.

Sea otters? In here? Surely they must realise that the water was poisoned? Animals sensed these things. Then she saw.

They were fighting over a floating sardine tin. The smell of it must have brought them in. Maybe the high water had made them adventurous. She rubbed at her sore wrists and ankles.

'No, no!' she remonstrated. 'You'll cut yourselves. The water will kill you.' They took no notice. She watched them for about half an hour before they left her, disappearing into the tunnel entrance.

As the sliver of light in the centre of the lake faded, Eleanor took off her thick socks and paddled across the treacherously slippery rock shelf to light a candle and eat the last of the food, some crackers, a triangle of cream cheese and a few crisps. Kitty had not come back. Well, cats weren't fond of water and it was also trickling down the rock chimney which had been her point of access to the cavern. The lonely woman missed the animal.

Sitting there in solitary misery in the flickering candle-light, looking up at the pillars and watching the glitter of the crystals, she wondered whether she would ever be free again. Supposing something had happened to Gonzo? He was her sole human link with the outside world. He would be angry when he saw that she had taken the rope bindings off. She rubbed her wrists again.

The otters. Surely they would die now after swimming in the poisoned red lake? She felt guilty that the smell of her old sardine tins had attracted them in. Innocent animals would lose their lives because of her carelessness. She wept for them, for her lost life, for her magazine and for her new husband. She sobbed for the grief that her absence was undoubtedly causing Aunty Rev and all the nuns.

*

'I had a good day today,' Celeste said, snuggling up against Roland on the sofa in her flat above the baby shop. 'Loads of customers. My early summer sale was a good idea.'

'Pleased you're doing so well.'

'Turnover is climbing steadily.'

'Good. Good.'

'Tomorrow the men are coming in to re-plank the balcony and that's the last of the repairs I was ordered to do.'

'Oh, the *Put and Keep* clause in the lease.'

'You were lucky he didn't go for you too.'

'I bet he will one day.'

'Actually, the bank balance is looking good.'

'Lend us a quid.'

'Neither a borrower nor a lender be,' she quoted. 'Shakespeare.'

'He clearly never had to scrabble for money,' Roland observed. 'I'm struggling a bit, to tell you the truth.'

'Oh, it'll pick up. Why don't you try and get yourself into one of the photography magazines? That would boost your image.'

'Not a bad idea. Clever girl.' He kissed the top of her dark hair. She tucked her legs up beside her and took his hand.

'Roland,' she said.

'Yes, Celeste,' he replied warily.

'Are you happy with us?'

'Yes, of course I am. Aren't you?'

'Oh, yes. It's very good.'

He stroked her shoulder as he gazed at the flickering, mock log fire. These June nights were still cool. She looked up at him.

'Is there a problem?' she asked.

'No. Nothing at all. Shall we see the news?'

He reached across her and picked up the remote control from the arm of the sofa.

'Police on the Mediterranean island of Milloncha have now issued a statement about the disappearance of Eleanor Landscar, wife of the billionaire entrepreneur Grant Landscar. They say that an open verdict was recorded at the recent inquest there as no body has been found. Mr.Landscar was unavailable for comment.'

'So that's that,' Celeste said.

'Poor old Eleanor,' Roland replied, his mind busy with images of Mrs. Thackman in her underwear.

'Fancy a bit?'

'You bet,' he said, plunging his hand up underneath Celeste's jumper.

*

'I think she's still making those nice earring of hers in the conservatory, Father Guyler,' Reverend Mother said.

'Shall I pop along and remind her that it's teatime?'

'Would you, Father. I expect she's forgotten the time.'

The priest, back in his wheelchair again due to dizzy spells, wheeled himself along the parquet corridor, through the small passage where the nuns' cloaks were hanging behind a curtain, and then into the conservatory at the side of the convent. He found Sister Catherine slumped over her work-table, a small pair of jewellery pliers still in her hand. She was rather blue in the face, panting and clutching at her chest with the other hand.

'Sister!' he said, rushing to her side.

'My inhaler! It's in my cell,' she wheezed.

'Stay there!'

Gripping the wheel guides tightly, he propelled himself as fast as he could back along the way he had come. There's something about the dignity of the office of priesthood the forbids impromptu impropriety but he really whizzed along, skidding on the polished floors, careering along the corridor in his black, ecclesiastical outfit like some holy hell's angel.

'Help! Help!' he called.

Temporarily abandoning her packing Synth heard and came out of her bedroom cell on the top corridor where the nuns' accommodation was laid out like a very clean prison. As she peered over the banister she rather hoped he'd fallen out of his wheelchair but he hadn't.

'Somebody! Anybody!'

She galloped down the stairs

'What's going on?' she demanded, puzzled by the priest's frantic demeanour.

'Sister Catherine's collapsed. She needs her heart spray. It's in her room.'

She rushed back upstairs again to the bedside table in Sister Catherine's cell and grabbed the phial, retracing her steps at the double, clattering down the staircase and rushing through the convent so that nuns appeared from everywhere to see what was going on.

'Sister Catherine's ill!' the priest shouted as he puffed past, following Synth. Like the Pied Piper he gathered a crowd of *religieuses* behind him, flapping their veils like bats as they came out of the dining room and followed. As soon as Father Guyler got back to the conservatory, he saw Synth taking the lid off the small canister and handing it to the gasping Sister Catherine.

'No!' he said. 'Read the label first! Make sure it's hers!'

He grabbed it back from the bewildered nun but It was her medication so he returned it to her and she pressed the dosage button, inhaling deeply.

Reverend Mother, who had been sitting at the head of the table waiting for her tea, also hurried along to the conservatory and joined the throng. The members of the order made way for her as she came forward through the chattering Filipino postulants.

'Stand back, Sisters.! Give her air!'

'Shall I call the doctor?' Synth asked.

'The number's by the phone in the hall. Yes, please.' Reverend Mother looked down with concern at her life-long friend. They had trained together at the Mother House. They had prayed together in the air-raid shelter in the grounds of St. Bede's during the war. They had opened the school together, trained the postulants and run retreats. So many memories! Was this the end?'

Sister Catherine looked up. 'I think I'm feeling a little better now, thank-you.' A murmur of approbation swept around. It almost seemed as if the plants in tubs nodded in approval.

'We've sent for the doctor, Sister. Would you be more comfortable with your feet up?'

Sister Catherine nodded and one of the postulants pulled over a wicker chair with a floral cushion on it. Then the Sisters carefully lifted the elderly nun's feet in their much-polished but very old buttoned-across shoes. One of the postulants appeared with a black cloak from the cubby-hole in the passage. They placed it over the frail-looking nun.

Reverend Mother turned to the members of her order and advised them to go and have tea. She would wait with the patient until the doctor came. Reluctantly, they all left, leaving the two elderly nuns alone together.

Father Guyler had whispered in Reverend Mother's ear that perhaps Extreme Unction might be in order. 'Let the doctor see her first,' she'd replied. 'She's looking a lot better now. 'The priest nodded and went to have his tea.

Alone in the warm conservatory, Reverend Mother took her friend's hand and patted it.

'Do you think I'm going to die?' Sister Catherine asked.

'No. You're not. It was just another of your angina spells. You'll feel fine tomorrow. Heaven isn't ready for you yet.'

'I need to tell you something.'

'Wouldn't you rather talk to Father Guyler? I can easily fetch him back.'

'That would never do. I think I should tell you, Reverend Mother. I cannot go to my grave with this burden on my mind.'

'Anything you say will be kept in utmost confidence. Tell me.'

'I don't know where to start.' Her lower lip trembled.

'At the beginning is always best.'

The patient hesitated and took some deep, rattling breaths and gave a cough. Reverend Mother gripped the other nun's hand tighter.

'You have time. Tell me slowly.'

Do you remember all those years ago when we went to Kridblikistan on the mission?'

'Yes, I do. Very challenging it was too.'

'You recall that you travelled out first with a group of sisters. I was to follow when term ended.'

'I remember.'

'Something happened while you were away. Something dreadful. I have kept it locked in my heart because I gave my word but now I think I should tell you, especially as Eleanor may not...'
Reverend Mother was quick to interject. 'Wouldn't you rather say this to Father?'

'No, no,' said the distraught nun, letting go of the spray inhaler so that it clattered to the floor. 'I have to tell you. I have to.'
Reverend Mother waited patiently. 'Go on,' she said.

'You remember Eleanor was working as a young journalist then, on day release from college?'

'Yes.'

'And you remember that Father Guyler was here too as our Pastor?'

'Yes, I do.' Reverend Mother's face wore a wary expression.
The patient struggled to contain her emotions, her face contorted in pain. The inhaler had only partly done its work.

'He left rather unexpectedly for India.'

'At the time I remember thinking it was all a bit sudden.'
Reverend Mother felt dread grow in her being. Surely not? Surely Sister Catherine wasn't going to tell her the most devastatingly awful thing, something she didn't want to hear.

'Eleanor was fond of Father Guyler.'

'I expect she was. We all were.'

'No. It was more like a crush.'

'How do you know?'

'Her eyes followed him everywhere.' Sister Catherine coughed behind her hand and then continued in a croaky whisper. 'When he left, she was heartbroken. She didn't eat properly for days.'

'I'm sure Father Guyler behaved with the utmost propriety.'

'Yes, yes. I'm sure he did but I think Eleanor was in love with him.'

'Eleanor? In love with a priest? Surely she would know that was wrong.'

'The heart doesn't always exactly know right from wrong in these matters, Reverend Mother.'

The Superior shook her head in part disbelief. Poor, poor Eleanor. That's why she had gone to Italy... to mend a broken heart.

'There's some more, Reverend Mother.'
Sister Catherine's eyes were rheumy with tears glistening.

'I am so, so sorry. I should have taken more care of her.'

'She was a young adult by then,' Reverend Mother said.
The patient pulled her hand away and wrangled her fingers together, twisting and pressing them in distress and then let out a bitter sob, her words almost incoherent.

'I didn't want her to go but she wanted to do something to cheer herself up. She took the bus into town and went to see a film.'

'She was quite entitled to do that.'

'But when she came out of the cinema, the bus didn't come so she started to walk back to the convent.'

Reverend Mother froze.

'She was raped, Reverend Mother. Somebody got out of a car and dragged her into a field and raped her!' Sister Catherine burst out, sobbing and wheezing.

'No. No. No!' the Superior exclaimed. 'Oh Eleanor! If only I'd been here...'

'She walked the rest of the way back here,' Sister Catherine gulped, 'all the way, not wanting anyone to see her. I heard her coming across the gravel as I locked up for the night. I let her in quietly. The other sisters didn't know. She didn't want anybody to know. All the way from the fields with no shoes on. Her feet were bleeding. She was in shock. She went to the doctor next morning. I made sure she had a bath before she went to bed. She insisted that I didn't call the police or tell you.'

Reverend Mother wept. Did these beasts never think about their victims? How such acts affect all those around them? How the pain and loss of innocence can never be expiated? How the shadow of disgust ricochets down the years?

Suddenly it was clear why Eleanor hadn't married before, why she'd devoted herself to her journalistic work, avoided emotional entanglements, perhaps even become a little bitter and deliberately unattractive in her dress style.

The convent doorbell rang. There were voices in the hallway and the doctor was shown in by one of the postulants who withdrew hastily.

'Now, what have we got here, ladies? Two crying nuns? Come now, it can't be that bad!'

Reverend Mother got up, dabbed her eyes and stepped aside, pulling herself together.

'Sister Catherine had one of her turns here about half an hour ago,' she said in a low voice.

He took out his stethoscope, felt the pulse and then asked permission to roll up the nun's sleeve for the blood pressure to be taken. Sister Catherine lay there with her eyes closed. The effort of relating the terrible news to her Superior had certainly taken its toll. Reverent Mother gave her consent. As head of the order in England it was within her remit to do so.

'How old is Sister Catherine, please remind me.'

'She's a year younger than I am. She'll be seventy-nine next month.'

'How long has she been on this medication now? Sorry I didn't have time to look at her notes. I came from a meeting.'

'About three years, Doctor.'

'Well, she seems to be stable now but I think there may be some heart damage. I've got the crash team outside so let's call them in.'

Quarter of an hour later, Reverend Mother watched as her lifelong friend was lifted onto the trolley and taken out to the waiting ambulance, the flashing arrival of which had alerted the sober teatime group to the fact that Sister Catherine was seriously ill.

For their Superior life would never be the same again. She knew that Sister Catherine's days were numbered and that she herself was the holder of the most dreadful secret. Forever she would have to pretend to Eleanor that she didn't know that her precious niece had been raped by some unknown man in a dark and lonely field. There was not a soul she could tell.

Chapter 25

A shivering Eleanor awoke from a fitful sleep. If the sea otters could swim in the red water of *Crimson Deeps*, then the lake couldn't be as poisonous as Gronzo had led her to believe. She rubbed her eyes, sat up, took off her woolly socks and rolled up her trouser hems. The rock shelf was still partially flooded with water trickling down from the grotto. She got up and paddled her way across to her rocky, crystal-laden bathroom and splashed the clean water on her face with a determination that today was the day when she would escape. She lit the final candle.

It was inevitable that Gonzo would come back and she didn't intend to be here when he did. She'd had enough of this misery, all the waiting, the possibility of further violence.

Somehow she had to overcome her life-long fear of water. Grant had helped a bit, cajoling her into the heated, indoor swimming pool at *Casslands*. She remembered him saying, 'Come on. Just crouch down and kind-a slip in.' He'd held his arms out to her and she'd slithered into the water. Dear Grant. He had hugged her close to his chest and kissed her tenderly as they stood waist-deep.

'Now, why don't I just hold onto your hands and you try a little kicking with your legs?' he'd said encouragingly but she couldn't be persuaded to take her feet off the bottom.

'Look,' he'd said as he'd confidently plunged off and swum like a professional across the pool while she'd clung to the rail at the side. 'You could try the breast stroke. That's easy. Just a matter of a little bit of coordination.'

So, to please him, she had put her shoulders under and gone through the arm movements but her feet had stayed firmly glued to the mosaic bottom of the pool.

How different were her circumstances today! She padded back to the ledge and looked out. She checked her watch. Gonzo never came early because of his duties at the *Villa Estancia*. She set about implementing the plan that had grown steadily in her head during the long hours of wakefulness during the night.

She collected the two large, empty orange-juice containers from the corner and, using bits of the hairy string, tied them by their handles to the tabs on the inflatable mattress. She made sure their lids were tightly screwed on. Then she checked the valves on the inflatable. They were well plugged. What else would float? What else would keep her buoyant? Polythene bags. She splashed back to the plastic box and retrieved a couple and blew them up, tying them to the inflatable. The plastic box! Of course! That would float! She tipped out the odds and ends of packaging in there and found, to her delight, a broken biscuit which she ate hungrily. Then she carried the box to the ledge.

If there was one thing that Eleanor never went without it was her shoulder-bag and that, she decided, was going to escape with her. It would have its own little boat in the shape of the big plastic box with its lid on firmly, floating behind her on a string.

There was no time to lose. Two long bread wrappers found their way over her hands and wrists up to the elbows. She would try and protect herself from the red water as she used her hands as paddles but if it contaminated her, she would take the consequences. Anything was better than this.

Fear found a home in the pit of her empty innards, gnawing like a bad-tempered dog with a bone. Her heart pounded. She was cold, so cold and the thought of lying on her stomach and propelling herself across the deep, dark, red lake, made her eyes fill with tears. If the inflatable turned over, she would drown. Her bloated corpse would be eaten by the otters. She shuddered. Mustn't think like that.

She pondered on the best way to launch her craft and decided that the plastic box should go in first. Then she swung the inflatable around so that the foot end was floating. With behind in the air, she transferred herself onto it. It felt highly unstable and she spread her legs as far as she could to try and equalise the weight.

Then, she eased the craft off and away from the rock ledge that had been her home for nearly six weeks. It bobbed about because the launch had created small waves. She could smell the plastic coating so near to her nostrils. Waiting, waiting for it to steady. With her right ear flat down, she dipped her bagged hands into the water and started to gently turn and manoeuvre her way forward, dipping and pushing back, trying not to splash in the acrid liquid.

It was hard to breathe like this. She lifted her chin slowly and turned her head to look back. The ledge was a couple of metres away. She tried not to think about the deep, deep lake beneath her, the lake that was now her means of staying alive. Her glance back showed the solitary candle glimmering like a beacon of hope.

The juice containers got in her way a little and she had to try and avoid them as she worked but it was a comfort to know that there were several things she could cling to if the inflatable went down. She just hoped there were no treacherous rocks hidden underneath.

The lake was calm and Eleanor proceeded slowly, peeping up now and then to see where the tunnel mouth was. Her strokes were short and delicate. Suddenly, there was a loud splash beside her and a sea otter looked as surprised as she was. Would it try and bite her hands in the water?

She patted the surface to encourage it to go away. Then there was another splash and another. The whole little family had come as a flotilla to guide her through the tunnel. Like a shoal of porpoise riding the bow wave of a sea-going vessel, they wove in and out ahead of her as she left the glimmering light of the cavern, the cathedral that was the edifice around *Crimson Deeps*, and moved slowly and inexorably into the black hole of the tunnel.

The torch had long ago given up the ghost so she had no means of light as she made her way forward in the inky blackness with only the echo of her laboured breathing bouncing off the walls with the sound of her hands and the activities of the otters ahead.

*

Grant Landscar went into the *Villa Estancia* kitchen to find Synth making some kind of paella for dinner tonight.

'Nice to see you safely back again, Synth,' Grant said from the doorway. 'Did you have a good flight?'

'Fine,' she replied, stirring away. 'Gonzo picked me up and brought me back here a couple of hours ago...' She paused and then looked at him with her candid, green eyes. 'Thank you so much for what you have done for my mother. She's really happy in the new care home.'

"That's swell. My pleasure. Please don't mention it! I kind-a missed your cookin' anyway,' he grinned. 'That smells good.'

'Well, as that Valeria girl seemed to have got all the ingredients, it seemed a waste not to make it now she's gone.'

'Shucks, we sure missed you,' he said with a whimsical smile, making as if to leave.

'Any news of Miss Eleanor... I mean Mrs. Landscar. I asked Gonzo but he didn't know anything.'

'No. No news so far but we live in hope.'

'If only I'd been here, maybe...'

'It's really nothing at all to do with you, my dear. They'd have got my wife anyway. Say,' he said casually, 'd'you happen to know where Gonzo's got to?'

'He said something about going out to check on the pool pump. He's probably in the pool house.'

'Thanks.'

Grant left the kitchen and went up to Gonzo's room. Nothing appeared to have changed. He looked around. The radio/tape-player was now on the window-sill. He walked over to it. It was set to tape/play. He pressed the button and a cultured English voice said:

'Repeat after me: How now brown cow,' followed by silence.

'The rain in Spain stays mainly on the plain.' Silence again.

'Please open the door.' So it went, enunciating banal phrases.

He stopped the tape, ejected it and read the label: *Speak good English without a trace of a foreign accent.*

Grant froze, looking out of the window. Was it possible? Could the laconic Gonzo be clever enough to do this? To kidnap his Eleanor? After all, he had been the last person to see her when the pair had taken Synth to the airport on the day his beloved wife had disappeared. Teddy Appleton-Smythe had texted him earlier to say that the signal had been picked up again by the satellite at 6 a.m.

and that it was pin-pointed in the immediate area of the villa. Suddenly everything was obvious. His immediate instinct was to throttle the man but he had to stay cool, to keep a clear head if he was to discover Eleanor's whereabouts.

*

In the pitch darkness, Eleanor's hand scraped the tunnel wall, tearing a hole in the plastic bag covering her right hand. She felt the tainted water seep in between her fingers, filling the bottom of the plastic bag and making it too heavy to use any more. She let it slip off with a hint of regret for the environment. As it went, she lost orientation and felt the blow-up bed rock violently. She heard the trailing plastic box containing her shoulder-bag hit the tunnel wall with a clunk. The rear end of the inflatable seemed to be hanging down into the water and her woollen-socked feet were soaking. She didn't dare to think what the poisonous waters of *Crimson Deeps* were doing to her skin.

She stopped for a moment, waiting for the surface to settle down. The sea otters had gone far ahead of her now. Slowly she started to pull herself along again, hitting her elbow on the floating plastic containers, getting a face-full of water which she spat out. It tasted dreadful. Like sour vinegar. The stench ran up the back of her throat, burning it, and the smell lingered in her nasal passages.

Timeless, she resumed her weary task, trying to keep the inflatable steady as the rear end trailed deeper into the water. Her trews were wet up to the knees. Then, all of a sudden she could go no further forward. Something was stopping her progress. She took her unclad hand out of the water and carefully put it out in front of her into the smothering, rank, darkness. She felt rock.

Sliding her hand to the right she felt sharp edges, not good for her little raft. Holding onto one of the inflatable's tabs, she extended her left hand in it's soggy plastic bag and felt again. The wall seemed to curve away and was smoother. Then it all came back to her. When Gonzo had brought her in here along the passages, there had been a sort of junction where three passages met. Was it her imagination, or could she sense fresh air blowing in from the left?

On instinct, she manoeuvred herself in that direction, trying to keep contact with the wall until she could follow the curve around. Yes, there was definitely a freshness in the air. Her eyes were stinging from earlier so she just kept them shut and paddled along.

Splash! Something furry slid past her right hand. The otters were back.

With renewed energy, and the wetness creeping up the back of her tee-shirt, she ploughed forward. The smoothness of the water in the tunnel gave way to an undulating feeling as she moved unwillingly and sinuously ever so slightly up and down. She could feel her legs dragging in the water. So on a whim, she decided to kick them about a bit. This created more turbulence but there was the impression of increased speed. Maybe there was some sense in this swimming thing after all.

Eleanor didn't know for how long she plodded through the water in this fashion but she was getting colder and more tired. Her teeth were chattering and the taste of the poisoned water was vile in her mouth. Her hands were freezing cold and she was losing sensation in her fingers.

A gust of cool air passed over her, further chilling the fragile body. The entrance to the cave must be near. Heartened, she clawed and splashed, fighting for her life. She would not drown in this dark tunnel. She would not let the forces of evil like Gonzo win. She would see her dear Grant again and Aunty Rev and her own lovely office at *Embroideryworld*.

A few more minutes of fervour and determination and she could see light. Yes, real light. It was reflecting off the rocky walls further along, glistening down onto the surface of the now sweeter smelling water. A small wave hit her in the face and it was salty. She clung to the edge of the inflatable that was fast becoming a de-flatable. Only the large, orange juice containers, polythene bags and big plastic box were keeping the whole contraption afloat. She struggled on.

The now useless inflatable was being hauled along under her like some slimy old crocodile and she beat her generously sized feet up and down like a rudder, propelling herself forwards, cresting and dipping with the now obvious waves.

A curve in the tunnel! The screech of a seagull! She was there, bobbing up and down in the cave mouth, her eyes nearly blinded by the brilliant Mediterranean sun and the cerulean blue sky. She was alive. Eleanor Landscar was alive! She had survived! Now all she had to do was find her way up onto dry land.

*

Grant asked Gonzo if he would join him now for a walk that afternoon to inspect a new patch of land he was thinking of buying next to the far side of the estate. It might be good for pig farming.

'The ground's a bit boggy but we could drain it,' he said.

'Sure, Señor. I know about pigs. I tell you if OK.'

'Shall we go then?' The quad bike transported them swiftly.

'What I'd like to show you is over there,' said Grant Landscar.

The got off the quad bike and Grant led Gonzo through a thicket and down a rough track, striking out away into some shrubbery. The estate manager was puzzled.

'Iss not good farming land, Señor Landscar.'

Grant looked at the man who clearly had Eleanor's pendant about his person, the man who had obviously been and stolen it from his wife's bedroom. How Grant kept himself from grabbing his estate manager by the throat... No, control. If he frightened Gonzo he might never find Eleanor again.

'Oh, it get's better in a minute. Come on! Keep up!' They plodded on.

'Over here,' Grant said, leading Gonzo down a slope to where an open, crooked gate gave way into a low-lying and marshy field. Grant took out the pendant tracker and pointed it at Gonzo.

'What-a you do, Señor? Why you point-a that thing at me?'

The tracker started to beep, louder and louder as Grant walked towards his estate manager.

'Why he make-a that noise?'

'Where's Eleanor?' Grant shouted at him. 'Where's my wife? What have you done with her?'

'I not know, Señor. You make big mistake. I good man.'

Grant's hand ripped down the front of Gonzo's shirt.

'Then why are you wearing my wife's pendant?'

'She give it me. Honest, Sirr.'

Grant surveyed the diamond-encrusted pendant.

'Eleanor would never have given that to you. She wore it all the time. You stole it from her dressing table. I know you did, AND you can cut out that "me poor foreigner" accent. I've found the tape in your room. It was you who made the phone calls to me and my daughter. It was you who arranged for the ransom notes and the flower in a pot, you and your friends. Where's Eleanor? Tell me NOW!' Gonzo put his hands up. The tracker continued to beep.

'I'm not telling you,' Gonzo said with his chin up. 'I want the money and then you will have your lovely wife back.'

Grant dropped the tracker and lunged at the man, grabbing him. Gonzo, surprised at the speed and ferocity of the older man fought back, clearly out-classing his employer.

Over they went in a bundle, rolling down the slope, crashing through the rotten gate into the marshy field beyond. The stetson flew wild. Grant ripped two fingers up Gonzo's nostrils and, as the man shrieked in pain, he let go and Grant's hands seized him by the neck, squeezing it with a primordial ferocity born of rage and frustration, shaking and pressing, putting his whole body weight into the task until Gonzo ceased to struggle.

Panting, the billionaire entrepreneur staggered to his feet, and looked around frantically. Gonzo had put him and his Eleanor through hell. He bent down and dragged the lifeless body through the gateway, rolling it until it fell into the welcoming arms of the bog where it lay half-submerged. Nature would drag it down in an hour or two. Filthy, Grant picked up his hat and tracker and meandered back to the quad bike, riding it homewards, pausing among the shrubs to sob for a while and sling the tracker into the dense undergrowth. He'd killed Gonzo, the only person who knew where his Eleanor was. Distraught, he parked up round the side of the pool house. He went in and took a shower in the pool room. He threw his clothes, shoes and favourite stetson into the incinerator and strode in through the kitchen in his designer underpants past a rather surprised Synth.

'I just fancied a swim,' he said, hoping he hadn't burned his boats along with his belongings.

*

Clinging to the remains of her home-made raft, the inflatable flapping around below her, Eleanor drifted up and down, breathing in the fresh sea air, hoping that the salty water would wash away any damage done to her skin by the poisonous waters of *Crimson Deeps*. She looked at the cliffs above her, wondering how she could get ashore, finally deciding that, after a little, she would try and kick with her legs and steer herself towards the rocks to the right of the cave entrance. If she could haul herself up onto there, at least she wouldn't drown. The sea otters had disappeared.

With a concerted effort she lashed out vigorously, hanging onto one of the plastic containers, steering with the other hand. A large wave came up terrifyingly behind her, sweeping her suddenly skywards and depositing her with a crash onto the rocks where she gave a yelp of pain as it withdrew with a hissing, slithering sound. She sat there for a moment and then realised that the sea could just as easily take her out again. Dragging her injured leg which was tangled up in the hairy string of the big polythene box that contained the famous shoulder-bag, she made a supreme effort and hauled herself out of reach of the sea.

She lay back on the sun-baked rocks, suddenly realising how much she had missed the warmth of the sun all these weeks in the cavern. Despite the pain, she could almost have drifted off to sleep. She suddenly panicked and worried that Gonzo might come back. Sitting up, she looked around and at the overhanging cliffs. Could she make it up there? She struggled on.

It was mid-afternoon by the time Eleanor had dragged herself along, grazing her hands and knees, her wrecked ankle tied up in the now very tatty headscarf and her shoulder-bag slung over her back. She had worked out that next to the cave was not the lowest part of the cliffs and she might find a better way up further along. She knew that the Mediterranean Sea had a small tidal range so there was no chance of a nice sandy beach appearing here.

'Ma-a-a-!' She looked up and saw a brown goat looking down at her, his beard wafting in the breeze. A goat path. Of course! She shaded her eyes and searched for the way. There were shrubs of aromatic inula with its clusters of yellow flowers clinging to the cliffs. Yes, she would follow the shrubs up the sloping face. With much effort she stood and limped her way forward, feeling for solid plants to cling onto, avoiding the sea holly's prickly leaves.

Another hour of painstaking climbing and crawling, clinging to the shrubs, and Eleanor found herself on soft turf. She collapsed with exhaustion and relief. She was out in the open and so, so thirsty. The grass was damp beneath her. She pulled some stems and sucked the paltry juice, needing more than was on offer. Her ankle throbbed and was very swollen. She'd lost her lucky lilac hat.

In front of her lay the deepening blue of the Mediterranean. Behind her some rolling farmland with fields of vegetables. She rose tentatively and hopped, falling over so often that she went back to crawling. There was a field of sheep to her right as she picked up a dusty track, deeply pitted with tyre tracks, brown puddles glistening. Dare she drink from them? Her common sense forbade it. Keeping to the grassy verge she crawled on until she came across one of the little Balearic windmill pumps creaking in the wind. There must be a habitation nearby. There must be. There was. A dog was barking excitedly as Eleanor came to the farm gate. The border collie ran back and forth and around in circles as they do. A woman appeared in the house doorway.

'Laddie, calm down. What are you barking at?' The woman looked towards Eleanor at the gate, not quite believing the dishevelled, scruffy sight clinging to the crooked post in a state of exhaustion with her eyes closed.

'Are you alright, my dear?' she called across in English before putting her head inside again and calling her husband. 'There's some woman out here.'

He appeared and they both hurried across to the gate, past the cavorting border collie and the waddling white, farmyard ducks.

'Look at the state of her...'
The bedraggled creature looked up. 'Help me, please. I'm Eleanor Landscar.'

Eleanor drank spring water until her thirst was sated. The escapee sat with her legs up on the floral sofa, covered in a patchwork quilt. The semi-retired English couple who ran the farm were kindness itself. Should they call the police? An ambulance? A doctor? The wife had bound Eleanor's filthy ankle with cold, wet bandages torn from a pillow-case and packed it with ice. She'd bathed her cuts and abrasions with antiseptic lotion.

'Please let me ring my husband,' Eleanor said. 'My mobile's flat. I have to tell him I'm alive. He must be worried to death.'

The farmer brought the phone to her on a long lead. 'I can't recall the number,' she said, distressed, her eyes wild with fear.

'Just sit quietly for a moment,' the wife said, 'and maybe it'll come back to you. It's the shock. How about a cup of tea?'

'I was so scared,' Eleanor whispered, starting to relate her traumatic story. 'Nobody knew where I was. Yes, yes, please. Tea. I need a cup of tea. I can't swim,' she said, 'and, in any case, the Gonzo man said the water in the cavern was dangerously poisonous from the aluminium works.'

'Oh, *Crimson Deeps*,' said the farmer enigmatically. 'They were going to prosecute us about that but I don't know what you mean about aluminium works. There aren't any around here.'

'But we agreed to put it right and make a donation to the mayor's charity,' his wife added, filling the kettle.

'Put it right?' Eleanor queried, munching on the comforting sweetness of an *ensaimada*.

The man handed a leaflet to the dishevelled survivor.

'I'm sorry,' she said, 'my eyes aren't very good at the moment. I got some of the chemical from the lake into them. They're very sore.' She took out her spectacles from her bag, put them on and read out the advertising on the front of the leaflet. It said, *Sophia Farm Speciality Pickled Beetroot*.

'You're beetroot farmers?' Eleanor was incredulous.

'If you look out through that window there, you can see our processing plant over on the horizon... that big corrugated iron roof... that's ours.'

'What's that got to do with *Crimson Deeps*?'

The woman looked guiltily across at her husband. 'We had a massive leakage from one of our tanks at the plant and the beetroot juice found its way down into the cavern. It used to be a tourist attraction but they had to close it because of the smell of the juice in the water. We were experimenting with making a beetroot flavoured drink from our left-over beet liquor.'

'You mean the water in the cavern wasn't poisoned?'

'Well, a little bit dodgy because we had to treat it with a solution of permanganate of elixir of potash. That used to be used quite regularly in water purification, you know. It'll be clear in a couple of years.'

Eleanor began to laugh, first giggling and then hysterically, tears running down her dirty face, making rivulets in the grime.

'You mean I've spent six weeks cooped up in the *Crimson Deeps* cavern surrounded by decomposing beetroot juice?'

She howled with laughter, doubled over, beyond pacification, hardly able to speak at the irony of it all.

'Please give me the phone again,' she said, trying to control her hysteria. 'I've just remembered the number.'

'Hello, Grant. It's me, Eleanor,' she laughed.

'Eleanor?, Oh my darling woman! You're alive. Thanks be. Where are you? Tell me where you are!'

Oh Grant, my dearest, I'm safe and well. Come and find me at Sophia Farm!'

*

Billionaire Grant Landscar's Wife found alive!

'Wife of billionaire entrepreneur Grant Landscar has been found alive and well on the Mediterranean island of Milloncha. Mrs. Landscar was kidnapped on her honeymoon nearly six weeks ago. Her kidnapper was a family employee who held her in a local underground cavern for the entire time. Following Mrs. Landscar's courageous escape, the employee, one Eduardo Gonzales, has disappeared. Millonchan Police suspect that he has left the island.'

Roland called out, 'Hey! they've found Eleanor Landscar alive!'

'Tell me some good news,' Celeste replied from the kitchen of her flat, coming through with a pizza on a tray.

'Early night after this?' she queried.

'Perhaps a night off?' Roland replied. 'I've got to be up early in the morning. I'm going bird watching.'

*

'You're an amazingly resilient woman,' the English doctor said to Eleanor in her bedroom at *Villa Estancia*, 'and a very lucky one indeed.'

He surveyed the skeleton thin body, the frizzy hair and the hollow cheeks of the billionaire's wife whose eyes sparkled with happiness as she sat up in her big, round bed. Grant was on the chair beside her, holding her hand.

'It's so lovely to have had a proper bath, to feel clean again,' she said.

Grant rubbed his strained shoulder. The fight with Gonzo hadn't done him much good. 'I can't quite take it in that you're back with me after all these weeks.'

'It was a nightmare,' Eleanor said. 'I can't believe it's over.' She turned to Grant. 'Aunty Rev. Did you ring her?'

'Yes, of course. She can't wait to talk to you tomorrow. She said to tell you that Sister Catherine is fine, by the way.'

'Fine?'

'You have a bit of catching up to do, I'm afraid. Sister Catherine had a little problem but she's OK now. Oh, and Pandy wants to talk to you... some idea she has about opening a sister magazine to *Embroideryworld.*'

Eleanor gave a sort of grimace. She wasn't ready to return to work for a very long time.

The doctor snapped his medical bag shut. 'My advice is that we admit you to hospital for twenty-four hours for a check-up but if you don't want to go, it's up to you.'

'I want to stay here,' Eleanor said firmly, grasping Grant's hand.

'Very well, but I'll call in tomorrow to check on you. Just keep drinking plenty of water, use the nose drops three times a day and slowly build up your tolerance to proper food again. Eat plenty of fresh fruit and vegetables and don't walk on that ankle.'

'I'll be good,' Eleanor promised.

'She will,' Grant added, nodding. 'I want her fit and well again.'

'I'll see myself out, the doctor said. 'Get a good night's sleep.'

Later, as Grant curled up beside Eleanor on the round bed, she snuggled down, enjoying the wonderful, luxurious softness of the mattress, the smell of clean sheets and the comfort of a soft pillow, she related to him in detail all about the cavern, the bats and the smell of the red waters of *Crimson Deeps*. She told him about the cold, the constant sound of water trickling through the grotto and the visits of the black cat that had lifted her spirits.

'Do you know,' she said, 'that Kitty actually came from *Sophia Farm*? The cat strolled in while I was on the sofa waiting for you. She jumped up onto my lap. She recognised me. When I asked the farmer if he knew where she went he said that he didn't but that she'd often come back smelling of tinned fish and one day had a string around her neck. The crisp packet with my note in must have got lost. They'd wondered where she'd been dining out.'

Grant hugged Eleanor to him, nuzzling her neck, sniffing the sweet smell of her skin. So, he'd forgotten to retrieve her pendant from Gonzo before he'd dumped his body. What the hell! As if picking up his thoughts, she pulled away slightly and looked down at him. 'And what about Gonzo?' she asked archly.

'He's disappeared. I think he stole your pendant, by the way.'

'Oh, what a pity!' She gave an imperceptible sight of relief. Grant went on, 'The police rang me earlier while you were asleep. They've been searching for him but he seems to have vanished from all his usual haunts. They questioned his friends. Apparently he'd been talking about going to America. They'll want to interview you when you're feeling stronger. Somehow, though, I don't think Gonzo will be troubling us any more.'

The evening sky hung like flaming, molten lead above the western hills. In the valley below, dry reeds rustled at the edge of the primaeval bog, their music punctuated periodically by the subtle plopping of gases escaping from the slime. Now and again, a frantic slapping filled the dusky air as a chocolate-coloured hand waved with futile and dying signals at the emerging stars. The stars understood nothing but how to shine benevolently and steadfastly onto the marshy surface of the bog as it closed over and resumed its tranquil, caked skin. The satellites took their course across the night sky, picking up the signal of a transmitter that slowly faded away. Somewhere a frog croaked. It was always so.

MARY B. LYONS

Extract from AIRSHOW ILEX

In the broom cupboard, Roland whispered, 'She's gone but I think we're here in the Press Centre for the night though.' The sound of his face being slapped was followed by a scuffle, a key rattling and the emergence of two perspiring and dishevelled people from incarceration

---

Extract from CARAVAN HITCHES

'I am the ghost of caravanners past,' the apparition said in an echoing, singsong voice. The moonlight shimmered on her silvery white gown as it floated about her in the evening air. Her face was pale, her hair long and white and she had deep, dark circles under her eyes. Paul stood stock still, the loo cassette handle gripped tightly in his hand. He felt the blood drain from his face and his heart pounded.

Extract from SPORTING HITCHES

The shackled girls came panting up to the scene of devastation. The chariot was on its side. The papier-mâché horses' heads were deteriorating into something resembling the Elephant Man. 'Nero' thrashed about in the water angrily while his trumpeter rummaged beneath the icy surface for his instrument. Jon-Jon lay pale and slumped with only his head and arms out of the water as he clung limply to a wheel in a semi-faint

---

Extract from BABY BOOM (Lullaby)

But your voice is gone and your patience too.
You sit on the stairs and weep.
They never taught you at classes how
To get the blighter to sleep.
So you go downstairs for a cup of tea
Put the TV on full hilt.
You clutch the cup with your feet propped up
Imbued with the worst kind of guilt.

CRIMSON DEEPS

Lyric and Melody © Mary B. Lyons 2011

Crimson Deeps, the water lies,
As red as blood, as my love dies
And in the dark, sinks like a stone.
By Crimson Deeps I weep alone.

The walls are black, the entrance dim.
I hug my dreams and think of him.
Naïve, believed his constant lies.
My soul in bitter sorrow cries.

Seaweed hangs in curtains wide,
Adorning rocks where wavelets glide.
Cold water drips in icy time
And echoes fill this cavern mine.

> I thought I'd found a soul mate,
> To share my whole life through,
> But I discovered too late
> That the stranger that I knew was you.

Long shadows fall on this poor fool
As I sit by the blood red pool.
Into the gloom, I call your name.
Afraid, I play your waiting game.

Stalactites from ceilings drape
And stab the night with ghostly shapes.
I shudder now, my fate to learn.
The candle fades but my heart burns.

> I thought I'd found a soul mate,
> To share my whole life through,
> But I discovered too late
> That the stranger that I knew was you.

Crimson Deeps, the water lies,
As red as blood, as my love dies
And in the dark, sinks like a stone.
By Crimson Deeps I weep alone.

The strong, lightweight, twin-sided,
fold-away, polypropylene, reading stand.
Also suitable for display and sheet music.
Sits neatly on your desk, table, bed-tray or
wheelchair tray. You can even put it over
the bath by sliding rods through the
triangular channels to read while you bathe.

**For details please see website
www.wordpower.u-net.com**

Study Buddy® is a registered Trade Mark
Wordpower™ is a Trade Mark
Study Buddy Design is registered at the Patent Office
Design Registration No. 2092939

Wordpower,
P.O. Box 1190,
SANDHURST,
GU47 7BW

Mary B. Lyons is a freelance writer, author, photographer, artist, illustrator, song-writer and broadcaster whose work has been published in the following:

The Times Educational Supplement
The Lancet
Hampshire the County Magazine
Police Journal
Surrey Monocle
Mail on Sunday (financial pages)
Omega
Machine Knitting Monthly
Hampshire Now
Royal Photographic Society Journal
Pilot
Funeral Director Monthly
Funeral Service Journal
Antique Collectors
SAIFinsight
Business Digest
Local and National papers

Mary has written many magazine and newspaper columns and currently has a regular column in a magazine. She has broadcast on BBC local radio and other stations, including hospital radio and Reading 4U. She has appeared on BBC television and also gives talks on a number of subjects to organisations and societies. If you wish to book her for a talk, presentation or photographic exhibition, and require a list of subjects, please write to: Wordpower, P.O. Box 1190, Sandhurst, GU47 7BW, enclosing a stamped, addressed envelope together with an estimate of possible audience size. Mary also performs her original songs with guitar to raise money for charity. Her hobbies include chess, art, design, music, machine knitting, costume jewellery design and all things technical.